tell me
it's *right*

KATIE WISMER

For the hopeless romantics who have never been in love

Also by Katie Wismer

Find your next read here: https://www.katiewismer.com/books

Sign up for My Author Newsletter

Sign up for Katie Wismer's newsletter to receive exclusive content and be the first to learn about new releases, book sales, events, and other news!

www.katiewismer.com

Playlist

Listen on Spotify: https://shorturl.at/YvfRX

Settling — Ripe
i think about you all the time — The Maine
Lost In The Wild — WALK THE MOON
Hot Mess — Friday Pilots Club
NUMB — Chri$tain Gate$
Swim — Fickle Friends
I Don't Care — Friday Pilots Club
i wanna love somebody — We Three
Ode to a Conversation Stuck in Your Head — Del Water Gap
STAY — The Kid LAROI, Justin Bieber
Days in the Sun — Ziggy Alberts
Dirty, Pretty, Beautiful — The Maine
HONEST — Jeremy Zucker
Papercuts — Landon Conrath
Anything but Ordinary — Avril Lavigne
Trampoline — The Unlikely Candidates
Cut Me Up — Friday Pilots Club
Change For You — Friday Pilots Club
Waiting for My Sun to Shine — The Maine
Bad Influence — Spencer Sutherland
flyby. — Virginia to Vegas, Mokita
Yes, I Was Drunk — Twin Atlantic
LANGUAGE — BOYS LIKE GIRLS
Project — Chase McDaniel
Sk8er Boi — Avril Lavigne
I'm over You — Bryan James

hold on — flor
Jericho — Landon Conrath
Typical — Sunderland, Max Waller
blame — The Maine
Say Don't Go (Taylor's Version) — Taylor Swift
CLOSER — Waterparks
Got Me Started — Troy Sivan
Move With You — Trey Kennedy
Never Grow Up (Taylor's Version) — Taylor Swift
Want Me — Stephen Dawes
Don't Feel Like Feeling Sad Today — YUNGBLUD
Hush Hush — The Band CAMINO
Stupid for You — Waterparks
Greek Tragedy — The Wombats
Work It Out — Joe Jonas

Chapter One

LIAM

I need to get out of the truck. I've been sitting here for a good ten minutes now.

The typical sea of designer suits and dresses brushes past me toward the monstrosity of a home ahead. Even the gifts they carry are overly polished in a way that should be wildly out of place for a six-year-old's birthday party. All polka dots and ribbons and shiny gold wrapping paper.

The house itself looks like a catalog ad for a party store. Streamers, lights, and balloons are spilling out the doors, windows, and over the sides of the balconies. But there's a method to the chaos—every glittery decoration hung just so.

I glance at the bag in my passenger seat. Neon green tissue paper and a cartoon car with a missing tooth.

"Liam!" A fist pounds against my window, and I lurch back. Miles's dorky smile stretches across his face—all freckles and dimples—as he presses his nose against the glass. "Didn't think we'd be seeing you here."

"Get off my truck."

There's an imprint left behind as he shrugs and pulls away.

He has to be, what? Twenty-three by now? But I swear he doesn't look any different than he did at fourteen. Must be the baby face. Or the too-short pants that show off his chicken ankles.

Why he and my brother Asher are still friends is beyond me. I'd been hoping it would fizzle out after high school. I might be only three years older, but their debauchery threatens to put me in an early grave.

Finally, I force myself to open the door and climb out.

Miles takes off at a jog, triple-checking the pockets of his khakis as he goes. A tick of his I'm all too familiar with. I give it half an hour before someone busts him and Ash with a joint in the bathroom.

The gift bag crinkles as I tighten my fist around the handle and start the winding trek up the drive. There were spots closer, but I didn't want to risk getting blocked in and forced to stay here longer than necessary.

I try to deduce a theme as I follow the music and chatter through the house—everyone must be gathered in the back-yard—but the place looks the same as always, just with added glitter and balloon arches lining the dual curved staircases at the entrance.

I guess the walls look different these days. But Christine's been slowly swapping out the art pieces since the day she moved in. Give her another few years and there won't be any trace of my mother left in the house at all.

"Liam!"

Ah, just who I wanted to see.

Christine skitters around the corner, looking like she's about to break an ankle in those shoes. They're as gold and shiny as everything else in here. Her dress is skintight and red, white, and blue, topped off with an American flag scarf knotted around her throat.

"You're just in time!" she squeals, and it's too late now, because she's barreling toward me with her arms spread wide. "The games are about to begin!"

Games? I peek around her at the open French doors moments before she yanks me into a hug. For such a small woman, she certainly knows how to knock the air straight out of you. Small stations are situated around the pool—a net, a Ping-Pong table, some kind of makeshift track.

An Olympics theme then.

I pat her on the back a few times until she releases me, and her eyes go comically wide as she takes in the bag I'm holding.

"Oh, you shouldn't have!"

As if I'd show up to my own brother's birthday without a gift.

She beams as I offer it to her.

"Where is Casey?"

"All the kids are out back! I was about to go check on the cake. They were putting some finishing touches on it earlier."

"Liam! You're here!"

Casey sprints down the hall, his little arms pumping at his sides. His swimming trunks are green, white, and red, and he has the same colors painted across his cheeks. I kneel as he lunges in for a hug, then ruffle his hair as he pulls away.

"Since when are you Italian?" I ask.

"Each of the kids picked a different country," Christine explains.

I resist the urge to ask why *she's* dressed like the Fourth of July then.

"Is that for me?" He points at the bag in his mom's hands.

"Uh, are you the birthday boy? Or is there someone else turning six around here that I don't know about?"

"Just me! Mom, can I open it now?"

Christine gives him an annoyed look, but she's smiling. "We talked about this. We'll open presents after the cake."

"Just Liam's, though! *Please.*"

She glances at me sideways, and I shrug. "I don't mind."

With a drawn-out sigh, she hands over the bag. Casey immediately rips the tissue paper out, but he's gentle as he removes the wrapped package.

"What is it?" he asks as he turns it over in his tiny hands.

"That would be the point of opening it," I say. "To find out."

He sticks his tongue out at me, then rips the wrapping paper off. I can feel his mom watching me, but I pointedly ignore her as Casey inspects the gift.

The sketchbook itself is plain—black cover, spiral binding —but as soon as Casey flips to the first page, his face lights up, and I exhale my relief.

Every few pages is a different drawing, broken down step by step as simple as I could make it. The biggest gamble was choosing which superheroes and characters to do, seeing as Casey's interests change on an hourly basis.

His head pops up like the best idea ever just occurred to him. "If I get as good as you, can I draw your next one?" He points at the tattoos on my arm.

Christine scoffs, then covers it up with a laugh. "Casey…"

"Absolutely," I say, meaning it. Can't be any worse than my first few.

His little nose scrunches up. "Can I watch you do it? Or does it get all bloody?"

I chuckle, knowing full well he wouldn't make it that far. Poor kid passes out just *seeing* the needle for a shot at the doctor's. "Not always."

"You should get back to your friends, don't you think?" Christine smiles and leans down to nudge Casey. "Don't want them to think you're ignoring them."

"Liam, are you gonna watch me compete? I'm gonna *dominate.*"

I quirk an eyebrow at the fancy vocabulary, even if he has trouble pronouncing it. "Of course! It's the whole reason I'm here."

He grins, exposing a missing tooth I hadn't noticed before. "It's gonna be awesome!" Then he pivots and sprints the way he came—the only speed he has these days, really.

"Thank you for coming," says Christine. "Really. I know things have been...tense, but it means so much to Casey. Especially since Taylor can't make it. And God only knows where Asher is." She gently tucks Casey's book in the bag. "And this was really thoughtful."

She says that like *I'm* the responsible brother now. My, how the tables have turned. I clear my throat and avoid whatever meaningful look she's giving me.

She's trying. I know. I can't fault her for it. But I'm also not interested in some woman who's barely five years older than me trying to act like a parental figure just because she's Casey's mom.

"Wouldn't miss it. Have you seen Leo? I think he said he's already here."

"Oh." She frowns. "I haven't. But he might be out back!"

I smile and step around her, knowing very well Leo is *not* coming today, but it does the trick. She waves and heads off for the kitchen, effectively ending the conversation. Though today would definitely be easier if Leo could come. I don't know what it says about me that my best friend has always been better at dealing with my family than I am.

But he's got his own family stuff this weekend, what with his sister moving in. I still can't fucking believe they decided that was a good idea. Gracie and Leo under the same roof

5

again? I give it two weeks before one of them kills the other. And my money's on Gracie.

I make it two steps onto the patio before I catch sight of my dad across the pool, which is almost enough to make me spin on my heel. A herd of screaming children rushes past me, followed by some woman telling them not to run, and that's when I notice who my father is standing next to.

The internal groan vibrates through every cell of my body.

The girl smiles along politely to whatever my dad is telling her while she sips a glass of champagne. Looks like one of the Hastings daughters. Like most of the adults, she's dressed like she's ready for the country club instead of a kid's birthday party.

If he's doing what I think he's doing...

As if sensing my thoughts, he looks up, meets my eyes, and smiles. Nothing about it is warm. He gestures for me to join them.

Yeah...absolutely the fuck not. He can play matchmaker with one of his many other kids. I pretend not to see him and slip back inside.

I've been in this house all of ten minutes and it already feels like ten minutes too long. The perks, I guess, of growing up here—at least I know all the right places to hide.

I swipe a beer out of a cooler before heading to the second floor. It's quieter, the music and voices drifting up muffled. I fish my phone from my pocket once I hit the bay window that overlooks the pool and pull up my texts with Leo.

Liam: You suck
Leo: That bad already?
Liam: I think my dad's arranging my engagement
Liam: And Christine is campaigning for teen mom of the year

Leo: Ah, the Candyman never rests

Leo: Oh come on. Christine's nice

Liam: Too nice

Leo: Did Casey open the present yet

Liam: Yeah

Leo: And he loved it, didn't he?

Liam: Stop trying to make me feel better

Leo: Right

Leo: You're a disappointment to the whole family

Leo: You have bad taste in music

Leo: And you really fucking need a haircut jesus christ

Liam: thank you

Chapter Two

GRACIE

How quickly I have become a complete failure.

I stare miserably up at the door, my arms cramping under the weight of the box in my hands. Maybe I should let it crush me. I would like nothing more than to flop onto the perfectly manicured lawn and lie there until I perish. To slowly waste away while these shiny suburban couples witness my demise. To—

"Stop whatever dramatic monologue you've got going on in your head and help me with these."

I glare at my brother over my shoulder. I suppose I should be kissing the ground he walks on right now. Leo hoists another box out of the moving truck. His white T-shirt is already soaked through with sweat, but somehow his blond hair is still perfectly coiffed. Mine, however, clings to my neck, the curls already taking on a mind of their own in this humidity.

"I wasn't—"

He plops the box on top of the one in my hands, and I grunt, my legs doing an awkward shuffle to keep from folding in on themselves. He juts his chin to the open front door. "Go on then."

Afraid he'll add another box if I keep standing here, I hurry inside, barely able to see over the load in my arms.

"Here, I'll take one of those." Leo's wife, Keava, appears in front of me and grabs the top box. I let out a sigh of relief.

"Thank you." I keep waiting for a crack in her perfectly pleasant face—even a quick *look* between her and Leo—but she just smiles and leads the way to the basement.

The house is fairly small and easy to navigate—the kitchen and living room on the first floor, two bedrooms upstairs, and the basement.

Which appears to have been their gym.

A treadmill, bike, and various weights are piled in the corner. It's an open floor plan with a bathroom in the corner, but at least there's carpeting and an AC unit.

"We'll get you a real bed in here soon," she assures me as she sets the box beside the air mattress currently inflating against the wall.

I've met Keava twice—at their wedding and Christmas one year. And neither instance involved spending much time together. Which just makes this situation that much more awkward.

She's even prettier than I remembered. Way out of Leo's league. Long brown hair, naturally tan skin, and a warmth to her that makes her instantly personable.

But I don't care how nice she is. At least a small part of her *must* be unhappy with me being here. She and Leo got married just over a year ago. There's no way she's thrilled about his baby sister moving into her basement.

When I don't respond, she smiles again and heads for the stairs. "I think I'll get started on lunch. Come on up whenever you're hungry."

Once she's gone, I set my box on top of the other and peel off the top.

My college diploma stares back at me.

I shove the lid back on.

Great lot of good that's done me.

Footsteps pound down the stairs, and Leo steps around the corner, three boxes piled high in his arms. He sets them on the ground, not even out of breath, and raises an eyebrow.

"Hiding down here so I do all of the heavy lifting for you?"

"I was coming back," I mumble.

He pauses, the amusement draining from his face as he puts his hands on his hips and glances around. "Is this okay? I know it's not a lot of space, but it's got to be better than Mom and Dad's, right?"

He doesn't meet my eyes as he says it, and I don't meet his as I reply, "Leo, it's great. I—thank you."

This, at least, feels like a step above *moving back home.*

Our parents have lived in the same house in Edgewater for more than thirty years, but Leo and Keava ventured a town away to Sweetspire, putting them closer to the city but still near the water. And if there's one good thing about returning to Jersey after four years in the Pacific Northwest, it's the beach.

We came this way plenty over the years since Sweetspire is twice the size, so it's not exactly *new,* but at least I'm not slammed in the face with memories everywhere I look like in Edgewater. Not that they're particularly bad memories, but being in that town feels like I'm forever stuck at sixteen.

Here feels like something new.

Even if it's only twenty minutes down the road.

A stupid grin covers his face as he tilts his ear toward me. "What was that? Didn't hear you."

I slap the back of his head as I surge up the stairs. "And you'll never hear it again."

"Babe, you can't give her that. She's underage."

Keava smirks at me across the kitchen table and passes the White Claw. The once-perfect kitchen is now flooded with my boxes, making the small space even more cramped, but Keava navigates it with ease as she slips the plates off the counter and joins us.

"Leo, I'm twenty-two," I say.

He stares at me, genuine confusion pinching his eyebrows together. "No shit?"

I take a bite of my grilled cheese. "You *just* came to my college graduation," I remind him around my mouthful.

He frowns like he'd never thought of it that way.

Keava rolls her eyes and smiles at me like we have some kind of inside joke.

I raise a hand before he can respond. "I'll always be twelve to you, blah, blah, blah."

Not that he's that much older. Four years on me and he thinks he's some kind of authority figure now, when *I'm* the one who used to cover for him when he snuck out in high school.

"Thanks for lunch, Keava," I add.

"Oh, it's nothing."

Leo stands up, leans across the table, and plants a kiss on the top of her head. "You make the best grilled cheese known to man."

A pretty blush fills her cheeks, and the two of them stare at each other across the table, googly eyes and all.

I've got to get out of here.

Their heads snap up as I stand. I awkwardly jab a thumb over my shoulder. "Think I'm gonna start to unpack."

"Of course!" says Keava.

Leo covers his mouth as he swallows a massive bite of his sandwich. "A friend agreed to come over and help carry some of the furniture down tomorrow. Is that…uh…okay?"

"I think I can survive a night on the air mattress."

"Right."

"You know where to find us if you need anything!" Keava calls as I head for the stairs.

The moment they're out of sight, I let the smile drop from my face. It's not that I'm ungrateful for them taking me in but being this *perky* is exhausting.

It's not that I haven't tried. For months leading up to graduation, I applied to every single job I could find. Well over a hundred. And…nothing.

Not even an interview.

No number of résumé tweaks or meticulously written cover letters or glowing recommendations got my foot in the door. Not when every entry-level job required five years of experience, and *oh yeah*, it's an unpaid internship and requires a master's degree.

So glad I spent four years and hundreds of thousands of dollars to get a degree just to be as qualified as I was before.

I slump onto the air mattress, and the distinct hiss of air leaking out fills the room.

Sighing, I lie back and stare at the exposed beams in the ceiling, the mattress slowly sinking beneath me. Maybe if I lie here long enough, it'll swallow me whole.

Chapter Three

GRACIE

I wake up on the floor with the air mattress folding around me. Sunlight slants in from the hopper windows near the ceiling and directly into my eyes. Groaning, I fish around until I find my phone.

5:30 AM.

Curtains are now at the top of the to-do list.

Footsteps sound above my head, so apparently I'm not the only one awake. Probably Keava. She teaches at the middle school, and I'm pretty sure they start around 7:00 AM.

It takes me a minute to wrestle myself out of the plastic burrito, and I stumble bleary-eyed toward the shower, side-stepping boxes as I go. The water comes out cold no matter which way I turn the knob, and it takes everything in me not to shriek as I hunch my shoulders and slip in.

On the bright side, I'm definitely awake now.

I don't think it's quite warm enough to break out the sundresses, but I slip one on anyway, figuring the long-sleeve shirt I layer underneath will cancel it out. After applying the few makeup products I manage to find, I head upstairs.

"Oh! Early riser!" Keava smiles at me from the kitchen as she pours coffee into a to-go mug.

I don't correct her. I just moved in. Immediately complaining isn't going to start us off on the right foot.

She steps around the counter and opens the fridge, her floor-length floral dress swishing around her as she moves. "You want some coffee?"

"Oh, uh, I'm actually more of a cold brew kind of girl. I saw a coffee shop around the corner on our way in. Do you think they're open yet?"

For some reason, my cheeks burn as Keava closes the fridge and looks at me. She probably thinks I'm freeloading and being stupid blowing my money on overpriced coffee. My meager savings won't last me long, but hopefully I'll manage to find a job before I run out completely. And if there's one thing I'm simply not willing to give up, it's working in coffee shops.

"Oh, Milano's?" She checks her watch. "They should be open by six. Want me to drop you off on my way to school?"

"That's okay. I figured I'd walk. Get some exercise."

"Great idea! It's super nice out this morning." She slips a tote bag off one of the kitchen chairs and heads for the door. "Hey, I even think they're hiring." She winks at me over her shoulder then slips into the garage.

My face burns again. She probably didn't mean anything by it.

I shove my laptop into my bag. If they have some nice seating, I can knock out a few more job applications this morning. Hopefully for something at least slightly related to design and not as a barista. Though I guess that wouldn't be the worst fallback plan.

Maybe I'd get some free coffee.

Sadly, that's the most exciting possibility I've heard all week.

Unsurprisingly, the coffee shop is quiet as I step inside two minutes after opening. A girl with long brown hair and a red apron smiles at me from behind the counter as the bell above the door announces my arrival.

"Welcome in! What can I get you?"

I eye the menu on the chalkboard behind her head. The drinks are spelled out in bright colors and cursive letters, doodles of carry-out cups and mugs lining the sides.

"A large cold brew with coconut milk and hazelnut syrup."

The girl smiles again as she types away on her register and takes my crumpled up ten-dollar bill. After dumping the change in her tip jar—probably another financially irresponsible move—I scout out a place to sit.

The shop is cozy and warm with plants and string lights hanging overhead. There's a fireplace in the corner with some leather chairs, but I head for the tables on the opposite wall after the barista hands over my cup.

I duck under the table to search for an outlet as the bell above the door rings.

The barista laughs, and I watch beneath the table as a skateboard glides into the shop, my view cut off below the newcomer's knees. All I can see are black Vans, tan skin, and long legs utterly covered in tattoos.

"You're late," says the barista.

He stops a foot from the door and kicks up the board. "Didn't realize you were keeping track."

That voice.

"Well, you're usually the first one in here."

Oh, God. My head hits the bottom of the table with an audible thunk. Wincing, I pop back out as the two of them look over at me.

Liam Brooks grins.

He somehow manages to look exactly the same and completely different. His dark, wavy hair is longer—and messy —though I'm willing to bet he purposefully makes it that way. That damn knowing smile is all too familiar, but he's got at least two dozen more tattoos than the last time I saw him—on his arms, his hands, his legs.

Jesus, how does he have time to do anything else?

"You hiding from me, Gracie?"

"I—no." I gesture to the charger in my hand and plug it into my laptop for emphasis.

"The usual," he tells the barista.

Then he saunters to my table.

You are not Leo's awkward little sister anymore. You are a grown ass woman.

A grown ass woman who is unemployed and living in Leo's basement.

I sit up straighter and focus on my laptop screen.

"I heard something about you coming back to town," he says, sinking into the chair across from me.

"I'm just visiting."

He presses his lips together, a smile threatening at the edges. "Congrats on graduation."

I peer up at him, but the amusement is gone from his expression. His eyes flit over my face just...curious. It seems he also added some piercings since the last time I saw him. One through his lip and a ring in his nostril. Though he might have just taken them out for Leo's wedding.

I realize a beat too late it probably looked like I was staring at his mouth and drop my gaze to my laptop. "Thanks," I mumble.

The barista appears with a large hot coffee and slides it in front of him. He thanks her and closes his hands around it, revealing a scorpion that wraps around his wrist and over the back of his hand.

"Been a long time, Little Leo."

There it is.

I roll my eyes, and he laughs, the sound full and deep. He started that stupid nickname when I was in third grade, and that's all *anyone* would call me for months. Even the teachers.

"Oh, come on," he says. "I had to."

"Glad to see you're still *the worst.*"

He spins my cup around so he can read the label. "You missed me."

"Don't you have somewhere you need to be?" I mumble. "An emo convention, perhaps?"

"Aha! She goes off to college and comes back with some teeth. I respect that." Before I can respond, he knocks two knuckles on the table between us and stands. "As a matter of fact, I *do* have somewhere to be. But I have a feeling I'll be seeing you around, killer."

"Hopefully not."

He laughs again, sets his skateboard down, and waves to the barista before gliding to the door. The bell rings as he opens it, and he pauses and glances at me over his shoulder. "Good to see you, Gracie."

Two coffees and nine job applications later, I find myself back at Leo and Keava's eerily quiet house. I restlessly pace around, trying to figure out what the heck to do with myself. I have plenty of unpacking left, but my options are limited with my furniture sitting in the garage.

Plus, unpacking makes this feel a lot more real. Permanent. Maybe I'm not ready to accept my fate yet.

My hands tremble at my sides, still burning off the energy from seeing Liam. I should have expected it. The Brooks mansion sits squarely between Edgewater and Sweetspire, so he's always spent a lot of time over here.

Leo and Liam have been a package deal ever since we were kids. I was hoping his single favorite pastime of getting under my skin would fade with age, but alas…

I pace out to the garage and set my hands on my hips, considering my options. Definitely can't get the bed down there by myself. Or the dresser. But I could handle a few smaller things. At least it would give me something to do.

After changing into leggings and a sports bra, I start with the lightest objects—lamps, the desk chair, some leftover boxes. By my third trip down the stairs, I'm sweating. If I could just get one of the pieces of furniture down, then I could start unpacking the boxes and get them out of the way.

Maybe the bedside table. It's heavy, but small enough that I think I can manage it on my own. Once I'm standing at the top of the stairs, fingers barely holding on to the edges and sweat dripping down my face, I realize I most certainly *cannot*.

No stopping now though. Might as well run with the momentum. I grunt, leaning back to balance some of the weight against me while also craning my neck to see the stairs beneath my feet.

A door opens somewhere behind me.

I miss the last stair. Luckily, the table lands right-side up on the ground. Unluckily, I pitch forward and ram into it. It knocks the air out of my lungs, and I topple off the side and land on my back.

Shit, that hurt.

"Gracie?"

Leo? He shouldn't be home yet…should he? What time is it? I groan and blink toward the stairs as someone jogs down.

They lean over me, and the silver chain around their neck hangs above my face. The tattoos disappearing into the collar of his shirt come into focus next…maybe some kind of wings?

Definitely not Leo.

The rest of Liam's face swims into view. A harsh line cuts down the center of his brow as his eyes sweep over me.

"You okay? You couldn't wait for me?"

Wait for me? I blink. Maybe I hit my head.

"What are you doing here?"

He leans back and offers a hand. Ignoring it, I scoot away and sit up.

"Didn't Leo tell you I was coming by? Said he needed help moving you in."

Liam is the friend he asked?

I'm going to kill Leo.

Good to see some things never change. He's clearly just as comfortable waltzing in like he lives here as he always was at Mom and Dad's.

Heat burns my cheeks as something occurs to me. He'd known I was moving in all along, that I wasn't *just visiting* like I'd said earlier, but hadn't bothered to correct me.

"Are you hurt?"

"I'm fine," I snap, pushing to my feet.

We stare at each other. He's still in the same shorts and black T-shirt from this morning. What does *he* do all day? Does he even have a job? His eyes slowly trail down me, and he pushes his hair back with his hand.

Then I remember I'm sweaty and standing here in nothing but my sports bra.

"Well," I say, crossing my arms over my chest, "consider yourself officially off the hook. I'm fine here."

A single eyebrow lifts as his gaze shifts to the table that nearly killed me.

"Leo's not even here anyway," I add.

"Looks like it's up to you and me then." With that, he jogs up the stairs and turns right for the garage, *not* the front door. "Push that aside so we can get the next thing down."

"Liam—" I sigh but grab the table and yank it farther into the room. By the time I turn the corner to follow him up, he's already on his way down, two of the heavier boxes I left behind stacked in his hands.

"Wait for me for the heavy stuff" is all he says as he passes.

As much as I want to protest and get him the heck out of here...I want to carry all these things down alone even less. Hopefully Leo will show up any minute now.

We work in silence for the next few trips, and I pause after setting a box down, trying to catch my breath. Liam sets two more near the gym equipment on the opposite side of the room, then turns, taking in the pathetic, mostly deflated air mattress on the floor. He walks over and pokes it, and it hisses as more air escapes the side.

"You *slept* on this thing last night?" I say nothing, and he turns for the stairs. "Come on. Let's get the bed."

I wait in the doorway to the garage as he considers the remaining pieces. He bends down, testing the weight of each in his hands.

"We're going to have to put this together," he mutters, seemingly to himself, then glances at me. "You don't know where Leo keeps his tools, do you?"

I stare at him blankly.

"Right. I'll grab the ones in my truck." He goes back to the metal frame in his hands. They're long and awkward, but not heavy. "All right." He stands, slipping the Ziploc bag with the screws and whatnot into his pocket, then hefts the frame pieces into his hands. "I'll be right back. We'll take the box spring down next, if you wanna shimmy that toward the door."

I check my phone once he's gone—Leo was supposed to be here half an hour ago—but do as he says, grabbing the box spring and awkwardly trying to nudge it along the floor. I'm nearly to the door when Liam reappears and grabs one of the corners.

"I'll head down first. Try not to shove me down the stairs, Little Leo."

I scowl but grab the other end. He walks down backward, the bag in his pocket jangling with each step, and I dig my nails into my end, trying not to let it slip.

Not that I would particularly mind dropping it on him. It wouldn't hurt.

Too much.

"Don't even think about it," he calls.

I wipe off whatever look was on my face as we reach the bottom, maneuver around the corner, and set it against the wall. He must've cleaned up the air mattress when he was down here before because the metal frame pieces are already laid out on the carpet, and there's a black bag of tools set off to the side.

As he fishes the bag of screws from his pocket, his phone rings. The moment his eyes land on the screen, his jaw flexes.

"Do you need to get that?"

"Nope." He jabs a thumb against the screen and tosses the phone onto the carpet. He doesn't look at me as he bends down and motions to the frame. "You wanna hold these two pieces together, and I'll secure them?"

The air feels much thicker now with his mood shift. We work in silence. He's on the last screw when his phone lights up again. I glance at it since it's right beside me, and a pretty redhead's picture flashes on the screen along with her name, *Hailey*. She looks...familiar, but I can't put my finger on it.

"Do you...?"

"Just hit ignore."

I raise my eyebrows but hit the red button.

So he's mad about a girl. Interesting.

A door bangs open upstairs. "I'm home. I'm home. Sorry I'm late!" Leo calls.

Liam smiles a little and rolls his eyes as Leo bounds down the stairs.

"Oh, shit. You guys really got to work."

"I will get out of your way," I say, hopping to my feet. I glare at Leo as soon as my back is to Liam, and he grimaces.

"Should grab the mattress next," Liam says from the floor.

I punch Leo in the chest as I pass, hard enough for him to stumble, and Liam snorts.

"That's really no way to say thank you," he mutters.

"You haven't actually done anything yet." Even though it physically pains me to do it, I pause before jogging up the stairs. "Liam though. Liam can have a thank-you."

He smirks at me from the floor. "Is that it or is the actual *thank you* still coming?"

"Don't push it."

Chapter Four

GRACIE

"You know, I don't ever remember being *that* obnoxious, even in middle school. Oh, hi, Gracie." Keava stumbles through the back door and starts piling her belongings on the kitchen table. She's somehow carrying twice as many things as she had when she left this morning. "Do you remember seventh grade?" she asks, heading for the fridge. "Demons. All of my kids are *demons*, I'm telling you."

I watch wide-eyed as she pulls a bottle of wine from the fridge, screws off the top, and takes a huge gulp straight from the bottle. Her head falls back with a sigh, then she sets the bottle on the counter in front of her, seemingly taking in the room for the first time.

"Where's Leo?"

I jab my thumb toward the basement. "He and Liam are finishing with the moving stuff."

She snorts. "I'm surprised Liam showed up."

I don't bother telling her it was actually Leo who nearly bailed on me and slide onto one of the bar stools, my muscles exhausted from going up and down the stairs. And I can definitely feel a bruise forming from that damn table.

She pulls a glass from the cabinet and glances at me as she pours the wine. "You want one?"

My eyes shoot to the bottle she just wrapped her entire mouth around.

"There's another bottle," she adds.

"You going to drink that whole thing yourself?"

She shrugs and shoots me a wink. "Probably."

I wave a hand. "I'm good."

"I was thinking we could order in for dinner. Chinese or pizza—you have a preference?"

"Either is fine." I chew on my lip, debating my next words. "Does the name Hailey ring a bell?"

Her eyebrows practically disappear into her hairline as her eyes dart from me to the basement stairs. "He talked about her?"

"No," I admit, shifting my weight. I don't know why I brought this up. "She was just calling a lot."

"Oh. Figures." She flicks her wrist at the questioning expression on my face. "Not really my place to say anything. And to be honest, I can't keep up with whatever is going on between the two of them these days."

Okay, so together. Or used to be together. Or something in between.

Not that it matters. Not that I care.

"Oh, hey, babe. Didn't know you were home." Leo bounds around the corner and plants a kiss on the top of Keava's head before ducking into the fridge for a beer.

"You guys all finished?" she asks.

Leo wipes the sweat from his forehead and nods. My eyes drift to the hall, but no one comes in after him. Did he already leave?

Not that it matters.

Not that I care.

Keava starts complaining about the kids in her class again as Leo digs a second beer out of the fridge and pushes it across the counter. At first I think he's giving it to me—weird, since he knows how much I hate beer—but then there's a voice beside my ear.

"Thanks." Liam takes the bar stool on my right.

"Liam," says Keava. "Chinese or pizza?"

"Chinese."

He's *staying*?

"I'll order it." Leo slides his cell from his pocket and disappears into the hall.

Keava sips her wine, her attention swinging back to me. "How's the job search going?"

I grimace, my face hot as I feel Liam look at me. Maybe I should've taken Keava up on that drink offer. "Nothing yet," I say, trying to keep my voice light. "But I sent out a bunch of new applications today."

"Well, fingers crossed." Keava smiles.

I have a feeling this question is going to be a daily occurrence.

I've been here twenty-four hours and it's already twice as humiliating as I'd feared. It's not like I need the reminder with my student loans looming over my head.

"You know," Keava continues, "I could ask around for you. See if anyone knows of any openings."

The burning in my face spreads down to my neck. "Oh really, that's okay—"

"The school has a daycare for the teachers, did you know that? I think they're looking for someone."

Daycare? Not that I have anything against it, but it's not at all related to anything I'm good at.

"And you could always keep taking your little pictures on the side," she adds.

Now the heat in my face turns into something else. *My little pictures.* My jaw clenches, but I don't bother correcting her. Yeah, I tacked on photography as a minor for fun, but all the jobs I've been applying for have been for graphic design or social media management.

But even if I *was* pursuing photography, that's a perfectly legitimate career too. I guess her attitude makes more sense now. She thinks I'm some artist with my head in the clouds and no intention of getting a job.

I pull in a slow, deep breath through my nose before responding. Maybe she didn't mean it that way. I don't want to piss her off, but I don't want to keep having this conversation more.

Liam beats me to the punch.

"Actually, Gracie and I were talking about bringing her on at the shop. That is, if she agrees to it." He turns and meets my eyes, expression entirely innocent.

"Oh?" says Keava.

I stare at him. *The shop?* I have no idea what that means. And judging by the way he's leaving the floor open for me to fill in the blanks, he has no idea what I do either.

I don't know why, and I don't care, but he's throwing me a life raft.

"Riiiiight," I say. "The website does look like it needs some work."

He nods seriously, though his lips are pinched together like he's holding back a laugh. "It does."

"Oh," Keava repeats as Leo rounds the corner, phone held proudly in the air.

"Chinese will be here in thirty. Mom and Dad texted and are gonna swing by too."

The grin overtakes Liam's face, his eyes glued to mine. "Plenty of time to hammer out all of those new job details."

"Pass the lo mein over here in case Gracie wants some more!"

"Mom, I don't need any more—"

"Well, you might get hungry again!"

The kitchen table is hardly big enough for six, but Leo brought in a few of the chairs from the deck so we could all squeeze around it. Dad pushes the plate across the jam-packed table, and Mom fusses with it until it's directly at my side even though I've already polished off my plate and am too full for comfort.

Mom is practically vibrating in the seat next to me. She's already said some variation of *We're so glad you're home!* three times, and I think it's physically paining her to hold back from saying it again.

"Well, if we're all finished..." Dad rises from his chair, removes his Giants hat, and reaches over to place it on Liam's head.

"You can't be serious," I say. "After we just ate all that food?"

Dad shrugs and points at Liam. "'Rematch anytime, anywhere'—I believe those were your words."

"I'd hate for you to throw your back out or something," says Liam. "You know, now that you're in your old age."

I shake my head as the two of them exchange unhinged grins and head for the rug in the living room. Leo jumps up to scoot the couch back to give them some extra space. The age-old Collins tradition of passing that ratty old hat to challenge someone to a leg wrestling match. I should've seen this coming the moment he walked in the door with it on.

I turn to Mom. "You're not going to try to stop them?"

She shrugs and hops up to get a better view. "I kind of want to see him get his ass kicked, don't you?"

"Let's go, Dad!" cheers Leo as the rest of us crowd around to watch.

Liam gives him a disbelieving look as he and Dad lie down, their hips beside each other but facing opposite ways. They each lift the leg closest to the other and tap it to the ground alongside the *three, two, one* countdown. At *one*, they hook their legs at the knee, and I hold my breath, waiting to see who will move first.

Dad lets out a guttural yell, his complexation turning red beneath his salt-and-pepper stubble, and slowly, he pulls Liam closer until he flips all the way over, the hat falling from his head in the process.

Keava lets out a whoop behind me.

Dad looks seconds away from pounding his fists against his chest as he grins and spreads his arms wide. "Who's next?"

Liam sighs as he gets up and leans against the couch beside me.

"You're going down, old man," says Leo.

"The age cracks are the best you all can do?" says Dad. "Really?"

I glance at Liam sideways as the next countdown begins. "You let him win," I murmur.

His lips twitch, but he keeps his attention on the stalemate currently happening in the middle of the floor. "Was it that obvious?"

Finally, Dad's the one to flip.

"Sorry to break your winning streak of...what was it? One?" says Leo.

"Come on, honey." Mom helps him up and pats him comfortingly on the back.

"Gracie!" Leo tosses me the Giants hat, then points at the ground next to him.

Liam takes the hat, props it on my head, and gives it a nice pat. "Give him hell."

I sigh, adjust the hat so it's not covering my eyes, and join him on the floor.

"And now, the reigning champ returns," Dad announces into his cupped hands.

I smirk as Leo and I raise our legs. At the end of the countdown, we hook, and it takes about a second until I have him flipped. You'd think he'd learn after all these years. He's always too slow. By the time I feel his resistance kick in, I already have the momentum in my favor.

"That must be a new record," Liam mutters.

"How? *How?*" Leo flops onto his back and lets his arms and legs splay out around him. "Your legs are half the size of mine."

I shrug and hold the hat up. "Mom? Keava?"

They both raise their palms and shake their heads.

"I know a losing battle when I see one," says Mom.

"You're a beast," agrees Dad.

"Liam!" Leo hops up and joins him by the couch. "Please beat my sister. I don't think her inflated ego will fit in this house anymore if she leaves here the reigning champ *again.*"

I don't bother reminding him the last time Liam was able to beat me was probably seven years ago. Liam meets my eyes for a moment before settling in on the floor beside me.

"Kick his ass, Gracie!" yells Dad.

"Don't you dare let me win," I say.

Liam grins. "I would never."

Three, two, one...

We hook legs, and I pool every ounce of strength. Liam doesn't move nearly as easily as Leo did, but even with the way I can feel his muscles flexing, he doesn't move me either. I manage to pull his leg an inch, but then just as quickly, he pulls me back. We stay locked like that—an inch one way, then the other. I grit my teeth, my hands curling into the rug beneath us, and my pinky brushes his.

A weird flash of heat rushes through me. I don't know why such small contact in comparison to the way our legs are wrapped around each other makes me falter, but it does.

But it makes him falter too.

I recover first and have him flipped over in the next second.

The room erupts in applause.

"She strikes again!" calls Dad.

Liam sighs, sits up, and braces his arms on his knees. "One of these days, Little Leo."

I smile and snatch the hat back. "Not on your life."

Chapter Five

GRACIE

The sun wakes me again the next morning, but this time, I roll over, throw a pillow over my head, and go back to sleep. If all I have to look forward to in the mornings is an interrogation from Keava, I think I'll start waiting until she leaves to go upstairs.

"You planning on skipping your first day of work?"

A scream lodges in my throat as I jolt upright and find Liam standing at the foot of my bed. I yank the blanket over my chest despite being completely covered in my oversize T-shirt.

"I—what are you doing here?"

He paces around and glances at my belongings—most of which are still in boxes—like he's browsing in a store. "Keava let me in."

"What are you doing in my *bedroom?*" I fish my phone out of the sheets and squint at the time. "At *six in the morning?*"

That, finally, makes him look over at me. His expression is entirely innocent, as if this is a perfectly normal thing for him to do. "Thought you might need a ride. Leo said you don't have a car anymore."

A very unnecessary reminder. I sold it toward the end of junior year when Mom and Dad were constantly arguing over whether they could afford to put Grandma in a nursing home, and I couldn't bring myself to tell them the money they'd been sending me wasn't covering the electricity...or food...or gas, so I couldn't drive the damn car at that point anyway. I'd taken on an unpaid internship that year in addition to my crazy class schedule, leaving no space for a job.

I don't respond at first, my brain still trying to wake up. "You...were serious? About the job?"

"I'll go grab some coffee. That'll give you about twenty minutes to get ready." He pops his eyebrows and heads for the stairs. "Meet me out front."

It doesn't occur to me until after I've showered, put on a quick face of makeup, and am standing in nothing but a towel staring at my clothes that I have no idea what Liam does.

I have no idea what I'm supposed to wear.

I have no idea what I've gotten myself into.

I close my eyes, trying to remember what he was wearing—I think it was a T-shirt. So, casual. Jeans are probably a safe bet. I fish a baggy pair out of a box and try to remember which one has my shirts.

A horn honks outside.

Shit.

I throw on the first thing I find—a plain black T-shirt. At least if I tuck it in and throw on a belt it'll look a little more put together.

Another honk.

Hair wet and shoes in my hand, I hurry outside to Liam's black truck idling against the curb.

"Took you long enough," he says as I hop in the passenger seat and lean down to slip on my shoes.

"Shut up."

"That's no way to talk to your boss," he muses, then taps the cupholders between us. There's a hot coffee on his side, and a large iced one for me.

I read the label—cold brew, coconut milk, hazelnut syrup—and slowly look up at him.

He doesn't look at me, just pulls the car away from the curb and shifts his weight.

"The barista said she remembered your order," he finally says. "She get it right?"

Something about the way he says it makes me...not believe him.

"Um, yeah. Er—thank you. I'll pay you back."

"Gracie, I don't give a shit about a five-dollar coffee."

I quietly take a sip and focus out the window. The sky is light pink with the sunrise, and the streets are pretty quiet. I expect him to take a left for the main street, or even the highway, but he circles back toward the coffee shop on the corner and parallel parks in front of it.

My eyebrows inch up my face, but I say nothing and follow him as he climbs out of the truck. Instead of heading for the coffee shop, however, he veers for the shop right beside it. I crane my neck to see the sign.

Brooks Tattoos.

I don't know how I didn't notice it yesterday. Maybe I'm just used to seeing the Brooks name on half the businesses in town, though this one looks nothing like their other logos. Not to mention the last kind of place I could imagine getting Mr. Candyman Brooks's approval.

I've never spent much time around Liam's dad, but I remember Mom and Dad always getting…weird whenever he came up in conversation growing up. Pained smiles, changed subjects, and always offering to let Liam stay at our house longer.

Keys jangle as Liam fishes them out of his pocket and unlocks the front door.

The lights are off when we step inside, and it doesn't escape my attention that the sign on the door says it opens at ten. Why the hell is he here at seven in the morning? He flips a switch, and the shop comes to life.

I don't know what I'd been expecting—something dark and scary and vaguely cave-like—but it's *cozy*. The shop itself is narrow and long, sectioned off with a sitting area at the front, a desk, and the tattooing stations in the back. Three, from the looks of it. The entire right wall is exposed brick, painted white, and covered in framed art, movie posters, and skateboards with paintings on the bottoms. Sunlight streams in from the wall of windows at the front, making the space seem light and open.

Liam sets his coffee on the front desk then disappears into a closet in the back. I shift my weight and linger in the entryway, looking around. My reflection in the mirror on the far wall stares back at me—probably for people to check out their tattoos once they're done—and all I can think is *What am I doing here?*

LIAM

I don't know if anyone has ever—in the entire history of the world—looked more out of place than Gracie Collins standing in a tattoo shop. She tries to hide it—she really does—but she's on fucking edge like she's afraid someone is going to leap out from behind the curtain and forcibly tattoo her face.

It had been impulsive, offering her the job. Especially when the shop is in no shape for it. But God, Keava can be such a bitch sometimes, and after I saw that spark of relief in Gracie's eyes, there was no way I was going to backtrack.

And the more I thought about it after leaving Leo's last night, the more I realized this very well may be the universe tossing me a life buoy.

Terrified, mousy, deer-in-headlights Gracie Collins has no idea, but she's about to save this place.

She's got that wide-eyed look on her as I head to the desk with the schedule and stencil paper. It's an expression I've seen on her a million times growing up, but something about it looks different now. Maybe it's because *she* looks so different.

She still had the baby face when she went off to college, and her features are still round and soft, but it's like they've settled into themselves now, complementing each other instead of fighting to take up space.

I realize I've been staring at her a beat too long and flip open the book to today's date.

"I have an appointment coming in at ten, and a few consultations this afternoon. But I have to get some admin things out of the way this morning." Like how the hell I'm going to pay her, and I'm sure there are a dozen or so forms she'll need to sign. All my artists are independent contractors, so that process was completely different than if I'm making her an employee. Which is pretty much what I implied last night, so that's probably what she's expecting. I spare her a quick glance. "You wanna clean up the stations in the back and make sure everything's sanitized? Familiarize yourself with everything. Supplies are in the closet."

Everything's already sanitized, but I don't need her standing there watching me while I try to figure this out.

"You hired me to be a *maid*?"

I roll my head to look up at her. "I hired you to make my life easier. Would it kill you to be a team player, Little Leo?"

"Okay, you've gotta stop calling me that."

I wouldn't do it if she didn't make it so *fun*. "As long as you're under this roof, I'm the boss, and I will do no such thing."

Surprisingly, she does it. I was expecting at least a little pushback, but her footsteps lightly thud against the floor, followed by the metal clings of the drawers opening.

I'm not even sure how much a position like this *should* pay, but if this is only for a few months until she finds something she likes better, it doesn't really matter. The shop's income can't afford it no matter what, so I'll just have to dip into the savings.

As I've had to do every month since we opened.

My inheritance from Granddad will last me at least a decade this way—especially since he left the building itself to me—but that's exactly what my father expects. For me to coast along on family money, then come crawling back once it runs out.

It was no secret why Granddad left so much of his fortune to me. It's not because I was his favorite. It's not because I most deserved it or because he thought I'd do good things.

It's because he knew I'd be fucked without it. Dad has been threatening to cut me off since I graduated high school.

It was one last chance for him to say *fuck you* to my father.

I knew it. Dad knew it. So did everybody else.

So I have between now and when that bank account hits zero to figure out how to make this place profitable. Because there is no way in hell I'm giving my father the satisfaction.

There are only three stations, so it doesn't take Gracie long, then she's back to standing in front of the desk and staring at me as I print off a bunch of forms for her to sign.

"Have you looked at the website?" I ask.

"I—no."

She somehow manages to always sound surprised. I let out a low laugh, spin my chair around to face her, and brace my arms on my legs. "Remind me what you went to school for."

"I—graphic and web design." She tilts her head to the side and narrows her eyes a bit. "And I minored in photography and social media."

"You had two majors *and* two minors? How the hell did you manage that?"

She shrugs. I figured she would've gone into something creative, and Leo's mentioned her marketing background, but all of that? I didn't go to college, but even I know that kind of schedule could drive a person off the deep end. At least she's used to being busy then.

I raise my eyebrows and blow the air out of my cheeks. "All right. Take a look at the website, then come back to me with some notes on what you think could be improved—the logo, the photos online, whatever is fair game. Just make me look good, okay? If you don't mind doing the office management type stuff…that would be helpful too."

"Does the shop have social media?"

I shake my head. I don't have any of it myself, and never plan to. Even if I were to venture into that world for the shop, I'd have no idea where to start.

"Well, maybe you should. I think it would do well."

"Why is that?"

"I—it could make a difference in bringing in new clients, and if you grow a platform, that could potentially bring in some other revenue. And you'd do well on it."

My lips twitch. "And why is that?"

Her cheeks pink, and she waves a hand, gesturing to the shop around us. "It's…photogenic in here. And you're…*you know*…and people would…" I can't help it. My smile grows with each of her failed sentences. She sighs. "Forget it."

"No, no. You're the fancy college grad. I trust you know more about this than I do. Like I said, you've got free rein. Just make me look good."

"You'd have to participate in the social media stuff," she mumbles. "People like…putting a face to things."

Literally nothing sounds worse, but seeing her excitement as she talked about it, the way her eyes lit up with ideas, it's the first time I've seen her like that since she got back here. I can't very well tell her no. And I know she's right. If I want the shop to start doing better, I have to be open to trying things I haven't done.

I rise from the chair and grin at the way she bristles and shifts her weight, like she's bracing herself for whatever comment I have coming next.

"You tell me when and where, Little Leo, and I'll do whatever you want me to."

Chapter Seven

GRACIE

There's a weight to the words and an intensity in his eyes that I don't quite know what to do with. Probably trying to make me squirm for his own amusement. I roll my eyes and step back to put more distance between us. "I didn't bring my laptop. Are you done with that?" I gesture to the computer. "So I can look around at what you have?"

"All yours." He glances at his watch as he grabs whatever he just printed, then slides the papers onto the desk in front of me, pops his eyebrows, and wordlessly heads to the back of the shop.

"What's this?" I call after him.

He doesn't answer, naturally.

I flip through a few of the pages, freezing at something particularly eye-catching on page three. It's paperwork for me —namely, my wages and places for me to sign for taxes.

"You're paying me forty dollars an hour?" I blurt.

Liam's head pops out of the door in the back, his eyebrows lowered. "Is that not enough?"

"Not en…" I swallow hard. I'd been mentally preparing for

a crisp minimum wage. This looks *legit*. I can't imagine getting a better offer for an entry-level position, well, anywhere. "Liam…" I shake my head. "It's too much."

"Think of it as motivation then." He flicks his wrist before disappearing into the closet. "Blow me away. Earn it." His head pops back out, and he points a finger at me, wincing. "Poor choice of words. That was not me coming onto you."

I let out a strangled laugh, my cheeks flaming at the implication. "Noted."

He nods once before ducking through the doorway yet again.

How much money is his shop bringing in? I suppose his dad could be funding things, but I'd be surprised. Both because of who Liam's dad is, but also who *Liam* is. Despite his family, he's never seemed content to coast along on a trust fund the way some of his siblings do.

He wouldn't offer if he couldn't afford it, right? But he hadn't been looking for someone, that I know of. He'd only hired me out of pity. Maybe he feels like he can't pull out now, like he's obligated to help me since we grew up together, since I'm Leo's sister, like he'd been joking when he'd offered but—

"You done with those?"

I lurch back in my chair, my heart in my throat. Liam is standing directly in front of the desk, the raised eyebrow suggesting he's been there for a while.

"I—yeah." I quickly scribble the last of my signatures and slide the papers across the desk to him.

He tucks them into a folder, which he shoves in the filing cabinet, then heads to the first station and starts pulling supplies from the drawers.

I frown as he arranges everything on the counter. It's barely past eight, and he said his first client isn't coming in until ten. I know absolutely nothing about tattoos, but there's no way it takes that long to set up.

I turn to the computer and type *Brooks Tattoos* in the search bar. The website is the first to pop up. It's not bad. Clearly made from one of the easy templates provided by the host, but it could look worse.

We can definitely do better though.

Right now, there's the home page, a contact form, an about page with the shop's location, and a few pictures of his work... but not much else. There aren't even clear shots of the inside of the shop. Not that I frequent tattoo studios, but if *I* were looking for somewhere to go, I wouldn't show up sight unseen. What if it was a dump and looked unsanitary?

Take photos of the shop, I add to my mental list of to-dos.

Liam appears at my side and feeds a thin sheet of paper into the machine beside me. I can't make out what the purple drawing is from this angle. It must be a stencil—at least I know that much.

He glances over my shoulder as he waits. "What do you think?"

"It's not as bad as I'd been imagining."

"Ah, so going off to college also turned you into a snob."

"I'm not a snob."

He grins, grabs the paper from the machine, and returns to the tattooing chair. He's already got ink lined up on the counter in little plastic containers, the tattoo machine—gun, needle, whatever it's called—set up beside it.

"Do you have someone else coming in this morning?" I ask.

"Nope." With that, he props one leg on the chair, rolls up his pants, pulls on some gloves, and starts shaving a section on his calf.

"You're going to do it on *yourself?*"

He shrugs, finishes cleaning off his leg, and carefully places the stencil. It looks like a skull, but turned to the side, and with a landscape of mountains inside of it.

Did he *just* draw that?

"We've got some time to kill."

I stand and drift a little closer as he positions the needle over his skin. Then, like it's no big deal, the machine buzzes to life, and he gets started. I watch his face for a reaction, but he doesn't even flinch. He just leans down, eyes focused, a small line creasing his forehead.

"I—doesn't that hurt?"

His lips quirk. "Doesn't feel great."

From what I can see, there are at least a dozen other tattoos on his leg. Did he do all of those too? His eyes flicker up to me for a moment, and his smile grows.

"Pull up a chair. It'll be more comfortable."

"Oh—I was just—"

He laughs. "Come on."

I grab the one from the front desk and roll it over, eyes glued to the needle as it moves across his skin. It's kind of mesmerizing. He pulls back, wipes the spot he just did with a cloth, and twists to start from a different angle.

"How'd you learn to do this?"

"Taught myself. First ones weren't great. Good thing you can't really see them."

My eyebrows rise at that, but I don't ask *where* they are, because I have a feeling that's exactly what he wants. We sit in silence, save for the buzzing of the machine as he does a few lines, wipes away the excess ink, repositions himself, then continues. It seems like he's doing the outline first.

"I'll be honest," he says suddenly, "I was surprised to see you come home. Thought once you got a taste of outside of Edgewater, none of us would ever see you again."

I pull my legs up on the chair and rest my chin on my

knees. "I kind of thought the same. I didn't..." I sigh. "I didn't expect it to be this hard to get my foot in the door anywhere."

His eyes flick to my face for a fraction of a second before returning to his leg. "What do you want to do? Dream scenario, where do you end up?"

I let out a breathy laugh. "That's a good question. And I guess that's the problem. I don't really have an answer."

"You'll figure it out. Graphic design is a huge field, isn't it? You could do pretty much anything."

"That was the hope," I say quietly, eyes flickering from the tattoo to his face. His features are somehow...softer when he's concentrating like this. "How did you know? That this was what you wanted to do."

"I didn't. Just took a leap of faith, I guess."

"Seems like it worked out pretty well for you."

He hesitates, his lips pressing together like he's considering something, but then all he says is "Didn't happen overnight, I promise." He sits back and wipes the ink from his leg again. "Anyway. Don't let Keava get to you. She can be..." He tilts his head back and forth like he's searching for the right word. "Insensitive. I don't think it's intentional. She's not great at reading the room." His eyes flick to mine. "*Don't* tell Leo I said that."

"I didn't know someone could be nice and unwelcoming at the same time."

He pops his eyebrows and starts on the opposite side of the tattoo. "That would be the perfect way to describe it." Once he's finished with the outline, he reaches for a different piece of equipment waiting on the counter. "Shading one is different," he explains as he readies the ink. "So hit me with it. How bad is the site? What are you thinking?"

"It's just really basic. You could add pictures of the shop, some more of your portfolio. Testimonials, that kind of thing.

Link your social feeds, once you have those. We can tweak some things on the back end to help with SEO. Oh! Do you sell merch? Or like aftercare products or whatever? We could set up an online shop. I could bring my camera in tomorrow to get some shots…" I trail off at the grin on Liam's face and realize I haven't taken a breath. I look away and flick my wrist, adding a nonchalant "If you want."

He shakes his head. "Can't believe you just called me basic."

That's what he got from all of that? "I—I didn't—"

"Gracie." He looks up at me, the corners of his eyes crinkling. "You've gotta stop making it so easy to mess with you."

I roll my eyes and push my chair over to the desk.

Filling the next few hours as Liam finishes his tattoo and we wait for his client proves to be pretty easy. Liam's records are a mess—some digital, some on paper, and his filing cabinet could use a serious reorganization. I don't know how he manages to keep track of his calendar every day. Half of his appointments are written on sticky notes on the desk, some are added to the calendar in his computer, and some are jotted in a notebook.

If he has a system to *anything* he does, it's lost on me.

Maybe it's an artist-brain thing.

And, like he said, he doesn't have a single social media account set up. Starting one from scratch would be a lot, let alone them *all*, so I make a pros and cons lists for which ones we should focus on first while also weighing how likely he would be willing to participate.

"Quite the little chart you've got going on over there." Liam braces his hands on the desk beside me and leans over my shoulder to take in my various lists and notes. "Once a teacher's pet, always a teacher's pet, I suppose."

I scowl. "You'll be thanking me once I'm done."

He laughs and pushes back from the desk. "I'm sure I will."

"Who do you have coming in at ten?" I ask, glancing at the clock. His client should be showing up any minute now.

He tosses his gloves in the trash. "A friend of my brother's."

The bells above the door chime a moment later, and a man walks in.

He's nothing like I would've guessed. He's pretty much Liam's opposite. All shiny gold hair and bright white smile. He looks like he spends more time in a gym than a tattoo shop, and I'd be willing to put money on him being voted prom or homecoming king at some point.

"Brooks." He pounds fists with Liam as he steps into the shop, then turns his dimpled smile on me. "Who's this?"

"This is Gracie. Gracie, this is Miles. She's gonna be helping me out around the shop."

Miles looks me up and down. "No offense. But *you* tattoo?"

"Oh, no."

"She's basically doing everything else for me."

Miles does a slow nod. Honestly, not sure who he is to judge. He doesn't seem to have any tattoos either, at least none that are visible. "Gotcha."

"I've got a few different versions of the design if you want to check them out," says Liam.

"For sure." Miles nods at me. "Nice to meet you, Gracie."

I wave awkwardly as he heads to the back with Liam.

It occurs to me that Liam and I haven't gone over any details of me working here. Like how many hours I'm supposed to work, or what I'm supposed to be doing. *Make me look good* isn't exactly a job description.

I'll need his passwords to get into the website and start

making any changes, but I *really* don't want to have to go ask him right now.

I glance over my shoulder to find Miles already looking at me with more than curiosity in his gaze. He shows no embarrassment or remorse that I've caught him staring. No, he just smiles when he catches my eye, and I quickly turn around, my face hot.

Menial work it is. I guess today is as good a day as any to tackle the filing cabinet. When I pry it open, a haphazard pile greets me—loose papers, folders, and random office supplies. I shoot a glare at Liam over my shoulder. His head is bent over as he lines up the stencil on Miles's back.

He better be paying me enough for this.

Chapter Eight

GRACIE

"Can you guys see me?"

"No. You're literally the dumbest smart person I've ever met, Trish. You have to turn your camera on. Seriously, how can you work in tech and not know how to work a video chat?" Alison flops onto her stomach on her bed, the camera shaking as she repositions her laptop in front of her.

"And you're the most impatient person I've ever met," says Trish. "I work for a tech *company*. That doesn't mean I do the tech part. Wait, those glasses are cute."

Alison beams and twists her face this way and that to give a better look. They're bigger than her old ones, the square lenses now twice the size of her eyes. "You like them? They're new."

"That hotel looks nice too," says Trish. "Where are you tonight?"

"Seattle."

"What!" shrieks Trish.

"I know, I know. If my flight time wasn't so early tomorrow, I would've popped down to visit you."

"One of these days I'm going to get on one of your flights and just spam that call button all. Night. Long."

My laptop blinks red at me, threatening to hibernate if I don't plug it in, and I urgently search the floor for my charger.

"Ugh, now where'd Gracie go?" whines Alison. "I'm all *aloneeeee.*"

"I'm coming! I'm coming!" I call, throwing aside dirty clothes and searching beneath the bed. I still haven't fully unpacked, and the room seems to get messier and messier with every moment I don't.

"And Martina is late, as per usual," Alison continues.

"You have a lot of complaints tonight," I call, crawling around to the other side of the bed.

"I haven't seen you guys in weeks. Even longer since I've seen you in person. *Excuse me* for missing you."

"Found it!" I call.

"Found what?" asks Trish.

"Trish, your camera is still off," says Alison.

I quickly plug the laptop in and jump onto my bed as Trish's camera flickers on, glitching a few times and making the twinkle lights along her wall smear across the screen. Alison slow claps for her, and Trish reappears with the middle finger.

"Should someone text Marti?" I suggest.

"Fuck her," says Alison. "If she can't be bothered to *make time for us*—oh hi, Marti!"

Marti's video appears on screen below mine, a green skin-care mask covering her face. She narrows her eyes. "Qué gracioso, el burro hablando de orejas."

Alison looks to me for a translation.

I shrug. "She called you a donkey."

"*A donkey?*"

Marti smiles innocently. "Only literally."

A loud yell sounds in the background of someone's video, drowning out whatever Marti was poised to say next. Trish's expression falls into a scowl, and she freezes in the middle of French braiding one half of her hair, which she has apparently dyed back to neon pink since we've been gone. The black stint didn't really suit her. It's a miracle she has any hair left with how often she changes her mind. "That's my lovely new roommate. Be right back." Her video cuts off again.

"Gracie, where are you?" Marti leans closer to the screen, squinting. "It looks...dark?"

"Oh." I laugh and rustle around in my blankets until I find my headphones, shooting a glance at the stairs. Leo and Keava are watching a movie in the living room, so they shouldn't be able to hear me down here, but just in case, I shove them in my ears. "Still settling in. The...uh...old light fixtures here broke, like, right after I moved in, and I haven't installed anything new yet."

"That blows," says Alison, whose face slowly shifts into a mischievous grin. "Why not have that new *boyfriend* come over and help you?"

"Boyfriend?" Marti demands. "Why have I not heard about this?"

I glare at Alison. "I never said *boyfriend*."

"You said you were seeing someone—same difference!"

I shoot a look at the stairs again.

"Did you meet him at work?" Marti asks. "How's that going anyway? What's the magazine you're working for called?"

"Okay, okay, I'm back." Trish's video reappears, saving me. She huffs as she falls into her bed, now holding a gigantic orange cat. "The new roommate and Gregory aren't exactly... well acquainted yet."

I swallow hard, hoping Marti will drop it. It's my own fault. I don't know why I'm bothering to keep up with the charade anymore. At first it started off with a few white lies over text. *Oh yeah, I'm dating. The job hunt is going well. Oh, you're apartment hunting? Me too!* With all of them landing jobs in their fields within *days* of graduating—not to mention their ever-exciting love lives that involve a new prospect every other week and new apartments in new cities—I just couldn't tell them the truth.

That not a single company has been interested in me. I've barely talked to a boy since college. And if it weren't for Leo, I'd be living with my parents right now.

And, I guess, if it weren't for Liam, I'd still be unemployed.

They're out doing everything you're supposed to do when you graduate college, and I'm here sitting alone in a basement.

I never intended to keep up the lies for long. Just keep them vague enough until I *did* find something, and then they wouldn't be lies anymore.

That was weeks ago.

Every day that I don't come clean, I feel like I'm digging myself farther and farther into this damn hole, and I'm starting to think they'll never *not* be lies. I'm going to be single and pity-employed by my brother's best friend for the rest of my life, and maybe if Leo is feeling generous, he'll let me turn his basement into an oasis for shelter cats so I can fulfill my destiny as a lonely, crazy cat lady where I'll pick up knitting and watching game shows in the afternoon—

"Helloooo. Earth to Gracie."

I blink back to the laptop to find all three of my friends staring at me.

"Did you hear me?" asks Marti, sans face mask. She must have gone to wash it off while I wasn't paying attention.

"She was contemplating the end of the world," says Trish.

"I *said*, I have news!" says Marti. "And speaking of the end of the world, Gracie, *You, Me, and the End of the World* is getting a movie."

"*What?*" I all but shriek.

"I don't know what that is," singsongs Alison.

"I think it's a book," offers Trish.

"Not just any book!" I scramble off the bed to dig through the box of books I haven't unpacked yet. When I find the right one, I proudly thrust it in the air.

It's one of the most beat-up books I own from how many times I've read it. The pages are full of tabs and highlights and notes in the margins, the pages yellowed from reading it on the beach over and over.

"That's not even the best part!" squeals Marti. "I don't think they've made the news public yet. I heard about it from my agent. She sent over the sides for the audition, and I recognized it immediately."

"Wait, *audition?*" I throw myself onto the bed. "You mean… you might…"

"I'm auditioning for Teagan!"

"Oh my God. Oh my *God.*"

"Will someone please explain to me what's going on," whines Alison.

"This is our favorite book, like, ever," gushes Marti. "We both read it when we were in middle school. It's one of the first things we bonded over freshman year. The author is actually from Gracie's hometown."

I hold up the book for them to see.

Trish leans forward, squinting. "Is that a *zombie?*"

Marti nods vigorously. "It's a romcom. Set in the middle of a zombie apocalypse."

"It's about this small town on the coast that everyone thinks is crazy because everyone there has been preparing for the end of the world and has, like, fallout bunkers and everything."

"And the main character has been training for this all her life with her dad, so she's this crazy badass—"

"And her love interest is her high school rival—"

"And they end up needing each other's help to survive—"

"Okay, okay, we get it," says Alison.

"You're never going to read it, are you?" I say.

Alison smiles innocently and shrugs. "I'll watch the movie! Especially if Marti's in it!"

"When's your audition?" asks Trish.

Marti waves a hand. "Oh, I'm just sending in a self-tape. I'll probably never hear anything back."

"No, no, I can see it!" I insist. "You would be so good. You have to keep us updated!"

She does an excited little shimmy. "Keep your fingers crossed for me."

"I think we should plan a girls' trip," Alison jumps in. "Like a reunion."

"Where to?" I ask.

"I vote a beach," Trish says immediately. "Portland will be in full swing with the rain before I know it, so I'll be craving some sun soon."

"I vote Vegas," says Marti. "You guys could come to LA for a bit first if you want, then we would road trip it."

"What about a boat? Like a cruise?" offers Alison.

"Okay, is it lame to suggest we bring the boys too?" says Trish. "This is the first time we're all dating at the same time, so it could be kind of fun, right?"

I stop breathing.

"Oh my God, yeah, you're right!" says Marti. "That could be fun."

"I kind of desperately want to get the fuck away from my family around the holidays, so what if we spent Christmas together instead?" suggests Alison. "Then we'd have like, what? How many months away is that?"

"Six months," I say, my shoulders relaxing. That's a perfectly reasonable amount of time to find a boy to bring...or fake a breakup, if need be. The rest of it, well, hopefully I can figure that out in six months too.

The alternative—being in this exact situation half a year from now—kind of makes me want to swan dive off the edge of my bed.

"Right!" says Alison. "So that gives us plenty of time to come up with a game plan."

Martina shrugs. "Works for me."

Trish cracks open a beer and raises it to her camera. "I'm in!"

"Gracie?" says Alison. "We're not doing it unless everyone agrees."

The chat falls silent, everyone looking at their screens.

Everyone looking at *me*.

I force a smile. "Of course I'm in."

Chapter Nine

LIAM

This girl is going to kill me. Gracie left her notes on the desk yesterday, and being the nosy bastard I am, I had to investigate. They were full of charts, pros and cons lists, and everything was color coded. Starting social media pages was at the top of her list, then she broke it down into which accounts she thought we should start first. Seeing as I've never been on any of them, naturally, I wanted to do some research before I saw her again so I could at least have an inkling of what she's talking about.

Her highest-ranked suggestion—some short-from video app—looks like an invention from the deepest pits of hell. The scrolling is endless. I tried to narrow the search by looking for other artists or shops similar to mine, and even that yielded millions of results.

The top-ranking ones being weird thirst traps of guys posing and zooming in on themselves in a mirror before transitioning to whatever piece they're doing that day.

Maybe I *do* have limits on what I'm willing to do to save the shop.

And I don't see the point. What are the odds a video like that would make a difference in the business? That it would convince someone to come to me specifically for a tattoo? I don't get it.

Okay, yeah, once I was down the social media rabbit hole, I also stalked Gracie a bit. Because that's what employers do, I told myself. They check up on who they're hiring. They usually do it *before* hiring someone, but semantics.

Gracie was always artistic growing up. Always taking pictures, planning elaborate birthday parties, customizing the hell out of her screensavers. She was also a good student—or whatever the step above a "good student" is—so it was safe to assume she'd be good at her job.

But damn. The first result that pops up from googling her name is her website. Upon further inspection, it seemed more like a digital résumé. It showcased her graphic and website design abilities, as well as a portfolio of her photography and previous social media work that she did through internships in college. It also linked to her personal social media—of which she has an account on what must be every site available. Every profile is meticulously branded and polished. How this girl hasn't already landed a job is beyond me.

I sigh and tuck away my phone. It's early enough that the skatepark is empty—it could also be since the crowds have been gravitating to the newer park by the water. That one's nicer without a doubt, but something about this place will always feel like home.

The smooth glide of my board's wheels against the concrete fills the silence as I kick off the ground and close my eyes for a moment, reveling in the feel of the cool morning air against my face. It's been a while since I had this place to myself.

I drop down in the bowl, letting my muscle memory take

over, but even after a while, it's not enough to turn my brain off.

I crunched the numbers after Gracie finished yesterday, something I've been avoiding for months. It was easier to stomach the idea without knowing how far we were in the red.

Maybe my dad's right. Maybe I'm not cut out for this. Maybe I'd be better off tattooing in someone else's shop instead of trying to run my own.

I hit the curve sooner than expected and lose my footing.

"Shit." I roll to the side so I don't completely bite it while my board flies off in the opposite direction. I slide down the wall until I hit the ground, then sigh and brace my arms on my knees.

"Brooks! I thought that was you!"

I groan as Fletcher rolls up and stops just above where I'm sitting. Once upon a time—give or take ten years ago—I taught him how to skate in this very park. He was the new kid in town, awkward and waiting to grow into his nose and ears, and a few years younger. I don't know why I took him under my wing. Maybe he reminded me of my younger brother. Or a version Asher could have been if I actually liked him.

"Tell me you didn't see—"

"You eat it like you've never been on a board in your life? Oh yeah, I saw." He grins as he sits and hangs his legs over the side. "What's got you so far in your head you forgot where your feet are?"

"Oh, you know, existential dread. The usual."

"Ah, I know it well." Fletch flips his cap on backward, flashes a toothy smile, and hops up with his board in his hand. "You mind? Or are you planning on setting up camp down there?"

"All right. All right." I get up to retrieve my board and watch as he stalls on the edge a moment before dropping in, his head lowered the way it always is before he goes for a trick. But after all that buildup, he just draws a few lines. "Was that Leo's sister I saw coming out of your shop yesterday?" he calls as he finishes on the opposite side of the bowl and kicks his board up.

I nod, already heading for the bench where I dumped my things. This hasn't cleared my head the way I was hoping it would, and if Fletch is here, it's only a matter of minutes before the others pour in.

"Let me guess, a butterfly? Song lyrics?"

"I wasn't tattooing her, you idiot."

He gasps. "An illicit affair? She does look all grown up now, doesn't she?"

I ram my shoulder against his as I pass. "Don't start. I hired her."

"*Hired* her? For what?"

I shrug and throw my bag over my shoulder. "Social media. Update my website. The kind of shit I hate doing."

"I didn't know you were hiring. Maybe I wanted the job."

I snort. "I'll keep you in mind if I ever want to go out of business."

The jab makes him smile wider. "So, is she staying?"

I fish my car keys out of my bag. "Huh?"

"Gracie Collins. She just graduated college, didn't she? Is she sticking around here?"

I asked her something similar at Milano's the other day. *I'm just visiting*, she said.

I don't know if she was embarrassed or being here doesn't feel permanent to her, if she's planning on skipping out the second a job offer—a *real* one with a boss who knows what they're doing and benefits and whatever else people consider before taking a job—comes through.

I know that must be her plan, but the thought still churns

in the pit of my stomach. I hadn't considered someone else stealing her out from under me before she gets to all of her plans for the shop. And now that I've dared to hope she could be the saving grace I need, I don't know what I'll do if she leaves town as quickly as she'd come. However much time I do get with her, I better not waste it.

Fletcher raises his eyebrows at my hesitation, and I shake my head.

"I have no idea."

But God I hope so.

Chapter Ten

GRACIE

On Saturday morning, I take off before anyone else is awake. Leo dug out an old bike from the garage so I'd have a way to get around town. For the past week, I've been relying on getting a ride from him or Liam. Seems he was already as sick of that as I was. So with a backpack on one shoulder and my camera bag on the other, I throw my leg over the bike and hope to find my way to the shore from here. Leo said it was walking distance, but Leo also runs half marathons for fun like an absolute psychopath.

The rest of Sweetspire seems as slow to rise as Edgewater always was. I don't see a single other person as I make my way toward the water. I, unfortunately, am getting used to waking up at six in the morning every day thanks to those damn windows.

The chilly morning air blows my hair behind my shoulders, and I close my eyes for a moment as I wind through the rows of houses, the smell of salt and sunscreen a steady comfort.

"Gracie Collins! Is that you?"

My eyes snap open, and I swerve. I let out a yelp as the bike jumps up onto the sidewalk, but luckily I manage to regain control and squeeze on the brakes.

I turn at the pickup truck idling beside me, then do a double take at the girl smiling sheepishly behind the wheel.

"Carson?"

"Where're you headed?" she asks.

"Uh, just the shore." I yank the strap of my camera bag higher on my shoulder before it can fall.

She nods to the side. "Throw your bike in the back. I'll give you a ride."

If not for the truck, I might not have recognized her. She's driven this giant monstrosity since sophomore year of high school, and it's as hard to climb into as I remember. It's been only four years since I last saw Carson, but everything about her looks different.

Every memory I have of her since elementary school includes her long blond hair in two French braids, but it's now dyed black and chopped into a blunt bob that barely skims her chin. Her face looks thinner too, her cheekbones more pronounced, and I'd be surprised if that wasn't filler in her lips, because they definitely never looked like that before.

"What are you doing out here so early?" I ask as I pull the door shut behind me.

"Oh, I was just heading home."

Home?

My confusion must show on my face because she shrugs as she pulls away from the curb. "I work nights." Before I can ask for more details, she adds, "And anyway, how long have you been back in Jersey? I had no idea you were here."

"A week or so. I, um, I moved in with Leo."

Her eyebrows shoot up.

"It's temporary," I add quickly.

The eyebrows come back down and pinch together.

We've made it to the water now, and she shifts the truck into park, but I don't climb out.

I don't know when or why we stopped talking. We were inseparable almost all our lives. By senior year of high school, we'd started growing apart—different friends, different hobbies—and by the time I left for college, somehow we went from talking every day to not exchanging a single word for four years. And the longer that silence between us grew, the harder it became to be the one to reach out.

"Look, Carson, I'm—"

"Gracie, I'm sorry I never—"

We both break off with an awkward laugh, and I look down at the camera bag in my lap.

"You coming out here to take pictures?" she asks.

"Yeah, and I just missed the water, I guess." I bite my lip, sigh, and add, "I'm staying at Leo's because I haven't been able to find a job after I graduated. And every minute I'm in his house I feel like more of a failure. I just—I needed the fresh air. Maybe I'll get some shots to add to my portfolio if any turn out okay. Sorry, I don't know why I'm telling you all this. You're probably exhausted and just want to get home. I'll—" I jab my thumb over my shoulder and reach for the door handle.

She lays a hand on my arm before I can climb out. "Have you had coffee yet?"

For a while there, that was our thing. Getting coffee and going for walks on the beach as we gossiped and swapped stories since we were in all different classes and barely got to see each other during the day.

"You know what? I'm not taking no for an answer." She hops out of the truck and circles to my side like she's going to pull me out if I don't do it myself. "You can leave that here, if you want. I'll lock it." She gestures to my things as I join her on the sidewalk. I leave the backpack but keep my camera bag, then follow her as she heads for the line of shops along the shore.

Most of them don't look open yet, but a tiny yellow house on the corner has lights glowing in the windows. A bell rings overhead as Carson steps inside first. There's so much more confidence in her walk than I ever remember there being. She commands attention as she walks with her head held high, shoulders thrown back, and an easy smile on her face.

Even with just the two of us in here, the space is pretty cramped. Two tables are against the far wall, with the counter across from them. I wonder if the owners live in the other parts of the house.

"Gracie? What do you want?" asks Carson with a glance at me over her shoulder.

I spout off my order then hurry forward and dig out my debit card before Carson can pay. She opens her mouth to protest, but I wave her off. "For the ride."

She rolls her eyes but smiles as the barista hands over her order—something in a large hot cup.

"You're not going to be cold carrying that out there?" she asks as the barista finishes my drink.

"It could be subzero temperatures and I'd still be drinking iced coffee."

She snorts and leads the way outside. There are decent enough waves this morning that I spot a few surfers in the water, but the beach itself is empty. Carson and I slip off our shoes before treading into the sand, and for a moment, the déjà vu is staggering enough that I forget where I am—*when* I am.

I watch the gentle morning sun reflect off the water, and an overwhelming sense of peace washes through me, so contrary to the heavy, suffocating feeling that's been weighing on my chest every morning that I wake up in that basement. There's something about being this close to the ocean that makes any problem feel small.

"So are you looking for work around here?" Carson asks as I sip my drink.

I try in vain to tuck my hair behind my ears as the wind whips it around my face. "Not exactly. I've been applying mostly for positions in the city. Either Philly or New York. For now, I'm working at Liam's shop on Main Street."

"*Liam Brooks?*" she practically screeches as she whips around and comes to an abrupt stop.

"I—yeah." I shrug.

"Liam Brooks," she repeats. "Leo's best friend, Liam Brooks."

It doesn't sound like a question, so I don't respond.

"Your biggest childhood crush, Liam Brooks."

"I—*what?*" I sputter. "I *never* said I had a crush on Liam."

She snorts. "Yeah, you never *said.*"

"I hated him growing up. And he hated me."

That gets a full laugh out of her.

"What?" I demand.

"Gracie, acting like you hate someone has always been your idea of flirting."

"I—that is not true."

"Mm-hmm." Her expression turns thoughtful. "Admittedly, I don't think you realize you do it."

"*Or* I was actually irritated by Liam always teasing me."

"Did it ever occur to you maybe that was his way of flirting too?"

I scoff and ignore whatever the hell that little flutter in my stomach is. Now she's really lost her mind. "You're being ridiculous," I mumble into my coffee.

"*Mm-hmm.*" She's full-on grinning now, and I shake my head and turn my attention to the incoming waves.

I absolutely never had a crush on Liam Brooks. He was annoying and smug, and he and Leo were always ganging up on me. And I absolutely never noticed when he had his growth spurt in seventh grade and suddenly his limbs weren't so gangly. Or when he stopped with the buzz cuts and grew out his hair in high school, which suited him much better. Or the way his eyes always looked different after his mom died.

"He runs a tattoo shop now, right? No offense, but what does he need you for?"

"Updating his website, social media marketing, that kind of thing."

She purses her lips and nods. "Well, that could be good, right? So many jobs won't hire you because you don't have experience, but this would technically be professional experience to put on your résumé." The look on her face twists from contemplative to mischievous. "So is he as hot as I remember?"

"Can we talk about you for a minute? It's been four years. Catch me up."

She squints and looks away with a shrug. "Stayed around home for the first year or so after high school. Once I had enough money to move out on my own, I came down this way to get a little more distance from my parents, and there's just more to do over here. I have roommates—three of us total. We rent a house a few miles that way." She points the way we came.

"How'd you meet them? Your roommates?"

An odd look passes over her face, but it's gone so quickly that I might have imagined it. "From work."

I wait, but a heavy silence descends like the one in the truck earlier. It's so foreign I don't know what to think. She was always the more talkative of the two of us, spilling every detail you never needed—or wanted—to know.

"So do you work around here?" I ask slowly.

"No, it's up almost near Newark. A little less than an hour commute, but I'm only there a few nights a week, and I like having some…space from it."

We've stopped walking now, and she stares out at the ocean, the gentle crash of the waves filling the silence. I step up beside her and chew on my lip. Years ago, I wouldn't have hesitated to push for more. But we're not close like that anymore, so I don't feel like I have the right.

"I guess it's better that you hear it from me," she murmurs. "It's not public knowledge around here, but with how gossip gets around, I've always figured it's just a matter of time." She rolls her coffee cup between her hands. "It's one of the gentlemen's clubs."

I'm not sure what I was expecting, but it certainly wasn't that. I nod slowly, trying not to stare at her, but I can't help it. My eyes trace over every difference as if I'll find something there to make processing this easier.

"The money's good," she says quietly. "A lot of the finance guys from the city come in pretty often. Some nights are worse than others but, I mean, you know what it costs to live around here. And without a college degree, finding a decent job…"

"You don't have to explain yourself to me," I say quickly. "I'm not judging. At all."

She gives me an unconvincing smile. "I guess I just want you to understand. I didn't plan this. I was looking for roommates at first to try to afford moving out—if I had to spend one more day with my parents, I swear one of us was going to commit murder—and I met this girl off a Facebook group, and we grabbed coffee. We got along really well. She's the one who introduced me to the place. Said she'd vouch for me to get a bartending job there. When I went in to interview, they said I could have a job, but not behind the bar. I guess I figured, what was the harm? If I tried it out for a week? And the money was so good those first few days…I was hooked."

"Are you…safe? The guys there, they don't try anything?"

She purses her lips. "The security there is good, but I'd be lying if I said there weren't some bad nights. But it comes with the job, I guess."

My stomach does a little flip, but I try not to show it on my face. I can't wrap my head around it. "I—thank you. For telling me."

She turns to look at me, and her eyes get a little misty as she smiles.

I'm the first to lean in and pull her into a hug. She falls into it like she was desperate for one, and I tighten my arms.

"I'm sorry we fell out of touch," I say.

"Me too."

"Maybe it was fate running into you today," I say as I pull back.

She smirks. "Maybe it was."

Chapter Eleven

LIAM

"You get stood up?"

I give Fletcher an unamused smile as he refills my beer. "Very funny."

So Leo's half an hour late. He's never been particularly punctual. He's always lived in his own little world that way. I'd be surprised if he knew what day it was. Add a new marriage into the mix, and I'm lucky he still agrees to meet up on a weekly basis.

I fear it's genetic with the Collinses. Even as kids, no matter if it was a playdate, a summer camp, or school, five minutes late was early for whoever was dropping him off.

Gracie being the exception, of course. Now that she's been getting herself to work, she's beaten me to the door nearly every day this week.

Fletcher disappears to clean up the other end of the bar as a group of women shoves their stools back and heads for the door. I check my watch. Ah, 6:00 PM.

Once the High Dive's three-dollar happy hour ends, it loses most of its appeal for people.

Not for me. It's one of the few places around here without my last name on the front, so I'll happily take sitting on a shitty bar stool that might break at any moment and sipping watered-down beer in near-darkness.

Light spills through the door as Leo *finally* stumbles his way in, highlighting the dust swirling in the air. He ditched the coveralls before coming, but there's no mistaking the grease coating his hands.

"Dude," I say as he slides onto the stool next to me.

He grimaces and reaches across the bar for some napkins. "I know. Sorry I'm late. Tommy fired someone *again*, leaving just the two of us with a slammed calendar all day. It's a miracle I made it out when I did."

"What'd they do this time?"

"Fucking breathed too loud, I don't know. Thanks, Fletch." Leo accepts the beer from him and takes a long drink. "What's up with you?"

"Oh, you know. Living the dream." Fletcher pops his eyebrows, wets one of the cleanup rags, and hands it to Leo.

Leo winces and scrubs at his hands some more. "How's the home improvement project going?"

"If you want to help knock some shit down, you can come see for yourself," says Fletcher.

"You never invited me," I say.

Fletcher braces his hands on the bar and raises his eyebrows. "Do you want to come work on the house?"

I smile. "Not even a little bit."

Leo laughs as the front door swings open behind him. Fletcher sighs and exchanges a wave with the newcomers.

"Regulars?" I ask.

"They sit at the bar for at least three hours and never tip," Fletcher says out of the corner of his mouth before heading that way.

"How's everything with the shop?" asks Leo. "My sister making you regret hiring her yet?"

"No, she's doing a really good job so far, actually."

Leo turns the corners of his lips down as he sips his beer. "It's only been a week. Give her some time."

I chuckle. "Why? Things not working out well with your new living situation?"

Leo tries to hang on to his smirk, but the fondness in his eyes whenever he talks about Gracie is plain as fucking day. I don't care what he says. I know he's thrilled she chose him over their parents. To anyone who doesn't know them, their relationship probably looks contentious—full of bickering and shit talking. But I know they both love every second of it.

"Okay, so it's nice having her around again," he mutters. "It was weird having her so far away for four years."

"How's Keava doing with it?"

He shrugs. "Good, I think. She's got three sisters, and I know she misses them. I was hoping she'd like having another girl around, you know? And since she and I got together while Gracie was off at school, they've never really had the chance to get to know each other."

I hum noncommittedly, my mind drifting to the conversation I had with Gracie the other day at the shop—to the weird vibe of Keava's questions in the kitchen, even as Gracie got visibly more uncomfortable by the second. I don't know why the memory makes me clench my teeth.

But maybe Leo's right. She and Keava are basically strangers to each other. It could just take some time for them to feel each other out. It's an awkward situation on both sides, and Leo's too fond of both of them to be anything but oblivious.

"And Gracie always said she wished you were a girl, so," I offer lightly.

He smirks. "And there's that."

"I'm a little surprised Gracie asked you, to be honest."

"Oh, it was my idea."

My eyebrows rise, and he shrugs. "I love my parents, but those two extra years I stayed with them while I wrapped up trade school?" He shakes his head and raises his eyes to the ceiling like he's watching it all back. "Made me feel like I'd never *feel* like an adult, you know? Just didn't want that for her. Especially because I could tell she's been taking the job hunt hard. Anyway, how's everything going with your family?"

"Who the hell knows?" I mumble as I drink my beer. "Called an *emergency family meeting* tomorrow night."

"Oh God. What for?"

"Your guess is as good as mine."

Leo hums thoughtfully. "Asher got someone pregnant."

"Or several someones. Maybe Taylor found a way to buy a personality."

Leo chokes on his beer. "Your family's hidden past with the Mafia has finally been revealed."

I throw my hands up. "*Finally.*"

"They just can't decide on the name for the new taffy flavor."

I nod solemnly. "It's been an ongoing debate."

"What are you two snickering about over here?" asks Fletcher as he digs beneath the bar for more glasses.

"Theorizing about what the latest Brooks family meeting could be about," says Leo.

Fletch waves a hand as he sets the glasses on the bar and fills them with water. "Oh, that's easy. They need Liam to model for the next ad campaign."

Leo bursts out laughing so loud the group at the other end of the bar turns to stare.

I scowl. "Why is that funny?"

But that just makes Leo laugh harder. He gasps as he wipes a tear from the corner of his eye. "Did you—*see*—the last—ad—your family—did?"

I frown, trying to think back, but I stopped paying attention years ago. Between the Brooks Candy Company and the million little businesses along the shore we've acquired over the last century, it's impossible to keep up with it all.

Now Fletcher's shoulders are shaking like he's holding back a laugh.

"What?" I demand.

"That collab they did with the candy-flavored hard seltzers?" says Fletcher. "The girls on the beach, with their bikinis made of…" He gestures vaguely to his chest.

"Oh, for fuck's sake." I slap Leo's arm, who's now bent over his knees, laughing so hard that no sound is coming out.

"I'm—picturing you—buck-ass naked—holding a lollipop over your—"

I raise my beer to my lips to cover my smile. "Neither of you are funny."

"All I'm saying is, if you do it, I'll frame it and hang it over the bar for free," says Fletcher.

Leo points at him. "Put one in your new house as décor."

"Make sure to get a copy to Gracie so she can post it all over your new social feeds," says Fletch. "You'll be *swimming* in customers."

I groan and cover my face with my hands.

"*Helloooo?*" complains a woman down the bar. "We're still waiting over here."

Fletcher sighs, scoops up the waters, and heads that way.

"Good riddance!" I call.

Grinning, Leo tries to pat me on the back, but I move a seat away.

"Run all you want. We are bonded for *life*." He holds up his pointer finger, exposing the scar from our stupid *blood brothers* ritual we did when we were ten.

I wag my own scarred finger in the air. "And it's all been downhill since then."

Chapter Twelve

GRACIE

I head into the shop Monday morning with a pep in my step. I lock the bike up front before striding inside with my backpack and camera bag slung over my shoulder and my head held high.

Liam can make fun of me all he wants, and maybe it's a little overzealous, but the more I think about it, the less working here sounds like a bad idea. Like Carson said, maybe this is an opportunity. If I can revamp the shop's presence online, I can use this as a real-life case study. A little *look-what-I-can-do* example to show other companies. Something that'll make me stand out enough to find the right job within the next six months.

The past week has been about finding my bearings. Learning the basics, making plans. Now it's time to get serious. And I know I can do this. When I'm through with this place, I'm going to have people who never even dreamed of getting a tattoo lined up down the block. I'm going to be dodging job offers left and right. I'll be able to hold it over Liam's head for the rest of his life that I doubled—no, *tripled*—the shop's income through my social media plans alone—

"You have something to keep busy with today?" Liam is standing on the other side of the desk, though his attention is squarely on his phone, and judging by the tension in his face, whatever he's looking at isn't good.

"I...was going to start setting up the different social accounts, make a plan for the website updates, take some pictures of the shop since it's nice and sunny today...why? Is there something else you want me to do?"

"Nope. Works for me." He finally glances up at me, but his eyes don't meet mine, and he gives me a closed-lip smile before shoving the phone into his pocket and heading for the back of the shop.

I stare after him for a second, not sure if I'm imagining the weird vibe, but he doesn't come back out. *It's none of my business*, I remind myself, then tidy up the desk and pull out my camera. I'll want to clean up and stage the inside of the shop more first, but I can grab some shots of the exterior. They'll be good to add to the website but also some easy first posts once I set up the new social accounts.

The bells above the door jangle as I step outside, and I tie my hair up in a ponytail before the breeze can make a mess of it. The sunlight is gentle and golden this morning, the way it falls on the building almost whimsical and picturesque. I can already tell these are going to turn out *so good*.

I try few different angles from the curb, then jog across the street for a wider shot. As I close one eye and peer through the eyepiece, the image blurs. I pull the camera away to wipe off the lens, but my vision doesn't clear.

Oh, God, no.

It's been so long since I've had one—years—but I recognize the aura for what it is immediately. Pixelated lines zigzag across my vision, slowly growing in size. I have maybe thirty minutes before the nausea and headache set in, but probably less until I can't see all together. I don't bother checking my bags for my medication because I know I won't find it. After years without a migraine, I stopped carrying it around. *Shit.* I couldn't bike home right now if I tried.

Sometimes my vision clears up after about forty-five minutes, so I guess I'll have to wait it out. My head will be on fucking fire by then, especially if I have to go out in sunlight, but I don't see any other solution.

The shop is quiet as I step inside and retreat to the bathroom to ride this out. No sign of Liam.

I close the door, rest my back against it, and slide down to the floor. I can't believe this is happening. Why now? After all these years? I mean, sure, I've been stressed, which used to be one of the things that triggered them. But I thought I'd outgrown them altogether once my hormones settled after puberty. That's what my doctors said, at least.

I squeeze my eyes shut, but the lines keep dancing behind my eyelids. Honestly, it's one of the most annoying parts of these headaches. Being forced to watch this damn light show until it makes me throw up.

I don't know how long I sit there with my legs pulled to my chest and my forehead pressed against my knees. Long enough for the pain to set in behind my eyes and at the nape of my neck.

Footsteps thud quietly outside the door. They disappear, then increase in volume like someone is pacing. After a moment, there's a soft knock on the door.

"Gracie?" calls Liam.

"Yeah?" I call weakly.

"Are you all right?"

I sigh. I'm going to be utterly useless for the rest of the day.

There's no getting around it. So much for taking the day by storm. And during my *second week* here too.

"Gracie?"

"No," I finally answer. "I—I'm sorry. I'm getting a migraine, and I don't have my medication. I'd just go home but I—" I huff out a frustrated exhale. "I can't see right now and—"

"Can I come in?"

"Okay." I scoot away from the door, but he doesn't open it right away. His footsteps sound like he's going in the opposite direction. Several moments pass before he returns and opens the door.

I cover my eyes and turn away as the piercing light fills the small bathroom, but he slips inside and closes the door behind him just as quickly.

"All right. Here we go." I startle as his hands brush my face. He pulls mine away, then slides on a pair of sunglasses that are a bit too big for me. "Come on. I'll drive you home."

I take the hand he offers and stumble to my feet, my balance off. He braces a hand on my back as he leads me to his truck parked out back.

It's not until I'm in the passenger seat, my hands pressed firmly to my eyes to block out the sun, that it occurs to me I left everything on the front desk. "My stuff—"

"I already got it," Liam says, and I feel him set my bag at my feet.

"I did manage to get a few good pictures," I say as the engine roars to life and he pulls away from the curb. "And the rest of what I was planning to do today I can do from home. It'll probably have to be, like, eight hours from now…"

"Gracie," he says, sounding…perplexed. "I don't care about the work. It'll get done another day. Don't worry about it."

I press my lips together as the car turns, not sure if the steadily building nausea is from my head or motion sickness.

"I didn't realize you still got these," he says after a while.

"I didn't either. It's been years."

"You know Mak started to get them after pregnancy? She'd never had them before. The doctor said it could just be temporary with her hormones out of whack and whatever. She said they were worse than giving birth had been."

I hum, not knowing how else to respond. I barely know Liam's sister, Makayla. She's the oldest of the Brooks, putting her a good ten years older than me. She also got the hell out of town the moment she turned eighteen, so the last time I saw her, I was in elementary school. I didn't even know she had a kid.

And I'm far too busy concentrating on not throwing up in Liam's very nice, very *clean* truck.

A low, primal groan escapes me as I fold forward and put my head between my knees.

"Gracie?" says Liam, a hint of panic in his voice now. "Do you need me to pull over?"

"How close are we?"

He turns the AC up higher and points the vents in my direction. "Two minutes?"

"I can make it." I have no idea if that's true, but I guess we're going to find out because there is no way—*no way*—he is pulling over and letting me puke out of the side of his truck. It's not like we're on some two-lane highway in the middle of nowhere. We're in the center of this very small, very gossipy town. I don't need the witnesses, and my pride can't handle being *that person* who threw up on some random person's yard or a public sidewalk.

But the second Liam pulls up to Leo's house, all bets are off. Liam tries to be helpful by opening the door and offering his hand, but I push past him, hurrying for the bathroom. I barely manage to open the toilet seat before the contents of my stomach surge up. I retch a few times, the action making the pounding in my head amplify, then slump against the wall, exhausted.

This is not good. In my experience, how a migraine starts sets the tone for how the rest of the day will go. If I can take my medicine and stay in the dark right at the start, it's like I cut the headache off at the knees and it never builds to its full potential.

Today, it's clear, will not be like that.

Liam knocks quietly on the door.

"You can leave my stuff out there," I murmur.

A pause, then: "I won't have you falling down the stairs on my conscience."

After flushing the toilet and rinsing my mouth in the sink, I swing the door open. "Didn't know you *had* a conscience."

His grin almost looks relieved as he steps aside to let me pass, and true to his word, he follows me to the basement. But even once I make it down the stairs, he doesn't leave. The sunlight is streaming through the windows in full force, and I curse myself yet again for not putting up curtains.

I groan and burrow under my blankets for cover.

"Hold on," Liam mutters, then jogs up the stairs.

I hear him return, but don't come out of my cave. That is, until he starts *hammering* something.

"What are you—?"

He's balanced on top of a stool he must have brought down from the kitchen with a hammer in his hand and nails between his teeth. He secures a dark blue towel over the first window, casting darkness over the bed, then moves his setup down the wall to tackle the other one. I wince, but the relief from the darkness far outweighs the pulses of pain from the noise.

"Good enough, yeah? Hopefully Leo won't mind a few holes in his walls." He grimaces. "And his towels."

"Thank you," I say softly. I don't think I could manage to do it myself right now, and I wouldn't have lasted long in this room. I probably would've ended up curled in a ball in the bathroom with a towel shoved in the space beneath the door to block the light.

"What else do you need?" He hops down from the stool and discards the hammer in the corner, looking around like he's eager for his next task.

"I'm good, Liam. Really."

"Oh, come on. There has to be something you use to help you feel better."

"Ice," I admit.

"Ice…"

"Like an ice pack." I wave a hand around. "I put them on my head."

"Right." He pauses with one foot on the stairs. "You want heat too? Is this an alternating kind of thing?"

"I doubt Leo has a heating pad," I mumble. Keava, maybe. But I don't want to go through her stuff.

His only response is the sound of him jogging up the stairs.

I dig around in the box beside my bed while he's gone until I find my medication, though it's probably pointless. It never makes a difference unless I take it within the first half hour or so.

Liam's quieter when he returns, like he's being careful with his footsteps. "Here we are."

I squint one eye open as he kneels beside my head, an ice pack in each hand. My vision has cleared enough to make out his facial features, at least. But that only means things will get worse from here. After my vision clears, that's when the pain really starts to set in. I prop one behind my neck, then use the other to press against my forehead.

He sets a heating pad on the nightstand. "I'll hold off on

warming this up for, what do you think, twenty minutes? Twenty ice, twenty heat?"

He says that like he's planning on staying that long.

"Liam...I can take it from here," I say slowly, not wanting to sound ungrateful, but my confusion pulls heavily at my voice. "And I'm sure you have more important things to do. Appointments. Clients."

"You trying to get rid of me? I'm hurt."

"No—I just—I—"

He lets out a soft chuckle and sits on the edge of the bed. "Gracie. Don't make it so easy, remember? Besides, a few of my other artists have clients today. They can manage without me for a bit. I don't have an appointment until later."

I scowl even though he can't see my face beneath the blankets. "You can't make fun of me right now. Haven't you heard you're not supposed to kick someone when they're down?"

"Gracie, I'd never make fun of you."

I scoff, then wince at the pain that shoots through my temples. "Liam, that's all you've done my whole life."

There's a pause. "I teased you growing up," he says quietly. "I never made fun of you."

I'd roll my eyes if that wouldn't hurt too. "There's a difference?"

"*Yes.*"

I don't know what to say to that, so I opt for nothing and adjust the ice pack to my eye sockets. I don't know if it actually helps with the pain, or the different physical sensation is just a nice distraction, but either way, it makes it more bearable. There's nothing worse than lying here with nothing to focus on but the pain.

"What does it feel like?" Liam asks after a while.

"Like I want to take an ice cream scooper and carve out my own eyeball."

"These usually last all day, don't they?"

I hum.

"What do you do then? Because you can't look at anything, right? So no TV or whatever."

I sigh. "If I'm lucky, I sleep through some of it. That's unlikely since this one started so early in the day. Quiet sounds don't bother me nearly as much as light, so I can listen to stuff to try to distract me. Music. Podcasts. Books. But sometimes even trying to process what I'm hearing hurts my brain too much. So I usually just lie here."

"All day?"

I shrug. "Don't have much of a choice."

"That sounds awful."

I press the ice pack to a different spot higher up on my head.

"Is me talking to you making it worse?" he asks when I don't respond.

"No," I admit. "You're actually…distracting me a bit."

"I've been told I can be very distracting. Here!" There's rustling on the nightstand, and I peek out to see what he's fishing around for.

My stomach flips as he pulls the book out from the rest of the pile and situates himself against the headboard.

"You are not reading me that book," I blurt.

He licks one finger, flips to the first page, then pauses. "*That* book."

"What?"

"You didn't say, 'You're not reading to me.' You said, 'You're not reading me *that* book.'" A devilish grin stretches across his face. "So why not? Why not this book?"

I look away.

"Gracie."

I say nothing.

"Is this a dirty book?"

He's never going to give it a rest now. My face flames despite the ice against my skin. "Maybe a little," I mumble against my pillow.

He flips the pages until he reaches the spot I dog-eared. "Chapter seventeen. Hm. Have we gotten to the good stuff yet?"

Silence.

"We have!" That damn grin grows wider as he crosses one ankle over the other and makes himself right at home in my bed. "All right. Catch me up. What's happened so far?"

I don't respond, but that apparently is not enough of a deterrent. "'Chapter seventeen,'" he reads. "'I wake up with his naked body in the bed beside me and about a dozen possibilities of how I could murder him and get away with it in my head'—Gracie, what *is this*?"

My hand shoots out from the blankets, but he holds the book out of reach.

I sigh. "It's enemies to lovers, okay? And you can't narrate and judge at the same time."

He hums as if it all makes sense now. "So why do they hate each other? What makes them enemies?"

I'm not sure why I'm entertaining this conversation. Maybe because his voice sounds genuinely curious and not like I'm about to be the punchline of the joke, or maybe because I haven't given much thought to the agonizing pain spreading through my skull for the past few minutes.

"They're more rivals than enemies. They're competitive figure skaters. They do pairs, but they're not each other's partners. None of the others really stand a chance against their two partnerships. For most competitions, it's pretty much a toss-up which one of them will get first or second. But the guy thinks this might be his last season, and the girl's partner is threatening to drop her if they don't win."

"Huh." He flips the book over to read the description on the back. "Figure skating," he mumbles to himself. "Do you watch the competitions and everything?"

I laugh a little. "No."

"So you don't care about the sport?"

"Nope."

"But you read about it."

"I mean, I don't *seek out* skating books. This one just had good reviews. And I liked the cover."

I've always been a sucker for the more symbolic, abstract covers. This one has a pair of skates dangling in the center, but it's the mix of colors and textures in the background—like watercolor paint—that really caught my eye.

He turns the book over to inspect it. One corner of his mouth turns down, and he nods his head to the side. "Okay, so I get it. The art is good."

He flips back to the marked chapter and starts reading. I stare at the side of his face, the blurry parts of my vision now lingering at the edges. I've known Liam practically my entire life, but I've never spent this much time around him alone. Most of the time we've spent together over the last twenty-two years hasn't been by choice. Which just makes this entire situation that much stranger.

But there's no denying how much the distraction helps.

He keeps his voice low and soft as I curl into a ball beneath the blankets and close my eyes. I think he'll stop after finishing the chapter, but then he moves onto the next, and the next, until I have no idea how much time has passed.

At some point, he pauses and goes upstairs for some water while I set up the heating pad. His footsteps are so quiet that I don't notice his return until the bed shifts beside me.

Before he can pick up the book again, I murmur, "Liam, why did you really hire me?"

He turns to me with a frown. "What do you mean?"

"Is this some weird loyalty to Leo thing? Or was it pity? Because if it was, we really don't have to—"

"It wasn't pity, Gracie. Okay, yes, at first I offered because I didn't like the way Keava was talking to you. But I also knew you'd be good at the job. And after, when I started doing some more research to see what I'd gotten myself into, it proved what I already knew."

"Research into…me?"

"Yes."

"So you stalked me."

"Yes," he says without missing a beat. "And you know what I found? That I'm the luckiest son of a bitch on the east coast because the most promising design graduate just fucking fell into my lap."

I roll my eyes despite my face heating under the compliment. But it sounds weird coming from him. "You're so full of it."

He doesn't respond for what feels like a long time, and when I glance up, he's not looking at me anymore. His gaze is focused somewhere across the room, and when he speaks again, his voice comes out softer. "I'm going to tell you something, Gracie. Something no one else knows. The shop's not profitable. It never has been. But I want it to be. I need it to be. So yeah, when I looked you up and I saw how good you were at what you do, it made me hopeful. Because maybe I hired you on a whim, but call it what you want, I think there's a reason for it. I think you and I can help each other."

The sincerity on his face is undeniable. I've wondered about the shop's income, how he was able to pay me so much when I rarely saw anyone in there. I'm willing to bet there's a lot more to it, but what it comes down to is: "You need me."

He ducks his head in acknowledgment. "I need you."

We stare at each other, and there's an openness in his eyes, almost a vulnerability, that I don't think I've ever seen before.

The shop isn't profitable, but he's able to afford to keep operating, to pay me, to take random days off like today. So there's money coming from somewhere. His family in some way, if I had to guess. And knowing Liam, he must hate that.

"I see a lot of potential with the shop, Liam," I say quietly. "It can get there."

He smiles. Not a smirk or a grin, just a soft, genuine smile.

"And thank you for taking care of me today."

His smile falters, and he leans back, adding a few more inches between us. After a long pause, he says, "Anytime, Little Leo."

Chapter Thirteen

LIAM

I hang around for another half hour or so until Gracie falls asleep before slipping out and hurrying to the shop for my afternoon appointment. The design is on the more complicated side—a mixture of vines, flowers, barbed wire, and chains—made trickier by the way it coils around my client's arm, but no matter how hard I try to concentrate, my mind keeps getting pulled back to Gracie's room.

The tension that had grown between us—whether it was even there or I'd just imagined it—disappeared in an instant when I dropped that nickname.

It needed to be done, but God, I regretted it the second it left my mouth.

It used to roll off my tongue so easily before. Now it feels like I'm grinding it out through my teeth.

Because the truth is, in the hours I spent at Gracie Collins's bedside today, not once—not even for a second—did it occur to me that she's Leo's sister.

But I'll do well to remember it.

The appointment takes up the rest of my afternoon, which

means, unfortunately, the timing works out perfectly. I pull up to the Brooks mansion about five minutes early, but by the looks of the cars in the drive, I'm the last one here. I debated not showing up at all, but when Dad announces an *emergency family meeting*, it's usually best to suffer through it than deal with everything you'll get from him after if you don't.

I frown as I head toward the front door, not recognizing the car parked closest to the front. Judging by the Pennsylvania plates, it's a rental. Is that…is *Makayla* here?

I push into the entryway without knocking, my hands starting to sweat. Dad's always had a talent for being overdramatic, so I didn't give much thought to the *summoning* out of nowhere. But if Mak flew in after not being home in nearly a decade, what if something is seriously wrong?

I stop short at the dining room, where everyone is already seated—Dad, Christine, Casey, Asher, Taylor, and—sure enough—Makayla, though her kid and husband aren't here. She grimaces when she sees me and drops her gaze.

That's not a good sign.

"Oh, Liam!" Christine beams as she rises to her feet. "So glad you could make it. We have a seat for you right here!" She gestures across the table to the chair between Taylor and Casey.

"Hey, Liam," says Casey with a big smile as I approach, and I rustle his hair as I sit.

"Hey, bro," offers my older brother, along with a slightly too forceful pat on the back.

"Taylor" is all I say.

"Glad you could finally make it," grunts Dad.

My eyes flick to the clock on the wall—two minutes until seven—but I grit my teeth. It won't make a difference.

The table has all the fancy shit on it, and everyone here is dressed like they're ready for Easter Sunday. The moment I walked through those doors in jeans and Vans, my opinions became obsolete.

Hell, who am I kidding. It happened long before that.

A server appears from the kitchen a moment later and starts pouring champagne.

I eye Christine, who's still grinning like she physically can't stop, then my Dad. They usually do red wine for these kinds of meetings.

"We won't hold you in suspense for too long," says Christine. "But before we get to celebrating, Makayla, would you like to do the honors?"

Mak smooths her hands down her sweater set and offers the server a closed-lip smile as they pour her glass.

"Well, Dad and I have been discussing the possibility of this for years. The Brooks Candy Company has been a national brand for generations. Of course, we've expanded along the boardwalk and around town with other businesses over the years, but we've gotten comfortable. Expansion hasn't been a priority. So we got to talking about what would be scalable while still staying true to the Brooks brand." She smiles and waits until everyone has their champagne before raising her glass. "To the new sister company with healthy candy alternatives, True Sweets!"

"Cheers!" says Christine as she clinks her glass against Makayla's then Dad's.

I exchange a glance with Asher at the other head of the table. He presses his lips together to hide his smirk then downs his entire glass in one swallow.

Taylor elbows me under the table. Sighing, I pick up my glass too and clink it against Casey's sparkling apple cider.

"Of course, this is more than just another business," Mak continues. "I really want to keep the Brooks heart in it." She turns to us with the same puppy dog eyes she's used her entire life. "I'd really like if we could all work on this together. Just the siblings. And I don't mean a little bit here and there. I mean full-time employment. A real role for everyone. One that plays to all of our different strengths."

Ah, here we go.

All eyes turn to me like they already know I'm going to be the problem.

"I think it's a great idea," I say.

Makayla blinks. "Really?"

"Sure." I shrug and set my drink on the table.

I don't give a fuck about candy—never have—and I certainly don't give a fuck about one that claims to have fewer calories or however they're going to spin this to convince people this is *healthier*. The thought of working for that day in and day out makes me want to repeatedly bash my head against a brick wall.

But it does seem like a natural next step for the business. It'll probably do well.

"I just don't have the room for anything else on my plate," I finish.

Silence falls over the table as the server returns with the first course.

"Liam," Mak starts, and I already know I won't like anything she has to say by that placating tone, like she's talking to her toddler. "This is a real opportunity—"

"I don't see why you need me."

"You would be great with design!" offers Christine, and I know she's just trying to be helpful, but I can't help but glare at her.

"Plenty of people design."

"But none in the family," Mak all but whines. "You're the only artist we have. And you're my *brother*."

"You've also got three more of those," I mutter. "Casey's a

budding artist." I pat the back of his chair, and he grins and sits up straighter. "Give him another ten years or so."

Now it's Mak's turn to glare at me.

"Liam," sighs Dad, and I'm surprised it's taken him this long to chime in. "No one wanted to push you after your grandfather's passing, but that excuse only lasts so long. You've had fun with your store, and I think we've all been incredibly patient. But it's time to stop fooling around and be the man this family needs you to be."

I don't even know where to start with that. He says that like the success of this family hinges on me and I'm being difficult, when in reality, he just hates having something out of his control. It would make his life so much tidier if I conformed like the rest of them.

I think he forgets that he might have taken over as the head of this family after Mom and Granddad passed, but he still only married into this legacy. He has created nothing. Granddad is the one who kept the brand alive when everyone thought it would go under.

"I'm sorry, is this a family meeting or an intervention?" Everyone else exchanges a look, and I bark out a laugh. "Everyone else already knew about this but me, didn't they?"

"I didn't!" offers Casey.

"Let me make myself very clear," I say. "The shop isn't going anywhere, and neither am I. It's doing well. I'm bringing on employees—"

Dad scoffs. "Pity hiring the Collins girl? Don't insult me. We all know what that was really about."

The Collins girl. As if he doesn't know her name. As if he hasn't known her for twenty-two years. I grind my molars. *He wants you to react.*

"Is that what this is for *you*?" I counter. "Pity hiring the black sheep so you can parade us all around town to make everyone think we're the perfect family?"

Dad slams a fist against the table and rises to his feet. "Grow the fuck up, Liam—"

"Okay, okay." Christine stands and holds out her palms like she's trying to calm wild animals. "Let's all take a breath. Mak has already started on some of the marketing materials and has some mockups. Liam, will you at least take a look at everything before deciding? Just give it that much of a chance?"

Makayla makes a noise in the back of her throat like she's trying to signal something to Christine.

Christine smiles at her, oblivious, and gives an encouraging nod. "Go on. Show him. I'm sure we'd all like to see it, right, guys?" She glances around the table for support, her eyes wide and smile tight.

"Yeah, yeah," coughs out Taylor. "I'd like to see it."

"Sure," offers Asher.

"I do!" calls Casey.

Dad's still glaring at me from the head of the table, but I sigh and hold my hand out for Mak's phone.

She stares at me for several seconds, and I can't figure out what that look in her eyes is before she slowly sets it in my hand.

The second my gaze falls on the screen, the sight hits me like a physical slap. The blood in my veins runs cold.

Taylor leans over for a look and chokes on his drink.

"Makayla," I say very, very calmly.

She sighs. "Liam, listen, it just—"

I point the screen at her face. "Why. The. *Fuck.* Is my ex-girlfriend your spokesperson?"

"Okay, listen—"

I toss the phone on the table, shove my chair back, and head for the door.

"Liam!" someone calls, and high heels click after me. "Liam." Makayla grabs my arm a few paces from the door and forces me to face her. "When I first asked her about this, it was before you guys broke up."

"And now?" I demand.

"Look, Liam, she's...her career is on the upswing. She's doing really well, and her socials audience is an exact match for our ideal customer. We'd never be able to find another model or influencer with her reach to do this for what we're paying her. We're going to reach an entirely new market with her. It's just business."

"Just business," I mutter.

I wrench my arm away and yank the door open. I shake my head once, twice, trying to calm the rage billowing up in my chest. She doesn't know the full extent of what happened with Hailey. No one does.

But that aside, to get far enough in the process with her to have these mockups without even asking me first? She never would have done this behind my back unless she knew she was doing something wrong.

"One big, happy family, huh, Mak?"

"Liam, I'm sorry to spring this on you like this—"

"Best of luck with the new business. Seems like it'll be a smashing success."

"Liam—"

I slam the door behind me.

Sweat drips down my face and falls onto the wood floor in front of me. My muscles ache as I push again, and again, and again. But I don't stop. Not until my arms physically fail midway through a push-up and I collapse against the ground.

It's just business.

I turn the music up louder in my headphones, loud enough I should probably be worried about causing permanent damage.

I switch to the pull-up bar hung over the bathroom door and grit my teeth as I haul myself up over and over. But no matter how much my muscles scream, it's not enough to drown out what's going on in my head.

Blowing up my phone is one thing. But weaseling her way in with my family? Into the business? Makayla may not have understood exactly what she was doing, but Hailey sure as hell did.

Maybe it was stupid of me to not fully realize it until now.

I'm never getting away from her.

I'm never going to be free of her.

Fuck, this isn't helping.

I drop back to the floor and rip my headphones off. Music continues to blare from them as I toss them on the bed and yank a shirt over my head.

I can't stay here. I can't *be* in this apartment, not when I can remember every place she used to leave behind little notes... can picture her laughing on the couch...hear her screaming at me from the kitchen as she took the plates out one by one and smashed them against the floor...see her blocking the door so I couldn't leave...

I snatch my keys off the counter and jog down the stairs to my car. Once inside, I plug my phone in to charge, and the screen lights up, revealing the half a dozen notifications I'm ignoring.

Asher, Makayla, Leo, Fletch.

I turn it off, then put the car in drive.

I don't know where I'm going. South, maybe. And as far as a full tank of gas will get me.

Chapter Fourteen

GRACIE

By some miracle, I sleep off the rest of the migraine. And by the time I wake, Liam is gone.

Not just from my bed. He all but disappears for the next few days, aside from a text letting me know the shop won't be open. When I replied asking why, he never messaged back. And when I asked Leo about it, he shrugged it off. Since asking more than once would be weird—or worse, he tells Liam I kept asking about him—I figure most of my work can be done from home anyway, and the sooner I finish, the sooner I can show off the results.

Carson snorts from across the table, and when I peek at her over the top of my laptop, she doesn't even try to hide her smirk.

"What?" I demand.

She lifts the gigantic neon mug housing her latte and takes a sip. "You're beating those poor keys like you're *trying* to get everyone in here to look at you."

My fingers freeze midword as I take in the coffee shop around us. People are, indeed, staring. I slip my headphones playing my *Classical Focus* playlist down and let them hang around my neck.

Since running into each other, Carson and I have started texting here and there. When I told her I was checking out a new coffee shop in Edgewater because it looked like a cozy place to get some work done, she offered to tag along, though she's sitting there flipping through gossip magazines while I chug enough caffeine to have me vibrating as I tackle my to-do list. But growing the social accounts could take some time. Getting them all set up and ready to go is only the first step. I figure if I can knock those and the website out before seeing Liam again, we can hit the ground running.

This place has better chairs than any of the Sweetspire shops—thick cushions, and wide enough to sit cross-legged—but the coffee itself isn't nearly as good. Of everywhere I've tried, Milano's still reigns supreme.

My phone screen lights up on the table, and I let out a groan through my teeth as I scan the text notification.

"Liam?" Carson asks, feigning innocence.

"Leo," I correct, snatching the phone off the table. He let me borrow his car to drive out here, but he underestimated how long I can hunker down in a coffee shop.

"Do you ever…let off steam?"

I peer at Carson again, and she's watching me with a scrunched brow and a look in her eyes like I'm an exhibit at a zoo.

"What do you mean? I'm fine. I'm completely steam-free." I go to take a sip of my coffee, but I'm already at the bottom. Of my second cup.

"You have no neck left." She gestures to her shoulders, and I realize mine are, indeed, hunched all the way up to my ears. When I relax them down, my muscles ache in protest.

She folds her hands together on the table and leans

forward. "You should come to my place tonight. We're having a few people over. You can meet my roommates. It'll be fun!"

I wince. "I'm not really great at parties. And it's a Wednesday."

She rolls her eyes. "It's not a party. And you'll be with me! And you could bring someone with, if you want. You said yourself you haven't been out much since you've been back. Live a little!"

Why are people always telling me that?

"Oh, come on." She reaches across the table and latches on to my arm. "Tell me you'll come. Please. Please. Pretty please?"

People are definitely starting to look at us again.

"Okay—okay!" I whisper-scream and swat her hand away. "Stop causing a scene or we'll never be able to come back here."

She snorts. "I think that ship has already sailed."

Talking Leo into letting me borrow his car again tonight is no easy feat, but all it takes is Keava reminding him it'll probably be dark by the time I head back for him to relent. She gives me an amused, knowing smile from behind the kitchen counter as Leo drops the keys into my waiting palm.

"There aren't going to be drugs at this party, are there?" Leo asks.

I roll my eyes. "No, Dad."

"And you know not to drink and drive."

"Leo. Who are you talking to?"

"And no boys!" he adds as I head for the door. "Definitely no boys!"

"Unless they're really hot!" calls Keava as I slip outside.

The address Carson texted me is about an eight-minute drive from Leo's, and my pulse skyrockets as I turn the corner and find the block lined with parked cars. It's easy to tell which house is Carson's from the lights, noise, and people lingering on the porch.

This is a *party* party. Not some *get together*.

I park a block away on the corner and stare at myself in the rearview mirror. I hadn't thought to change out of what I've been wearing all day—cut-off jean shorts, a flowy halter top, and sneakers. I quickly undo my pigtail braids and let my curls spill over my shoulders, then fish around in my purse until I find some light pink lip gloss.

"Oh, this is such a bad idea," I mutter under my breath. It's not too late. I could start the car again and get out of here.

But then I'd have to face Leo and Keava with my walk of shame back into the house.

"Hey! Gracie!"

I jump at a knock on my window. I squint against the streetlights as a familiar face peers in at me. Liam's brother, the one about the same age as me. Another guy stands behind Asher, but I can't see his face.

"Hey, Asher."

He hooks a thumb over his shoulder. "You coming to this party?"

Slowly, I nod.

"Want an escort?" he offers as he opens my car door.

Now would be the time for a witty reply, but having none, I give him a tight smile, grab my purse, and climb out.

"Oh, hey," says his companion.

"Miles, right?" I tug my purse onto my shoulder just to give me something to do with my hands. "From the shop?"

"Yeah." He flashes a stupidly perfect grin. "You remembered."

"I didn't know you were friends with Luna and Raquel,"

says Asher as he takes my other side and gestures for us to walk ahead.

Those must be the roommates.

"Actually, I'm friends with their roommate, Carson."

"Oh, that's right!"

He says every sentence so cheerfully, like he's genuinely delighted by everything. It's...odd. Maybe because it's such a contrast to Liam, who's so unreadable most of the time, given away only by the occasional eyebrow raise or smirk.

Despite him being only a year older, I haven't spent nearly as much time around Asher—or any of the other Brookses, for that matter. They all went to private school, and to say we ran in different circles would be an understatement.

"How do you know them?" I offer.

"Ash's been trying to convince Luna to go out with him," Miles whispers to me conspiratorially. "She's been running him around like a dog."

"She's just playing hard to get," says Asher. "And I'll chase her all she wants as long as she lets me catch her in the end."

"And you're, what? The wingman?" I ask Miles.

He chuckles. "Hardly. I'm here to get the crash and burn on video so it'll go viral."

Asher smacks him in the back of the head as he surges ahead onto the porch steps.

"See you around, Gracie," says Miles, his eyes holding mine for a beat longer before the two of them slip inside.

I text Carson to let her know I'm here before forcing myself to step through the door. There are a handful of people I don't know on the couch in the living room, and I pass a few more as I make my way to the kitchen at the back of the house. It's nice, if a little old. Reminds me of a lot of the places people rented in college—squeaky floorboards, minimal furniture, empty alcohol bottles used as décor.

It seems more like the first breaths of a party, not one that's well underway. As suspected, bottles and cups are lined up on the counter, and I quickly make myself a drink—mostly orange juice, but with enough vodka to hopefully take the edge off.

"You're hereeee!" squeals Carson as she hurries through the kitchen door with a beer bottle in each hand.

"You didn't think I'd actually show up, did you?" I ask as she tugs me into a suffocating hug. I grunt in surprise and awkwardly pat her back a few times until she lets me go.

"I had my doubts," she admits, then sways on her feet. I reach out a hand, but she manages to steady herself against the opposite counter.

"You good?"

"Oh, grand." She flashes a smile full of teeth, then throws back the rest of one of her beers.

"You look cute," I offer.

"Oh, this?" She does a little spin in her strapless black dress, then pops one of her combat boots out to the side. "You too. Very effortlessly boho chic. The Converse really tie the whole thing together. Or maybe it's the hair."

She must be even drunker than she looks.

"*Anyway*, come, come."

I clutch my drink to my chest as she grabs my hand and leads me up the stairs.

The door to the primary bedroom is wide open with two other girls inside. They're both sitting on the ground in front of a floor-length mirror, their makeup spread around them.

"Girls, this is Gracie, my friend I was telling you about. This is Luna." She gestures to the little redhead in a lacy dress covered in tiny red strawberries. "And Raquel." The second dark-haired girl pauses applying her bright red lipstick and waves.

Luna finishes adding butterfly clips to her hair and stands. I know I'm staring at bit, but I can't help it. Not after that talk with Asher on the way in. She's just...not at all what I pictured. The smile she offers is polite but not overly warm.

"See you down there," she says, then slips from the room.

Raquel and Carson exchange a glance I don't understand, then Carson shrugs and lounges on the bed.

"You grew up around here like Carson, right?" asks Raquel as she turns to the mirror and dabs some fake freckles along her nose.

"Yeah. What about you?"

"I moved up here from Delaware a few years ago."

"Why'd you move here?" I ask.

"Yeah," chimes in Carson. "Why would you willingly move to Jersey?"

Raquel gives her an unimpressed look. "I was *supposed* to move here because my girlfriend got a new job."

"Supposed to...?"

"They broke up less than a month after she moved," whispers Carson.

"I can still hear you."

Carson raises her palms like she's at gunpoint. "It's true!"

"Hence being desperate enough to room with her." Raquel points her eyeliner at Carson before dropping it into her makeup bag.

Carson just smiles and bats her eyelashes.

"Are you guys coming or what?" shouts a voice from downstairs.

"All your chatting is gonna make me miss the game!" Raquel jumps up, grabs a red Solo cup from the windowsill, then takes off toward the stairs at a run.

I glance sideways at Carson. "Game...?"

"Oh yeah!" She hooks her arm through mine and practically skips after Raquel. "I didn't mention that?"

"Mention what—"

When we reach the bottom of the stairs, the living room looks entirely different than it did when I walked in. All of the furniture is pushed to the outskirts of the room, leaving a circle of eight folding chairs propped in the middle with their backs to each other.

Is this fucking musical chairs?

"You bet your ass it is!" calls Raquel, and I blush when I realize I said that aloud. "Here's how the game works." She claps her hands and waits as people drift closer from other areas of the house. "There will be two teams of four. The trick is, you want to stay in the game, but you also have to work together. If you eliminate a teammate, you finish your drink. If you're a member of the losing team, you finish your drink. Any questions?"

"And no excessive violence!" calls Carson beside me. "If you draw blood—or break any of our things—you're streaking on the beach! We'll have three judges watching everything very closely, so behave yourselves!"

"Boys versus girls?" offers Miles from the kitchen doorway.

A girl in denim shorts, a bikini top, and a cowboy hat snorts beside him. "What a boy thing to suggest."

"I don't care what team I'm on as long as I'm playing!" Carson announces and plops herself in one of the chairs for emphasis.

"I'm in," says Asher, taking the seat beside her, followed by Miles, Bikini Girl, Luna, and a few others I don't know.

Once there's four girls and four guys standing around the chairs, Raquel removes one and points to the beefy guy sitting by a Bluetooth speaker in the corner. "DJ?"

"You've got it."

A rap song bursts through the speakers, and the players

scramble to position themselves so they're not standing beside teammates as the game begins.

"Gracie!" calls Carson. "You're a judge. Keep an eye on those two for sure." She points at Asher and Miles.

Fine by me. Better than being in the thick of it. I drift a step closer with my arms crossed over my chest.

The music cuts off abruptly, and chairs screech across the floor as everyone dives for a seat. Miles and Asher grab ones easily, but the other two guys are bodychecked by Carson and Luna.

I wince, and the room lets out a collective *Oooo* as they hit the floor. The tall guy with glasses pushes to his feet first, and he grimaces as he takes his seat.

"He eliminated a teammate!" calls Raquel.

"Drink! Drink! Drink!"

"Fuck you guys," he mumbles, then takes the red Solo cup someone hands him and gets to chugging. The beer spills down the sides of his mouth and over his chin, but after a few moments, he lowers the cup, gasps for air, and shakes his head like a dog coming out from the rain.

"We let you guys have that one," says Asher. "Chivalry and all."

"You're just making it even more embarrassing for yourselves," quips Luna.

Asher beams like he's just thrilled she's acknowledging his existence.

The next several rounds pass in a blur of squeals, thuds, and chants as people chug their drinks. Then it's down to Miles and Carson, and a hush falls over the room as the final song starts to play—the Macarena.

"Who the fuck picked this?" calls Raquel.

Miles grins, showing off his dimples, and does the dance as they circle the chairs.

"Don't you dare be a gentleman and give it to her!" yells Asher.

The music cuts off, and even though Miles is on the opposite side of the seat, he slides around in a fluid motion, grabbing the chair a millisecond before Carson lands on top of him.

She stares at herself in his lap as if not comprehending what she's seeing, and all the guys in the room erupt in cheers and applause.

Miles smiles and meets my eyes across the room. And before I realize it, I find myself smiling back.

If you angle your head just right through the line of houses and trees, you can see the ocean from their front porch. The house vibrates with music and laughter behind me as they start up round two. I sip my drink, hoping no one will notice I escaped for a moment of peace and fresh air. And truthfully, if they roped me into playing, there's no way I'd be able to drive home after a round of that game. And I'm not putting myself in that position in a house full of basically strangers, especially not when the one person I *do* know is absolutely trashed.

"Oh, you need a way better hiding spot than this if you don't want them to find you."

Miles grins as he steps onto the porch and closes the door behind him. I'm beginning to think that grin is his default expression. I mean, if I had those teeth and dimples, I'd probably be showing them off as much as possible too.

"I believe congratulations are in order."

He bows his head and leans against the railing beside me. "Not quite your crowd, huh?"

"Oh, no! No, they're—it's just—I just needed a minute."

His smile turns knowing, but softens. "Not mine either."

An incredulous laugh gets caught in my throat.

"What? You don't believe me?"

"No," I admit. "I don't know if I've ever seen someone look more in their element. Life of the party, some might say."

"Oh? Some?"

I take a sip of my drink.

"So what I'm hearing is, you've been watching me tonight."

Thankfully it's too dark for him to see how red my face must be.

"Go on a date with me."

I freeze with my cup a few inches from my face.

"Tomorrow night," he continues, voice perfectly casual. "I can pick you up at seven. Dinner. Somewhere nice."

Slowly, I turn to look at him. He stares back, hands casually in his pockets, head tilted to the side as he waits for my answer. The moonlight falls perfectly on his profile. A little *too* perfectly. Maybe I'm hallucinating. That would make a whole lot more sense.

"Why?" is the only word I manage to get out.

His eyebrow lifts. "Why?"

"Why me, I mean."

That gets him to smile. "Because I've been watching you tonight too."

"*There* you are, man!" Asher stumbles through the door and shoots me a nod when he notices me standing there.

"No luck with Luna?" asks Miles.

"The night is still young," Asher insists, then glances both ways down the street before fishing something out of his pocket.

Miles stiffens beside me. "Ash..."

"You want some?" he murmurs as he prepares a line of white powder on the railing.

Is that *coke?*

Miles glances at me sideways.

"Gracie?" offers Asher.

"I'm good," I say immediately.

Asher's eyes flick to Miles, and Miles gives a single shake of his head.

Asher shrugs, leans forward, and snorts the powder in one go. He stands up straight with renewed light in his eyes, then grabs Miles by the elbow. "Come on. I need a wingman."

"I really doubt that'll help," mutters Miles, but he lets Asher pull him toward the door. He hesitates before stepping inside and glances at me over his shoulder. "Tomorrow? Say yes, Gracie."

Every insecurity inside of me is screaming *This is a bad idea,* but somehow I find myself uttering a breathy "Yes."

GRACIE

"Liam! Would you stop being so awkward?"

He huffs out a breath and kicks the skateboard into his hand, his other fist resting on his hip. "I'm not a model!"

"Oh wait, maybe hold that pose." I lower to my knee and reframe the shot. It's just how I imagined it—the contrast of the industrial look of the skatepark with the sunset and ocean water in the background. "Just pretend I'm not here."

"That's impossible with you barking orders," he mutters and runs a hand through his hair.

I grab as many shots as I can. *This* I can work with. When he's distracted and yelling at me and not focusing on the fact there's a camera pointed at him, I might actually grab some good candids.

Everything else is…painful to look at. Especially with all the extra scowling he's doing today.

"I really don't see what the point of this is," he adds. "It's a tattoo shop. It's not like I sell skating gear."

"Turn a little so I can see the backs of your legs more."

"Oh, you like these?"

"I meant the tattoos," I say flatly. "Now start running like you're going to do a trick thingy."

"Trick thingy," he repeats under his breath with a shake of his head. But he does what I ask.

I don't care if he sees my vision for the pictures as long as he keeps doing what I say.

What he doesn't understand is social media marketing is about more than just showing a product. You have to get people to care. To connect. They want faces, names, personalities. They want a reason to choose you over someone else.

And, I hate to admit it, Liam Brooks looks good on a skateboard. I'd be stupid not to take advantage of that.

"Okay, come back! I want a close-up of your arm holding the board. Stand...here!" I point to the spot that'll give just a hint of interest in the background.

When he steps in front of me, he's grinning.

"What?" I demand.

He shakes his head, that damn smile still in place. "I've never seen you this bossy."

"Shut up."

"Careful. I might be into that kind of thing."

"Would you just turn around?" I twirl a finger in the air for emphasis. "Hold the board how you normally would down by your side."

"You're making me feel like a piece of meat."

"Do you want me to do my job or not? Face forward."

He obliges, and I shift side to side, trying to find the best shot.

The truth is, I'm just relieved nothing feels weird between us today. After three days of radio silence, he texted me the upcoming schedule, and I sent him what I managed to accomplish while I was off and asked if I could shadow him the next time he went skating for some pictures.

He hasn't told me where he disappeared to, and I haven't asked. Not that I'm not painfully curious, but I could tell from the hesitation in his body language when he showed up today that he didn't want me to. It seems we're also going to pretend him taking care of me at my bedside on Monday never happened, and I'm fine with that.

"Okay, fine," I sigh, rising to my feet. "I think I'm all good here."

He throws his head back in a dramatic sigh. "Thank God. You hungry? Think I'm gonna grab some lunch before heading back to the shop."

I pause putting the lens lap on the camera. He's asking me to eat? With him?

"I—yeah, I could eat."

"That sandwich shop on Main okay?"

I nod as I dig my phone out of my bag to see what all the buzzing's about. It's been going off nonstop for the past ten minutes. There's a string of missed calls and FaceTimes from Marti, followed by some texts in all caps.

I gasp and cover my hand with my mouth.

"What is it?" Liam demands.

"Oh my God," I whisper, my hand shaking as I jab at the screen until it opens the texts. "Oh my *God*."

"What is it?"

I hear Liam's footsteps get closer, but I swat at him when he tries to look at my phone as I read the text over again to make sure I understood it right.

"What the hell is—"

"Jared Morgan was cast as Hunter."

"I—what?"

My eyes snap up to his, and I let out a frustrated groan as I realize there's no one around who will fully appreciate this news. I need to call Marti back, but preferably not somewhere in public where people will stare at me for screaming.

"There's this movie adaptation being made for a book that a friend and I really love," I explain in a rush, but Liam's face just scrunches up further in confusion. "And we've been waiting on casting news, and they finally announced who will be playing the male lead. Jared Morgan." I hold my phone out so he can see the screenshot Marti sent me.

Liam cocks his head and squints. "Didn't you have posters of him on your wall in high school?"

My jaw drops open, and I yank my phone back.

As a matter of fact, I did, and there is no way he should remember that.

"So, this is good news?"

I throw my hands up and let out another string of unintelligible noises. "It's…shocking."

He quirks an eyebrow. "Shocking?"

"He's been in a ton of legal battles with these women who claim he did terrible things—*he* claims they've been stalking him and they never even met. No one has been willing to cast him in anything in *years*. There are, like, several documentaries on how drastic his fall from grace was. I can't believe you don't know this."

"You're right. This stuff really is right up my alley," he deadpans.

I lift my chin. "You pretend to be above it, yet you recognized a picture of him immediately."

He smirks and heads toward his truck in the parking lot. "So are we happy he got it or not?"

"I don't know." The teenage girl version of me who was mildly obsessed with him? Absolutely. The version of me now who isn't sure if he did those things…*and* there's a chance—

even if it's microscopic—that Marti could end up working with him? Conflicted.

She seemed excited about it based on the texts though. She *was* saying on a video chat the other day her agent thought she had a much better chance at the role if they secured a big name for the male lead. If they have one well-known actor to help draw an audience, they might be more willing to take a chance on someone like her.

"Heard Leo and Keava are driving up to Philly for the weekend," Liam adds.

"Her sister's wedding," I say absently as I chew on my thumbnail. "They're heading out tonight for the rehearsal dinner."

"We can throw your bike in the back."

Once I get the lock undone, I reach down to carry it over, but Liam beats me to it and hefts the bike into the truck bed.

"You throwing a party while he's gone?"

"As if I'd tell you. You'd report back to Leo."

"That sounds like a yes to me."

"No. I'm just glad he won't be around tonight to interrogate Miles," I mutter under my breath.

Liam goes still. "Miles Cushing?"

Shit, I have no idea why I said that.

"You know him?" I ask lightly, though of course he does. Miles is friends with his brother, not to mention the first time *I* met him was in Liam's shop. I try to laugh it off. "Oh wait, never mind."

He meets my eyes as he opens the car door for me, and I can't quite read the look on his face. The humor in his eyes is gone now though. "I didn't realize you two…talked."

I shrug as I climb into the truck. "He's taking me to dinner tonight."

Liam hesitates before closing the door, then he's back to

scowling as he rounds the truck and climbs in the driver's side. "Where are you going?"

"Um, I can't remember the name. It's not in town."

A strange tension descends over us as he starts the car, and his jaw keeps flexing like he's holding back from saying something.

"What is it? You *don't approve?*" I tease.

His scowl deepens as he pulls onto the road. "All I know is every time my brother's gotten into trouble, Miles has been right at his side."

A flash of last night appears in my head. How casually Asher whipped out drugs, like he does it all the time. And maybe he does.

But Miles had seemed uncomfortable. And he said no.

Maybe Asher is the bad influence is on the tip of my tongue, but I don't know if that's crossing a line. Liam doesn't talk about his siblings much. I have no idea how close they are.

"Luckily I only agreed to dinner, not a marriage. Yet."

He gives me an unamused sideways glance. But to my relief, he drops it. "You're not planning on posting these all over the new website, are you?"

I bat my eyelashes. "Only if you're mean to me."

The scowl returns, and I sigh. "I promise to let you look them over and veto any you don't like once I'm finished editing them, okay?"

His shoulders relax a bit at that. "Just don't make me look like a douche," he mutters.

I pat his leg. "Don't know if there's much I can do about that. I'm not a miracle worker."

I swat Liam's hand away for the *third* time. "Would you knock it off? You have your own chips!"

"Yours are better." He smirks as he manages to steal another from the edge of my plate and pops it in his mouth.

Our timing seems like it was just right today. Beach Bunz isn't a very big restaurant to begin with. Add in a crowd, and you can barely squeeze through the door. It was bustling with activity when we first stepped inside, but by the time we finished ordering at the counter, it cleared out enough for us to grab one of the small tables out front beneath the gigantic rainbow umbrellas.

When they leave the door propped open like this, the whole block smells like freshly baked bread. The day's heat is in full swing by now, but the shade and breeze are so comfortable I could sit out here all day. I eagerly dig into my sandwich—the best white bean and avocado I've ever had, even though it falls apart as I try to eat it.

"So your friend Marti already sent in her audition for this zombie movie?" says Liam. "Those books sold a lot—so this is like a big deal, right?"

I nod as I chew. "Millions. They've sold *millions* of copies. She's downplaying it. I think because she's afraid to get her hopes up. But *I* think it's a big deal she even got to audition. I don't know anything about how all that works, so maybe she's right and getting an audition doesn't mean much."

His eyebrows rise as he takes another bite of his sandwich. I'd expected him to go for one of the seafood ones they're known for, but he ended up getting the same thing as me. Judging by the way he's already down to the last few bites, he must like it. "She in LA now?"

"Yeah, she's from there originally. Her family's really cute. It's like a village. All her aunts, uncles, cousins—they all live on the same block. I spent Thanksgiving with them one year."

"Oh yeah, I remember you didn't come home for it last year."

My eyes flick up to meet his. He breaks the contact almost immediately and refocuses on his sandwich. He's been expertly steering the conversation away from anything to do with him since the moment we sat down.

And I thought I could mind my business, I really did, and yet I find myself blurting out, "Where were you?"

He tosses another chip in his mouth. "For Thanksgiving that year? With your family, as usual."

"Don't play dumb with me."

Finally, he meets my eyes, and it's like I can see the thoughts churning beneath the surface as he decides if he's going to tell me. I know the moment a corner of his mouth kicks up that he won't. "Why? You miss me?"

"Desperately," I deadpan.

His smirk grows as he tosses his napkin on his plate, but the look in his eyes is different now. There's a heaviness behind them that wasn't there before, and I mentally kick myself for bringing it up.

He checks his watch and sighs. "You ready to head back to the shop? Next appointment's in twenty."

He'd seemed fine at work on Monday. What could have possibly happened from the time he left my bed to later that night when he texted me about the shop being closed?

But I let it drop, because of course I'm not the person he'd want to talk about it with. I force a smile as he piles the rest of our trash together to throw out.

"Yeah. Yeah, let's go."

Chapter Sixteen

GRACIE

Well, it's finally happening. After a near twenty-three years of complete and total celibacy, I'm going on my first date. It's not that I have *zero* experience, per se. Make outs, hangouts in dorm rooms, and weird gray area "talking stages" with guys aside—there's never been anything official.

I pause with one foot on the basement stairs. Staying in this little hole in the ground has never sounded more appealing.

This is a mistake. Miles is going to realize it too about thirty seconds into our date. We're going to lapse into awkward silence so thick that he actually falls asleep at the table, hitting his head on the way down, then we'll have to call an ambulance, and everyone in the restaurant is going to see that I'm the first person in history to literally bore someone to death—

The doorbell reverberates through the house.

I close my eyes and let out a slow breath. I did not spend the last hour bent over the bathroom mirror to chicken out now. Smoothing my hands over the baby blue silk of my dress,

I put one foot in front of the other, urging myself forward before I have the chance to talk myself out of it.

Miles beams as I swing the front door open, and I'm immediately glad I opted for the dress instead of the jeans and sweater I'd been considering. He's in a pair of gray slacks and a navy button-up, and my knowledge of men's footwear is lacking, but the leather looks shiny and expensive.

"You look beautiful," he says, then pulls a single red rose out from behind his back. "For you."

Like the cliché I am, I blush.

"We should get going if we want to make our reservation."

I accept the arm he offers to lead me to the giant black SUV waiting by the curb. Goose bumps spread down my arms in the cool night air, and I pull my wrap tighter around myself. The fabric is measly and thin, but I figured we'd be inside for most of the night, and none of my jackets looked remotely good with this dress. It is a bit unseasonably cold for June, but at least it's not winter.

He opens the passenger door and offers a hand to help me climb into the monstrous thing, which would have been a feat by itself, let alone with the six-inch heels. But I manage to wrestle myself inside and let out an audible sigh at the warmth of the car as he closes the door.

It's cleaner than I would've expected, though the lemon air freshener hanging from the rearview mirror is a little overpowering. But it's the thought that counts, right? If he went through the effort of cleaning for me, that must be a good sign.

He smiles as he slides into the driver's seat, and I twist my fingers a little tighter together in my lap. *Don't be weird. Don't be awkward. He already likes you at least a little. Otherwise, he wouldn't have asked you out.*

A radio station playing the Top 40s hums lowly in the background as he pulls away from the house. Is this the kind of music he listens to, or is he playing it for my sake?

"Can't believe you've never been to Winters," he says. "You're gonna love it."

I smile, my cheeks already starting to cramp. I should say something, maybe ask him a question, but all I can think is *Do you go there often?* and if those words come out of my mouth, I will have no choice but to throw myself out the door of this moving vehicle.

"So tell me about what you do at the shop for Brooks!"

This, at least, is an easy conversation. The drive to the restaurant is nearly half an hour, but it passes quickly as I tell him about the random assignments Liam has given me so far and my plans for his website and social media. It's easier to talk to him with his focus on the road instead of me. The moment I meet his eyes, it's like I forget how to form words.

"And what do you do again?" I ask, tugging at the hem of my dress. "Liam said something about construction?"

Miles snorts. "That's a nice way of describing it. Makes it sound kind of impressive, right? Building shit."

"But that's not what you do...?"

He tilts his head to the side. "My dad owns a real estate development company. So I mainly help out on the office side of things for now. You know, learning the ropes, working my way up to managing a project on my own."

"Ah." I nod, though I can count on one hand the number of jobs I know less about than *real estate development.* "A very underappreciated occupation, if you ask me. Some might even say noble."

"You know what? You're right. Gonna make the guys at work start addressing me with a title."

"My Lord?" I suggest. "His Grace? The Right Honorable?"

He lifts an eyebrow. "The Right Honorable?"

I shrug. "Sometimes I read historical romance."

"Wait, wait. What's the word for those? Bodice breakers?"

"Bodice rippers," I mutter.

He snaps his fingers. "Right! Is it like that? Are they…racy?" He wiggles his eyebrows with the last word, and I immediately regret saying anything.

Maybe I will jump out of this car after all. For the second stupid time tonight, I blush.

He lets out a full-on cackle as he glances at me sideways. "I knew I liked you for a reason."

Thank God I went with the dress. The restaurant is fancy. Like, *fancy*, fancy. The kind that makes me feel like I'm playing dress-up in my mom's high heels and I should just *run along now* since it's already past my bedtime.

Miles walks through the door like he's done it a hundred times before and gives a curt nod and his reservation to the host.

"Right away, sir. If you'll follow me."

He leads us through a sea of white tablecloths, flickering candles, and patrons dressed like they're going to the Oscars. I tug on the hem of my dress and gulp. They can probably tell from a cursory glance that I fished this out of a clearance bin at a thrift shop. The plates we pass are the square white kind with more empty space than food on them, the presentation *just so.*

Which might be fine and dandy on a cooking competition show, but I can already tell this is going to be one of those menus without prices on it.

And I'm still going to leave hungry at the end.

Miles pulls out a chair as we reach our table and gives a slight bow of his head. "My Lady."

I snort, and it sounds so inappropriate in this atmosphere. My hand flies up to cover my mouth as I take a seat.

"Red or white?" Miles asks as he sits across from me and plucks the drink menu from the center of the table. He nods like I responded, then turns to the approaching waiter. Before the poor man can get a word in, Miles says, "We'll take a bottle of the Pinot Noir."

The waiter's eyes flick to me for a moment before he utters a quick "Right away, sir" and disappears into the shadows. The place is so dimly lit I can barely see past the surrounding tables.

I force my face not to react as I glance down at the menu. Fancy words that don't register with my brain...and no prices.

Miles peers at me over the top of his menu. "The salmon here is good. And it'll go well with the wine. Or the duck."

Duck?

The waiter materializes, brandishing the bottle and going off about the *notes* and other wine-lover words that mean nothing to me. He pours a tiny amount for Miles to taste and waits for his approval before pouring the rest of our glasses.

"Do we know what we'd like to eat?" he asks.

"We'll take one of the duck and one of the salmon," says Miles as he slides the menu out from in front of me and hands them both off.

The waiter nods. "Excellent choices."

"That way you can try both," Miles explains.

Okay, so the sentiment is kind of sweet. I try not to bristle at him ordering for me—the drink and the food. Maybe girls like that on dates? *Should* I like that? Either way, I'm definitely not eating either.

"Oh, actually, I don't eat meat!" I say with a smile and a shrug, hoping it comes off light. "I was thinking one of the pasta dishes—"

"They're known for their duck," Miles cuts in. "Best I've ever had. Come on." He winks. "One night off. They won't mind. They're already dead."

I blink, momentarily stunned, and now the waiter is pointedly not looking at either of us like he's as desperate to get away from this table as I am. Miles still has that goofy smile on his face as if that was a completely normal, nonpsychotic thing to say.

Maybe he just says the wrong thing when he's nervous and he's more anxious about this date than he's letting on? That's a stretch, even for *I-always-give-people-the-benefit-of-the-doubt* me. Or maybe he hasn't been around many vegetarians and doesn't realize there's absolutely nothing funny about his joke.

"The—the pesto pasta is fine," I sputter, and the waiter all but runs to the kitchen.

Miles shrugs, unperturbed, and holds up his glass. "To you, Gracie! Congrats on your new job. And welcome home."

I force myself to brush it off as I clink my glass to his and take a sip. I pretty much never drink red wine, but it's not nearly as bad as I'd been expecting.

But the word in his little speech that really trips me up is *home*.

Technically speaking, yes, I'm from here. My family lives here. Anyone who looks at me would describe what I've done as "moved back home."

But it doesn't feel like it. Returning feels more like a defeat than a homecoming.

I spin the wineglass around in my hands. Aren't people on dates supposed to ask each other questions? I wait, but Miles says nothing.

"So, um." I clear my throat. "You went to school with Asher?"

Miles bobs his head. "We met through the swim team freshman year."

Asher and Miles are only a year older than I am, but I never really crossed paths with them growing up since they went to the private school across town. Liam was the only Brooks who dared to slum it at public school, and that was after getting expelled his sophomore year.

I wasn't at the high school yet, but that was before Leo got his license, so he still rode with me and Mom. I don't think I'll ever forget the look on Liam's face the first time Mom picked him up to drive him to school with us. It was so different than every other expression I'd seen him make. There was just... nothing behind his eyes.

No one ever told me the details of the fight that got him expelled, but the timing always made it seem like it had something to do with his mom dying.

God, why am I thinking about Liam right now?

I blink back to the table. If Miles noticed my attention drifting, he doesn't show it. He's far too preoccupied with refilling his wineglass. I watch him, searching for the things I'd originally thought were attractive about him. Attractive enough at least to agree to this date. But looking at him from across this table somehow feels vastly different than last night.

"Did you swim all through school?" I ask when he offers nothing else.

He bobs his head. "All four years of high school, then swam at Tufts on a scholarship."

"What made you want to move back here after graduating?"

He shrugs and takes another gulp of wine. "Always planned on coming back. Family business and all. Dad said once I got my business degree, he'd let me take on a larger role."

I pause, waiting to see if he's going to ask me anything in return—something easy, like where I went to school, or asking me the same question about why I moved home after graduating—but he just stares at me.

Okay then. I chip away at my nail polish under the table. "Well, you were right. This place is really nice."

He beams. "Just wait until you taste the food. Hey, you've barely touched your wine."

I force a smile and take another sip. I was so nervous about tonight I haven't had an appetite all day, and I'm enough of a lightweight as it is. The last thing I need is to drink this whole thing on an empty stomach.

Maybe the lull in conversation isn't as awkward as I'm making it out to be. I've always felt the need to fill the silence with new people, but maybe he's someone who's comfortable not talking just for the sake of talking.

Granted, this is a first date where you'd supposedly want to get to know the other person.

Was it all in my head that he'd seemed more interested before? The party, the car... Maybe I've already disappointed him somehow and he's counting down the seconds until it's over and *that's* why he's making zero efforts at conversation now. Is it the dress? Did I say something wrong on the drive here? Is he more annoyed I didn't go with his menu suggestion than I realized?

"So, do you still swim?" I offer.

"Oh, fuck no. Well, maybe a bit at a darty with a beer." He winks.

"A...darty?" I repeat stupidly. Obviously I've heard the term before. I'm not *that* clueless. Trish and Marti were big fans in school, and they managed to convince me to tag along here and there. But I have this weird, nagging feeling in the back of my mind as I think about the party the other night. How he'd said it wasn't his scene.

"You know." He swirls a hand in a circle. "Day party. Didn't you have those at...wait, where did you go to school?"

"Oregon!" I sit up a little straighter, then wince at how eager that sounded. "Just outside of Portland."

"Ah."

And...that's all he says.

The waiter drifts toward us in my peripheral version, and I send up a little prayer of thanks to whoever is listening as he sets the food in front of us. I'm starving, and at least eating is better than sitting here with him staring at me.

I take a swig of my wine. It looks like it's going to be a long night.

Chapter Seventeen

LIAM

"Fletch, it's a fucking deathtrap in here." I duck beneath a plastic sheet a few feet inside the front door. The entire living room has been stripped to its foundations, and it looks like he's taken one of the walls out entirely. A few work lights are set up, casting shadows over the rest of the space, and Fletcher is nowhere to be seen.

"You just don't see the vision!" he calls.

I follow his voice toward the kitchen at the back of the house, one of the few rooms that's starting to come together. I never saw the house before he started the renovations, only pictures. It was outdated, cramped, and falling apart—the perfect house for Fletch's first solo flip. I'm not sure if it's still considered that if he's planning on living in it afterward.

He grins as I step around the corner. "You brought beer."

"You told me to. Three times." I set the six pack on the counter and look around. The new countertops, appliances, and cabinets are in. Now it looks like he's down to installing the hardware and light fixtures.

He shakes his head and opens a bottle. "You missed all the fun. Demo is the best part."

"I'll take your word for it. You need a hand?"

I consider myself fairly handy, but it's nothing compared to Fletcher. His parents do this for a living, and he's been helping since he was a teenager. He probably could've built this entire house from scratch by himself if he wanted to.

He waves me off when I go for the cabinet handles sitting on the counter.

"If you don't want me to help, why am I here?"

He bends down to screw the handles into the lower cabinets. "To entertain me, obviously."

At least it's better than what I was doing before I got his text—sitting alone in the dark shop, ditching sketch after sketch halfway through until I had a mountain of crumpled-up pages lying beside the trashcan, checking the time every ten fucking seconds.

I glance at my watch. 9 PM.

Absolutely nothing significant about that time.

"Li?" I blink back to the room to find Fletcher leaning against the counter, beer in hand and staring at me. "You good?"

"Of course." I grab a beer for myself and resist the urge to check my phone. I don't know what the fuck is going on with me today.

Fletcher's eyes narrow.

"So the kitchen looks basically done, right?" I add. "What's next?"

He stares at me for another second like he's debating pushing it, but then that easy smile is back as he sips his beer. "Living room next. Bathroom down here is already done." He nods to the hall that connects the living room and kitchen.

"We're doing from back to front on this floor, then we'll start on the second."

I pace through the hall to peek in the bathroom. He replaced everything—shower, toilet, sink, counter. It's still small, but it looks nice. Sleek, modern. Nothing particularly personable about it.

"*So*," he says as I step into the room again. "How are you doing? Heard about the Makayla and Hailey thing."

"Asher," I mutter under my breath.

"You want to talk about it?"

"Nothing to talk about."

"Okayyy." He lifts his palms in a placating gesture. "Off-limits, I get it." He slides another few handles off the counter and gets started on the row of cabinets overhead. "Where the hell did you get off to the past few days then?"

"I don't know what you mean."

"I think you do."

I twist the bottle between my hands and ignore the look I can feel him giving me. "So I decided to get out of town for a few days. Get some fresh air."

He hums. "I get that. Anywhere in particular?"

In truth, it's a bit of a blur. I started driving that night, figuring I'd get it out of my system and turn around within an hour or two.

But then I just kept driving, and driving, and driving.

Filled up on gas. Stopped at a motel when I couldn't keep my eyes open anymore. Then woke up and did it all over again until I felt like I could breathe, then I turned around.

"Savannah."

Fletcher freezes with his arm midway to the cabinet. "As in...*Georgia*?"

I nod.

"You drove all the way down to Georgia," he repeats.

"You want me to draw you a map or what?"

He blinks a few times, shakes his head, then resumes screwing in the handle. "All right. Just for future reference, I'm a great road trip companion."

"You would've been yapping the entire time."

He grins. "Exactly. No falling asleep at the wheel on my watch."

I chuckle and shake my head. "I'll keep that in mind."

"So how's Gracie Collins working out at the shop?"

My stomach drops, and I glance at my watch again without thinking.

Fletcher catches it because he always fucking catches everything.

"Good, I think," I say, my voice light. "Everything I've seen her do so far is a million times better than anything I could come up with. And she hasn't quit yet. You sure you don't want help with those?"

Fletcher waves me off with a smirk as I take a step forward. "You'll put them on upside down or something. No."

"You're such a control freak. You'd be done in half the time if you let someone else help."

"Where would the fun be in that?" He moves on to the lower cabinets beside the fridge. "Now, stop trying to change the subject and tell me about Gracie."

I rock back on my heels. "She's like a drill sergeant. Is making me be in all these pictures and stuff."

A smile tugs at one corner of Fletcher's mouth as he stands and leans against the counter, and I don't at all like that look in his eyes. "That's not what I meant."

I sip my beer. "Then what did you mean?"

"I *mean*, I happen to know Gracie is on a date with Miles Cushing tonight, and in the five minutes you've been here, you've checked your phone eight times."

It takes everything in me not to bristle at Miles's name. Hearing it makes my imagination run wild. It digs up every memory I have of the kid, every fucked-up thing he's been caught up in. The hazing he used to do to the younger kids on the swim team—pissing in their Gatorade bottles and filming them as a group of seniors forced them to drink it. Not to mention the drug arrests, the trespassing, the vandalizing school property. Not that he ever went down for any of it.

Maybe that's what rubs me the wrong way the most. His damn cocky smile and that *I-can-get-out-of-anything* glint in his eye. I can't even fathom what someone like Gracie would see in him.

"I don't see how those two things are related," I mumble.

"Right." He sets his beer on the counter, crosses his arms, and shrugs. "I've always liked Gracie. We didn't have a lot of classes together, but she was nice. Quiet, but nice. Weird fucking match with Miles though."

Fletcher's never acted younger than me, so it's easy to forget the age difference. That he was in the same year as Gracie, so of course he'd run into her more than I did back then. A weird, prickly feeling sets up camp in my chest at the thought.

He's not smirking at me now, exactly, but he's baiting me, and we both know it. He's always read between the lines better than anyone I've ever met, like he just somehow knows *everything*. So I can either keep digging myself into a hole of lies here while he pretends not to notice, or we can both drop the bullshit.

"I'm...concerned," I admit.

He hums.

"I don't like Miles."

He hums again. "Me neither."

"And she's..." I trail off, not knowing how to end that

sentence. *Too good for him* doesn't begin to cover it. I don't even like the idea of him *looking* at her. I settle for "My best friend's sister. And Leo's not in town. Don't think he knows about it."

"So naturally the protective duty falls to you by default." Now he's smirking at me. "Do you know where they are?"

I scowl. "No."

He nods. "Liam."

I swallow a mouthful of beer. "Hm?"

"She doesn't need a bodyguard."

I say nothing.

"She can handle herself. I'm sure she's fine. In fact, I don't think this has anything to do with you being worried about her."

I scoff. "You're way off base, man."

He stares at me for a moment like he can see right through me, but I see it in his eyes the moment he decides against whatever he was going to say. He nods to the side instead. "I could use some help with the deck out back if you want to hammer some shit."

That actually sounds like exactly what I need.

GRACIE

Miles was right about one thing. The food is divine. And the more I drink the wine, the more I like it.

The more bearable the whole night becomes.

The conversation comes a little easier the later we get into the night, though we mostly just talk about the food and other places he likes around town.

There's also a good chance my expectations are unreasonably high from my reading habits. Maybe this is what dating is like.

I try not to acknowledge how soul-crushing that prospect is.

It feels twice as cold when we leave, and I wrap my arms around myself as I follow Miles to his car. He staggers a bit as he weaves for the driver's side, and my steps slow. He hadn't seemed that drunk in the restaurant, but he…he wouldn't drive me home if he wasn't okay, right?

The wind picks up, and I shiver as my teeth start chattering. It's enough to spur me forward and climb in. I bite my tongue to keep from asking if he's good to drive as he starts the car. Would that be offensive to ask? Is it stupid not to?

"You really do look gorgeous tonight," he says as he pulls out of the parking lot in a perfectly straight line and acceptable speed.

My shoulders relax. "Thank you. And thank you for dinner."

Fortunately, he hadn't let me look at the bill when it arrived.

"Of course. I'm glad you liked it." He reaches over and squeezes my knee.

Then he leaves his hand there.

I stare at his fingers on my bare thigh as he merges onto the main road, frozen in my seat. Maybe if the date had gone better, I would be thrilled at this revelation, but right now, his hot, meaty hand feels like dead weight against my leg, and the longer it sits there, the stronger the urge to fling it off becomes.

I focus on the night sky out the window. The stars are so bright out here. If the wind didn't make it so cold, I could just lie outside and stare at them for hours.

Miles flexes his fingers against my thigh, and I stiffen.

"It's a beautiful night, isn't it?" he offers.

I hum my agreement.

"I swear no one else is ever on this road," he adds. "Always so quiet."

I haven't noticed many other cars on the two-lane highway —not now or on the way here. The restaurant is one town over, and there's not a lot in between.

Finally, he pulls his hand away from my leg to rummage around in his pants pocket. "Do you smoke?"

My eyes flick from his pocket to his face. "I—no."

"Do you mind if I do?"

My mouth hangs open. I know very well he's not talking about a cigarette. Not that I'd appreciate that either. "While you're driving?" My voice comes out small and high-pitched.

He laughs, removes his hand from his pocket—sans joint—and rests it back on my leg, higher up on my thigh this time. "I'll take that as a no. You got it, boss."

The clock on the dashboard says it's 10 PM. It took about thirty minutes to get here, and we've been in the car for, what? I'd like to say ten minutes, but realistically, it's closer to five.

God, I hate the way I want to cry right now. I was so excited for tonight, and now I'm counting down the minutes until it's over.

His fingers dig into my inner thigh as his thumb makes light strokes. My stomach flips, and not in a pleasant way. I don't know how to ask him to stop, but I also don't know if I can take this for twenty more minutes.

How can he honestly think something is going to happen? Or does he see nothing wrong with how dinner went?

"So, are you still living with your family?" I ask because apparently I am incapable of not filling the silence.

I cross my legs.

He doesn't take the hint and leaves his hand there as I do.

"Oh no." His smile is too wide and full of teeth. "Don't worry. I got my own apartment in town."

I realize too late how that question came across. *Fuck.* But I should wait to confirm he's taking me to Leo's house until we're closer, right? So I don't make it awkward?

"You know, Miles, I—"

"Hold that thought, gorgeous."

I brace my hand against the door in surprise as the car slows and pulls off onto the gravel shoulder. My eyes widen as I turn to look at him.

"Is there something wrong with the car?"

"Oh! No. No. Sorry to worry you." He squeezes my leg and chuckles as he shifts the car into park. His grip is starting to get uncomfortably firm, and his fingers somehow managed to climb a few inches higher. "It's just been such a nice night. Thought maybe we'd make it last a little longer."

It takes everything inside of me not to let my thoughts show on my face. *Such a nice night?* Were we on the same date?

"You're so different from the other girls around here, Gracie. It's refreshing."

Now my eyes are really threatening to bulge out of my head.

I'm so different? How would you know? You haven't asked me a single question about myself!

Not knowing what else to do, I laugh. It comes out awkward and forced and too high, but like everything else this evening, Miles doesn't notice. He unclips his seat belt and starts leaning toward me.

Oh my God. He wants to *hook up* in his car *on the side of the road?*

I turn my head and try to laugh it off. "I'm not really a kiss-on-the-first-date kind of girl."

He stops a few inches from me, close enough that I can smell what he had for dinner, and snorts. After he searches my face for a few moments, his smile dims. "Wait, you're serious?"

I nod.

The smile snaps back into place. "That's just because you haven't seen how good of a kisser I am yet." He leans forward, undeterred when I turn away again. "And I've been told I'm quite good at a few other things."

The reality of my situation starts to trickle in. I'm in his car in the middle of nowhere. He's twice my size. And he's clearly not picking up on any subtle hints.

His hand pushes farther up my leg, trailing under my skirt, and he presses his lips against the side of my throat.

"Miles," I say, and I hate the way my voice shakes. "I'm really not comfortable with this."

He kisses my collarbone, his other hand coming up to weave in my hair. "The nerves wear off. Promise."

The blood drains from my face. He's just...not getting it. Or choosing not to.

"No, Miles, I mean I don't want to do this at all." I grab his hand that's nearly all the way to my hips and push it away for emphasis.

The look on his face when he pulls back makes every alarm bell in my mind go off. It's his eyes. They're just...dark.

"So that's your game, huh?"

I blink rapidly and shift my weight, trying to put more distance between us. "I—I'm not playing a game. I just—I just take things slow, is all. This is moving too fast for me."

"Don't you think we're a little old for this? I pick you up, bring you flowers, take you to the nicest place within fifty miles, I pay for your food."

My hands tremble as I tug the hem of my skirt lower. "I really just want to go home now."

"Unbelievable," he mutters under his breath as he shakes his head.

We sit in silence for what feels like forever, but he doesn't put the car in drive. He faces forward and wraps his hands around the steering wheel in a death grip.

"You know what? No." He whips toward me and juts sharply with his chin. "Get out."

"*What?*"

"Get. Out. Of. My. Car."

I look from him to the dark nothingness outside the window. "Miles, you can't—"

"Yes the fuck I can. It's my car. You thought I was going to be your chauffeur and meal ticket tonight—"

"That is *not* what I—"

"*Get out, Gracie.*"

I flinch at the volume of his voice in the small space, and hot tears spring to my eyes.

"Get out!" He reaches across me and shoves the door open.

In the process, his elbow clips me under the chin. I rear back, my mouth filling with the taste of blood.

He grabs my purse from the floor and chucks it out the open door.

"You can either climb out yourself or I'll do it for you."

I scramble with my seat belt and trip over my feet as I hurry out of the car, a mix of tears and blood streaming down my face. I barely have both feet in the gravel before he's speeding off with my door hanging open. It slams shut as he twists the car.

The rev of the engine echoes as he drives away. Within moments, the headlights disappear, and then I'm in complete darkness. My mouth throbs, and the coppery taste of blood overwhelms my senses. I gingerly fish around with my tongue to find my lip split.

I don't know how long I stand there, unable to move. Long enough for goose bumps to blossom over every inch of exposed skin, and then I start to tremble. From the cold night air or the adrenaline subsiding, I don't know.

Because surely this isn't happening. This can't be happening right now.

A shaky breath passes my lips, the sound suddenly too loud in the quiet. I take a step back from the road, and my heel digs into the gravel at a weird angle, making my ankle roll, and it's enough to snap me out of whatever trance I'd been in.

I hunt for my purse on the ground, and once I find it, my

hands are shaking so badly that it takes three tries to get the clasp undone. The first thing I notice when I dig my phone out is the angry red symbol in the top corner of the screen—low battery.

Oh God.

Unlocking it, I immediately flip it to low power mode, then freeze with my finger poised over my contact list.

Who am I supposed to call? Leo and Keava are in Philly for the wedding. Mom and Dad are in New York for some restaurant opening. Carson is at work all the way up in Newark tonight. This town is so goddamn small that no rideshare apps function out here.

I don't...I don't...

My breaths come in short and fast as I take in my surroundings. I don't even know what road this is, my service is hanging on by a thread, and my battery has already lost a percent. I'm down to ten.

The only other person I know in town is Liam.

Tears sting my eyes, but I swallow them down. I can't afford to panic.

I tap his number. It rings and rings, and with every moment that passes, my heart sinks deeper into my stomach.

I don't have a plan B. I guess I could start walking the way Miles drove off, but a half-hour drive going like fifty miles an hour? How long of a walk is that? Twenty-five miles?

I don't know the number for the cab company, and I don't know if my service—or battery—can handle a Google search.

If I wait for someone else to drive by, I could be here all night, and even if someone did happen to show up, I don't know if I could bring myself to get in the car. I've seen way too many crime documentaries for that.

Fuck.

Do I call 911 next? How fucking mortifying. I finally go on a date and end up needing a ride home in a police car.

"Hello?"

I nearly drop the phone. "Liam?" My voice cracks around his name, and whatever resolve I'd been clinging to breaks. Tears stream down my cheeks, and I hiccup, trying to catch my breath.

"Gracie? *Gracie?* Are you okay?"

"I—I—" Down to eight percent battery. "I don't know where I am," I gasp. "My phone is about to die."

"Slow down, slow down. What happened? Where are you? What do you see?"

"The side of the—road. Kicked me out of—the car. I see—nothing. There's nothing. It's just—dark. God, I'm at—I'm at seven percent."

I sink onto the ground and tuck my knees into my chest as I try to catch my breath.

"Gracie, I need you to listen to me. You're going to share your location with me. Then you're going to stay right there until I come to get you."

I nod quickly before realizing he can't see me. A whimper escapes me as I send the invite to share my location. My battery is down to five.

"I got it—I got it!" There's rustling on his side. "I'll be there as soon as I can."

"Okay," I whisper.

"Are you somewhere safe to wait? Is there anyone else around?"

"There's no one here." I shiver as the wind picks up. "There's nothing out here."

Except maybe wild animals waiting in the bushes to jump out and tear me apart.

The phone cuts off before he responds. I yank it away from

my ear, expecting the screen to be dark, but my battery is still hanging on.

What if he doesn't come? What if he can't find you? whispers a voice in the back of my head.

But then my phone starts to ring, and I jump as it shatters the silence.

"Hello—?"

"I'm here" comes Liam's voice, followed by a car door slamming and an engine revving to life. "I always fucking lose signal here. Just stay on the line with me until your phone dies, okay?"

"Okay," I say, my voice barely a whisper.

"Gracie." His voice is suddenly hard, firm. "You're going to be fine."

"Okay."

"I'm going to be right there."

I squeeze my eyes shut and pull my wrap tighter around my shoulders. "Okay."

"It says you're about twenty-five minutes out."

I nod, my teeth starting to chatter.

A few moments of silence pass between us, save for the howls of the wind, some chirping bugs nearby, and the low hum of Liam's car through the phone. I press my forehead to my knees, trying to keep my breathing calm.

Lowly, he asks, "Are you okay? Did he hurt you?"

I gently touch my lip, and my fingers stick in the drying blood. The pain feels distant now, unimportant. I'd almost forgotten about it.

"I'm fine," I rasp.

"Gracie…"

"I'm fine," I repeat, forcing my voice to come out a little more evenly, but when I glance at the screen again and see a single percent of battery staring back at me, my chest starts to shake.

"Gracie—"

My phone dies.

My head drops against my chest like it's too heavy to hold up anymore, and the tears fall from my cheeks into the dirt. But the longer I sit here, the more violent the shivers become, so I push to my feet and pace back and forth, trying to force some warmth into my limbs.

I want to go back to a few hours ago and slap myself for deciding against a jacket because it didn't *look good* with my dress. Hell, I should slap myself for thinking this was a good idea in the first place.

But kicking me out of the car and leaving me here like this? *Who does that?* I guess part of me thought he'd turn back after a few minutes, but that window has long since passed. Not that I'd want to get in his car if he did, but I flinch at every branch cracking in the distance, my heart lodged in the base of my throat like my body is preparing for a threat to lunge out at any second.

I search my purse for anything I could use as a weapon, but I don't know what good some pepper spray would do me against a bear. Are there even bears around here? Wolves, maybe?

With every step, my heels sink into the uneven ground, threatening to throw me off balance. Sighing, I pull them off and toss them beside my bag. They're open-toed and strappy, so it's not like they were keeping me warm anyway. But after a few minutes—maybe seconds, I can't tell—I realize the pacing isn't helping. I'm shivering, my teeth are chattering, and my toes are starting to feel numb.

I crouch next to my things and wrap myself in a ball, hoping to conserve what little body heat I have left.

Liam will be here soon, I remind myself over and over. *He'll be here. He will. He will.*

When I lift my head again, headlights appear on the horizon. My breath catches in my throat, and I scramble to my feet.

The lights grow quicker than I would have expected, like he's driving much faster than he should be. I take a few steps back from the road, my arms wrapped around myself. As it gets closer, the car takes on the familiar form of Liam's truck, and what was left of the apprehension in my shoulders finally relents as he pulls up. And I can't help it—I let out a sob. He jumps out of the car so quickly I'm not sure it fully stopped first.

He hurries toward me, stripping his bomber jacket off as he goes, leaving him in a thin white T-shirt. He wraps it around my shoulders as he reaches me. I can't stop trembling as he tightens his hands on my arms, his entire body going still as he takes in whatever damage is visible on my face.

I don't remember choosing to do it, but I collapse against his chest. He pulls me in, one hand cradling the back of my head. I can't tell if the frantic heartbeat is coming from his chest or it's my own echoing in my ears.

He loosens his grip and gently says, "Get inside."

I start to turn back for my things, but he nudges me toward the car. "Go on. I'll get those."

I do as he says and let out a soft moan as I climb onto the heated seats and turn the air vents in my direction. I quickly wipe the tears from my cheeks as he climbs in a moment later and sets my things at my feet.

"I'm—I'm sorry. I didn't know who else to c-call. Leo is out of town and—"

"Gracie." I suck in a surprised breath as he takes my face in his hands and looks me up and down. "It's okay," he says softly. "Christ. You're freezing."

He yanks the beanie off his head and pulls it onto mine instead, then takes a few moments to adjust my hair so it's not stuck in front of my eyes.

"I'm f-fine," I insist, but my chattering teeth ruin the intended effect.

He pulls his leg up to untie his shoes next. He rips a sock off, then gestures to me. "Give me your foot."

"Liam—"

"Foot."

My poor toes are so cold I can barely move them, so I don't stop him as he takes my leg and works the sock onto my foot, then does the same thing for the other.

His eyes search my face, and I brace myself, waiting for him to ask and silently pleading with him not to. I don't want to have to say it aloud. I don't know how I'd put what happened tonight into words.

But in the end, I see it the moment he decides something, and he nods toward the seat belt behind me and shifts the car into drive.

"Buckle up."

I stare out the window as we drive, though there isn't much to see. The darkness swallows any details in the distance. The pit in my stomach grows heavier with each moment that passes in silence, the drive stretching on even longer than I remember it being on the way here. I try to imagine myself out there, stumbling my way back in the dark and the cold. How far would I have made it before I gave up? No other cars have appeared.

I shiver and force myself to stop the line of thinking.

Liam must think I'm still shaking from the cold, because he cranks the heat up higher and turns the remaining air vents in my direction. But the chill has sunk well beneath my skin, burrowing deep into my bones in a way that feels like it'll never leave. It weighs on my eyelids, making it harder and harder to stay awake as the steady hum of the truck's engine threatens to lull me to sleep.

But when we make it back to Sweetspire, my head jerks up as we reach the light before my neighborhood and Liam turns in the opposite direction.

He spares me a quick glance before refocusing on the road and tightening his fists around the steering wheel. "Leo and Keava won't be back for a few days," he says. "I...well, I don't want to leave you alone right now. And I want to make sure you get that lip cleaned properly. Is it all right if I take you to my apartment?"

I probe at it and wince. It hurts more now that I've warmed up. I'm afraid to look.

"But I can just take you home, if you'd rather," he adds when I don't respond.

As much as I want to curl into a ball in my bed and never come out...I think about being in that house right now. The darkness. The quiet. And I realize being alone is the last thing I want.

"No," I croak. "That's okay."

Chapter Nineteen

LIAM

She follows me up to the apartment like a zombie. I don't even know if she can hear me talking to her. I subtly sweep her for other injuries as I open the door and follow her inside, but there's nothing visible other than her busted lip. Did *all* of that blood come from her mouth?

Jesus Christ, that must hurt.

Blinding rage threatens to swallow me whole. I clench my hands into fists as I steer her to one of the kitchen chairs so I have some good lighting to clean up her face. She offers no resistance, her socked feet shuffling along the hardwood, and she all but falls into the seat.

I set her bag and shoes in the chair next to her, then hurry to find the first aid kit in the bathroom. *Just focus on the task at hand.* If I think too hard about how she ended up here, about what happened to her face, I won't be any use.

She's staring at the table when I return, and she doesn't acknowledge me as I pull up a chair beside her. She still has my jacket tightly wrapped around her shoulders. Her hair is tucked beneath the collar, but a few strands fall out and frame her face. Makeup is smeared all around her eyes from crying.

Focus on the task at hand.

"Can I take a look at that?" I ask, trying to keep my voice gentle.

She blinks, finally noticing me. Her eyes are so wide she still looks like a deer in fucking headlights. Is it the shock...or does she really not feel safe here? I ignore the twinge in my stomach and slowly extend my hand toward her face. Sudden movements probably aren't a good idea right now. But she doesn't flinch or pull away as I tuck the hair behind her ear. Propping my fingers under her chin, I tilt her face up toward the light.

Her eyes squeeze shut as I dab at the blood around her mouth with a wet cloth, trying to clean it up enough to see what we're dealing with here. I've had my fair share of cuts and bruises from my early skating days—and some more recent incidents, to be honest—but I'll know pretty soon here if I'm out of my depth.

She winces as I get closer to her lip.

"Is it bad?" she whispers as I set the towel on the table. "I'm too afraid to look."

"No, Gracie," I murmur. "It's not bad at all." Thankfully, I don't have to lie. She must have bit her tongue or something too to get all that blood because the damage to her lip is minimal. It's more swollen and bruised than anything. A saltwater rinse and an ice pack and she should be fine.

But there shouldn't be any damage in the first place. Did he *hit* her? I grit my teeth as a million scenarios play out in my head.

"Are you hurt anywhere else?"

She drops her gaze to the table and shakes her head. I can't tell if she's telling me the truth.

"What happened tonight?"

It's the wrong thing to say. Her shoulders hunch in, and it's like I can see her shutting down further before my very eyes.

"I'm going to get you some salt water to rinse out your mouth and some clothes to sleep in, okay?"

She nods without looking at me. Maybe she just needs more time to process. I know pushing for answers isn't helpful to her right now, but I can't get the image of her shivering and bloody on the side of the road out of my head. It's taking everything in me not to track down Miles and beat him to a pulp right now.

She doesn't say anything else, not as she rinses her mouth, not as she changes clothes in the bathroom, not as I help her into my bed.

"I'll be right on the couch if you need anything." I set a glass of water on the nightstand. I should go now. Let it rest. Let *her* rest. But I can't help myself. I lower to my knees beside her head.

"Please don't tell Leo about this," she whispers.

I blink and rock back an inch. That's definitely not what I was expecting.

"You can talk to me, you know," I say.

Her eyebrows pull together.

"Please, Gracie," I add. "Talk to me."

She looks away, and silence stretches between us for long enough that I think that's that. But right before I'm about to push to my feet, she says, "On the drive home, he was getting really handsy and wasn't taking no for an answer. He pulled off to the side of the road, and when I kept saying no, he got mad. He told me to get out of the car. When I didn't move fast enough, he reached over me to shove my door open and his elbow hit my chin. I don't...I don't think he actually meant to hurt me."

Didn't mean to... As if that makes the story any fucking better. As if leaving her deserted on the side of the road in the middle of the night is a perfectly acceptable thing to do.

Fucking Miles. He's always been immature and pain in my ass, but this? And it's my fault she met him in the first place.

I force down a deep breath.

Her lip already looks twice as swollen as it did when I picked her up. I slip the ice pack off the nightstand. "Do you want this?"

She reaches for it wordlessly, though a flicker of amusement passes over her eyes.

"What?" I murmur as she presses it to her lip.

"Déjà vu."

I crack half a smile. "Let's not make this a regular thing, yeah?"

"You don't like being my nurse?" she teases.

"I'd put on the skimpy little uniform and everything if you asked me to."

She swats my arm, and I chuckle, more relieved than anything that she seems herself again. She had me worried there for a second.

"Thanks, Liam," she says quietly. "For picking up, for coming to get me, for everything. I don't know what I would've done if...just, thank you."

I reach for her hand before I think better of it, but she doesn't pull away as I lace my fingers through hers. Her hand feels so small in mine, her fingers cold from the ice pack. Her nails are painted light blue, the same color as her dress. They hadn't looked that way at work earlier, which means she did them just for this date, and he wasn't remotely worth it. I rub my thumb back and forth along the back of her hand.

I don't say anything else, and neither does she. I can't

imagine any words that could make this right. What am I supposed to say? "I'm sorry this happened"? "You didn't deserve this"? What good will that do her?

But I don't move, and she doesn't let go of my hand. I just sit on the floor beside her and wait until she falls asleep.

Chapter Twenty

GRACIE

The sunlight pouring in from the window across the bed wakes me, and I start to roll over until I notice the pressure on my hand.

Another hand.

The one that belongs to Liam.

Who is sleeping sitting up, his head resting against the bedside table and his poor spine in a very awkward contortion.

And his hand is still in mine.

I don't move. I don't *breathe.*

I've never had a chance to see the intricacies of his tattoos up close. The ones on his hands, especially, since they're so much smaller than the others. Most of his tattoos seem complex—full of details and shading. But the ones on his hands are minimalistic, in a way, the scorpion wrapping around his wrist being the outlier. The rest are thin—birds and lines and intricate patterns that look like they might be coordinates or constellations. They blend seamlessly over his long, slender fingers, the perfect mix of ink and empty space. He didn't take his rings off, and I can feel the warm metal of the one on his pinky against my skin.

His fingers tighten around mine—just barely—and my eyes snap to his face, but he's still asleep. His eyebrows draw together, and he shifts, trying to find a more comfortable way to prop his head against the nightstand. He suddenly looks so much...younger. His lips are parted, his features soft.

Keeping an eye on his face, I gently extract my hand from his. For some reason, my stomach sinks as soon as I break the contact, like he'd been some kind of buffer, and without him, memories of last night come rushing in. My face throbs in remembrance.

I have no idea how bad it looks. I couldn't bring myself to look in the mirror last night.

I climb out of bed on the opposite side so I don't wake Liam and slip into the bathroom. He loaned me a pair of sweatpants and a T-shirt last night, and the too-long legs drag beneath my feet with each step. Steeling myself with a deep breath, I close the door behind me, flick the light on, and face the mirror.

The girl staring back at me is a disaster. Liam did a good job of cleaning the blood off, but my skin is stained pink in places, though some of it is probably a bruise forming. My bottom lip is swollen to twice its usual size, just on the left side. The worst is my makeup. I'd put on way more than usual, wanting to look good for my date, and now my mascara and eyeliner is everywhere *but* my eyes.

I grab one of the washcloths from the basket beside the sink, wet it with warm water, and get to work scrubbing at the makeup. I doubt water alone will get rid of it, but I'll do what I can.

I pause as I finish the first eye. I hadn't paid much attention when I was in here last night—hadn't paid much attention since the moment Liam picked me up, really. It was like the moment my body realized it was safe and could switch out of fight-or-flight mode, I just shut down. I can't remember a single thing Liam said or my responses, if there were any.

The bathroom is *immaculate*. It's tiny and cramped, but I don't think my bathroom—hell, any part of my living situation —has *ever* been this organized or clean. The counter is clear aside from the basket with the towels, and every surface shines and smells faintly of cleaning supplies.

And he had no way of knowing I'd end up here last night, so it's not like he cleaned because he was anticipating company. Is it just like this all the time?

Come to think of it, every time I've been in Liam's truck, it's been pristine.

Is Liam Brooks…a neat freak?

The thought is irrationally funny to me.

When I step out of the bathroom, the floor beside the bed is empty. I glance around the apartment for Liam. The place looks different in the light. It's not quite a studio, not quite a one bedroom.

It's an L shape with the bedroom area on an elevated plat-form and tucked in the back. The bathroom sits between it and the living space, where he has a leather couch and two matching chairs facing a mounted television. The kitchen and a small seating area are beside the front door, and I head that direction as the sound of glass clanking together fills the silence.

Liam's in the kitchen with his back to me. He opens a few cabinets, then the fridge, then sighs and puts his hands on his hips.

The floor creaks beneath my feet, and he turns.

The intensity of his gaze as it locks on me makes me

stumble to a stop, and I cross one arm over myself, hooking it around the opposite elbow. I don't know why I feel so awkward all of a sudden. There's something about standing here in his T-shirt first thing in the morning that makes me feel like...

Well, like something completely different happened last night.

"I keep forgetting to get groceries," he says. "So I don't really have anything for—"

"It's okay. I'm not hungry."

"How are you...how are you feeling?"

"Fine," I say a little too quickly, then fold myself into one of the kitchen chairs. "Thanks again. You know. For last night. And everything."

"Of course."

I nod.

He nods.

I pull my knees into my chest and wrap my arms around my legs. I'm not going to bring up the hand-holding if he's not, but for some reason, it's all I can think about right now.

I clear my throat. "What time does the shop open today?"

He frowns and takes a step forward. He opens and closes his mouth before he says, "Gracie...you can have the day off."

"No, I'd really rather work," I insist, meaning it. If I don't, I'll end up in Leo's house alone all day with nothing to do but hyperfixate over every detail of last night, and I don't know if I'm ready to do that. "If you have stuff for me to do, I'd like the distraction."

He nods slowly and crosses his arms over his chest. "I can drop you off at Leo's. Do you mind getting yourself to the shop? Say, eleven? I have a few things to take care of, otherwise I'd pick you—"

"I've got the bike."

"Right."

I nod.

He nods.

And the strange tension in the air holds strong for the entire drive home.

Chapter Twenty-One

LIAM

I don't know what the fuck is wrong with me today. From the moment Gracie stepped around the corner, I haven't been able to string a coherent thought together, let alone get one out. I drive her to Leo's in silence, cursing myself the entire time as I scramble for something to say.

But in the end, she just gives me a closed-lip smile and hurries inside, still in my clothes, her dress and shoes from last night draped over her arm.

It's a confusing as fuck image.

But I also really, *really* don't have time for this today.

I hadn't realized what time it was until Gracie and I were in the car. I do the math in my head as I hurry across town, but no amount of breaking the speed limit is going to get me there in time.

The parking lot is full but quiet when I arrive since school started and everyone is already inside. I flip the visor down and check my hair before stepping out of the truck, smoothing my hands over my shirt, then jogging to the front door.

A rainbow carpet lines the entryway, and a woman with

short gray hair smiles at me from the front desk as I rush inside.

"Sir. *Sir*," she calls before I can get very far. "You can't go any farther without a visitor's pass."

"Right. Um. I'm Liam Brooks." I shove my hair out of my face and step in front of her desk. The entire thing is behind a wall of glass like this is a maximum-security prison and not an elementary school. "I'm sorry. I'm running late. But I'm here to see my brother, Casey Brooks. I signed a form for today, so I should be on the schedule or whatever."

"Oh, for Career Day?"

I nod.

"I'll just need to see your ID."

I fumble with my wallet and slide my license through the tiny slot at the bottom of the glass. I bounce my leg and check the time on my phone as she rolls her chair away to make a copy of it. Casey's teacher probably only has so much time allocated for this today. Odds are if I show up too late, Casey won't get to do it at all.

The worst part is, if that happens, he probably won't even get mad at me.

"Here you go." She slides my ID and a visitor's pass—a peel-and-stick name tag—through the slot. "Room 111. Do you need help finding it?"

"I'll manage. Thank you."

I stick the name tag to my shirt as I hurry down the hall. Luckily, Casey's classroom is one of the first. The door is shut, and a young blonde woman in a long dress is talking at the front of the room. I hesitate before rapping my knuckles against the door.

The woman pauses whatever she's saying and glances my way. I wince and wave as I meet her eyes through the small window in the door. She turns back to her class, holds up a finger, then hurries toward me.

I step back as she opens the door, but she cracks it only a few inches.

"Liam Brooks?"

I nod. "Hi. I'm so sorry I'm—"

"Late."

I try to peer over her shoulder for Casey, but I can't see past the first row of kids. "I really am sorry. Something…unexpected came up, but I got here as soon as I could."

She sighs, steps into the hallway with me, and closes the door behind her. "We've already moved on."

"Look, I know you're busy and you have a schedule for the day and I'm screwing it up, but if I could please just have a few minutes? Not the whole time, but this means so much to Casey. He's been talking about it for weeks. I'm the one who messed up, not him. Please."

She scoffs, like, very audibly, and crosses her arms over her chest. As if I've said something ridiculous.

"This has become a real trend with your family, you know? I've heard a lot of similar excuses. There's always something important going on. Always something that keeps you all from getting *anywhere* on time. And I'm just supposed to, what? Accommodate you because your dad owns half the town?"

Great. Dear old Dad's already left an impression, it seems. And this teacher—I peek at her name tag—Ms. Berry, is glaring at me like I dumped pig's blood on her at the prom. I know a losing battle when I see one. And I'm not keen on causing a scene in a goddamn elementary school. For fuck's sake. As if the past twenty-four hours couldn't get any worse.

I basically rushed Gracie out the door this morning. She looked a little better than she had last night—that haze over her eyes was gone, at least—but there was something distinctly traumatized about the way she carried herself. And for noth-ing, apparently.

"Casey is a *sweet*, sensitive kid," she continues. "What kind of message is this sending to him? His mom is late to pick him up half the time, his dad just didn't show up to his parent teacher conference, and now his brother—"

"Look, I know. *I know.*" It comes out more forcefully than I meant it to, and she stops midword.

I'm all too familiar with what it's like growing up with Candyman Brooks as a father. At least when I was Casey's age, I had Mom. Christine loves Casey, there's no doubting that. But she's basically a kid herself. She acts like one, at least.

But Casey's teacher is right. Of course to her I look no better than them. And maybe I'm not.

I scrub a hand across my face and sigh. "You have no reason to take my word for it, but this isn't usual for me. I'm never late. I'm sorry. Can I—can I at least see Casey for a minute before I go? So he knows I was here? So I can tell him I'm sorry."

Her shoulders deflate as she drops her arms to her sides, as if she's disappointed I'm not arguing further.

She looks me up and down. I bristle under the scrutiny, but finally, she opens the door and steps aside to let me pass. "You two get five minutes."

I don't remember having Career Day when I was in school, so I didn't know what to expect. A few dozen small children ogling me and asking to touch my tattoos, apparently. Casey was thrilled though. Told the class I get to "draw on people for money," then proceeded to point to every tattoo that was visible and explain it to the class, including his commentary about which ones he likes and doesn't like. That part was a real hit. The other kids were all too eager to jump in and let me know which ones don't look good.

As for Ms. Berry, I swore she was hiding a laugh behind her coffee cup as she sat back and watched the entire room roast me.

But the light in Casey's eyes, the sheer joy on his face from getting to be the center of attention, hell, I'd let him talk shit all he wanted.

But as soon as I climb into my truck, reality filters in.

I have a few hours to kill, so I swing by the skatepark between Casey's school and the shop. It's late enough in the morning that it's busy—especially since it's summer and most of the public schools are already on break. Poor Casey's got a few more weeks though.

I stay in the parking lot beside the skatepark, frowning at the crowd. I never used to mind it, but when I'm trying to clear my head, it's exhausting. A few guys I used to squeeze in sessions with are across the park, and I have half a mind to go catch up. They gave me shit a few weeks ago about never coming around with them anymore.

And maybe I would, if it weren't for the group next to them.

I could spot my weaselly little brother anywhere with that ridiculous haircut. It's shaved on both sides and stupidly long in the middle, but it somehow doesn't budge in the breeze with all the hair gel he uses.

And standing beside him with his usual cocky, shit-eating grin is Miles. Asher says something, and Miles throws his head back with his laugh like he doesn't have a care in the world.

He has no idea what happened to Gracie last night. Has no idea if she ever made it home, if she's okay. Probably hasn't given her a second thought since he kicked her out of his car.

She could be lying dead out there for all he knows, and as long as he wouldn't get blamed for it—as long as his dad could get him out of it—he wouldn't care.

Everything that happens next is a blur.

There's pain in my hand, and the sound of a car door slamming. I force my fist to release my keys enough to shove them in my pocket as I make short work of the distance.

I don't plan to do it. I don't plan to do anything at all.

I'm just moving. Moving and breathing hard and seeing blood dripping down Gracie's terrified face and then—

"Brooks!" Miles grins when I reach him, Asher having already skated off and leaving him alone for a moment. He frowns and glances at his watch. "The shop not open today?"

My fist lands square across his jaw. Someone gasps behind me as Miles goes down and lands on his hands and knees on the pavement. He doesn't get up right away. When he does, he lifts a hand to his mouth. His tongue flicks out to lick his lip, and it's stained bright red with blood. I can't help but picture Gracie's bloody mouth—but hers looked even worse than that.

I should've hit him harder.

He sighs, dropping the bullshit friendly act. "If this is about your receptionist—"

"Her name is Gracie," I say through my teeth. "And you don't even know what happened to her after you left, do you?"

He blinks, and his eyebrows draw together, the first hint of concern finally coloring his expression. "Look, dude, I was fucked up that night. I wasn't thinking clearly, and…"

I tune out whatever else he says. If he thought his words would calm me down, they had the opposite effect. Not only did he throw Gracie out on the side of the highway like some roadkill, but he was driving her while he was on drugs?

I grab the collar of his shirt in my fist, and he stares up at me, nostrils flared, but he doesn't fight back.

"You could've killed her," I say lowly. "Do you understand that?"

"Look, I don't know what she told you—,"

"She didn't have to tell me anything because I'm the one who found her on the side of the road, bleeding and half frozen to death. Not that you care. Not that you checked to see if she made it home last night."

"Hey, Liam. What's going on here?"

I don't acknowledge Asher as he walks up to us.

"Nothing, man," says Miles, that shit-eating grin back in place. "Stepped a little too far into your brother's territory, apparently. If I'd known you were already fucking her, I never would've asked her out. It was a waste of a night anyway—,"

I shove him away roughly, and he trips over his board and lands hard on his ass. I should turn around now. I should walk away, get in the truck, and *go.*

And maybe if he'd shown even an ounce of remorse, I would've.

"*Liam,*" warns Asher, who must recognize the look in my eyes. He tries to step between us, but I push him aside. Miles grins up at me from the ground like he's fucking daring me to do it.

And God help me, I do.

Chapter Twenty-Two

GRACIE

The shop is empty and dark as I pull up on my bike. Frowning, I lock it up and search for the extra key Liam keeps in a fake rock near the corner of the store. He didn't offer any details about whatever errands he had to take care of, so maybe those are running later than expected.

Which is fine. I was planning on cleaning up to take a few more pictures today, and it'll be easier without him here.

I head toward the closet to get the cleaning supplies and wince as I catch sight of myself in the mirror. My lip is swollen, though it looks better after the painkillers I took this morning. The bruising is rapidly getting worse. It's a deeper red, nearly purple, and it makes my mouth look twice as big as usual. It's a good thing I'll be *behind* the camera.

The shop was pretty tidy to begin with, so I finish up within twenty minutes. I double-check my phone to see if Liam texted to let me know he'd be late, but there's nothing. He *did* say to meet him here at eleven, right?

The small red light on the shop phone is on, which I think means there's a voicemail. I hesitate, not knowing what to do.

I'm not sure why he'd call here instead of my cell, and handling the phone isn't really in my job description.

I click to listen to it anyway, then leave the phone on speaker.

"You have three new messages."

I chew on my lip.

"Real fucking mature blocking me, Liam," spits a feminine voice. "You do realize that's not going to make this go away, right? Man the fuck up and stop running away from all your problems for once in your life."

"I—oh." I try to shut it off—this definitely isn't for my ears —but the next one starts playing automatically.

"You've always been such a coward. Good to see nothing's changed. You're so fucking pathetic, Liam. This isn't going away. *I'm* not going away."

My spine stiffens. I don't recognize the voice, but I'm pretty sure I know who it belongs to. And I'm too far in to stop listening now.

The final message starts with a drawn-out sigh. "I'm sorry, Li. I'm just frustrated. You know how I get. I just want to talk to you. Don't you think I deserve at least a conversation? Can you please hear me out about this? I still love you. You *know* I still love you. And *I know* you still love me too, so I'll back off and wait until you're ready to talk. You know where to find me."

Not a second after her voice cuts off, the phone rings. I jump and curse under my breath as the shrill sound cuts through the air.

After a few rings, I sigh and grab it. "Brooks Tattoos?"

"Gracie, thank God."

My heart drops into my stomach at the tone of Liam's voice. I pull the phone away from my ear and inspect the number on the screen, but it's not one I recognize.

There's a hint of static, and then: "Gracie? Are you there?"

"*Liam?* Where are you calling from? Why are you calling me on here?"

He sighs heavily, and there's a long stretch of silence before he says, "The Ocean County precinct. This was the only number I knew off the top of my head."

"The *police station—?*"

"Yes. I don't think they're going to give me a lot of time, so I need you to listen to me. There's cash in the safe in the back of the shop that should be enough to post bail. I need you to bring me the yellow envelope. The code is 7742. There's also a spare key for my truck in there. I...well, I need you to head over to the park about two blocks from the shop and pick it up. Can you do that, please?"

Post bail.

As in he's been *arrested*.

"Liam," I whisper, knowing full well there is no one around and if anyone wants to listen from his side, they're probably recording it. "Are you okay?"

"I'm fine."

"If you're fucking pranking me right now—"

"I swear to you, I'm not."

"Why the hell were you arrested?"

He sighs deeply, and there's a long pause before he says, "Will you come or not?"

I already have my phone out to look up whatever park he's talking about on the map. "Liam, of course I'm coming."

My heart races as I step through the doors as if I'm the one who did something wrong. But once I say why I'm here, it turns rather uneventful—mostly sitting in one of their impossibly uncomfortable chairs and waiting, leaving my mind with nothing to do but spiral and try to figure out what could have landed Liam in here. I just saw him a few hours ago.

The place is dingy, to put it nicely. The yellow-and-blue-tiled floor and buzzing florescent lights overhead look to be a few decades old, at least.

I rise to my feet as Liam steps around the corner but freeze as I take in his face. He's covered in dried blood. His face, his hair, his shirt, and as he lifts a hand toward me in a half wave, I realize, his hands. His knuckles are *mangled.*

Wind rushes into the room as the door opens behind me. A man in a suit shoves through the waiting area, and a storm brews in Liam's eyes at the sight of him. Liam crosses the room toward me, but then Suit Guy steps in his path, forcing him to a stop.

A muscle in Liam's jaw ticks as he slowly peels his gaze up to meet the man's in a way that could only be described as menacing.

"I hope you know you just threw your entire future away," snaps the man as he thrusts his meaty finger into Liam's face.

Liam stares at him, unblinking, that same dark, deathly rage brimming in his eyes, but he doesn't respond. The man keeps his finger up, but he takes a step back.

"Come on," Liam says lowly to me as he steps around the man, something urgent about his movements now, like he can't get me out of here fast enough.

We're nearly to the door when someone else steps around the corner.

I freeze with one foot out the door.

Miles is barely recognizable. He looks like he should be in a hospital. One eye is completely swollen shut, his lip is more busted than mine is, and half of his hair is matted with dried blood.

My gaze slowly swings to Liam as the pieces click into place. He's already looking at me, his mouth set in a grim line.

He presses a hand to the small of my back, and I can feel the heat of Miles's attention on me now, but I don't turn. I just follow Liam out the door.

Neither of us says anything in the car. One look at his hands tells me the shop is closed today, and maybe many days after that. The skin is broken and bloody, and his joints are already starting to swell. He holds the steering wheel loosely like he can't quite close his fists.

He parks outside Leo's house, but still, we say nothing. I don't get out of the car. I haven't begun to process the situation. I'm still in the police station, frozen the moment I saw Miles walk around the corner.

Miles, who Liam apparently beat the shit out of. Because Liam looks bad, but Miles looks a million times worse.

I wet my lips and glance at his hands resting on the steering wheel, then turn and open the door.

"You might as well come inside to clean up," I say without looking at him. "Those look terrible."

It's not until I'm already in the entryway of the house that I hear his car door open. I head for the kitchen and search through the cabinets for whatever first aid stuff Leo has. I'd laugh at the way the roles have reversed in less than twenty-four hours if any of this was at all funny.

"I can do it," Liam says from the hall.

"Sit."

He takes a bar stool in silence as I join him with my makeshift first aid kit and plastic bag full of ice. I grab one of his hands and start dabbing at his knuckles with a cotton ball soaked in peroxide. He lets out a low hiss through his teeth but doesn't pull away.

When I've finished and moved onto his other hand, he says quietly, "I didn't plan this."

His brow is furrowed, and he's staring intently at the counter.

"So your errand for today *wasn't* to track down Miles and beat him to a pulp?"

Slowly, he shakes his head. "Casey—my little brother—he asked for me to present with him for Career Day. I was on my way back and stopped at the skate park to clear my head before work. And I saw Miles there. And he just...I shouldn't have let him get under my skin like that. I snapped."

I've never witnessed it for myself, but I'm not oblivious. I've heard the stories. The other fights, the detentions at his old school, the expulsion that landed him in public school with the rest of us. But hearing about it and seeing the bloody aftermath are two very different things.

He's never seemed violent, at least not around me. I don't know if I've ever seen him truly angry. I don't understand how the calm version in front of me could turn into the person who did *that*.

Swallowing hard, I wet a new cotton ball.

"Gracie," he says lowly.

I focus on his knuckles as I dab at the cuts.

He inhales sharply, then so low I almost don't hear him, he says, "I need you to know...this isn't...this isn't me anymore. I don't want you to think that this is me."

I set the bloody cotton balls on the counter. I have no idea what to say, so I wait for him to continue. His brow furrows as he searches my face.

"It used to be," he says. "The fights—but I haven't—it's been ten years since the last one."

"When you got expelled."

It wasn't a question, but he nods.

There's a cut through his eyebrow that I hadn't noticed before, and I jut my chin to ask for permission to clean that one too.

He nods and clenches his jaw as I get to work.

I don't meet his eyes as I say, "There were a lot of rumors about what that one was about."

His shoulders kind of…deflate at that. Enough to make me pause what I'm doing.

"It was a week after my mom, and my first day back at school. My dad thought it would be good for me to *get back to normal* or whatever. Some stupid freshmen were talking shit in the halls. Gossiping about how my mom crashed the car on purpose to get away from my dad—or that *he* did it and staged the whole thing to look like an accident. I just—I blacked out. The next thing I knew one of their jaws was broken and I was sitting in the dean's office getting kicked out. My dad paid everyone off to keep things quiet and stop the kid's family from pressing charges."

I press my lips together against the sudden nausea churning in my stomach. I've finished cleaning all visible wounds, so I focus on slathering some antibiotic ointment on a Q-Tip. Just thinking about losing my mom has my eyes burning, let alone having to listen to her death turn into the latest piece of small-town gossip. And at sixteen years old?

I start dabbing the cream on his knuckles, and I think that'll be the end of the conversation, but then in a strained voice he says, "For the record, I'm sorry I dragged you into this and that you had to come get me. And I'm sorry I got arrested for it. I know what you must think of me now, but…I'm not sorry I did it."

I know what I'm supposed to think, supposed to feel.

Angry, disgusted. Afraid, maybe? I shouldn't condone violence or feel any satisfaction at seeing Miles's bloody and broken face.

And yet.

"I just don't want you to be afraid of me," he whispers.

I hold his gaze. I must have drifted closer without realizing it because now there's barely any space left between us. I'm standing between his legs, the heat of his body surrounding me, his face a few inches above mine even though he's sitting. And I just…can't bring myself to feel any of those things.

Because despite the million memories I have of him giving me a hard time over the years, I also have a lot of other ones. The kind we pretend never happened.

Like when he'd found me on the playground in seventh grade after a group of bullies dumped my lunch out and stomped all over it. He'd wordlessly dropped his in front of me and walked away, even though it meant he'd go without.

Or the ride home he gave me in high school when he found me waiting outside after Leo got his first girlfriend and forgot about me.

And my personal favorite, my freshman year, a junior named Oliver Davis asked me out on a dare and left the entire lunchroom laughing at me when I said yes. A few weeks later when Oliver tried to do a prom proposal for some senior girl, he got through his whole little musical number, with *Prom?* written on the chests of the basketball players behind him, and a fart-sound simulator stashed in his backpack went off the second he opened his mouth to ask.

No one was ever able to prove that one was Liam, but the smirk on his face as he watched the whole thing go down said enough for me.

Liam Brooks has made me feel a lot of different emotions over the years, but fear has never been one of them.

"I could never be scared of you, Liam."

His gaze softens before shifting to the cut on my mouth.

"You might want to go to the hospital," I murmur. "I'm not exactly qualified—"

"They're not that bad. I can tell." Slowly, he peels his gaze up from my lips. "Thank you. For the help."

I stare back wordlessly for a moment, two. His eyes flick between mine like he's searching for the answer to an unasked question. Maybe I'm looking for it too.

Finally, I say, "Why did you call me? Why not your family, or Leo?"

"They only let me make the one, and I knew you were at the shop waiting for me. I didn't want to leave you hanging." The corners of his mouth turn down and he shakes his head. "And...I don't know. I guess I just immediately thought of you."

That sends a strange, confusing jolt of warmth through me.

Logically, I know bringing someone else into it would've raised questions about what happened with Miles, and I'd asked him to keep it a secret. And picking his son up from jail would be far too scandalous for perfect and polished Mr. Candyman Brooks. Or at the very least, he'd hold it over Liam's head for the next ten years or so.

Calling me was the convenient, smart choice.

"I'm not going to thank you for defending my honor or whatever," I say, stepping back and breaking the layer of tension in the air. Because saying it out loud would make it too real.

That I liked it far more than I want to.

Chapter Twenty-Three

GRACIE

The shop stays closed through the weekend, and I busy myself with more job applications, tweaks to the new website and socials, and a trip to the bookstore to stock up. They closed the only shop in Sweetspire, and now the closest one is over half an hour away on the other side of Edgewater.

I manage to cover the worst of the bruising on my face with makeup now that Leo and Keava are back, and thankfully they don't look closely enough to notice. I have half a mind to swing by and say hi to Mom and Dad while I'm over here, but they *would* look closely enough to notice, and I really don't have the energy to dodge questions right now.

I sigh as I step through the doors, waiting for the smell of paper and wooden shelves to work its way through my veins and give me that high I can't find anywhere else. It's a smaller shop with a café in the back and few store cats roaming through the aisles. I smile as a large orange one struts up to me, tail held proudly in the air, and rubs against my legs, purring.

But still, for maybe the first time ever, browsing the bookshelves and sipping my iced coffee doesn't bring me joy. There's not anyone else in here right now, giving me the whole place to myself, and for some reason, I can't force myself to enjoy it. I stare at the rows upon rows of colorful spines on the shelf, but I can't focus enough to read the titles.

I meander to the front of the shop where the display tables are. I grab a few with covers that catch my eye on the romance one and check out without reading the blurbs just to have something as I take a seat in the café to read for a bit. I'm not quite ready to go home, and I'm not in a sunny enough mood to go sit on the beach.

But instead of cracking my new books open, I find myself in a Google rabbit hole.

What's the difference between assault, aggravated assault, and battery?

What happens when someone presses charges?

Can you go to jail for beating someone up?

What if he deserved it?

This is all my fault. And if Miles's dad is true to his word, Liam is going to pay the price for it.

I stare at my phone like I'm waiting for a notification to appear.

I haven't seen or heard from Liam at all since patching him up in the kitchen. That was two days ago.

Which before, wouldn't be that unusual. But for some reason, going that long without talking to him feels different now.

It's almost physically painful to resist the urge to reach out. But he might not want to hear from me. Maybe the reality of the situation is sinking in too and he blames me.

I hope you know you just threw your entire future away.

Sighing, I grab my bag of books and head to Leo's car. This excursion hasn't been nearly as helpful as I hoped. I try rolling the windows down, blasting upbeat music, and taking the longer route with a better view of the water to snap myself out of it, but my mind is stewing the entire drive back to the point of feeling obsessive.

I just wish I knew why Liam was—

—sitting on Leo's couch?

I freeze with one foot in the door as Liam's and Leo's heads turn in my direction. They're lounged on the couch with some sports game on the TV.

"Hey!" Leo calls as I finally get my feet to work again and close the door. "We ordered some pizzas that should be here any minute. Got half veg for you."

"Thanks," I mumble.

Liam meets my eyes as I step into the kitchen, then smirks as his gaze falls to the bookstore logo on the bag. He looks a lot better today, though I can't see his hands from this angle. I can't help but wonder how bad Miles's face is.

I hope he looks like roadkill.

Liam stares at me a moment longer, his eyebrows lowering at whatever he sees on my face.

Wordlessly, I take my books and head for the basement stairs. I'm nearly to the bottom when I hear Liam say, "I'm gonna run to the bathroom."

"No need to announce yourself," says Leo.

Footsteps creak on the floor overhead, but then they start down the stairs, so light I almost can't hear them.

I'm sitting on the edge of my bed when Liam's head appears around the corner.

"Hey," he says quietly.

"Hey."

He doesn't come far into the room, just a few steps from the stairs, and crosses his arms over his chest as he leans a shoulder against the wall. "Find anything good?"

"Huh?"

He nods at the bag beside me. "At the bookstore."

"Oh." I stare at it. "I—I don't know. I just kind of grabbed a few random ones."

When I meet his eyes, he's frowning.

"Are you all right? You seem off."

"Oh," I say again, feeling off. Feeling…confused. About a lot of things, really. But namely why he's down here talking to me. And why he had to lie to Leo about it. And why I was so relieved the moment I walked in the door and saw him here. "Have you…have you heard from Miles's family or anything? About pressing charges?"

He blinks and pulls his head back an inch. *"That's* what—you're worried about *me?"*

"Well, yeah," I all but laugh. As if picking him up from jail isn't as far from my normal routine as you can get.

He stares at me in a way that makes me feel like I'm under a spotlight. Slowly, he peels off the wall and sits on the bed beside me. "I haven't heard anything from them yet."

"But you think they will. Press charges."

He nods once. "I'm not worried about it, so I definitely don't want you to be. I'll deal with it when it comes."

How can he possibly not be worried about it? I peek at him out of the corner of my eye and find him already staring at me, namely, my mouth.

To see how visible your injuries still are, the same way you were looking at him.

"What did you tell Leo?" I ask, letting my hair fall in front of my face to hopefully conceal the way my cheeks are burning. I gesture at his hands. "There's no way he didn't notice."

"I told him I got into it with Miles at the skatepark." My head whips around. "I said nothing about you," he hurries to add. "But I figured gossip moves fast around here, and he'd probably hear about it, so I tried to keep it as close to the truth as I could. Just made up some excuse about him getting Asher back into drugs."

I nod slowly. "And he bought that?"

He shrugs, and his shoulder brushes mine. "Seemed to. It's not far off."

For some reason, having him this close has my heart beating faster, like I'm doing something I'm not supposed to. He runs his hands up and down his thighs like a nervous tick. His knuckles are bruised and swollen, enough that he's notably not wearing any of his rings today. He wets his lips and opens his mouth to say something, but then the doorbell rings.

He holds my eyes for a beat longer before murmuring, "The pizza."

I nod.

He nods.

He hesitates, his gaze so intense on my face that I can't look away, but then he blinks and rises to his feet, and the moment dissipates.

He heads for the stairs and calls, "I've got it!"

Chapter Twenty-Four

LIAM

My calendar is a mess with all the rescheduling we've had to do lately. I'm just lucky my clients were willing to be so flexible with me. That many cancelations would've been a serious hit this month. Poor Gracie's been running around like a glorified personal assistant all week trying to keep me organized. And if she hadn't slipped out during my previous client to grab a coffee and sandwich for me from Milano's, I wouldn't have eaten anything today at all.

She has her hair up in a ponytail, and it bounces around her head with every step as she sanitizes the stations between appointments. The sight of it loosens something in my chest.

Maybe because until today, I've only seen her wear her hair down since the incident with Miles, like she was using it to hide behind.

Today, she has a little light back in her.

Maybe it has more to do with the interview she had this morning. She played it off—*it was just over video chat, it didn't last long, it probably won't go anywhere*—but I know that's the first nibble she's gotten with all of those job apps she's been sending out for months.

So of course she's excited about it.

And of course I'm happy for her.

Of course.

But I guess I'd been hoping—hell, expecting—to have her around all summer. It hasn't even been quite a month yet, and she could already be leaving?

We finally get a break around three before my next appointment at four, and I lay my forehead against the front desk and close my eyes.

Gracie pats my back, and I relax a little into her touch. "Just one more to go today, right?" she says. "And it's Friday. The weekend will be a nice break."

I nod without lifting my head. This next appointment is bound to take several hours though. It's the second session on this client's leg piece that covers her entire upper thigh.

The bells above the door ring, and all of my muscles tense. *Oh God, she's early.* But when I look up, it's Christine's high heels clicking against the floor as she makes her way inside, Casey at her side holding her hand.

"Hey, Case." I shoot a questioning glance at Christine. In the years I've had this place, I don't think she's ever stepped foot inside. Don't think she's ever individually sought me out at all. "What are you guys doing here?"

"I was just on my way back from picking Casey up from a playdate, and I was hoping you and I could talk. I know you're busy. It won't take long. Promise."

Maybe Makayla or Dad sent her to try to sell me on the new business again. Or to rope me into something else. Some gaudy party or family appearance, if I had to guess. I'm about to protest—I really just don't have the bandwidth for this today —when she adds, "It's about Miles Cushing."

I stop short.

Casey, oblivious to the new tension in the room, releases his mom's hand and rushes toward me.

"Hey, buddy." I bend down to give him a hug, then find Gracie's eyes over my shoulder. Whatever lightness I'd seen in her today is gone at the sound of Miles's name. Her features are pinched tightly together like she's bracing for impact. "Gracie, this is my brother Casey and his mom, Christine."

She offers a shy smile and wave.

"Hi, Gracie!" Casey beams and goes right in to hug her next. "Our names rhyme!"

"So they do." Her eyes dart from me to Christine, clearly coming to the conclusion this is not a conversation for his ears. "You've probably been here before," she says slowly, "but can I show you some of the new stuff I've been working on in the back?"

"Do you tattoo too?"

"Well, no," she says. "But I work for your brother. I take pictures, and—"

"You have a camera?"

"Yeah."

"Can I see it?"

"Sure." She smiles uncertainly at me over his head, and I mouth a quick *thank you* as they turn and head for the back of the shop. Casey grabs Gracie's hand like he's known her for years.

My stomach sinks as soon as they're gone and I have to turn back to Christine. If *she* knows about Miles, I'm guessing everyone else in the family does too. I'm sure they see it as just another screwup to add to my tab. Honestly, I'm surprised it took this long. The arrest happened a week ago.

"Michael Cushing came by the house earlier."

I sigh and rub my eyes. "I'm surprised you're here and not my dad then."

"He's out of town. He doesn't know."

I eye her warily. "You didn't tell him?"

She shakes her head and chews on her lip. "Do you want to tell me what happened? Because I have a feeling the version I heard isn't the full story."

I glance at Gracie over my shoulder. Casey's sitting on the table farthest from the door with her camera in his lap. She's hunched beside him with her hands at the ready in case he drops it, but I can tell from the tilt of her head that she's listening to every word up here.

I don't know the legality of what happened between Gracie and Miles, if there would be any way to punish him for that. Being a douchebag isn't illegal. Reckless endangerment, maybe. Or driving under the influence, but what proof do I have for any of it? Maybe I should've encouraged her to go to the police that night. But in the moment, all I'd thought about was making sure she was okay.

When I turn back to Christine, she's already followed my gaze.

"He deserved worse," I mutter. "If he wants to press charges, let him."

"He won't get that far. I'll make sure of that." There's a fierceness in her eyes I don't think I've ever seen before.

"No offense, Christine, really, but what could you possibly do?"

She gives me a flat smile and lays both hands on the desk. "Oh, you have no idea how scary and convincing I can be. And I have a feeling Michael's son's behavior isn't something he wants to be the latest town gossip. Reputation matters, especially for someone like him. What clients are going to hire him with a delinquent son running around? Don't think I don't know what he and Asher get up to. But I need you to tell me exactly what he did before I talk to Michael again."

I glance at Gracie, feeling like it's not my place to share if she doesn't want me to. She blushes a pretty pink color when I catch her already looking my way. She looks from me to Christine, her teeth worrying at her lower lip, and nods.

"Can I take a picture with you?" Casey asks.

Gracie blinks back to him. "Are we smiling or is it a silly one? You have to press this button here…"

I turn to the very last person I would have expected to come to my rescue and sigh. "Okay."

Chapter Twenty-Five

GRACIE

It quickly becomes clear Casey is an even better eavesdropper than I am and too smart for his own good. He smiles and pretends to be interested in the camera in his hands, but his eyes shift and his head tilts every time a voice drops a little too low to hear easily. As Liam and Casey's mom drift to the green velvet chairs in the waiting area in the corner, I offer to take Casey to get ice cream three shops down.

He's also about as far away from Liam's personality as you can get. He's friendly and bubbly and takes my hand with a huge smile as we head outside, then swings our arms between us as we walk.

"What flavor are you thinking?" I ask.

"Do I get one scoop or two?"

"Let's start with one. But I'll get a different flavor so you can try mine too."

"Okay!"

I reach for the door, but he beats me to it. It takes him a second to get it open, then he holds it wide and waits for me to pass.

"Aren't you the little gentleman?"

After several minutes of serious contemplation, he settles on brownie batter and I get birthday cake.

"It's on me," he announces as we reach the cashier, and to my shock, he pulls a mini leather wallet from his shorts and fishes out a ten-dollar bill.

"Oh, Casey, I'll get it. Save your money."

His little jaw falls open. "I'd never let the girl pay. Here." He waves the money toward the cashier, and I sigh as she takes it. "You can put the change in the tip jar," he adds.

I shake my head a little as he takes my hand and leads me to one of the tables outside.

"You know, this might be the best date I've ever had."

He beams and shoves a spoonful into his mouth. We sit in silence as we eat, and I push the rest of mine to his side of the table once he finishes his. Hopefully his mom won't be mad at me. I've never actually seen Liam's stepmom until today. Though she looks a lot younger than I was expecting, she seems nice enough. And she's clearly raised Casey well.

"I already knew who you are," Casey says.

"You did?"

He nods seriously. "Your brother is friends with my brother."

"That's right."

Casey's eyebrows pull together. "Everyone's mad at him because he doesn't want to work with Makayla—that's my sister. But he's really mad at them too."

I glance around the empty sidewalk, feeling very, very out of my depth. "Oh, I—I didn't know that."

"What is a black sheep?"

I reach for some napkins to try to help with the chocolate all over his mouth now.

"How can a person be a sheep?" he presses.

"It—well, it means someone who's a little different. Someone who maybe doesn't fit in with the rest of the group."

"Like Liam," he says.

I nod slowly. Where the hell did that question come from?

"What does pity hire mean?" he asks it casually, not looking at me as he digs around the bottom of the bowl for every last bit of ice cream.

"What?"

He looks at me. "Liam *pity hired* you. What does that mean?"

My stomach drops. "Where did you hear that?"

Kids usually parrot things they hear, right? I don't know who he overheard talking, but I could give a pretty good guess.

"Or downgrade? What does that mean? If Liam *downgraded* with you?"

I let out an unintelligible noise, my cheeks hot. I had no idea I was such a topic of conversation at the Brooks household. I don't know why I'm surprised. I accused Liam of hiring me out of pity myself, but there's something about his entire family laughing about it that cuts a lot deeper.

But *downgraded*? That doesn't sound like they were talking about the job.

I feel suddenly nauseous, unable to help myself from picturing Liam's ex Hailey. Aside from her picture appearing on Liam's phone, a while back I may or may not have looked her up on social media. The hundreds of thousands of followers aside, she's undeniably stunning. Of course his family would see me that way after her.

Not that anything's going on between me and Liam. Not that I was ever stupid enough to think there might be...

Or maybe I am. Maybe I have been starting to think that maybe, just maybe, after the migraine and Miles and spending the night holding his hand...

But whatever moments were there I must have imagined.

I don't respond, and Casey's eyes go round and wide.

"Was that a mean thing to say? I'm sorry!"

"Oh, no, Casey, it's okay. Are you done with these?" I grab the empty bowls before he can respond and turn for the trashcan beside the street.

But I can't shake this feeling of…humiliation clinging to me. I can't help but wonder if that's how Liam's always seen me too. Leo's pathetic little sister looking at him with puppy dog eyes while his type is the kind of pretty that can make a living from just existing because of how much people like to look at her. He must think I'm such a joke.

The door to Liam's shop opens, and Casey's mom steps out. She smiles and struts toward us.

"Thank you," she says as she reaches a hand for Casey.

"I don't want to go yet," whines Casey.

"Up. Now."

He groans but does what she says. "Goodbye, Gracie!" he calls over his shoulder.

"Bye, Casey," I say softly and wave.

Chapter Twenty-Six

LIAM

I hurry through the shop with my arms full of supplies to set up for my next client. That meeting with Christine took longer than I expected, and I don't know how much of it to believe.

She says she feels bad about how dinner went, that she had no idea Hailey was involved, that she wanted to help to try to make things right.

But I learned a long time ago not to take anything my family says at face value. At the same time, Christine's never had that calculating air about her.

The bells above the door ring as Gracie returns, and I let out a sigh of relief. I don't know how I'd get through this day without her. She's standing frozen less than five steps inside, looking like she's seen a ghost.

I stop in my tracks. "Gracie?"

She blinks and focuses on me, but she's still white as a sheet.

"You okay?"

She blinks again, finally seeming to snap herself out of it, and heads for the front desk. "Yeah."

Ah, shit. "Did Christine say something to you?"

"No."

She sounds nothing like she did before she left with Casey. What the hell happened out there? I pile everything on the tray and head over to her.

"What's wrong?" I touch her arm, and she jerks away hard enough that I stumble back a step. "Hey—"

"Nothing. Come on. You only have ten minutes until Mina gets here."

Her voice sounds all wrong, and her hands shake as she organizes the already pristine desk. "Come on, Gracie. Just talk to me."

"Everything's fine," she snaps, then pushes to her feet and hurries toward the back of the shop.

"What's wrong?"

"Why do you care so much?" she demands.

I let out an incredulous laugh. What could have changed so drastically in the past ten minutes? Even with all the craziness, we were getting along so well today, or at least I thought we were. Maybe I'm just oblivious.

"Oh, come on," I say, trying to lighten the mood. "The ice cream couldn't have been that bad."

It's the wrong thing to say. I know it the second her shoulders tense, but worse is when she whips around and I see how glassy her eyes are.

My stomach drops.

"Everything is just a joke to you," she murmurs.

The words are barely audible, but they hit like a punch to the gut. It's the same damn thing my dad's been saying all my life.

Stop fooling around.

It's time to be serious.

You treat everything like a joke.

Grow up.

And maybe there's some truth to it. Maybe I'm not serious enough at times. But with the shop, with Gracie, that's never been the case.

And I thought she knew that.

But maybe she sees the same thing my dad does when she looks at me. When everyone looks at me.

"Everything's a joke to me? I'm the one trying to have a conversation with you, but you just expect me to be able to read your mind and magically know what's wrong."

"Nothing's wrong."

I flick my wrist. "Yeah, the tears are really selling that."

I wince as soon as I say it. That didn't come out right at all.

Her eyes harden. "You know what? Fuck you, Liam. And fuck trying to save your shop. I don't know why I've even been trying so hard when it's obvious this is all a game to you. Consider yourself off the hook for your summer charity project. I quit."

She storms toward the closet for her bag.

Summer charity—

Oh. *Oh.*

"Gracie."

She throws her bag over her shoulder, and the second she turns toward me, I don't think. I just move.

I close the space between us, grab her face with both hands, and crush my mouth to hers.

She goes rigid, but that lasts only a fraction of a moment, and then her lips part for me. I've imagined kissing Gracie more times than I care to admit, but the reality of it?

Earthshattering.

I can feel her uncertainty, her confusion.

But she kisses me back.

She kisses me back.

I kiss her harder, letting my fingers weave into her hair and breathing in the fresh floral scent of her.

I don't know what she heard, why this is coming up again now. And it doesn't matter. I can never seem to say the right thing, so all I can hope for is to be able to *show* her. That maybe feeling sorry for her played a hand in offering the job, but it stopped being about that from the first moment she walked through that door.

The moment I saw her work and felt some hope that I could make this place work after all.

The moment she started putting her plans into action and I knew I'd made the right choice.

The moment she changed from quiet and uncertain to barking orders at me.

The moment hours passed as I sat at her bedside without even noticing.

The moment I saw her on the side of the road, or when I spent all night holding her hand because I couldn't bring myself to let go even once she fell asleep.

And I'm quickly realizing kissing her now was probably the wrong thing to do too. Because now that I've started, I don't know how I'll ever stop. Nothing, not a single thing that has ever happened in my life, has ever felt more right than this.

She pulls back an inch, then another, her blue eyes wide as she stares into mine. They're not as light as they seem from far away. There are layers to them, like the gradient of the sky right before sunset.

Now would be a good time to say something, but I can't string a coherent thought together. I just stare back, slightly breathless and completely failing at not looking at her mouth again.

"You have never been a charity project," I murmur, silently pleading with her to believe me. To see it in my eyes.

She steps away, forcing me to drop my hands, and when she breaks the eye contact, I feel it like a physical loss.

"I should go," she whispers, then all but runs out the door.

Chapter Twenty-Seven

GRACIE

4:14 PM *Liam missed call*
Liam: Please call me back
5:00 PM *Liam missed call*
Liam: Gracie, talk to me
5:45 PM *Liam missed call*
6:00 PM *Liam missed call*
Liam: Please

"Finally." I flip the page with a sigh and burrow deeper into my blanket burrito, but not so far that I can't reach the straw poking out of my wineglass. It's a lot to juggle, what with also trying to keep the reading light currently clipped to my book at the right angle while also not covering any words on the page, but the enemies *finally* became lovers and now everything is right in the world.

Except for, of course, everything else.

But that—that I'm not thinking about.

No, tonight I am binge reading, drinking an entire bottle of wine myself, and I'm only leaving the warmth of my bed for absolute dire circumstances...like needing to pee.

With a groan, I untangle myself from the blankets, carefully set my wine and book on my nightstand, and shuffle to the bathroom.

The moment my brain is undistracted, memories of what happened earlier force themselves to my attention.

Pity hire.

Downgrading.

But then...Liam. Looking at me in utter disbelief as soon as I said it. And then...kissing me.

Kissing me.

I don't know why I ran. Maybe because crying in front of him about it was humiliating. Crying about it at all was stupid. That would be the one word to sum the entire thing up. *Stupid.*

I know Casey probably heard those things from Liam's dad, maybe his siblings. I don't know why I overreacted like that. Why I took my embarrassment out on him. Then I panicked and ran like an idiot.

My fingers trail to my lips as I stare at my reflection in the mirror and it's like I can still feel him there. And that...that does strange things to my body. My stomach is wound tight as a fucking spring, my heart rate is concerningly high, and my skin is all hot and tingly. Because I've been touched by men before, but never like *that*.

The kiss probably lasted only a few seconds. I honestly have no idea. The second his lips were on mine my brain just stopped working.

Why did I run?

I pace the length of my room, too wound up to go back to my book now. Too afraid to look at my phone in case he reached out again—or worse, he didn't.

I tried to respond. I did. I typed out a message, deleted it.

Tried again, deleted it.

Stared at the screen for a solid ten minutes until my eyes started to burn.

I feel like I need to *run*, but the treadmill is loud and Keava and Leo are sleeping, plus it's late and I watch way too much true crime to go outside by myself.

Short on other options, I end up back in bed. But I pause as I reach for my book, my eyes drifting lower to the drawer in my nightstand.

Fuck it.

A quiet buzz fills the room as I throw the comforter over me to muffle the sound because if they hear me upstairs I will simply have to smother myself with my pillow.

God, this really isn't helping.

I close my eyes and try to force my muscles to relax, to think of hot book boyfriends and banter and slow-burn sexual tension.

Of hands on skin and lips on necks and the way Liam's hands held my head so firmly, no trace of uncertainty—

I suck in a sharp breath, trying to force the image away, trying to stop imagining what might have happened if I hadn't left. If I'd kissed him back—*had* I kissed him back? I can't even remember. I must have.

If we'd stood there much longer, if I'd let myself touch him the way I wanted to, if his hands had trailed into my hair, his body pressing mine against the wall...

I clamp my mouth shut against a moan.

But what does it, what finally pushes me over the edge, is the memory of his eyes staring into mine as I'd pulled back, so deep and intense and earnest. He has the greenest eyes I've ever seen. I've always thought so.

The silence of the room is stark once I shut the toy off, and I lie there panting for several moments, waiting to come down.

But I don't feel better. Not even a little bit.

Chapter Twenty-Eight

GRACIE

"You don't think this is a bit overkill?" I mutter.

Carson shushes me and refocuses on the brush she's currently ramming into my eye socket. "I'm blending. Okay, now look up."

I wince and try not to blink as she moves onto my lower lash line.

"What's got you all melancholy?" she asks. "It's a holiday! There, appreciate my masterpiece." She spins my chair around to face her full-length mirror.

At least my makeup isn't as in-your-face as the literal American flag she has painted on her cheek. A pop of blue eyeshadow sits in the inner corners and along my lash line, and she filled in the rest of the space with glitter and tiny white stars.

Beyond that, my skin has *never* looked this flawless and glowy when I do my makeup. I twist and turn to inspect her work from all angles.

"You're a magician."

She beams in the mirror behind me, then claps her hands on my shoulders.

"Come on, get changed. I want to get there before the hot dogs get cold. I heard they'll have veggie dogs too!" she calls before disappearing into her closet.

I pull on my trusty red tube top from college and the pair of denim shorts she's letting me borrow—covered in white stars and white fringe hanging off the front pockets, naturally. Carson opts for a red, white, and blue bikini and sheer beach cover-up, then hooks her arm through mine and leads us downstairs.

The Fourth has always been a big holiday around here— mostly because it's one of the few holidays in the summer so it's a good excuse for a beach party—but it's never really been my thing. This year feels different though. Carson's excitement is contagious, and I'll take any distraction I can get right now.

The shop is closed for the long weekend, which means it's been days.

And I still haven't talked to Liam other than finally responding to say I needed some time. Days have passed, but I'm no closer to having a response than I was the moment it happened. Just giving him the silent treatment until I figured it out seemed cruel though.

The day is already in full swing when we arrive, loud enough to hear even when we're several blocks away. Upbeat music from a live band carries over the sea of people, umbrellas, and barbeque. The party stretches from the boardwalk to the beach and every little nook and cranny it can squeeze into. It sounds like the parade is going on in the distance too. I tighten my grip on Carson so I don't lose her in the crowds.

Not that she makes it easy on me. She is a woman on a mission, swerving in and out of people trying to find the best line to get a hot dog. By the smell of it, there's no shortage of them.

The sun is really beating down today. I shade my eyes with my hand as we find a spot in line. Carson fills me in on all her work gossip as we wait—one of the dancers is pregnant, a regular customer's wife came storming in and dragged him out, a new girl started working there and she's been teaching them all tricks that no one's ever seen before…

"Oh, wait, didn't I hear you and Miles Cushing went on a date? *Why* are you letting me blabber on instead of giving me the details!"

My stomach dips, but in no small act of grace, we reach the front of the line, and I give the worker a probably too enthusiastic smile. "One beef and one veggie, please." I wave Carson off when she reaches for her wallet and hand over a bill. "Consider it payment for your makeup services," I say with a shrug.

We pivot for the beach once our hot dogs are sufficiently coated in ketchup and mustard, and she gives me a little smirk as we pause to slip off our flipflops.

"*Soooo.* Miles?"

I grimace, but I should've known better that she wouldn't drop it. The more I evade it, the more she'll want to know. Better to make it sound boring so she'll move on.

"Nothing worth talking about, I'm afraid. Bad date. Won't see him again."

"Ugh." She hooks her arm through mine. "I should've known. He's too hot. It's like once you pass a certain threshold of hotness, they become too insufferable to date."

I hum noncommittally.

"Oh, there they are!" She points to her group of friends already camped out on towels under a row of umbrellas, a cooler sandwiched in the sand between them.

"Hey, all!" Raquel waves over her head. I almost didn't recognize her with the oversize sunglasses and floppy hat. Judging by the way her skin already looks tanned to a crisp, they've been out here awhile.

The three other girls smile and say hello—I think two were at the party a while ago, but I can't remember any names—as Carson fishes our towels out of her bag and starts setting up. Her other roommate, Luna, is noticeably absent.

"We were thinking of hitting up the High Dive," says one of the girls. "They're doing two-dollar red, white, and blue shooters until sunset."

"Only if someone cuts Mina off," says Carson. "I don't want a repeat of last year."

The girl on the far end scoffs. I do a double take when I notice the tattoos covering her leg that are obviously still healing. She throws a towel over it as she readjusts herself to shade it from the sun. That style... I thought her name sounded familiar. She was Liam's client.

Liam.

Even thinking his name has my stomach churning.

"I washed your clothes for you," Mina says.

"What about the memory of getting puked on, huh? Who's going to wash that out of my brain?"

"Gracie, you want something to drink?" offers Raquel. "We have beer and wine coolers."

I blink back to the beach and smile as I take one of the strawberry ones and smooth out my towel next to Raquel. "Thanks for letting me crash your group."

"Crash our...girl, you're part of the group now!" She bumps her shoulder against mine and lowers her voice. "The girl who looks like she's about to shove her fist down Carson's throat is Mina, and that's Bev. They work at the club too but live up near Jersey City. Came down here to escape the big Fourth crowds."

Bev props her red heart-shaped glasses on her head and smiles at me. "You dance too?"

"Oh, no. Carson and I have known each other since we were kids."

"Oh, cute! Childhood besties. Wish I had one of those. The girls I knew growing up were raging cunts." She laughs at whatever she sees on my face, then reties her bikini around her neck and jumps to her feet. "Promise I'm a girls' girl. *They* weren't. I'm hitting the water!" And with that, she takes off for the waves at a run.

Raquel pats my leg. "You get used to her."

I sip my drink as the girls start talking about some guy who comes into their work a lot. It's kind of a relief to be out of the conversation for a minute anyway. I lean back on my elbows and people watch. The beach is much busier than a normal day, but not nearly as bad as the bigger celebrations farther north.

Mom and Dad used to take us to those when we were kids. The day was full of fried Oreos and amusement park rides and sparklers. These days they opt for a little backyard get-together since they have a good enough view of the fireworks from their porch. Mom always makes the best pasta salad anyway.

Carson says something I don't hear, and everyone laughs. I smile along like I was paying attention.

Mom and Dad were really encouraging about me not spending today with them, saying I should go out and cele-brate like *the young folks.* But I can't help but wonder what they're doing right now, if Leo and Keava are there yet, if—

"First round's on me!" Carson squeals as everyone climbs to their feet and starts packing their things.

"I'll grab Bev," Raquel mutters, then takes off toward the water.

Carson appears at my side once she's finished folding her towel, and she tosses her arm over my shoulders. "So Gracie, you ever done a blowjob shot?"

Everyone is wasted and the sun hasn't even gone down yet. Well, everyone but me. After the first red, white, and blue thing that tasted like straight up toothpaste, I've managed to artfully dodge each round of shots with quick trips to the bathroom or simply getting "lost" in the crowded bar.

The High Dive is one of the few bars left around here without the Brooks name attached to it, and it shows. Rather than the sleek, upscale feel the rest of them have, the High Dive seems to relish in its dinginess. All of the windows are covered with thick velvet curtains, and other than a few light fixtures hanging above the booths on the outskirts of the room, the space is lit with various neon signs.

After my third disappearing act, the bartender met my eyes with a smirk, clearly catching on. We went to high school together, actually. Fletcher, I think his name is. He fills my shot glasses with water for the rest of the night, and the girls are too far gone to notice.

It was busy when we showed up, but we're well past standing room only now. I can't even see the pool tables, just hear the crack of the balls in the distance. I thought maybe after I gave it some time, the whole thing would get more fun, but it's just...not.

I check the time on my phone for the hundredth time tonight and finally pluck up the nerve to grab Carson and say, "Hey, I'm going to head out! I'm not feeling too great!"

I have to shout it over the music, and she blinks drunkenly at me for a moment like her brain is struggling to process the words.

"I can walk you home!" she says.

I don't have faith she can walk at all at this point. If it weren't for Raquel also being mostly sober, I don't think I could bring myself to leave her at all.

"I'm gonna grab a taxi!"

Hopefully they planned for a lot of business tonight and it doesn't take forever.

She pouts but hugs me goodbye, and I squeeze my way through the crowd toward the door, leaving a chorus of "Bye, Gracie!"s in my wake.

When a driver pulls up to the curb outside the bar, instead of Leo's address, I give him Mom and Dad's.

I close my eyes and lean my head against the window as the music fades behind us.

It doesn't occur to me this might be a bad idea until we're pulling into my parents' driveway and there's an extra truck parked there.

A very familiar, very pristine truck.

If the ride over here weren't so damn expensive, I'd have half a mind to turn right around and head home.

The porch light flickers on as the door opens, and my father appears with a giant American flag top hat on. "Gracie! Hey, Gracie's here!" he calls through the door.

I wince and extend an arm to hug him as I join him on the porch.

He smiles down at me. To my relief, he doesn't ask about the cab or why I'm not with my friends. He says nothing about my random appearance at all, just squeezes my shoulders and leads me inside. "You're just in time. Mom was about to cut the cake. And we haven't done sparklers yet or anything."

The house is empty as we head through the hall to the sliding glass doors. The sight of the backyard loosens a knot in my chest that I hadn't realized was there. It looks exactly the same as it always does—corn hole set up in the middle of the yard, the grill off to the side, a wooden picnic table on the deck full of food on red, white, and blue plates.

But no sign of Liam.

Leo and Keava wave from their game of corn hole, but I beeline for the table and load up a plate of the pasta salad.

"Save room!" cries Mom as she hurries over with the cake.

Judging by how tall it is, that thing has at least three layers in it. The outside is pretty tame—white frosting covered in sprinkles and careful rows of icing piped along the edges. Strawberries and blueberries are artfully placed on top, along with a mini American flag.

She sets it on the table and goes in for a hug.

"Oh, sweetie. I'm so glad you came! It wasn't the same without you here."

"How long did you spend on this cake?" I ask, leaning in for a closer look.

"Pfft." Mom waves her hand, but it's Dad who calls, "Two days!" before ducking inside.

"Well, in that case, I'll happily have cake for dinner," I say.

Mom kisses me on the cheek, then gets to cutting.

The door creaks behind me, and I polish off the last of my pasta salad just in time for Mom to plop a giant piece of cake on my plate.

"Sounds like a plan to me."

I jump, having expected my dad. But when I turn, it's Liam standing two paces behind me. The moment I meet his eyes, I'm frozen, unable to look away. It feels like we stare at each other forever, then one corner of his mouth lifts, and softly he says, "Hey."

"Hey," I squeak.

"We cutting the cake?" Leo bounds over, and the moment breaks.

I blink and turn, taking my cake to the farthest spot at the table. The cake might be delicious, but I have no way of knowing because trying to chew as Liam sits across from me is impossible and it just tastes like ash. Everyone else chats and laughs, but I don't hear a word. I can't hear anything other than my pulse in my ears. I feel the weight of Liam's gaze on me, but I focus on my plate.

My phone buzzes in my pocket. I glance at it under the table, my stomach flipping at the sight of Liam's name.

I can leave.

My eyes snap up to his, and my brows pull together as I subtly shake my head.

Another buzz.

Can we talk? Front porch?

Slowly, I nod.

"I'm gonna grab another beer," says Liam as he pushes back from the table. "Anyone want anything?"

"Just a rematch," says Keava with a wide grin.

He points at her. "My ego cannot take getting my ass kicked twice, but thanks."

"Mom, this cake is so good," says Leo around a mouthful. "Best you've ever made."

She glows under the praise and wiggles a little in her chair. "I added a few special ingredients this time. You'll never believe what they were! First—"

I stand and give Dad a closed-lip smile along with a murmured, "Restroom," before following Liam. I don't give myself time to hesitate or overthink—I head straight for the porch.

He's already waiting there when I step outside, sitting on the railing as his head tilts back to take in the last of the orangey-pink sunset lingering in the sky. He doesn't turn, but he must hear my footsteps. I stare at his back for a moment before pushing myself forward and taking a seat beside him.

"I'm sorry," he says after a moment. "I probably should've given you a heads-up."

"I should've assumed you'd be here."

He's spent more holidays with us than not for as long as I can remember.

But that was before I knew what it felt like to have his tongue in my mouth. I squeeze my hands together in my lap and swallow hard. His eyes track the movement.

"Leo said you were going out with friends."

"I did. It just..." I trail off, not sure how to explain it. How *that* version of today felt like what I was supposed to be doing, how I was supposed to embrace being young, but the entire day I felt like I was trying to fit into shoes that were too small for me.

"It's never been my scene either," he says with a shake of his head. "Look, Gracie." He sighs, and every muscle in my body tenses for what comes next. "About the other day..." He presses his lips together and winces like he's struggling to find the right words. "I'm sorry. I know I'm your boss, and Leo's friend..."

I brace myself for some derivative of *it was a mistake, it won't happen again, I don't know what came over me, let's just forget about it.*

"And I don't know when...why...I just—" He sighs and runs a hand through his hair. "All I know is the second I showed up here, I started looking for you. And now I'm sitting next to you, and I know I should go back inside, but I don't want to get up. And not hearing from you the past few days, it's all I've thought about. I think I've been holding back from saying anything for a while because I don't want to make you uncomfortable..."

"You do make me uncomfortable, Liam," I whisper.

He blinks and rears his head back.

"But not...in a bad way."

Everything falls silent. Slowly, he reaches up and cups the side of my face. His eyes hold mine as his fingers twist into my hair, and he trails his thumb down my cheek.

"In this kind of way?" he asks lowly.

I can't speak. I can't breathe.

I nod.

Something behind his eyes shifts, a wall coming down, and my breath hitches as his hand drifts farther back and cradles the base of my skull. He leans closer, close enough that I can smell his cologne, can see the faint freckles on his nose and the flakes of gold in his eyes.

The tip of his nose brushes mine, but he stops there, his breath washing over my cheek as he murmurs, "In this way?"

My heart is threatening to beat out of my chest. Vaguely, I register the fireworks going off in the distance.

I nod.

His lips are a whisper away, and they brush mine as he says, "In this—?"

I close the last of the distance between us and kiss him. I don't know what comes over me, but suddenly my desperation to feel his mouth on mine overrides everything else. Just to see, just to know if last time was a fluke. If I'm remembering it wrong. Building it up to be something more than it was.

But no. One thing is certain. Liam Brooks knows how to kiss. Not that I have much to compare it to, but there is no way, *no way*, anything could be better than this.

Gravity loses hold on my insides, and I'm just falling, melting, flying.

The few drunken make-out sessions I had in college were all rushed and sloppy—like I was a meal to be devoured, no matter how ugly or messy the process.

But Liam takes his time. Every movement is slow and deliberate as he gauges my reactions, but the more I relax against him, the tighter he holds me, the deeper he kisses me, the more everything else ceases to exist. He kisses me like he's giving something, not taking it.

When he pulls back, I feel dazed, stunned, like my brain is stuck trying to reboot.

His gaze flicks to my lips, and a small smirk appears.

"What?" I murmur.

He shakes his head, his fingers weaving through my hair. "I just have the feeling you're going to flip my entire life upside down."

"In a bad way?"

The smirk grows as he leans in to kiss me again. "I don't know. But it's a way that I want."

The front door opens, and we lurch apart.

Leo and Keava appear around the corner a moment later, smiling and holding hands.

"Oh, hey!" says Keava as she peers at the fireworks overhead. "Wow, good thinking. Much better view up here."

Leo lifts their intertwined hands. "We're gonna head to the beach for a bit." He points at Liam. "Still on for the game tomorrow?"

Liam salutes him.

Leo pauses with one foot on the steps as he takes in the driveway. "Unless...Gracie, do you need a ride home?"

"I'll take care of her," says Liam.

"You sure?"

Liam waves him off. "It's on my way."

"See you at home, kid," calls Leo as they take off.

We sit in silence until their taillights disappear into the night, and even then, neither of us says anything. But the ghost of a smirk lingers on Liam's face as he reaches over and takes my hand.

Chapter Twenty-Nine

LIAM

We stay for another hour or so after Leo leaves, watching the fireworks and eating Mrs. Collins's masterpieces. I sit on the porch with Mr. Collins as Gracie and her mom laugh and dance around each other with their sparklers in the yard. It opens a hole in my stomach that I try, and fail, to shove down.

I've been coming to the Collins house for holidays for years, but the Fourth of July is one that started long before my mom died. She'd come with me, sometimes my siblings too, before they got old enough that it was cooler to go do things with their friends instead. Sparklers were always her favorite part. Some of my favorite pictures of her are the ones we took together every year on this day.

The lights smear across my vision, and I can picture her out in the yard too, one in each hand, beaming so wide you could see every last one of her teeth. I didn't inherit much from her, unfortunately, but that smile is the one thing I do have.

And, well, I have her to thank for the family that basically adopted me. Leo and I never would have become friends without her and Mrs. Collins conspiring together after they met at a baking class and realized they had kids the same age.

Not that we hit it off immediately. That first playdate was a disaster, and I couldn't shoo Leo out of our house fast enough. I was in a superhero phase, and all he cared about was the stupid train set—which belonged to Taylor, so I wasn't even allowed to touch it.

I don't know what it was that made my mom insist we try again. She must have seen something that we couldn't. Maybe she could tell, even back then, that I was never going to fit into that life like the rest of them and I needed someone on the outside.

I clear my throat and shift in my chair. Mr. Collins lays his hand on my shoulder without looking at me, like he can tell what I'm thinking.

Gracie looks over midlaugh, the light from her sparkler making her face glow and her eyes shine. She looks so fucking beautiful it makes my chest hurt.

When it's time to take her home, I keep my hands to myself as we climb into the truck and her parents wave us off. But once we're down the street, I can't help but reach over and lay my hand on her knee. I feel her looking at me and spare her a quick glance before returning my attention to the road. Even in the dim light, I can see the faint blush on her cheeks, and I like the sight far more than I should.

We sit in comfortable silence with nothing but the low hum of the radio in the background and the glow of the stars over-head. But as we get closer to Leo's house, I feel the energy shift. Gracie bounces her leg and chews on her lip.

Before I can ask her what she's thinking, she says, "There's no point in telling Leo, right?"

I glance at her as we pause at the stop sign a street away.

"Because...because I'm probably leaving soon anyway," she continues. "And I don't want things to be weird, or to make a big deal out of it, so what would be the point? And I don't even know what I'd tell him because, well." She wrings her hands together in her lap. "I don't really know what, exactly, is going on here."

I stare straight ahead as I park along the curb outside her house. To be fair, I don't know what's going on here either, but I do know her words hit like a punch to the gut for more reasons than one.

Her eyes are round and wide in that trademark deer-in-headlights look of hers.

I clear my throat. "I...yeah, I won't say anything. If that's what you want."

She's back to chewing on her lip. "Is that okay?"

Her breath catches as I cradle the side of her face and lean in. My eyes flick to the house behind her—dark, so Leo and Keava aren't back yet.

I feel like the only answer I *can* say is yes. It's not like she changed the rules here. I always knew it was a matter of time before she left. Knew there was nothing simple about kissing Leo's sister.

Leo's sister.

Even thinking those words now feels wrong. Because that's not who she is.

She's Gracie. And for the first time, she feels more mine than his.

Leo will never see it that way.

And maybe she won't either.

"Whatever you want, Gracie," I murmur.

The tension in her body subsides, and her eyes soften as they meet mine.

God, I can't think when she looks at me like that.

"Thank you for the ride home."

I kiss her on the forehead even though everything inside of me aches for more as I pull away.

Chapter Thirty

GRACIE

"Nope. No." Liam steps back from the front desk and crosses his arms over his chest. "Just delete the whole thing."

I roll my eyes. "Liam, this is a good thing."

He points at the phone in my hand. "A dozen strangers on the internet commenting *Daddy* on a video of me is *not* a good thing."

I fight to keep a straight face. Especially after hearing him say it. "You're bound to get some weird comments when something goes viral. That's just what happens. Did you even read the other comments?"

He covers his eyes with his hand like he physically can't take any more.

Admittedly, the video did venture into a less-than-ideal demographic for a while. Not that it was entirely surprising. We've posted similar videos in the past—basically a before and after, starting with footage of Liam doing the tattoo, then transitioning to the finished piece. I threw a trending sound over the top, so you couldn't hear the actual conversation going on, but I managed to catch a moment where Liam's tongue flicked to the corner of his mouth, then he smirked, glanced up at his client, and laughed, and...well, I may have been guilty of watching it several times myself. Not to mention it was golden hour, and the way the light fell on him highlighted his cheekbones, tan skin, and tattoos in a way that was mesmerizing.

Was it a little shameless? Maybe. But watch time matters, especially in those first few hours after you post, and gaining momentum from the wrong demographic helped us get a wide enough reach to find the right people, so that's all that matters.

"'I'm visiting the shore next week, where can I book?' 'Sick work, man.' 'Can't wait to work with you,'" I read as I scroll, purposefully skipping over the even worse thirsty comments that he thankfully hasn't seen yet. Not to mention the over-the-line ones I've already reported and blocked.

He peeks an eye between his fingers. "Those are just comments. That doesn't mean—"

"The shop's email is blowing up with inquiries. Over a hundred people have signed up for the mailing list I set up on the website—and that's just since last night. You've gained over ten thousand followers. Plus, the video itself made a few hundred dollars from the views alone. Liam, this is what you hired me to do. You don't have to like it, but you do have to trust me."

His grimace shifts into a smirk. "I like it when you're bossy."

I open my mouth, close it. The wider his smirk grows, the hotter my face burns, and I lower my gaze to the black fabric of his T-shirt.

It's been easy to compartmentalize the other night as long as I stayed focused on work. Well, maybe not easy. My stomach started doing enough somersaults to join the circus the moment I saw him this morning, but I've been doing a damn good job of ignoring it.

I wasn't sure what to expect from him today after my word vomit.

There's no point in telling Leo, right?

I don't want to make a big deal out of this.

I wanted to kick myself as soon as I said it, but then he'd agreed, so I obviously couldn't take it back. Because the fact of the matter is, no amount of keeping this quiet will make this *not* a big deal for me.

It's confusing, without a doubt.

Complicated, for sure.

But a small deal it is not.

The way my heart aches as he looks into my eyes makes it very clear this situation has all the potential in the world to break me into a million little pieces.

Because the one thing I said that *is* true is: I might be leaving soon.

"Don't flirt with me," I mumble.

His smirk turns into a grin. One of his breathtaking ones that shows all of his teeth and creases the corners of his eyes. "Go out with me after work."

I mock gasp as I lose the fight against keeping my smile back. "Stop hitting on me."

He grabs both arms of the chair and leans until our faces are inches apart and the silver chain around his neck dangles between us. My cheeks burn under the intensity of his gaze, and I can feel my heart in my throat. "Just to the skatepark. I have dutifully done everything you've asked for that godforsaken app. Now you're going to try something for me."

I balk. "You are not putting me on one of those death traps."

He nods seriously. "I am."

"I will die. You get that, don't you? Actually die."

"Gracie. I won't let you fall."

"When I'm careening to my death at a hundred miles an hour, I don't think you'd be much help—"

"I won't. Let. You. Fall," he repeats, his voice low.

All possible responses simply evaporate from my mind. The way Liam so calmly holds my gaze, like staring directly into my soul is the most normal thing to do, has me holding my breath. There's something about the way he looks at me that feels different than anyone else. It feels like so much more. The amusement that was in his expression a moment ago is gone, replaced by a rare softness I don't think he lets many people see.

The bells above the door startle me out of whatever trance I'd been in.

"Hey, man," calls Leo's voice.

That *definitely* snaps me out of it.

Liam steps back while I sit up straight and turn to the computer.

"Hey, Gracie," adds Leo as he props his sunglasses on top of his head and steps inside, a Milano's coffee cup in hand.

His voice sounds...normal. Not suspicious. Like he didn't just walk in on something weird. I guess he wouldn't be able to see the desperate desire to pounce on his best friend like a wild animal from the outside.

"What are you doing here?" I ask.

"You could at least pretend to be happy to see me. We're family, you know."

I frown, and he rolls his eyes with an exaggerated exhale.

"I was in town dropping off lunch for Keava. Thought I'd swing by and let you know we won't be home until late."

"Hot date tonight?" says Liam.

"Don't start with me."

My gaze bounces between them, and Liam has that same smirk he always wears when he's giving me a hard time.

"Where are you guys going?" I ask slowly.

Leo sips his coffee and grimaces. "The middle school is putting on a musical tonight. Apparently, a lot of Keava's students are performing, so…"

"That's going to be awful."

Leo gives me a flat look. "Obviously. But she wants to be supportive. It's sweet."

Liam muffles a laugh, and Leo's eyes swing to him. "What happens when Casey grows up and decides he wants to be an actor or something? You're telling me you're not going to be in the front row for every damn show?"

Liam shrugs. "Yeah, fair enough."

Leo's eyes narrow. "You're in a good mood today."

"Should I not be?"

His eyes narrow further.

"Don't you have work, Leo?" I cut in.

"Oh, sorry, was I interrupting something here?" He says it on a laugh, like the idea is absurd, but I still stiffen in my chair.

Liam checks his watch. "Ah, shit. I do have a client coming in ten. Gracie, can you sanitize station one while I find wherever the hell I put that design?"

"All right. All right. Message received." Leo raises his palms and turns for the door. "Try not to kill each other while I'm gone!"

Liam and I glance at each other sideways as the door closes with a quiet thud.

"Gracie, come on, let go of the book."

Liam's standing on the outskirts of the skatepark, his board in one hand, a helmet in the other. I adjust the strap of my purse over my shoulder and hold my book tighter to my chest.

I always take one with me, but this one is a little too thick to fit in my bag and I don't want to damage it.

He nods at the wooden picnic table behind me. "I'm sure the enemies to lovers or whatever will still be there after one run." He holds the helmet toward me.

I wouldn't just need elbow and knee pads for that. It would have to be a full Bubble Wrap body suit. Not to mention my little flowy dress is hardly skateboard-ready attire.

Liam tilts his head to the side and flashes what he probably thinks is a charming smile.

Okay, maybe it is. A little.

"Live a little, Gracie."

"That's exactly what I'm trying to do! Live. Something that could very well cease if you put me on that thing."

He plops the helmet on my head without warning, but I don't stop him as he adjusts my hair out of the way and secures the clasp beneath my chin.

"Safety first," he murmurs, then sets the skateboard at my feet. "I'm not going to shove you headfirst into the bowl. Just try standing on it."

I glance around the rest of the park. The last thing I need is an audience witnessing me fall flat on my ass. But it's quiet, with only a few other people skating around, none of which are paying attention to us.

After setting my things on the table, I test one foot on the board. My hands reach out on instinct as I add the second foot, but Liam's already there, his hands on my forearms to keep me steady.

"There you go," he murmurs as the board sways beneath me until I find my footing.

"I can't believe you find this fun," I mumble.

Ignoring that, he says, "Try leaning most of your weight on

your right foot, and you're going to kick off the ground with your left."

"Liam..."

His hands tighten on my arms, but he steps back to give me some room. And for some unknown reason, I do what he says.

My stomach dips as my balance falters, but Liam holds firm and walks alongside me as I move.

"I hate this. I hate this a lot."

"No you don't."

I step off the board entirely, then stop it with one foot before it can go rolling off.

"Try kicking it up."

That, maybe, I can manage. I've seen him do it enough times. I hit the end not quite hard enough, so I have to lurch forward and grab it. When I meet Liam's eyes again, he's got that same damn look on his face.

"Why are you smirking at me?"

He shakes his head, as if in disbelief. "You have no idea, do you?"

I clutch the board a little tighter. "I have no idea what?"

He takes the helmet's chin strap in his hands but pauses before undoing the clasp. I am hyperaware of how close he is to me but try not to let it show on my face. One corner of his mouth remains raised, but the amusement in his eyes softens. The strap clicks as he releases it. "How goddamn cute you look in this."

My brain barely has a chance to process the words before someone bounds up behind Liam and slaps him on the back. "Good to see you, man!"

"Hey, Fletch," sighs Liam as he runs a hand along the back of his neck.

He turns to me with a hand extended. "Fletcher. We went to—"

"School together. I remember."

He smiles, all warm and goofy and full of dimples. "He's got terrible patience, but he's a pretty good teacher. I'd listen to him. Though I am a bit disappointed I'll no longer be his one and only protégé."

"Don't think you need to worry about that. One lesson was enough for me."

"Oh no, it looked like you two were just getting started."

Liam raises his eyebrows at me.

"Hold on. I've got something that might help." Before I can respond, Fletcher takes off toward the parking lot at a jog.

"You roped your friend into this too?" I demand.

Liam raises his palms. "I had nothing to do with this."

Fletcher returns with a handful of elbow and knee pads, and squints at me as he approaches, like he's calculating something.

"These are technically children's sizes," he murmurs, holding one up to my elbow. "But I think they should fit."

"He teaches kid camps," Liam explains.

"Are you saying I'm child-sized?"

"Your elbows are!" Fletcher declares as he attaches the Velcro.

I take the rest of the pads from him to put on myself. They're all too tight, but it'll work.

"Feel better?" asks Liam.

"Yes," I admit. "Do I look ridiculous?"

"Not at all," says Fletcher.

"There's still no way in hell I'm doing that." I point at the pit of doom he previously called *the bowl.*

"Oh no. We never do that on the first day."

"Fletch," says Liam.

"Right." He pats Liam on the back and waves before grabbing his board and heading for the opposite side of the park. "I'll be over here if you need me!"

I reclip my helmet, and Liam offers his hands. With a dramatic sigh, I take them and step onto the board.

"You'll be a pro in no time," he assures me.

"Uh-huh."

"Flat surfaces only—just get used to shifting your weight and moving around."

I kick off, and he takes a step back to give me room. In a moment of panic, I tighten my hands around his, and he holds mine just as tightly.

"I'm not letting go until you tell me to," he says quietly.

After a few minutes of back and forth on the pavement, the sheer terror of it all subsides, and I try on my own a few times. Turning around feels completely out of the question, but I do manage to subtly serpentine. Every time I step off the board and look back at Liam, he's beaming like I just did the most impressive trick he's ever seen.

Eventually, Liam's the one to call it for the day, and I'm almost a little sad.

"I'll get them back to Fletch later," he says as he helps me remove all the pads.

"This was…fun," I mutter as I slip the helmet off and hand it to him.

He grins. "Yeah?"

"Terrifying."

"Of course."

"But fun."

That grin remains fully stretched across his face the entire walk to his truck. He offers a hand to hold my things as I climb in. It doesn't occur to me until I'm seated and buckled with the door shut what a bad idea that was.

Liam climbs into the driver's side and turns the book over in his hands, his eyebrows high as he reads the description.

"Give it back," I sigh.

"No figure skaters," he muses.

"Liam."

"Am I reading this right? He's a *dragon*? How does that work? Logistically?"

I grab for it, but instead of holding it out of reach like I'm expecting, he hands it over without a fight. The look on his face is almost...thoughtful.

"What is it about these books that you like so much?"

"Is that a trick question?" I mumble as I tuck it beside my bag at my feet. I'm well aware of how much other people see it as a cliché. Yet another girl in love with love.

"No trick."

"I don't know, I just..." I lean back and push my hair behind my ears. "I feel like there's a lot of hate in the world, so I like anything that shows the best sides of humanity. And I think love brings out the best in people. And the characters in romance books...I don't know. I guess I like that they're willing to fight for it. To put everything out there, make these insane grand gestures—they act like love is the most important thing in the world. And I feel like we've lost that a lot in real life."

I clamp my lips together before I can say anything else embarrassing.

"A hopeless romantic, huh," he says.

"You think it's dumb."

"No." I chance a sideways glance at Liam. He's not smirking, not grinning. Just smiling as he starts the car. "I don't."

GRACIE

The shop is so busy for the rest of the week that even with an artist working at every station, for the first time since I started working here, Liam has to turn people away. Undeterred, most of the ones who came in for walk-ins end up making an appointment for later. By Wednesday, he asks me to stop posting on socials in the hopes it'll slow momentum down.

It does no such thing.

He opens early, closes late, and I'm not entirely convinced he hasn't been sleeping in one of the chairs overnight.

"Okay, enough. No more."

I flip the sign in the window to Closed as a group of four girls who look like they might still be in high school reach the front door.

"Please! We just want something small!" calls the blonde at the front.

"We're closed." I turn the lock for emphasis. "Try again tomorrow. Or call and make an appointment."

The girls all groan and pout, but mercifully, they leave.

When I turn around, I find Liam perched on the end of the

front desk with a bemused smile. The rest of the shop is quiet and dark, since his other artists left an hour and a half ago when we were *actually* supposed to close.

"Don't smirk at me," I say as I head to the back to collect my things.

"You're cute when you take charge." He grabs my hand before I can pass and pulls me to a stop in front of him.

I fight against my stupid traitorous lips as they attempt a smile. I poke him in the chest instead. "You need to learn to say no. And take a day off. When's the last time you slept?"

"You worried about me, Gracie?"

As a matter of fact, I am, but I'm not going to tell him that. He can't keep up with this pace for long.

His eyes flit between mine. "What are you doing tonight?"

I glance at the book peeking out of the top of my bag. I might not be the one tattooing, but I've spent just as many hours in this shop with him this week, and by the time I make it home at night, I'm too exhausted to do much else but zone out in front of the TV with Leo or head straight to bed. My poor book hasn't been touched in far too long, and I've been missing out on the prime summer days. My need to be near the ocean is starting to feel like I'm in withdrawal. Seeing it from a distance on my ride home isn't cutting it. "I thought I'd read on the beach."

It occurs to me he's still holding my hand, and like he's just realizing it too, he threads his fingers through mine and squeezes. "Want some company?"

I mock gasp. "You mean you're actually going to take a *break?*"

His smile turns a little sheepish. "I was gonna bring my sketchbook and work on some designs."

"All right, fine." I pat his cheek twice and pull away. "Just don't slow me down."

"Yes, ma'am."

I throw my bag over my shoulder and point a finger at him. "And you can't make fun of my dragon book."

He slips the keys from his desk, spins them around his finger, and winks. "That I can't promise."

We set up on the quieter part of the beach, down past the pier. I spread out on the towel, savoring the feel of the sun on my face and the salt in the air. The peace from it is immediate. It's hard to believe it took moving away for me to realize it—how much my soul longs for the water. I guess it was easy to take for granted when I had unlimited access to it growing up. But four years away painted the world in a different light. Not everyone gets this. In fleeting moments, maybe. A weekend trip, a yearly vacation. But to live and breathe day in and day out with the sea air in your lungs is something different entirely.

Liam lies perpendicular to me and rests his head on my stomach, his sketchbook propped on my leg. The sound of the waves crashing on the beach and his pencil scrawling against the page threatens to lull me to sleep. I keep having to backtrack and reread the same page. I'm a chapter in when his pencil pauses.

"Tell me about school," he says.

I blink up from my book. "School?"

"Yeah. You don't talk about your time on the West Coast much. How did you like it?"

I smile a little, both at the memories and the earnest way he asks the question, like he genuinely wants to know. Despite only being home for just over a month now, college already feels like a lifetime ago. The all-night study sessions in the library, the occasional frat party my friends would drag me to, the late-night fast-food runs.

It was the place I really found my footing. I'd never seriously considered photography until I took a class freshman year, and it wasn't until I watched my friend Jo—who was a senior when I was a freshman—go on to start her own photography business and thrive after graduating that I felt confident enough to pursue something creative.

The school itself was small—the student body barely bigger than that of my high school—and I definitely missed the sun during the rainy parts of the year. But for those four years, that place felt like home.

Things felt simpler there.

"I liked it a lot, actually. But I realized early on I wouldn't want to stay there long-term, you know?"

He cranes his neck to give me a crooked smile. "Missed that Jersey charm, huh?"

I snort and push his head back around.

"People drive any better out there?" he asks.

"Unfortunately, no."

"I bet our bagels are better."

"They are. Do you...do you ever wish you'd gone? To college?"

I stiffen, hoping he doesn't take it the wrong way, but he just tilts his head from side to side.

"Sometimes I wonder about it. Just to have had the experience, I guess. Don't know what I would've studied."

"Art?" I offer.

He shrugs. "Don't think I would've been able to suffer through all the general education stuff they make you take. My dad would tell you it's a miracle I graduated high school."

He says it casually enough, but there's tension in his body

that wasn't there before. Probably more to do with the topic of his dad than school.

Because he can be as self-deprecating as he wants, but I happen to know Liam is a lot smarter than he pretends. Any low grades in school would've been due to him not wanting to invest his time into something he found pointless, not his inability to do it.

I can remember more than one occasion where I'd been sitting at the kitchen counter, stumped on a math or science problem. And after watching Mom, Dad, and even Leo fail to help, all it took was a glance at my homework and Liam would have it figured out in under a minute.

"You might have liked them. At least for me, they had less busy work than in high school. And you had a decent number to choose from."

He hums. "You keep in touch with anyone?"

"Yeah." My voice comes out a little too high. I clear my throat. "I'm closest with my friend Marti, but I have a few other friends I still talk to. We all video chat sometimes."

He rolls over to look at me. I pretend to be very interested in my book.

"You are a terrible, terrible liar."

My jaw drops open. "I—I am not lying."

"You're *concealing* something. Same thing, basically."

I shut my book with an audible thunk. "I am not."

"Your voice only does that weird high-pitched thing when you are."

I open my mouth, close it. I guess I shouldn't be surprised he knows that.

He sits up and lays a hand on my leg. "I'm sorry. I'm not trying to give you a hard time. Are you guys fighting or something?"

I sit up too and squint against the sun reflecting off the

ocean. And I realize I don't want to lie to him. Both because lying is what got me into this mess in the first place, but also because there's something about talking with Liam that makes admitting it aloud easier. He might hide behind his jokes and sarcasm sometimes, but I've never felt judgment from him.

I sigh. "No. I've gotten myself into a weird situation with them."

He sits quietly and waits for me to continue, his thumb stroking idly along my thigh.

"When we graduated, it felt like they all hit the ground running. Found jobs, places to live, new relationships. I didn't want to be the *one* person in the group chat who completely fell on her face. It started out with a few white lies that I thought would be more temporary circumstances than they were."

Liam nods slowly. "So they don't know that you're back here?"

I shake my head.

"That you live with Leo?"

Another shake.

"And the shop…"

I wince. "They think I work for a magazine in Philly, and that I'm dating some guy I met through work."

He nods again.

"Not that I wouldn't want them to know about that one," I hurry to add. "I had just already told them before I got the job with you and…"

"It felt like too late to backtrack," he offers.

"Yeah."

He frowns and scoots to my side so he can look out at the water too. "So this has been going on since you graduated?"

"I mean, it's not like it's constantly brought up, but yeah. That's when it started."

He glances at me sideways. "That was months ago."

My shoulders slump. "I know."

His frown deepens as he stares out at the waves.

My face grows hotter with each moment of silence that passes. I don't know why I said anything about it. "I know it probably sounds stupid—"

His hand shoots out and grasps my knee. "I'm not thinking that." He turns, his eyes finding mine, that troubled furrow deep between his eyebrows. "I was just thinking you shouldn't have to do that. If they were good friends to you, you wouldn't feel like they wouldn't be there for you."

"It's not that. They're great. I guess I was embarrassed."

The wind kicks up, blowing my hair in front of my face, but Liam catches it before I have the chance and tucks it behind my ear, then leaves his hand against the side of my face. Quietly, he says, "You don't have anything to be embarrassed about. But I do think you should tell them the truth. They're your friends. I'm sure some of them feel like they don't have their lives as figured out as it seems too."

A begrudging smile forces its way onto my face. "When did you get smart?"

He scoffs and smiles back. "I've always been smart."

We stay like that, smiling and sitting a little too close, but I can't bring myself to move. Even though we're out in the open and anyone could see us, maybe that's part of what makes it fun. Liam leans an inch closer, and my breath catches.

"How's the dragon book?" he murmurs.

"I've been having a hard time focusing on it," I admit.

His smile grows. "Need me to narrate for you again?"

I laugh, then movement over his shoulder catches my attention. I lurch back and suck in a sharp breath. "Liam." I squeeze his arm then point behind him.

He turns as the two figures walking along the path swim

into view. I thought something about that walk looked familiar. Leo and Keava are walking hand in hand, each holding an ice cream cone. They haven't noticed us yet, but they're getting closer.

"Come here." Liam jumps to his feet and reaches a hand toward me. I take it, scrambling and leaving my shoes and book behind as he pulls us a few yards away beneath the pier. The hot sand burns my toes as we run, and I let out a breath of relief at the temperature change once we hit the shaded area.

My heart hammers in my chest as I poke my head out. I don't know why I feel so...guilty. It's not like we were doing anything. But still. Despite how much time together Liam and I have been spending for work, if Leo saw *that*, there's no way he wouldn't find it suspicious.

Keava and Leo turn onto the pier, close enough now that I can hear their laughter.

Liam doesn't let go of my hand, but he puts a single finger over his lips as their footsteps sound overhead.

"...that's exactly what I told him!" laughs Keava. "But you know he never thinks before he jumps, and..."

They keep walking, and I watch their shadows disappear through the cracks.

I finally exhale once they're gone.

"Close call," Liam whispers.

I laugh quietly and nod, the adrenaline still flooding my system.

He rakes a hand through his hair and cranes his neck like he's trying to see where they went. "They're hanging out on a bench down there."

I eye our abandoned belongings. In perfect view from the end of the pier. This end of the beach is empty enough that if we went out there, even just to collect our things and leave, all it would take is Leo or Keava glancing over here for a split second for them to see us. All six foot whatever of Liam is kind of hard to miss.

When I turn to Liam again, he's already looking at me.

"You want to wait it out until they leave," he concludes.

I shrug. How long could it possibly take them to finish a few ice cream cones?

This is getting ridiculous.

I'm not sure exactly how much time has passed, but the sun is now setting on the horizon.

We've resumed our earlier position—me sitting with my arms propped behind me, Liam's head in my lap, though it took only a few minutes for him to start snoring.

I knew he was overworking himself, but he must have been even more exhausted than I realized if all it took was a few moments of quiet for him to pass out.

I lightly run my fingers through the soft strands on his hair, and he hums low in his throat for a moment before the quiet snoring resumes. I smile and leave one hand on the back of his head.

I can't see the end of the pier from here, but no one has come or gone since Leo and Keava went down there, so they must still be on the bench. Being all romantic and googly-eyed watching the sunset, if I had to guess.

Maybe we should've made a break for it.

I sigh and lie back on the sand, careful not to disturb Liam, and admire the vibrant streaks of pink and orange lingering in the sky. Their reflections skate across the waves gently lapping against the shore. It's peaceful, and quiet, and—

"*Gracie.*"

I startle awake at someone shaking me by the shoulders. When I open my eyes, everything is dark.

"Gracie, wake up."

It takes my brain another moment to process it's Liam's voice, and that's the sound of the ocean behind him...

And those are the night stars overhead.

"Oh my God." I scramble into a seated position and look around at the eerily vacant beach. I must have fallen asleep too. "What time is it?"

"Come on." Liam helps me to my feet, then I hurry after him to where our things are discarded a few yards away.

"Liam—" I start, my voice already several octaves too high.

"I know. I know. Come on."

My bag and shoes in one hand and my other gripping Liam's, we take off at a jog toward the parking lot, empty save for Liam's truck.

"Shit," I hiss as he starts the car and the time flashes on the clock—nearly midnight. "Leo is going to be so mad."

Liam speeds down the road as I dig around in my bag for my phone. Unsurprisingly, the screen is covered in missed calls, voicemails, and texts from Leo, wondering where the hell I am, each more frantic than the last.

I shoot him a quick text that I'm on my way back now, hoping that'll calm him until I get there and can explain, but that just invites a whole new string of messages. The texts pop on the screen, one after the other in a never-ending rampage.

"You want me to..." Liam starts.

"No, no, I've got it. Park a little down the block so he doesn't see you."

Liam presses his lips together like he's holding back from what he really wants to say, but he does it, then hops out to help me get my bike.

We both pause for a moment as I take the handlebars from him.

"I'm sorry," he says.

I shake my head. "It's not your fault."

"I'll call you later?"

I nod and hurry off down the street. It's not until I reach Leo's house that I hear him restart the truck. The lights are on as I stash the bike in the garage and head inside. The second I open the door, Leo lunges up from the kitchen table, Keava shortly behind.

"Where the hell have you been?" he demands. "Do you have any idea how close I came to calling the police?"

"Leo—"

"I get it—you're not a kid and you don't need a curfew, but you couldn't have called?"

"I'm sorry—I'm sorry! I ran into Carson after work, and we ended up hanging out and watching TV, and we both fell asleep. I texted you the moment I woke up and realized."

I wince at how easily the lie rolls off my tongue.

Leo seems to buy it though because he sighs and rubs his eyes.

"I'm so sorry. I didn't mean to worry you."

He sighs again and slumps into one of the kitchen chairs. "You had me...I was imagining a lot of worst-case scenarios."

"Sounds like I'm rubbing off on you."

He gives me an unamused smirk. Well, he tries to. His eyes tell me he thought it was at least a little funny.

I cross the distance between us and hug him from behind. "I really am sorry."

He pats my arm a few times. "I owe my new gray hair to you."

I glance up to find Keava watching us with her head tilted

to the side, and there's something about the look in her eyes that tells me she doesn't quite believe me.

Chapter Thirty-Two

GRACIE

Liam: Be ready at 6:30
Gracie: …ready for what?
Liam: For me to pick you up
Gracie: For. What?
Liam: :)

My bathroom sink is drowning in used makeup wipes. Every time I get a few steps into my routine, something goes wrong and I whip one out, wipe it off, and start over.

It's just an off day. It has absolutely nothing to do with the fact it's already six o'clock.

We've been dancing around what happened on the Fourth of July for nearly two weeks now. Despite the skatepark and the beach and the flirting, the handholding and the *looks* he gives me and the texts he sends even when we're in the same room…

He hasn't kissed me again.

And man, my overactive imagination has *loved* cartwheeling through every possible thing that could mean.

In the end, I do the same makeup I do every day for work. Anything different and he'll probably notice, then he might think I'm trying too hard, and—

"Oh my God, get it together," I mutter under my breath and force myself out of the bathroom as if I can physically leave the overthinking behind me.

I keep the outfit casual too—some jean shorts, a cropped tank top, and a zip-up hoodie. I pace around my room, not wanting to go upstairs yet but out of things to do, and if I let myself look in the mirror again, I'll start messing around in a never-ending cycle. Keava and Leo already left for their biweekly dinner date night, so the house is quiet.

The pacing is not calming. My hands are sweating, and my heart is beating too fast, and I don't think I was even this nervous before my date with Miles. *Why* am I so nervous? It's just Liam. I'm around him almost every day, have been long before this job.

It's just Liam.

But also: this is Liam.

Older than me, cooler than me, already knows everything embarrassing that's ever happened to me, Liam.

The doorbell rings.

The only thing that gets me up the stairs is inertia.

One foot in front of the other. Don't think about it. We're just moving, moving, moving—

I swing the door open without allowing myself to hesitate.

Liam is standing on the porch with his hands casually tucked in his pockets. For some reason, the image is entirely... foreign. I don't think I've ever seen him use the doorbell and wait outside before.

"Hey." He smiles and nods sideways toward his truck. "Ready to go?"

"I'm guessing it's pointless to ask you where..."

"Yep," he says cheerfully, then heads to get the car door for me.

He says nothing else as we drive, just lets the soft radio music fill the space between us. I tightly wind my hands together in my lap and peek at him out of the corner of my eye. As always, he's the picture of calm and relaxed. He has one hand thrown over the top of the steering wheel, and he bobs his head absently to the song as his eyes sweep the road.

And he looks...*nice*. I can't really put my finger on what it is. He's wearing pretty much the same thing he always does—loose-fitting jeans and a T-shirt, though he has a shirt with a collar layered on top this time. His hair is as messy and tousled as always. Same silver rings and chain around his neck.

He must feel my attention on him because he shoots a quick look my way with half a smile. "We're almost there."

I peer out the window. Wherever we're going, it's close to Leo's house. If he keeps going straight, we'll hit the water. He veers right before we hit the main area, then drives along the coast for a few minutes. Golden rays make him glow as the sun prepares to set behind him.

"Here we are." Gravel crunches beneath the tires as he pulls into a small parking lot that backs up to thickly wooded dunes. I squint through the window and spot a narrow, sandy path that cuts down the middle.

"Did you bring me out here to murder me?"

"I found this place last summer," he says as he hops out of the truck and circles to my side. He offers a hand to help me down, but even once I'm standing beside him, he doesn't let go. "It's quiet," he continues as he pulls me toward the path. "Hardly ever see anyone else here."

"You're not making me feel better about the murder thing."

He laughs and tightens his hand around mine in a way that has my stomach doing flips.

I can't see the water at all over the brush, but the sound of the waves grows louder as I follow him through the sand. When we break through the foliage at the end of the path, I stop short.

The sun is just starting to set over the water, painting the sky in electric hues of pink and orange, but it's the colorful display on our right that I can't look away from.

There's a wide red-and-white-checkered picnic blanket spread out on the sand. An array of snacks, drinks, paints, and two blank canvases sit on top, along with a small sign with block letters wedged into the sand.

Can I be your boyfriend?

I stare at it as if my brain can't comprehend the words.

Liam steps up beside the display, looking nothing like he had in the car. He shifts his weight and swallows hard as he meets my eyes.

He's *nervous*, I realize. I don't know if I've ever seen him nervous.

I stare at him. He stares back.

Slowly, my lips curl. "You did the grand gesture," I murmur.

He returns my smile. "Had to consider my audience. You didn't answer the question."

I let out a small laugh as he leads me to the blanket.

"Gracie…" He pauses and wets his lips. "I know we talked about not making a big deal out of this. And I haven't been able to stop thinking about it since, because the thing is, I *do* want to make a big deal of it. I haven't had any interest in dating in a long time. And then you come back into my life like a fucking storm." He smiles as he says it, and his thumb traces small circles on the back of my hand. "And I don't want this to be something that just passes through. I know it's more compli- cated than that. I guess what I'm saying is, I want to give this a real try. If you do."

I know now's the part where I say something, but I'm frozen, mute. I think I'm barely breathing at this point.

He leans back. "If I've misread everything—"

"You haven't." I tighten my hand around his before he can let go. "You haven't misread anything. I...like you. A lot. And it scares the hell out of me."

"For what it's worth," he murmurs, "I'm nervous too."

"Liar. Nothing makes you nervous."

His gaze flicks from my eyes to my mouth. "You do. So, is that a...?"

"Yes," I whisper.

Finally, *finally*, he leans forward and presses his lips to mine again. My eyes flutter shut, and I melt into it. Into him. I thought maybe after kissing the same person a few times, the novelty would wear off. That it would start to feel, well, as bland and normal as the other men I'd kissed. But with Liam...every gentle brush of his lips, every exhale, every trace of his tongue, threatens to make my knees buckle. I feel his mouth curl into a smile against mine before he pulls away.

"I would like to propose a contest," he says.

My eyebrows fly up. "A contest?"

He hands me a plastic champagne flute and pops the cork, then juts his chin at the paints and canvases as he pours us each a glass. "I do your portrait, you do mine."

"You want me to paint *you*? That's completely unfair. You're an artist."

"So are you."

I scoff and grab a grape from the charcuterie board he positions between us. "I take pictures, not make them."

He tsks and shakes his head. "Too afraid to lose to even try. I thought better of you. Really. Besides, I never draw people. I'm terrible at them. Believe me, it's a level playing field."

"You know what? Fine." I snatch up the best-looking paintbrush. "How long do we get?"

He shrugs and nods at the setting sun. "Until we lose the light."

We fall into silence as we set our stations up, the drinks and food nestled on a small tray between us. Liam chews on his lip as he looks from me to the canvas and sketches with a pencil. His hair falls into his eyes as he works, and even as he looks at me, I can't tell he's not *looking* at me, looking at me. He's completely consumed with the task at hand.

I swipe a few colors across mine with a large brush, then get to blending them. I stand no chance at making this realistic, but I might be able to semi-pull off something abstract. Hopefully I retained something from those required art classes in college.

I press my lips together as I take everything in. The sunset. The picnic. The art. The sign. The sea breeze full of the salty scent of home.

It's cheesy, cliché, over-the-top, and nothing like Liam…but it's everything that I love. And I don't know why it comes as a surprise that he knows that.

I lean over and kiss him on the cheek.

He pauses with his paintbrush in the air.

I smile as he meets my eyes. "This was really sweet. Thank you."

He drops his eyes for a moment. If I didn't know him better, I'd swear he looked a little self-conscious. "I know it probably doesn't compare to your books but—"

"It's better," I say, meaning it. It's everything I was beginning to think was never going to happen for me. Wasn't sure if it was *real*.

Slowly, he narrows his eyes. "You're trying to distract me."

"You never said that was against the rules."

His smile grows. "I clearly underestimated you."

"Clearly."

He leans in to kiss me, but I push myself back with a grin and return to my station. He grabs my leg before I can tuck it beneath me, then lays it over his thigh so my foot rests in his lap. He says nothing else as that concentrated look falls over his features, but he leaves his hand resting on my ankle, his thumb stroking back and forth.

And suddenly everything is quiet. It's like every cell in my body was vibrating as fast as it could, static blasting in my ears, my skin hyperaware of every sensation around me to a nearly overwhelming degree—but when I feel his touch, everything just *stops*.

We stay like that until the last of the light drains from the sky.

"You're such a liar," I mumble.

Liam chuckles as he starts the truck and pulls out of the parking lot.

I squint and hold his painting up, inspecting it. Not only is the portrait of me detailed and proportionate and *perfect*, but he added the sunset and waves in the background too. It looks like it was professionally done.

His hand settles on my thigh as he turns onto the main road. "Yours turned out great too, what are you talking about?"

Granted, I did surprise myself a little. His portrait is in a completely different style. I didn't even bother trying to get into the details of his features, instead opting to get the outline of him as accurate as I could before experimenting with wide and multicolored brushstrokes, letting the sunset blend in with him.

It's not that I've never tried painting before. I took plenty of art classes in college, but I was never a natural at them. Something about the canvas has never spoken to me the way a camera does.

But tonight, admittedly, was fun.

"I still think you won," I sigh.

He pumps his fist in the air.

I rest my head against the seat and look at him. "What's the prize?"

He purses his lips, considering. "You have to do what *I* want for our next date."

"You're going to put me back on that death trap, aren't you?"

"Oh, don't act like you didn't like it. We'll see. To be determined."

Liam keeps one hand in mine for the rest of the drive, but the closer we get to the house, the larger the unspoken part of tonight grows between us.

As he parks his truck beside the curb—several houses down from Leo's—he sighs and turns to me. "I want to tell Leo, if that's all right with you. And I'd like him to hear it from me. As much fun as I've been having with you...I've hated feeling like I'm hiding something from him."

"I know. I have too."

He gives me a tight smile before stroking his thumb across the back of my hand once then releasing it.

"You seem worried," I say. "You don't think he'll take it well?"

His eyes dart to Leo's house down the street as a crease forms between his eyebrows. The lights are on inside, so Leo and Keava must be home now. "I don't know. I just need a little bit to figure out the right way to tell him, okay?"

I nod. "Thanks for tonight, Liam. I had a really nice time."

He smiles, softening whatever that look in his eyes had been. "Me too. I'll call you tomorrow, okay?"

I climb out of the truck once I realize he's not going to kiss me or open my door like he did before. He smiles and waves before he takes off, and I hesitate on the curb, a weird mix of disappointment and confusion in the pit of my stomach.

Chapter Thirty-Three

GRACIE

"You got in late last night."

I freeze with my spoonful of cereal halfway to my mouth as Leo turns the corner into the kitchen. My brain quickly dissects every quality of his voice—inflection, cadence, volume, tone. Unless he's trying to hide it, he doesn't sound suspicious.

His hair is a tousled mess like he just rolled out of bed, and judging by the wrinkled T-shirt and shorts, he did. "You with Carson?" he asks as he ducks into the fridge.

"Mm-hmm." I wince, grateful his back is to me so I don't technically have to lie to his face. Surprisingly, I haven't had to lie to him much despite the sneaking around Liam and I have been doing the past few weeks. At least one of us works late most nights, and what free time he does have, he's usually off with Liam or Keava.

He smiles as he pulls out the milk carton and pours himself a bowl too. "I think it's great that you two are hanging out again. You two used to be inseparable."

She was never around as much as Liam was growing up,

but if the Collinses were going to add a fourth honorary child to the mix, it would've been her.

"Yeah. It's been really nice."

"So, I was thinking about hitting the water today. Want to come?"

I give him an unimpressed look. "You know I can't surf."

He shrugs. "We'll take the paddleboards."

I narrow my eyes. "What's your angle?"

A laugh gets caught in his throat. "My *angle*?"

"Yeah. You feel bad about something? Are Liam and Keava busy? I'm your last resort?"

A strange look passes over his face. If I didn't know him any better, I'd swear he looked *guilty*. He shakes his head and presses a hand to his chest. "It's hurtful that you think so little of me. If you recall, at one point, you *liked* doing things with me." He pushes the cereal around in his bowl for a moment, the amusement on his face fading. "I know we've both been busy since you got back. And I know I haven't been the best at balancing everything since the wedding. But I just…thought it might be fun."

I think that's as close to a *I miss hanging out with you* as I'm going to get.

"I'm pretty rusty with the paddleboards."

Now it's his turn to give me an unimpressed look. "You literally just have to sit on it." He sighs dramatically. "But we could do something else, if you'd rather. Just please don't take me to a bookstore."

"It wouldn't hurt you to read. Do you even remember how?"

He narrows his eyes but doesn't take the bait. "With how long it takes you in there, I could make it through an entire book then and there."

Okay, so he's not wrong.

My heart warms. He's not throwing out an invite to something he was going to do today regardless—he's actually trying to make plans with me.

We used to do all kinds of things together growing up. He's the one who took me out on a paddleboard for the first time. He taught me to ride a bike, how to tie a shoe. And as much as he made fun of my *girly* romance movies, he built forts with me and sat through them just the same.

Things changed when he graduated high school, then even more when I went off to college. Life got busier. More complicated.

"I guess we can do the paddleboards," I mutter.

"Yes!" He grins and pumps his fist in the air. "I'll drive and get them loaded up. Meet me out front in ten?" He doesn't wait for me to respond before shoveling the last bite of breakfast into his mouth and sprinting upstairs to change like a little kid.

No doubt he's going to hold me to those ten minutes by the second, so I hurry to finish and head downstairs. I have a feeling fighting to keep up with him is going to be a theme today.

Seeing the ocean from the beach and sitting in the middle of it are two entirely different things. Something I so easily forget with how little I venture past those first few feet of waves. But despite my concerns about not getting on a board in a while, I paddle my way to the still water with ease, then pause to breathe it all in. The fresh air is *marvelous,* and the sun soaks into my face in a way that lights me up. I feel my lips turn up at the corners.

Leo's board comes up beside mine. "See? Like riding a bike."

"This was a good idea," I admit.

"You're just going to lie there all day, aren't you?"

I settle onto my back and close my eyes. It's comfortably warm today, but not too hot. "Maybe."

Water ripples around me as he paddles off, but it isn't long before I hear him coming back. "Fletch is teaching one of his surf camps over there," he says with a laugh. "Don't think I've ever seen so many wipeouts in a row."

I peek one eye open. Sure enough, Fletcher and an older man are a ways down, closer to the beach, half a dozen or so kids surrounding them on small boards.

"You were once one of them," I remind him.

"Nah. I've always been naturally gifted."

I snort and settle on my back, regretting the strappy bikini I chose. It's going to make a lot of weird tan lines.

I expect Leo to paddle off again, but then he says, "You noticed any girls coming into the shop lately?"

"Uh, besides the majority of Liam's customers?"

"You know what I mean. Repeat visitors?"

I frown, not sure what he's trying to get at. I lower my sunglasses and roll my head to the side to get a look at his face, but he's turned away from me, his attention somewhere on the beach.

"I think Li's seeing someone," he explains.

My heart careens into the pit of my stomach. He's fishing here, but for what? Does he already know it's me and just wants me to admit it? He doesn't *sound* suspicious, but...Leo's always been good at hiding his emotions. Liam must not have talked to him yet though, otherwise why not ask me outright? And Liam would've told me if the conversation happened, how it went.

I force myself to keep my voice light as I ask, "What makes you think that?"

He shrugs. "He's been...happy lately."

I snort. "And that's unusual?"

The corners of his lips turn down and he nods his head from side to side. "Kinda."

No, he doesn't know anything. Not for sure, at least.

I relax a bit against my board.

"So you *did* have an ulterior motive for this little bonding trip," I tease. "What, you want to know if I have any secret insider knowledge?"

He groans and rolls his eyes. "Forget I said anything."

"No, no, you've got me where you want me. Trapped in the middle of the ocean. Pump me for information."

"*Do* you have information?"

I shrug. "No. *But*, if there's something going on, I'm sure he'll talk to you about it when he's ready. Or you could always —this is groundbreaking, I know—ask *him* about it."

"Okay, okay, Dr. Gracie. Message received." He rolls off his board with a large splash before I can respond, and I laugh and cover my face as it rains over me. He pops up a second later and shakes his hair out like a dog. "There is something else I wanted to talk to you about," he says as he tugs himself on board.

I hum, but when he doesn't say anything else, I remove my sunglasses and sit up.

He sits with his knees pulled into his chest and drapes his arms around them, his face screwed up like he's debating his next words.

"Spit it out."

He smirks and roughs a hand through his hair. "It's a secret, so you have to keep it to yourself, okay?"

"Oooo, a secret."

He gives me a flat look, but I can tell by the twitch in his lips that he's fighting a smile. "Keava and I have decided this is the year we want to start a family."

My jaw drops. "Is she...?"

"Not yet, but we're hoping soon. So we don't want to tell anyone until it happens, obviously—she knows I'm telling you," he rushes to add.

"Leo, that's so exciting." I splash him. "How many?"

That gets a full laugh out of him. "Let's start with one, then we'll go from there."

A whirlpool of emotions swirls in my gut. Excited and happy for them, of course. Stoked at the prospect of being the cool aunt. But also...I *cannot* still be in that house once they add a newborn to the mix. And I don't want them to feel like they need to put their lives on hold for me either. The house is small. They're going to need the basement. If they turn the second bedroom into a nursery, they'll need the space.

I know Leo would never kick me out, would never ask me to leave. But I don't want him to feel stuck with me, like I'm overstaying my welcome.

Yet another reason for me to figure my life out. And soon.

"No one else knows?" I ask.

He shakes his head.

"But you told me?"

He shrugs and smiles. "Of course. You know I've never been able to keep secrets from you."

I smile back despite the absolute turmoil wreaking havoc inside of me.

I am the very worst human being to have ever existed. Truly. Right at the top of the pyramid.

Because he's right. For better or worse, we've never kept secrets from each other. And now I'm sitting on an atomic bomb of one. I bite my lip, fighting against everything inside of me screaming to tell him everything.

But I promised Liam I would wait.

And Leo looks so happy right now. This was a moment for

him to share something exciting about his life with me. I don't want to derail that.

"I'm really happy for you, Leo. And I know you're probably going to give godparent to Liam...but I am officially throwing my hat in the ring here."

He snorts. "Gracie, shut up. You know you're top of the list."

I blink, suddenly a little teary-eyed over a kid that doesn't even exist yet. "Really?"

"Of course." He rises to his feet, and I don't at all like that look in his eye.

"No—don't!"

But it's too late. He's already launched himself at me. His arms wrap around my waist, and his momentum sends us both crashing into the water.

GRACIE

"You know, I actually really, *really* hate surprises."

Carson huffs from the driver's seat beside me. "Well, I love them, so stop complaining."

She swats away my hands before I can mess with the blindfold again.

"Oh, silly me. Here I was thinking it was *my* birthday."

"And if left to your own devices, you would've spent the day cooped up in bed reading a book."

I mean, I don't see the problem with that.

The car jerks as she hits a curb, and my hands fly out to steady myself against the door.

"Whoops!" she giggles.

We've already been driving for at least fifteen minutes based on the number of songs on the radio I've counted. She didn't tell me anything about what she has planned for tonight. Just the time she'd pick me up.

I might be giving her a hard time about it, but it was actually pretty touching that she remembered the day, let alone wanted to spend it with me. We used to spend all of our birth-

247

days together growing up, but it's been years. And even though the past few months of rekindling that friendship has been going well, it still feels like we're finding our footing again.

Aside from a few *happy birthday* texts from my long-distance college friends, I wasn't expecting much more than something small and casual with my family.

Well, until a text came in shortly after I woke up.

Liam: Outside your window.

Sure enough, when I pushed the hopper window aside, I found a small box sitting on a towel like he was worried about the package getting dirty.

I'd grinned like an idiot as I brought it inside, but that was nothing compared to when I opened it. The card alone would've been enough.

Gracie,

Having you around is the best thing that's happened to me in a long time.

Happy Birthday.

Liam

I gently opened the tissue paper, revealing a new strap for my camera. It was bright and colorful—all pinks and blues and purples, like watercolors. As I ran it between my hands, I realized smaller designs were interspersed among the colors—ocean waves, seagulls, hearts, stacks of books, and in the corner, almost too faint to see, were Liam's initials.

I should've recognized it from the style of art immediately.

He designed it. He drew the whole thing. Like one of those complex sleeves he tattoos on his clients, all of the images complemented each other and blended seamlessly together, all individually detailed and stunning, but when you zoomed out, it was a perfect, coherent picture.

How long had he been working on this?

"Gracieeeee. You're not spiraling right now, are you?"

I blink back to the car—or, well, the darkness of my blindfold. "Of course not. Just because I don't need to talk as much as I breathe like you do."

She chokes out a laugh. "Okay, birthday girl. I'll let you have that shot. But only that one. Did Leo do something for you this morning? He better have."

"He took me out for brunch."

"Oooo, yum. Waffles and mimosas?"

"Obviously. Are we almost there?"

"Mom, are we there yet?" she teases.

"I'm starting to think you don't have plans for us at all and this is an actual kidnapping."

"Take a breath, Chicken Little, we're here." The car slows to a stop as she says it, and beyond the hum of the radio, I pick up the distinct crunch of gravel beneath her tires.

"Can I take this off?" I reach for the blindfold, but she swats my hand away again.

"Not yet!"

"My makeup is probably all smeared now," I mumble as she opens my door for me.

"It's silk. You're fine."

She helps me down from the car, then loops an arm around me as she guides me forward. My high heels sink into what is definitely gravel beneath us, and the cool night air raises a chill on my bare legs.

Carson insisted on a dress, so wherever she's taking me, it must be nicer than the usual bars around here. I lost track of time in the car, but it felt like we were driving for at least twenty minutes, plenty of time to get out of town.

The air smells like it's going to rain, but it's less salty here, like we're farther away from the water. It's also quiet. No music, no voices, no cars. So not at a bar or a restaurant.

Carson keeps one hand on my elbow, the other on my back, as she leads me forward. "Step up," she instructs. "Just two steps."

Whatever I climb onto—a porch?—groans under our weight.

I stop walking.

"Almost there," she says.

I cock my head to the side. That groan sounded awfully familiar.

I had a feeling the second she pulled that blindfold out this was a surprise party situation. My parents were a little *too* encouraging about me spending today with friends instead of them.

Carson hurries me forward like she can tell I'm figuring it out.

The sound of a doorknob turning, then a soft surface replaces the wood that was under my heels a moment ago. Carson stops me with her hands on my shoulders, then unties the scarf.

"Surprise!"

I blink, my eyes fighting to adjust to the light as a chorus of voices surrounds me.

Everyone is crowded in my parents' living room—Leo, Keava, Mom, Dad, even Grandma in her wheelchair.

As well as my friends.

I stare blankly at Trish, Marti, and Alison, who popped up from behind the couch in sparkly dresses and ridiculous pointed party hats.

"I—what are you guys doing here?"

"Your mom called," says Trish as she rushes forward to give

me a hug. "We were planning on surprising you for your birthday anyway, so it was perfect!"

She knocks the wind out of me with the force of her hug, and I pat her a few times, noticing Liam for the first time lingering behind the rest.

"Happy birthday!" adds Marti as she and Alison pile in for a group hug.

"Oh, me too! Me too!" Carson jumps into the mix, and then I'm just a trapped sardine.

And what should be a happy, carefree moment is instantly soured when I meet Marti's eyes. Wide and brown as usual, but there's a noticeable concern to them.

Because they must know.

Whether they put it together themselves or from talking to my family, all it would take is the smallest tug of a thread for my mountain of lies from this summer to come crumbling down.

"Come on, come on, let's show you around!" squeals Carson, oblivious, and hooks her arm through mine.

She leads me to the dining room first, where the table is elaborately set up with flowers, string lights, and pink and white balloons full of confetti. Little display towers full of treats are interspersed between the decorations—Rice Krispies treats, donuts, cake pops. I meet Mom's eyes over my shoulder and smile. It must have taken her days, if not a week, to bake all of this.

"I'll get the drinks!" offers Dad. "We got sparkling rosé, your favorite! We set up the firepit and projector out back so you guys can watch a movie later, if you want to."

Leo and Liam jump in to help pass the champagne flutes around, and once everyone has one, they turn to me.

I groan internally. If this is about to turn into an embarrassing speech thing...

But thankfully, Mom takes the reins. "To Gracie! Happy twenty-third! Cheers!"

I clink my glass against Carson's on one side and Trish's on my other, but it's Liam's eyes across the circle I keep going back to. Judging by the distance he's keeping between us, he hasn't talked to Leo.

"Dinner will be served in about an hour," announces Dad. "The first course, at least."

"First course?" I demand.

He exchanges a conspiratorial smile with Mom before the two of them disappear into the kitchen.

Leo crosses the room to me and nods for me to turn around. "You need to open my gift before the sun goes down." He keeps nudging between my shoulders until I follow him to the front door.

"Why is it outside?" I ask. Even once we reach the porch, he keeps pushing me forward. "If this is some kind of prank and you're just locking me out of the house, I swear to God, Leo—"

I stop short as he jogs ahead of me, pauses in the center of the driveaway, and leaps around with his hands held wide like he's presenting something. Other than a packed lawn full of cars, I don't see anything.

Leo lets out a dramatic exhale at whatever he sees on my face. "Oh, come on." He waves impatiently for me to join him. "You know how many hours I had to put in to rebuild this thing? Don't tell me you don't like the color or something."

"Wait, the *car*?" Despite Leo living and breathing engines and all that mechanical stuff that might as well be an alien language, I don't know the first thing about cars. But *this one?*

It's black and that perfect size between a sedan and SUV. I can already tell with a peep through the window that it's nicer than the car I had in college.

"This is my present? Don't mess with me, Leo."

He grins. "So you *do* like it."

"Like it...oh my God, Leo!" I throw my arms around his waist and tug him into a hug. With me living rent-free in his house for months now, I wouldn't have blamed him if he hadn't gotten me anything at all. "This is amazing. I can't believe you built this. Thank you so much."

He pats me awkwardly on the top of the head. "Now you can stop stealing mine. And with the weather cooling off here pretty soon, didn't want you stuck with just a bike."

I pull away and smirk at the way he's avoiding eye contact now.

I nudge him with my shoulder. "Love you too, bro."

The next hour passes quickly as I catch up with everyone, sip wine, and devour a few too many chocolate-covered strawberries. We take about a million pictures until everyone has something they're happy with to post on social media—with the drinks, with the decorations, with each other. But what *I'm* most looking forward to is the cake reveal. Mom's something of an artist with all baking, but especially cakes. I'm expecting nothing short of a masterpiece.

I'm starting to think Liam isn't going to talk to me one-on-one tonight at all until I'm refilling my drink alone in the kitchen and he walks in behind me.

"Hey," he says quietly as he props a hip against the counter.

I peer at him out of the corner of my eye. "Hi."

"I'm sorry about Leo. I didn't want to ruin today for you in case it didn't go well. I promise, I'm talking to him first thing tomorrow."

I nod slowly and sip my drink. It makes sense. It's logical. So then why doesn't it lessen the knot in my stomach that's been there since the other day at the beach with Leo? If I'm really being honest with myself, it's been there long before that.

"Gracie." His touch ghosts along the small of my back. "Are we okay? If you'd rather I talk to him right now, I'll do it."

I sigh and let myself lean into his touch. "No, you're right. I just...I'm feeling worse and worse about hiding this from him."

"I am too. I promise." He ducks his head until I look at him straight on, and he tucks a loose strand of hair behind my ear. "You look beautiful. I'm sorry I haven't been able to show up for you tonight the way I wanted to."

"I get it. And thank you for the gift this morning. It was really nice."

His thumb trails down my cheek. High heels clank against the tile behind him, growing louder. He drops his hand just as Carson appears around the corner.

"Time for dinner!" she says with a smile that lets me know she was definitely eavesdropping.

Liam heads out first, but she grabs my arm before I can follow him.

"Carson..." I start under my breath.

But all she says is *"Nice* work, Collins" before leading us both to the dining room.

Mom is lingering in the opposite doorway as I step inside. She nods for me to follow her to the front room, where Dad and Grandma are already waiting.

"We've already set the table," she says. "Would you mind too much if you get started without us?"

"We need to get Grandma back to the nursing home," Dad adds, one hand on his mother's shoulder. "It's been a long day for her."

I wave them off. "Of course."

Grandma is all but asleep in her chair already, but I kneel

down to her level and gently pull her into a hug. "It was so good to see you, Grandma. I love you."

"Oh! Gracie Belle!" She chuckles as she pats me on the back, then lets out a surprised gasp as I pull back. "You're *beautiful.*"

I squeeze her hands. "Of course I am. I look like you."

She explodes in a fit of giggles, and I lean forward to kiss her cheek.

"It shouldn't take long," Mom says behind me. "We'll be back before the second course."

After all the snacking everyone's done for the past hour, I'm not sure how any of us are going to make it through the *first.*

I wave goodbye, then hurry to my spot at the head of the table when I realize everyone's been patiently waiting for me to get started. The plates are already filled with street tacos, and despite my not being very hungry, my mouth starts watering at the sight of them. The same could be said for everyone else, apparently, because the room lapses into silence, save for the clank of dishes as everyone inhales their food.

"You said you have movies set up?" asks Carson on my right. "Which ones?"

Leo shrugs from the opposite head of the table. "Whatever you guys want."

"So a romcom then." Marti shoots me a knowing smile, and Trish laughs beside her.

"You guys can't make fun of me on my birthday. It's against the rules."

"I agreed to no such rules," says Carson as she sips her wine.

"Gracie, I've been meaning to ask you," says Alison on my left as she finishes her own glass, "how's the new job and everything going?"

"It's, uh, it's been good." I fight to keep my voice light, but the tightness in my throat ruins it.

"What magazine did you say it was again?"

"Magazine?" asks Keava.

Trish elbows Alison beneath the table, and she sends her a questioning look. Carson grimaces and sinks a little lower in her chair.

"Can we talk about this later?" I say under my breath.

Alison cocks her head. I can't tell if she's having one of her semi-bitchy moments and doing this on purpose, or if she genuinely hasn't picked up on what Marti and Trish clearly have. "Um, what about the new boyfriend?" she asks instead. "I was kind of hoping we'd get to meet him here! Do you guys have plans for tomorrow instead or something?"

"Boyfriend?" asks Leo.

Jesus fucking Christ. I swallow hard, my face on fire as I feel all eyes at the table on me. Well, I've been wondering when it would all come crashing down, and it looks like this is it. It's already twice as mortifying as I thought it would be. It feels like one of my nightmares, standing on stage in a packed auditorium, but I don't know what I'm supposed to do.

"I, um—"

The room feels kind of fuzzy, and I realize I'm breathing too fast. My fight or flight response is screaming at me to get up and run. I lock eyes with Liam across the table. I can't quite read that look on his face. His brow tight and jaw set off to the side like he's...deciding something. Before I can stand, he does.

"That would be me." He holds my gaze for a second longer before turning to Alison and extending a hand. "Don't think we had a chance to meet earlier. I'm Liam."

I stop breathing.

Alison says something I don't hear. My attention is now locked on Leo, whose face has gone scarily blank as he looks between me and Liam.

Mercifully, Keava jumps in. "I think we could all use a break before any more food, yeah? We already have the seats set up out back. Girls, can a few of you give me a hand, and we'll take some drinks out there?"

Her eyes are on Marti, Trish, and Alison, and though they barely know Keava, even they can tell it isn't a suggestion. Carson takes one look at Leo currently glaring at Liam and jumps up from her seat too.

"I'll help!"

Once everyone else is outside, Keava hesitates at the door, one hand extended toward me. "You too, Gracie."

"I'm good here."

Her fake smile disappears, and she jerks her head roughly to the side.

I meet Liam's eyes, and he nods.

Keava ushers me outside and closes the sliding glass door behind us, but I break free of her hold before she can pull me away.

"Leo…" starts Liam, his voice muffled through the door. "I was going to tell you."

I wince. Not a great start. I should've stayed in there. Liam's never been the best with words. Keava tries to pull me away.

"You know, this involves me too," I snap.

"I know," she says softly and drops her hand. "Just…just give them a minute."

I strain my ear, wondering if they're speaking too quietly to hear, but no, I think Leo is being silent.

"I'm really sorry it came out like that. And I'm sorry I didn't tell you sooner. We just—I was planning on telling you tomorrow—"

"No."

The cold firmness in Leo's voice stops Liam midsentence. Liam sighs. "Leo—"

"*No*," Leo repeats, louder, harder. "You promised me, you *promised me*, you would never go there with her."

Liam sputters. "That was—that was in high school."

I blink, stunned. *High school?* Why was that even a topic of discussion back then?

"She's not like all the other girls you've burned through after Hailey, okay? She won't *survive* you, don't you understand that?"

A jolt runs through me, my cheeks flaming. I'm not sure what part of that sentence does it.

All the other girls you've burned through.

Or *she won't survive you*, like I'm some sort of naïve, breakable child.

"This isn't like that at all, Leo. Do you really think I would've gone there with her if this meant nothing to me?"

"I have no idea. Clearly, I have *no idea* who you are or what you're capable of—"

"Leo, come on. You know me. You're being unreasonable."

A hand brushes my arm and I jump, thinking it's Keava trying to pull me away again. But Trish gives me a sheepish smile as she edges forward, clearly trying to hear too. The other girls aren't far behind.

"Am I?" Leo all but barks out a laugh. "I don't think I am. Because if you honestly believed that, if you really saw nothing wrong with what you're doing, you wouldn't have kept it a secret. How long have you been lying to me? How long have you two been doing this behind my back, huh?"

"Leo, I'm *sorry*—"

"How long?" he demands. "Is this why you gave her a job? So you two could have an excuse to sneak around?"

"No. *No.* Gracie's damn good at her job, you know that." There's a pause, then quietly: "We didn't...it wasn't until around the Fourth of July."

"Nearly a *month*? I can't fucking believe this," Leo mutters. "You're supposed to be my best friend."

"And you're supposed to be mine, Leo. Yeah, I feel bad that you found out this way, and maybe I should've told you sooner, but do you really think so little of me that this would be the worst thing in the world?"

God, the *hurt* in his voice cuts straight into my heart. I don't realize I'm stepping forward until Trish tightens her hand around my arm. She widens her eyes and shakes her head.

"She's my little sister, Liam. And you're no good for her."

"Maybe I could be."

A beat of silence passes, then quieter, Leo says, "For your own sake, Liam, I hope you can change, but you're not going to do it with Gracie."

"It's really not up to you to make that call."

"I cannot *believe* you—"

"I love her, Leo. I'm in love with her."

There's a long, agonizing stretch of silence.

Had I heard him right? Did he really just say...?

"You need to leave," Leo says coldly.

"Leo—"

"Now. Don't make me throw you out. I can't even fucking look at you."

I shake Trish off and shove the door open.

Leo barely spares me a glance as he paces along the wall. "Not now, Gracie."

"Don't you dare *not now* me as if this has nothing to do with me. I actually think this has nothing to do with *you*, but you're making it all about you!"

He stops midstep. Stares at me. God, I wish it were a glare. Wish he looked angry, that he'd yell some more.

The surprised hurt on his face is gutting.

Liam is staring intently at the floor, every line of his face pulled tightly together.

"If you want me to get on board with this," Leo says lowly.

"I'm not going to. And that should mean something to you, Gracie. When have I ever not looked out for you?"

"Don't let this ruin your night, Gracie. I'll go."

Liam heads for the door without another word, and I stare at my brother, silently pleading with him.

But he says nothing. Does nothing.

It isn't until the front door closes behind Liam that I make up my mind.

I go after him.

"Gracie!" calls Leo.

I slam the door behind me.

GRACIE

I don't have to worry that I'm too late, that Liam already left, because he's frozen at the end of the porch. As I get closer, I see why.

A woman is standing in the driveway.

One with red hair and a very familiar face.

Because I've seen her picture appear on Liam's phone time and time again with each call that he declined.

She gestures wildly with her hands while she talks, and Liam flinches—physically, visibly flinches away. Heat sparks in my chest, and my heels click loudly against the porch as I approach. Liam whips around with wide eyes, but they soften in surprise when he realizes it's me.

The redhead's eyes turn into slits as I stop at Liam's side. "This is a private conversation."

"This is private property," I counter.

"So this is why you haven't called me back? I *knew* it. I knew it the second I saw this." She waves her phone around, but I can't see whatever she has pulled up on the screen.

"How did you even find me here?" Liam demands.

"I went to your apartment first. Was planning to swing by Leo's, then I remembered I follow Keava's accounts." She shrugs and crosses her arms. "She posted on her stories."

Okay...that's incredibly stalker-ish.

"You need to leave, Hailey," says Liam.

"So ending a nine-year relationship doesn't even warrant a conversation, huh?"

"We've *been* over," snaps Liam. "There's nothing left to talk about."

"We've been on a *break*." She flicks her wrist toward me. "Something you've clearly taken full advantage of. You said you needed some space to think. To think about *us*. To figure out how to make this work."

Every word that comes out of her mouth is dripping with spite and vitriol, the same way it did in those voicemails. And I don't know a damn thing about her, but everything about her energy feels wrong.

And yet. Her words poke at something soft and vulnerable inside of me.

I turn to look at Liam's face.

Is that what Leo knew that I didn't? Why he didn't want me involved with him?

"Do you...do you want me to...?" I start to take a step back, suddenly feeling very stupid. Like I inserted myself somewhere I don't belong.

But Liam's hand shoots out and lands on the small of my back. His eyes are wide, earnest, as they stare into mine. "No," he murmurs. "No."

Hailey scoffs and paces through the gravel.

Liam's jaw hardens as he turns to her. "If you came all the way down here for this, you wasted your time. Since apparently I wasn't clear enough before, this is over, Hailey. Completely. I don't want to hear from you again. I don't want to see you again. And I definitely don't want you showing up around the people I care about. So you can either leave now or I can call the police."

She laughs, the sound loud and mocking. "The police? Really, Liam? Is this act supposed to impress your new girl? You've always been so fucking dramatic."

"If he doesn't, I will," I say. "Get the fuck off my parents' lawn."

Liam blinks at me, surprised. Honestly, I'm surprised too at how hard my voice comes out. But the patronizing way she was talking to him snapped something inside of me.

I whip out my phone for emphasis.

Her nostrils flare as she glares at me, and after several moments of tense silence pass, she turns around and climbs into her car.

Liam and I don't move until her brake lights disappear in the distance.

"I'm sorry," he whispers. "About your birthday. I've really screwed everything up—"

"Shh." I lay my hand on his arm. And when he turns, he looks at me like a desperate, cornered animal. "Come on. Let's go."

Liam drives us to his apartment, but we don't get out after he parks. He didn't say a word on the way over here, and neither did I. I didn't know what to say, if saying anything would help or hurt. I've never seen that look in his eyes before, and his grip on the wheel the entire way over here was bone-crushing. I can't tell which he's more affected by—Hailey showing up or that argument with Leo. Maybe it's both.

"I need you to know that Hailey and I were never just on a

break," he says suddenly. "We've been broken up for nearly a year. And even before that, we were on and off."

I nod but say nothing.

"And what Leo said—I know you heard all of that—it's not true. I know why he thinks that, and I've never corrected him because...well, he doesn't know..." He sighs and roughs a hand through his hair. "It's complicated. I just, I don't want you to think of me like that. Because I've never—after Hailey—"

"Liam." I lay my hand on his arm. "Take a breath. It's okay."

He stares at my hand for a moment before gently laying his on top. "I didn't mean for you to leave your party."

"I wanted to." I tighten my fingers around his arm. "How about we start with one thing at a time?"

He nods.

"Why did she show up tonight? What was she showing you on her phone?"

That, finally, loosens the tension in his shoulders. He lets out a disbelieving laugh and shakes his head. "*That.*" He fishes his phone out of his pocket, swipes around for a second, then hands it to me.

It's pulled up to one of the shop's social media pages. I haven't logged in since work a few days ago, but there's a post from today. One I didn't schedule.

I click on it, and blink in surprise when my face appears. It's of me at the beach the other day, my eyes closed as I smile and the sun sets behind me.

Wish our social media savior—ahem—manager a happy birthday!

Liam shifts his weight in his seat. "You said I should practice posting, and that personalities and faces are important, and I just thought it was a good picture and—"

I laugh at the nervous edge to his voice. "*This* is what she was so upset about?"

He laughs too and covers his eyes as I hand the phone back.

"Anyway, she's back in town for this thing with my sister. They're working together on a new branch of the business. And this is just something Hailey does. Every time we break up, if she feels me moving on, she likes to pop back in."

Every time we break up.

"How many times have you ended things?"

He shakes his head. "Since we first started dating in high school? At least half a dozen."

I don't know why my stomach twists at that. Liam must see it on my face because he hurries to add, "This time is nothing like those, I swear. This one was for good."

I wish that made me feel better.

"Please come inside. I'll explain everything. Answer any questions you have."

I don't respond, but I let him take my hand and lead me up the stairs. He doesn't let go, not even after we're inside his apartment and on the couch, and there's a slight tremor in his fingers.

He said there were things Leo didn't know.

I'm starting to think there's a lot of things that maybe no one does.

"Look, I don't know how to do this. I don't have any idea where to start, so I'm just going to start talking, okay?"

I run my thumb along the back of his hand, desperately wanting to believe there's an acceptable explanation for all of this, but I can't get Leo's words out of my head.

If you want me to get on board with this, I'm not going to. And that should mean something to you.

Because no matter how angry I am with him for how he handled things tonight, his opinion *does* mean something to me. It means everything to me, actually.

But then I think of the past few months with Liam...all of

our conversations and little moments, the way he took care of me, how he remembered all the tiny details about me that no one else ever has...I don't want to lose that either. But was any of it real if I've been in the dark this entire time?

Liam keeps his focus on our hands and lets out a long breath. "Hailey and I met my sophomore year of high school. She's two years older. She was my first everything, but she'd dated other guys before. So everything with her...I guess I just assumed she knew more. That that was how relationships were supposed to be. I thought it was normal."

His forehead creases as he says it, and he pauses long enough that I wonder if he's waiting for me to respond. But then he adds, quietly, "It took me a long time to figure out that it wasn't. Normal. The fighting, the yelling, the hitting, the insults, the going through my phone, the silent treatment, the not wanting me to go places without her..." He sighs. "We'd started dating a few months before my mom died. I wonder a lot if things would've been different if that hadn't been the timing. Because even when things were bad between us, she was there for me. In a way no one else was. And I kind of... clung to that. And I think that made it easier for her. She didn't want me spending time with other people, and I was at such a low point that I didn't want anyone else around. She was my whole world, and she knew it.

"Anyway, after she graduated high school, she went to a community college about an hour down the road, so we stayed together. Even if it wasn't that far, the distance was tough. She'd get mad if I took too long to respond, if I didn't drive up to see her enough... We broke up a lot during that time. Once I had some distance from her, I started to see I felt *better* when she was gone. But I also had this, I don't know, attachment to her. It was hard to let go. After pushing everyone else away for so long for her, if she was gone, I didn't have much left."

For the first time since he started talking, he meets my eyes.

I remember those years, vaguely. Leo's first two years of high school, Liam was around as usual. I saw him a lot less those final two years, but I'd assumed that was because they'd both gotten their driver's licenses and didn't need to ride with me and Mom anymore.

Hailey I have virtually no memories of. At the time, I'd assumed it was because she went to Liam's old private school, and it's not like the kids there tend to socialize much with the Edgewater public schools.

Of course I remember the first time I heard Leo use the words *Liam* and *girlfriend* in a sentence, but social media wasn't that big back then, and twelve-year-old me hadn't honed her internet stalking skills yet.

"After she finished college, she went up to New York," Liam continues. "Wanted to pursue modeling. We agreed to try the long-distance thing again. It seemed to be going well. She seemed more trusting, less controlling. I thought maybe it was because she'd grown up a little. Then I drove up to surprise her for Valentine's Day, and realized she was seeing someone else. She apologized, of course. Promised it was a mistake. Just a one-time thing. I don't know why I bought it. Why I was willing to still try after that. I was so...clueless. I actually thought that us always going back to each other meant something important." He barks out a laugh that has no amusement in it. "But the final straw was when I found out she'd been seeing him the entire time. He helped her get a job. She knew him before she moved up there."

I scoot closer to him on the couch until our legs touch. I can't tell if he wants me to touch him, to talk. He seems barely aware that I'm here.

"And Leo..." He swallows hard. "What Leo thinks he saw after she and I broke up is me going out and sleeping around with basically every woman in town. Hailey was the only girl I'd ever been with. And after we broke up, I was fucking terrified I'd never feel like that for anyone but her. So I went out. I met women. I tried to force myself to feel something. I took a few of them home, but I could never bring myself to go through with anything. One-night stands felt so...detached." His eyes flick to mine then away. "Except one. I tried it once, and it just made me feel worse. So, I, um, I think that's everything. And if this is too much—"

I throw my arms around his shoulders and pull him close. My chest shakes on my inhale, and I feel tears burning in the backs of my eyes, but the overwhelming emotion flooding my veins is rage.

"She's so goddamn lucky I didn't know all of that before seeing her tonight," I whisper. "Or I probably would've punched her."

He lets out a startled laugh.

"Does Leo know about...?"

"No, I don't think so. I'm sure he put some things together. He saw how much we fought and how often we broke up. But..."

"You've never talked to him about it."

He shakes his head, and I run a hand down his hair. "Why not?"

"I don't know. I guess..." The way he looks up at me, all of his usual ease and confidence gone, breaks my fucking heart. "Maybe I was embarrassed. And I think part of me believed a lot of the things she was telling me. About how things were my fault. That I was pathetic. And I just...didn't want my best friend to think those things about me too."

"I'm sorry," I whisper, tears rapidly building in my eyes. "About tonight."

"No, no, Gracie." He cups my cheek.

"I don't want to come between you and Leo. I never wanted—"

"And I don't want to come between *you* and Leo. But it's going to be okay."

"How can you be so sure?" I don't know if I've ever heard Leo that angry, seen him like that. Especially not directed at Liam. I figured telling him would make things weird, at least for a while, but I never thought...

"This was a shock to him. Leo's always needed some time to process things. And I get where he's coming from. He loves you and he's worried about you and he wants to keep you safe. He just needs time to see that's all I want too."

I blink the tears away. "And if he doesn't?"

"He will. I'm going to make him see that, Gracie. I promise you, I'm going to make things right with him. But I'm not going to walk away from this either." He swallows hard as he looks from my eyes to my lips. "You know how I told you you're the best thing that's happened to me in a long time?"

"Yeah?"

His hands skate up and down my back, and I shiver as his fingers trace along my bare skin where my dress ends.

He shakes his head, looking up at me with something that looks like wonder in his eyes. "That wasn't true. You're the best thing that's ever happened to me, Gracie Collins. The best thing."

My nose burns at the threat of tears. "You're my best thing too," I whisper.

We lean in at the same time. I try to put everything I don't know how to say into the way I kiss him. How much more he deserves. That he has nothing to be unsure or embarrassed about—*she* does. That he never should have had to shoulder all of this alone.

"I'm so sorry I ruined your birthday," he whispers against my lips.

"You didn't ruin anything." I kiss him harder, deeper.

His hand tangles in my hair, and I straddle his lap, pulling myself as close to him as I can.

He groans low in his throat. Every part of me is somehow cold and on fire all at once. I have no idea what I'm doing. All I know is I don't want to stop kissing him. I don't want him to stop touching me. I don't want to do anything in the world except this, this, *this*. The fervor he kisses me back with melts away any thoughts, any fears. This is a side of him I've never seen before, and now that I've gotten a taste, I'm dying to know every piece of it.

His arms fold around my waist, pulling me flush to his chest, then he stands. Before my feet can brush the ground, he flips me so my back hits the couch and his weight presses down on me, my legs parting around his hips. The hard press of him between my thighs has my breath leaving my lungs in a rush.

I gasp as his hands run along the silky fabric of my dress, down my ribs, my hips, and hook beneath my thighs. His lips trail to my cheek, my jaw, my throat, places I've never been kissed before, his hands finding places I've never been touched, and my body flames with feelings I've never felt.

For a moment, my brain is stuck in a loop of *I've never, I've never, I've never*, and it's enough to break through the haze of want.

Liam pauses with his face inches from mine. "Do you want to stop?"

"No, it's—it's not that. I just—"

He waits, his thumb rubbing my arm.

I don't have to say it. His eyes widen slightly, and he pulls back another inch. "This is your first time," he breathes.

I don't think I've ever been more mortified in my life that it was that fucking obvious.

Liam must see it on my face because he quickly shakes his head. "I don't want to rush this, Gracie. I don't want to rush *you*. I don't want to do anything a single moment before you're ready."

I've heard something similar from other guys before, ones who didn't mean it. Ones who thought saying that would make me change my mind, and when it didn't, they disappeared from my life.

But they never looked at me the way Liam is.

I never trusted any of them the way I trust him.

And I never wanted any of them the way I want this right now.

"I know," I murmur. "And I'm not rushing."

He gives me a small, cautious smile as I pull his lips to mine.

"You're sure?" he whispers.

I nod.

"If you want to stop, just say the word."

"Liam, shut up and kiss me."

And God, does he. He kisses me so hard I feel it in my soul. His hands dance across my body like they want to touch all of me at once—down my arms, my sides, my legs, up into my hair, the sides of my face. I grip his shoulders, the muscles flexing beneath my hands, then trail down his back, his sides, and he shivers beneath my touch. I pull at the hem of his shirt, desperate for more, to feel his skin against mine.

He leans back on his knees and pulls the shirt over his head with one hand. My mouth runs dry. He pauses as I hesitantly run my hands along the planes of his stomach.

His body is a beautiful mosaic of his art. It tells a story. The progression, the growth of his craft. The growing confidence in the placements that are more visible. I want to know about every single one, the story behind it. It would probably take all day.

His next kiss is achingly slow and tender. It makes everything inside of me feel like liquid.

"All right, birthday girl," he whispers. "Hold on."

He loops his arms beneath my thighs and scoops me up in one swift movement. I barely manage to lock my arms around his neck before he stands, and my gasp turns into a laugh as he heads for the bedroom.

"Of course I'm not doing this on the couch," he says.

LIAM

Nothing has ever looked better than a breathless and disheveled Gracie Collins in my bed. Her hair is mussed from all the times I've run my hands through it, her lip gloss smeared from my inability to stop kissing her.

And that fucking dress.

I've been holding on to my sanity by a thread since the moment I watched her walk in the door. It's thin and silky and hugs her body in ways that shouldn't be legal.

I grab her legs and pull her to the edge of the bed, then sink to my knees.

"You comfortable?" I ask as I trail my lips from her ankle to the inside of her knee.

She hums as I slowly drag my hands up the sides of her legs, taking her skirt with them.

"Good." I kiss her inner thigh, her hip. "Because we're going to be here a while."

She watches me as I slip my thumbs beneath her underwear and slide them down her legs, both of us already breathing hard. Has she thought about this as much as I have? Because I've been desperate for this long before tonight.

Despite the brave face, I can tell she's nervous by the tension in her body, the slight tremor of her hands. Slowly, I slide my hands up her legs, trying to let her get used to my touch, and rise up to kiss her. She kisses me back, her lips fitting perfectly against mine, and she traces her hands over my chest in a way that has me shivering.

Slowly, I work my way down her body, kissing her chest, her arms, her hips. I take one of her hands with me, link my fingers through hers, and leave them pressed against her stomach.

I nudge her legs open farther once I'm on my knees and hesitate. I don't ever want to forget a single detail of this moment.

She squirms under my stare, and a half smile rises to my lips. Then finally, I take her pussy in my mouth. She sucks in a sharp breath as I trace her with my tongue, and I let out a low groan at how exquisite she tastes. I was already planning on being down here a good long while, but *fuck*, I could do this all night.

I start slow, searching for what feels good for her. And it's so goddamn hot that she's not shy about it at all. The breaths, the moans—there's absolutely no mistaking when she likes it.

I test sliding a finger inside of her, and her hips lift to meet my hand like she'd been waiting for it. I grin against her clit— that's my fucking girl—and gradually quicken my pace, then add a second.

Her chest heaves as her breaths quicken, and it's all I can do to just watch her. I don't know what this girl is doing with me, but I'm sure as hell going to do everything I can to make it last.

"Liam," she moans, her hand tightening around mine at the same time her pussy clenches around my fingers.

I ease off, slowing my pace, not wanting this to be over already. She lets out an impatient whine.

"I told you to get comfortable."

She laughs breathlessly.

"I'm just getting started."

"Liam—*oh*." Whatever she was going to say disappears into her moan as I dive back in, my strokes harder, faster.

I'm caught between how badly I want to watch her come and selfishly wanting to wait until I'm inside of her for her to do it. Hopefully she'll be up for both. She might never have had sex before tonight, but I read some of those books of hers—parts of them, at least—and I think it's fair to assume there's a lot more to Gracie Collins than meets the eye in this department.

"Oh God," she gasps. "Please don't stop."

She still hasn't let go of my hand, and I tighten my fingers around her, silently promising not to since my mouth is currently too preoccupied to respond. My own impatience wins, and this time when I feel her toeing the edge, I don't back down. I keep my pace steady as I stroke her inner walls, my tongue tracing the same circle until I have her shaking beneath me.

Her other hand tangles in my hair as she comes, holding me to her. All I care about is the way my name spills from her lips, over and over and over again like it's the only word she can remember. I want to brand the sound of it on my soul, to let her dig so far into my chest, there's no shadow or corner she hasn't touched.

I could do that a thousand times, and I still wouldn't get enough. I ease off when she starts to shrink away, redirecting my kisses to her inner thighs, her hips—any inch of skin I can get my hands on.

"You have no idea what you do to me, do you, Gracie?" I murmur against her stomach.

She hums and runs her fingers through my hair.

"Come here." I tug her into a seated position and wind my arms around her, searching for the zipper on her dress. She goes for my belt at the same time, and our movements turn frantic, desperately trying to peel off the remaining layers between us.

Any hesitation I'd sensed from her on the couch is gone now. I frame her jaw with my thumbs, tilting her face up to me. "You're sure?"

She smiles softly and lays her hands over mine. "Yes."

If anything, I think I'm more nervous than she is. I've never been someone's first before, and she deserves for this to be perfect.

She presses her forehead to mine, and the way she looks into my eyes, it's like she can hear what I'm thinking.

"I wouldn't want it to be with anyone but you," she whispers.

She situates herself on the bed as I rifle through the night-stand for a condom. She watches with her teeth sunk into her lower lip as I kneel before her and roll it onto myself, a small wrinkle forming in her forehead. She gets a little tense as I lean over her, so I kiss her slowly, deeply.

"You're in control here, Gracie," I whisper against her lips. "Nothing happens a moment before you want it to, okay? I've got all night."

I go back to kissing her jaw, her neck, her perfect little breasts. She looses a shaky breath, her hands on my arms, and I trail my fingers between her legs, testing to see if she's still too sensitive or if I can start rubbing her clit again. If I can't, I don't know how else to help make this not hurt other than making sure she's as relaxed as possible. And I really, really don't want to hurt her.

"Liam?" she whispers.

I pull back enough to look at her face, and she brushes her thumb between my eyebrows, smoothing the muscle there.

"It's okay. You're not going to break me."

"I just want this to be good for you." I shake my head. *I want it to be a hell of a lot better than that.* "Better than good."

I can't quite figure out that look in her eye as she smiles up at me. "It already is."

Chapter Thirty-Seven

GRACIE

I was so goddamn nervous. At least, I was at first. But once we got started, that all slipped away. And now seeing Liam practically unravel with overthinking, one of us has to keep it together. I don't know what switch flipped in his brain, because he certainly didn't seem nervous when he made me see God a few minutes ago.

I kiss him slowly and run my hands through his hair, over his shoulders, along the muscles of his arms as they brace against the bed on either side of my face. He relaxes, and I move my hands to his chest, moaning into his mouth as my fingers trail down lean muscle.

His hips grind into me, and I lift mine as an invitation.

"You're ready?" he whispers.

I nod. The same way I convince myself to do anything I'm scared of, I just have to surge ahead before I let myself think too much.

He never stops kissing me. Not as he lines himself up with my entrance, not as he slowly pushes in an inch, then another. Not as he slides a hand down to my clit.

The combination of sensations steals my breath.

"Am I hurting you?" he murmurs.

"Not at all," I gasp.

His lips trail down my neck and chest until he takes my nipple into his mouth. The flicks of his tongue as he slides in another inch make my head fall back. My body stretches around him, but the sensation isn't discomfort, and it isn't pain. Whatever it is, it's new, and I don't want it to stop. It all comes together—his slow, testing strokes, his fingers, his tongue, like he's playing my body like an instrument. I don't know how he could've possibly been that nervous when he's this *good* at this.

Vaguely, I register that noises are coming out of me, but I can't stop them. Whimpers, moans, I think some sound like his name.

He seems to grow more sure of himself after a minute, and his pace increases as his lips land back on mine. I sink my teeth into his bottom lip, and he groans low in his chest, the sound vibrating through my body.

"You feel so fucking good, Gracie," he breathes. "You doing okay?"

Much, much better than okay. But all I can manage is "Yes."

In all my friends' accounts of losing their virginities in high school or college, their stories were full of jackhammering and lying there for a few minutes and waiting for it to be over.

Liam's hips meet mine in slow, sensual movements that have my lungs forgetting how to breathe. He shifts and experiments with different angles, different speeds, different force, until he finds whatever moan of mine he likes best and sticks with that.

"That's it. I've got you."

"That feels so good," I gasp.

I feel his mouth curve into a smile against my neck, and he

grabs one of my hands, links his fingers with mine, and presses it into the pillow above my head.

All I can think is *Thank God.*

Thank God I didn't sleep with any of those losers in college.

Thank God I waited.

Because there's no way any of them would've compared to this.

"I love you," Liam breathes against my skin, so low I almost don't hear it, don't know if he means for me to.

But still, I murmur, "I love you, Liam."

I recognize the relief in his eyes and regret not saying it sooner.

We crash together in a hungry, desperate kiss full of tongue and teeth and gasps. My nails dig into his back as he drives into me harder, faster, the heat in my core building until it's impossibly hot. I hope he's as close as I am because I can already tell I'm not going to be able to move anymore after this.

Please don't stop. Please don't stop. Please *don't stop.* I don't know if I manage to say it aloud, but his grip on my hand tightens to a nearly painful degree, the movements of his hips starting to jerk.

I think I stop breathing. All I know is I don't just come over the edge. I'm shoved off the cliff, suddenly and violently, and then I'm falling. I think he finishes too. I think he groans my name.

Every part of me trembles as I gulp in a breath, and Liam slows to a few more gentle thrusts before stilling between my legs. His head falls to my shoulder with a shaky exhale, and we lie there for a moment, panting and holding each other. My heart pounds in my chest, and I can feel his just as clearly against my palm.

Slowly, he pushes himself up and smoothes his hands over my hair, his smile uncertain as he searches my face.

I bite my lip. "Is it always that good?"

He throws his head back, his laugh full and relieved. "No." He kisses me. "It's not." Again. "But I have a feeling with you and me, it will be."

What I've done doesn't fully occur to me until I'm sitting on Liam's couch in one of his T-shirts. Liam returns to his spot next to me with a glass of water, and I cover my face with my hands.

"Oh my God," I moan.

"What? What's wrong?"

I stare up at him with wide eyes. "That was so rude of me. To just walk out on my own party. To leave all of my friends there—some who flew all the way here from the West Coast just to see me! And I just walked out! Where's my phone? I should—I should call, or—"

"Gracie." Liam takes my face between his hands before I can get far and forces me to look at him. "Breathe. I'll find your phone."

After a few seconds of searching through the couch, he pulls it out from between the cushions and hands it over.

"Shit, it's late," he mutters as he checks his own phone. "Damage control might have to wait until the morning."

I chew on my lip and send a few copy-and-paste texts to apologize and let everyone know I'll fill them in tomorrow.

"Hey." Liam gently taps beneath my chin with his knuckles. "Everyone who was at that party loves you. They'll understand. You want to order food and watch something?" My eyebrows inch up, and he laughs. "I'll take that as a yes." He takes the seat beside me on the couch, pulls out his phone, and leans forward on his knees. "What are you in the mood for? There aren't a lot of vegetarian spots around here, are there? And there are only a few places still open. What about sushi? Do they have stuff for you?"

I peer at his phone over his shoulder as he scrolls through a delivery app and pulls up the sushi place a few streets down. "Oh yeah. Their asparagus one is really good. The sauce is delicious."

He clicks on the roll. "This one?"

I rest my chin against his shoulder and nod.

"Perfect. That's what I'll get too."

"Liam, you don't have to. I mean, you can get whatever you want."

He turns, putting our noses an inch from each other, and searches my face. "It doesn't bother you when people eat meat in front of you?"

I look away and lean back. Obviously I don't like seeing it. Or being around it. Or, God, smelling it. But I get enough jabs and jokes when people find out I'm a vegetarian as it is. Bringing more attention to it is the last thing I want to do.

He ducks his head to meet my eyes. "You're just too nice to ask me not to, right?"

My face burns at how easily he can read me.

"Gracie, I want the asparagus roll. You know, I think the only thing missing in my life right now is some asparagus, actually."

"Do you even like asparagus?"

He shrugs and finishes making the order. "I will now. So." He settles into the couch, then grabs my legs, pulls them across his lap, and hands me the TV remote. "What'll it be, birthday girl?"

I chew on my lip and sift through the options. *Something I haven't seen before or an old favorite...*

"Can I ask you something that's none of my business?" Liam says.

"Sure." I switch to a different app that's usually better about having new releases.

"This being your first time...why is that? I don't believe for a second you didn't have guys throwing themselves at you in college."

I stop scrolling.

"You don't have to tell me. I just wondered if there was a reason."

I inhale slowly, considering my words. It's a fair question, but I've never tried to put together the words for an answer.

"There were a few guys in college," I say slowly. "And we fooled around a little bit. But the first time I ever got close to having sex, I ended up telling him I wasn't ready yet. And, you know, he was nice about it in the moment, but then afterward he pretty much ghosted me. We talked sometimes, but nothing like it had been, until he stopped reaching out altogether."

I hated the way I could still feel butterflies in my stomach every time his name popped up on my phone, how that turned into a gaping pit in my gut when I finally realized I was never going to hear from him again. I'd held out hope for weeks—far longer than I should have.

"And he'd seemed so genuine before that," I say softly. "But as soon as he realized he wasn't going to get to sleep with me, he turned into this completely different person. So then whenever there were other guys, and I actually did, you know, want to sleep with them? I would tell them no. Just to see if they reacted the same way." I swallow hard. "And they did. All of them. I just wanted to see if they would wait—they wouldn't have even had to wait long!—if a single one of them cared about me more than they cared about that, and it never happened. So I decided I would rather stay a virgin than have my first time be with someone like that. At some point I stopped bothering with dating. It felt...pointless. Shallow." I give him a wry smile. "The hopeless romantic in me couldn't take it."

He frowns, the tension in his forehead carving deep lines, and his hands tighten around my legs. "I'm really glad you didn't. Not just because selfishly I'm glad it was with me. I hate that you experienced that. I don't understand how a single one of them could have gotten to know you and not fallen completely in love with you." He brings me into his chest and kisses the side of my head. "I'm crazy about you, Gracie," he murmurs in a voice almost too low for me to hear. "And I'm still going to say that tomorrow and every day after."

My throat tightens. I hadn't realized how much I needed to hear that. He traces the backs of my hands, his fingers playing idly with mine. Such a simple action, but it makes the last of the tension in my body deflate, like this, finally, is what convinced it we're safe right now.

In fact, being with Liam, I don't know if I've ever felt safer in my life.

The sushi arrives halfway through the movie—a recent romcom release—and Liam ends up liking the asparagus rolls so much that I have to fight him away from stealing pieces of mine too.

He tries to pull me against his chest, but I wiggle away.

"Would you just get over here?" he says with a sigh.

"You're trying to distract me so you can take the last piece."

"Fine. Finish it, then come here."

I narrow my eyes at him as I chew, and he lifts an eyebrow while he waits. When I'm done, I cautiously scoot closer, not sure if he's trying to lure me in to put me in a chokehold or wrestle me to the ground or something.

He stretches an arm out to make room for me. "So paranoid."

"I grew up with Leo. Sue me."

But as I settle against his chest and he props his chin on the top of my head, all he does is pull up the camera on his phone.

"I'm sorry I didn't get one at the party," he murmurs. "I don't want to not have a picture with you on your birthday."

I look up at his face as he snaps the picture. Simple words, and he says them casually enough, but the romance-book girl inside of me is melting. Because despite how hard and intimidating and cool he may seem on the outside, I think Liam Brooks is as much of a hopeless romantic as I am.

Chapter Thirty-Eight

GRACIE

I feel a little bit like a creep. Liam sleeps peacefully on his back, even once the sun starts streaming through the windows. No matter how hot it got in the night, we stayed wrapped around each other, but the duvet and sheets ended up shoved to the bottom of the bed, leaving Liam in only his boxers and me in his T-shirt.

Now I can't stop staring at him. I think my mouth is watering.

His lean build is so...deceptive. I could *feel* how strong he is around me last night, but I didn't fully realize until now that I can *see* it too. My eyes trace every strong line of his body—the subtle outline of his muscles, the intricate patchwork of designs covering his skin. I've never gotten to see them all and really take them in. There's so much to look at. I don't know much about tattoos, but some are more faded, the lines less crisp, which leads me to believe they're older. He's clearly not a fan of color—they're all black, at least from what I can see.

He makes a sound low in his throat as his head turns

toward me on the pillow. He doesn't open his eyes, but his lips curl, and I know I've been caught.

"Come here," he murmurs.

I inch forward to tuck myself beneath his arm.

"Closer."

I press a little harder against him until there's no room left between us.

"Closer."

I snort, then throw a leg over his hips and roll until I'm straddling him.

That gets his eyes open. He grips my thighs, and the wolfish grin on his face softens as his gaze meets mine. Slowly, he trails his hand up my hip, over my ribs, and into my hair. No matter how many times I feel his skin against mine, it sparks heat through me like it's the first time. He sits up enough to let his lips brush mine as he says, "This is dangerous."

"Why is that?" I whisper.

He pulls my mouth down to his, and a small whimper escapes me as he kisses me slowly, deeply. When he pulls away, he says, "Because I like having you in my bed far too much to let you sleep anywhere else now."

"Are you telling me you're kidnapping me?"

He nods and ducks his head to kiss my shoulder.

I push against him until he's on his back again. His chest rises faster with his breath, and the heat in his gaze as he looks up at me has my stomach tightening. I trail my fingertips over his skin, starting at his hips, gliding over his abs, his chest, tracing the lines of his tattoos.

"You couldn't have done these all yourself."

"No, anything I couldn't reach easily, someone else did."

I tilt my head. "Did you do your first one, or did someone else?"

He mirrors my movements, his hands skating along my legs. "Someone else."

"Which one was it?"

He curls his fingers around mine, then drags my hand up and places it on the inside of his left biceps. There are a few tattoos there, but in the center is a single stemmed flower. There's something almost delicate about it compared to the rest. It's hidden against his body when his arms are down, so I've never noticed it before.

I lean in closer, taking in the thinner lines, the detail in the shading. It's much more faded than the ones around it.

"What kind of flower is it?"

He hesitates a moment before saying, "Water lily."

Lily. His mother's name.

I trace my fingers over it, then meet his eyes. "For your mom?"

He smiles softly. "Got it a week after the accident."

"It's beautiful." I feel his gaze on my face as I go back to exploring. There doesn't seem to be much rhyme or reason to most of them—a snake, an olive branch, a constellation. "Which one is the first one you did?"

"Above my right knee."

I scoot down to see. "Oh, the butterfly?"

He laughs as I lean in to inspect it. "Don't look too closely at it."

"Why? It looks great to me."

The bed shifts as he sits up. One hand rests between my shoulder blades as the other points to the edges of the tattoo. "See how it's kind of blurry? The lines aren't that clear? It's blown out. Went too deep."

I hum. Now that he pointed it out, I see what he's saying, but I never would have noticed it on my own. "You designed all of them though, didn't you? Even the ones you didn't tattoo yourself?"

He nods.

I smile, shaking my head.

"What?"

I throw my hands up. "That's so *cool*." I go back to inspecting the ones along his thighs. "You're so talented." I glance at him when he doesn't respond, and if I didn't know any better, I'd swear he looked a little red.

I climb onto his lap again and take his face between my hands. That finally gets him to smile, and he leans down to press a kiss to my collarbones.

"You think you'll ever get one?" he murmurs against my skin.

"I don't know. I'm kind of afraid of how much it would hurt."

"You'd be fine." He kisses my throat. "You're tough." My jaw. "If you did get one, would you let me do it?"

"Of course. I wouldn't trust it with anyone else."

He beams like a kid opening a Christmas gift, and I laugh. "If I got one, where do you think I should put it?"

He hums like he's thinking about it, tightens his arms around my waist, then flips me onto my back. I let out a breathy laugh as he pushes my shirt up to my stomach, then leans in and presses his lips to the dip inside my hipbone.

"Maybe here," he murmurs. Slowly, he trails his mouth up my stomach until he presses his lips to my ribs right beneath my breast. I shiver as his breath ghosts across my skin. "Or here." He links his fingers with mine, then lifts my arm so he can kiss the inside of my wrist. "Or here." He finds the spot beneath my elbow next. "Here."

I squirm against the bed, my breaths coming in fast now. I

know he notices, but he just continues his leisurely perusal of my body, pressing an open-mouthed kiss to each new spot he finds—below my collarbone, inside my ankle, the outside of my forearm. Finally, he finds his way back to my mouth, but the kiss is brief, sweet, not what every cell in my body is screaming for right now.

His eyes flick between mine. "How are you feeling?"

My eyebrows pull together.

"About last night," he adds.

"Good," I say, my voice quiet and small, but I force myself not to look away, even as I feel my cheeks heat.

"No regrets?"

Regrets? "Of course not. Do you…?"

"Not at all." He presses his lips to my forehead. "I just wanted to make sure. Are you okay? You sore at all?"

"A little," I admit. "But I'm fine."

"Can I make you breakfast?"

I nod, trying not to let my disappointment that he's getting up show on my face. Especially now that he has my body wound far too tightly for comfort.

He presses one last kiss to the top of my head before rolling himself out of bed. But he doesn't move toward the kitchen. He turns back to me, grabs my legs, and pulls me to the edge of the bed.

"Liam—"

"Hope you don't mind if I have mine first." The last thing I see before he lowers to his knees is his wolfish grin, then his face disappears between my legs.

"Do you want me to come in with you?"

I look from Liam's thumb tracing circles on my hand to his

face. A small voice in the back of my head screams *yes*, but only because I don't want to say goodbye to him yet.

But logically, I know this is something I have to do on my own. And this is only the first stop on the apology tour today.

I kiss him on the cheek and unbuckle my seat belt. "I've got this."

He doesn't look entirely convinced, but he lets me go.

"Call me later and tell me how it goes?" he says as I hop out.

I nod and head for the house before I can think too much about it. My new car sits in the driveway, so Leo or Keava must have brought it back for me.

It's quiet when I walk through the front door, and at first I think no one's home. But as I head for the basement stairs, I catch sight of someone sitting at the kitchen table. My steps slow. I know he heard me come in, but he doesn't turn. I resist the urge to hide in my room and head toward him.

Leo's sitting alone with an untouched cup of coffee in front of him, his arms braced on the table. It isn't until I take the chair beside him that he finally looks up.

"Can we talk?" I ask.

The bags under his eyes are dark, like he barely slept, and my chest pinches.

"I'm sorry about last night," I continue when he doesn't say anything. "I don't want to fight with you, Leo."

"We're not fighting," he says quietly.

"Then what are we doing? You can barely look at me."

"Because you're wearing my best friend's clothes," he says with a flick of his wrist.

He takes in the hoodie and matching sweats, and the lines around his mouth deepen. I grimace. I'm not sure what would have been worse—showing up in Liam's clothes like this or still wearing last night's dress.

I sigh and wind my fingers together. "I'm really sorry that

this is how you found out. And I'm sorry for not telling you sooner. Don't blame Liam for the not-telling-you part—that was my fault. I—I didn't expect this to be that big of a deal."

He lets out something between a scoff and a laugh. "Gracie." He exhales slowly and closes his eyes. "You see the best in people. I admire that. But what you have to understand is, Liam is not what you're looking for—"

"You don't know that."

He laughs again, nothing about it sounding amused. "Yeah, actually, I do. I know everything about him, which is exactly the problem."

"You don't," I say quietly. "You don't know everything. And *that's* the problem."

He opens his mouth, closes it.

"Make me understand. Why are you so against this?"

"Gracie, you should've seen the trainwreck his last relationship was. You were too young to really understand all the details—"

I scoff. "Don't do that."

"What? You were! You were *twelve* when they started dating. And I don't want that for you. Especially for your first relationship. I don't want you to think that's what it's like. I don't know what it is when it comes to girls, but Liam self-sabotages. I've never seen him in something healthy."

I don't want you to think that's what it's like. It's so eerily similar to something Liam said that it makes me shiver. But it also makes my heart ache. For Liam. Because that was *his* first relationship, and what Leo's so afraid of for me is exactly what he went through.

"Have you ever considered there's more to his side of the story?"

He frowns but says nothing.

"This isn't going away." I push up from the table. "I love you, Leo. I'm grateful that you're trying to look out for me. But I'm not going to stop seeing him. And I hope you can come to accept that. For me, but also for him. He's your best friend, for Christ's sake. You *know* he's a good person. Can't you give him a little more credit?"

More anger seeps into my words than I'd been intending, but the more I think about it, the angrier I get. Leo's his best friend. They've known each other for most of their lives. Liam has had no one to talk to about everything he's been through, and no wonder he didn't feel like he could go to Leo if Leo was going to be as judgmental as this.

Leo's eyebrows lower in confusion.

"Talk to him, Leo," I call as I head for the stairs. "Make this right."

"Where are you going?"

"On tour!"

The girls are staying at Mom and Dad's house in my old bedroom and the guest room. I feel even worse than I already did when I show up and realize there's an extra air mattress set out, like they were expecting me to sleep over with them.

Last night was one of the best nights of my life.

And it was one of the most selfish, thoughtless things I've ever done.

Everyone's already awake and finished with breakfast— pancakes, courtesy of Mom—when I show up. I cringe at the thought of whoever filled my parents in when they got back last night.

Oh, Gracie? The guest of honor? The entire reason we're all here?

She ditched us to be with her boyfriend. Who happens to be Leo's best friend. Who she didn't tell anyone about. Also, she's a big lying liar who lied about everything she's been up to this summer.

Mom smiles at me from the kitchen as she loads the dishwasher, and laughter pulls my attention outside. My friends are huddled together with cups of coffee in the seating that was set up for the movie last night. Carson's still here too, nestled in close to the others as if she's been part of the group all along. I guess I shouldn't be surprised they all hit it off.

"There's some leftovers, if you want some," offers Mom.

"I'm not hungry. Here, let me help with those." I reach for the remaining dirty plates, but she waves me off.

"I think you have something more important to take care of." She raises her eyebrows and looks pointedly at the sliding door.

I wince. "What did you hear?"

"Enough," she says lightly. "Are you all right?"

I nod.

"Do you want to talk about it?"

I grimace. "I just saw Leo."

She adds another plate to the dishwasher. "He'll come around. You know how he is."

My eyes flick between hers. "So you don't agree with him? That this is a bad idea? Me and Liam."

She shrugs. "I think you're old enough to make that choice for yourself." A small smile grows on her face. "Can't say I'm that surprised. Now, those girls came a long way to celebrate you. I think you should be spending your time talking to them, not me."

My throat tightens. "I know."

She grabs my wrist before I can leave. "I'm happy for you, sweetheart. But you can't let the rest of your life disappear for a relationship. You can't let that be the only thing that matters."

I nod, kind of wishing she'd yell instead of this kind, calm voice she's using. The anger would be a lot easier to take than the clear disappointment in her eyes.

The girls all look up as I step onto the deck.

Marti's the first to speak. She offers a sleepy smile and lifts her coffee in the air. "She's returned!"

Bless Marti. Leave it to her to always break the ice.

Carson waves, but the others, unfortunately, don't look nearly as forgiving.

"Everything okay?" asks Trish.

Dad brought out the nice outdoor furniture—arranging the larger wicker couch and love seat together to form an L around the projector screen. All four girls are huddled together on the bigger couch beneath a blanket, so I take the love seat.

"I'm the worst," I say.

Alison's eyebrows lift as if in agreement.

"I can't tell you how sorry I am for taking off like that. I wasn't thinking."

"It's okay," says Marti with a shrug, but it looks forced, even for her. "Bummed we didn't get to do the cake though. Your mom saved it in case you wanted to do it today instead."

I don't know why this detail over everything else has tears springing to my eyes.

The icy exteriors over Trish's and Alison's expressions crack.

"Oh, come here." Trish scoots closer to Alison in the middle and holds open the end of the blanket.

"I'm really sorry," I say as I slide in beside her. "I don't know how yet, but I'm going to make it up to you."

Trish lets out a long breath. "I suppose we've all done stupid things for boys."

"Not me," says Alison.

"We didn't see you the entire first three months you dated Josh," Marti reminds her.

She grimaces.

I'd nearly forgotten that was his name. We all just called him Senior Douche.

Trish holds up a hand. "I can forgive the running off into the sunset with hot skater boy. It's your birthday. You get one free pass. What *I* want to know is what's really been going on with you this summer. Why did you lie to us?"

"I was embarrassed," I whisper.

"What?" says Marti. "Why?"

My eyes bulge. "*Why?* Because you three all have your lives so figured out. You made transitioning out of college look like a piece of cake, and I fell flat on my face. I just...I was hoping I'd get things a little more together by the time I saw you guys again."

Trish screws her face up. "I, for one, do *not* have my life figured out."

Marti all but cackles. "I'm an unemployed actor whose career peaked when she was seven! I have three roommates in a two-bedroom house!"

Alison shrugs. "My job isn't remotely related to my degree, *and* my parents still pay all my bills."

"So you ended up moving back home," says Marti. "So what? Doesn't seem so bad here. I like it."

"And your new job obviously comes with...perks." Alison wiggles her eyebrows.

I whip around to Carson, who gives me a sheepish shrug. "I filled them in a bit."

"Sorry for spilling the beans in front of everyone last night," Alison adds. "You know I'm not the best at picking up subtle hints."

"Stop being so nice to me." I cover my face with my hands. "Yell or something."

"*I'd* rather get all the dirty details about what happened after you left last night," says Marti.

"That argument was kind of hot, not gonna lie," mutters Alison. "'*I'm in love with her!*'"

I scowl at her imitation of Liam's voice.

"Puh-lease tell me there was at least *some* fooling around after that," she continues. "Even if it was only PG-13."

"It wasn't PG-13," I say before I can think better of it.

All four of their jaws drop.

Marti squeals, grabs Trish's hand, and shakes it.

"Look at that blush!" Carson points at my face.

"Is it true? Can it be?" Alison grabs my cheeks between her thumb and pointer finger and twists my face this way and that. "Are you...a *woman?*"

"Oh, shut up." I wave her off, but I can't help the stupid smile on my face.

"No, no! Don't shut down on us now!" whines Trish. "I need more. How was it? He looks like he'd be good at it. Did you...?" She makes a clicking sound with the side of her mouth.

"We are at my parents' house," I whisper-scream. "You guys are all wildly inappropriate."

Trish grins. "So that's a yes."

Marti lets out a wistful sigh. "I can't believe you never told us how hot he was. How did you grow up around that and not jump him the second you hit puberty?"

Alison's grin turns downright diabolical. "Did he talk you through it? Reenact your books for you?"

I slap her on the arm. "Okay, okay. Enough."

Thank *God* I didn't let Liam come with me for this conversation.

"Nope," chirps Alison. "This is your punishment for leaving us."

Carson nods seriously. "We get to give you a hard time for the rest of the day."

"Orrr you can be generous and share the details with us," offers Marti, complete with hands folded beneath her chin and batting eyelashes.

I pinch the bridge of my nose with two fingers. "Fine. But that means we're breaking out the cake for breakfast."

Driving the girls to the airport a few days later is bittersweet. They stayed another two nights after my birthday, and I slept at my parents' house to hang out with them. A marathon sleep-over like that is no easy feat for my poor introvert heart, even with people I love. But as I park beside the terminal and climb out to help get their suitcases from the truck, my eyes inevitably fill with tears.

"None of that!" Marti waves a hand in front of her face, her own eyes glassy, then pulls me into a hug. "We'll see each other at Christmas."

"Whoop!" Alison pumps a fist in the air. "Girls' trip!"

"Don't forget." Trish points at me.

"I won't. I promise." I set the last of their suitcases on the curb and all but hold my breath to keep from crying as I give them each one last hug.

"FaceTime date next weekend?" says Trish.

"Absolutely."

I wave as they head inside, then let the tears fall as I climb into the car. The silence feels so much emptier in their absence.

I hesitate before shifting the car into drive, trying to collect myself. I don't know why my emotions are going haywire. I'll miss them, sure, but I think my body is just confused now. Being around them made me feel like I was still in college, and now I have to snap back to reality.

A reality that's not all bad, but it's so far from where I want to be. This temporary situation with Leo has already stretched on for months. If I'm not careful, I might blink and find a lot more time than that has passed.

Chapter Thirty-Nine

GRACIE

"You know, I don't think I've ever seen you in a suit before."

I regret the words the second they're out of my mouth because I *have* actually. Once. Nearly ten years ago.

At his mother's funeral.

Liam doesn't seem to notice though. He presses his lips together in a bashful smile and readjusts his hair.

We're some of the first to arrive, along with the rest of Liam's family. I crane my neck back to take in the massive hotel before we step inside. A night here is probably worth a month's rent. But the Brookses wanted to make a *splash* with this launch for True Sweets, and apparently the Brooks mansion was far too small for that.

With most of the attendees coming down from New York, I'm surprised they kept it in Jersey at all. Liam's dad said it was something about showing they're proud of their roots or whatever.

I'm even more surprised Liam agreed to come. Of course I said yes when he asked me to go with him, and despite how uncomfortable I am as we walk through the doors, I do everything I can to appear at ease. I can *feel* the tension in Liam's body, wound tight like a spring, so one of us needs to keep it together.

The ballroom is an explosion of color when we step inside. Long, narrow tables with fancy gold place settings and name cards stretch through the vast space, and obnoxious backdrops for photos appear every few feet along three of the walls. A small stage sits at the far end of the room with the new True Sweets logo behind it in neon pink lights.

"Oh good, you're here!" Christine smiles at us before finishing her conversation with a waiter in a black and white uniform. She points to the back corner, and the man disappears that way. "Wow, you two look great." She hugs Liam, and he stiffens and awkwardly pats her on the back. "And Gracie! I'm so, *so* glad you could make it." She throws her arms around me next, and when she pulls back, I brace myself for what I'll find on her face.

But her smile seems…genuine.

Not that any of the Brookses have ever been outwardly hostile to me, but after getting those bits of information from Casey, I can't help but wonder *who* he picked that up from. Who here secretly thinks I'm a downgrade from Liam's previous girlfriend.

"We're set up out back too," says Christine. "That's where your brothers and Makayla are, last I saw. The influencers and VIP guests are set to arrive first in about half an hour to get started on content, and we're having a private cocktail party for them. Everyone else should start trickling in about an hour after that. We'll be serving dinner in here later, but the drinks and snacks are already set up outside if you're hungry!"

"Everything looks amazing, Christine," says Liam.

Her shoulders detach from her ears with her exhale.

"Really? Good. I have to hunt down the DJ, but I'll see you two later!"

We wave as she hurries off through the same door the waiter used earlier.

"I thought this was Makayla's event," I mutter once she's gone.

Liam presses his hand to my lower back to lead us outside. "Mak's always been better at dreaming things up than carrying them out. And this." He raises his eyebrows and glances around at the disco balls, human-sized pink feathers, and walls covered in flower arrangements. "Has Christine written all over it."

The terrace has a similar look—giant pink flamingo floats in the pool, tables overflowing with decorative containers of candy, and backdrops designed around the True Sweets logo obviously intended for the influencers to post with.

"Look who showed up." A tall, dark-haired man slaps Liam on the back. It takes me a moment to recognize him as Liam's older brother. They look nothing alike aside from the color of their hair. I can't tell if it's the sharp cheekbones and jaw that give him that haughty air, or if it's the way his nose seems permanently angled to the sky.

"Taylor," Liam says unenthusiastically.

"Might as well grab one of these." Taylor raises the beer in his hand. "Gonna be a long night." With that, he heads over to a pretty blonde woman standing at the bar. A few others are scattered throughout the space—a woman in a pink floor-length gown who I think is Makayla, along with her husband, judging by the way she's hanging off his arm, Asher, who's currently flirting with the female bartender, and a woman with a clipboard and an earpiece who's pacing around and inspecting every detail.

"Casey?" I ask.

Liam shakes his head. "No kids. He and Georgina—Makayla's daughter—are sharing a babysitter tonight."

The only other noticeably absent Brooks is the Candyman himself, and if Liam isn't going to bring him up, I sure as hell won't.

Hailey also isn't here yet, but considering what Christine said about the influencers—and what Liam's told me about her basically being the face of this new campaign—I'm sure it's only a matter of time.

"You want something to drink?" Liam offers.

"Sure."

He kisses my temple before heading for the bar, and I pace along the outskirts of the pool, taking it all in. The terrace has a gorgeous view of the ocean, and with all the sparkly decorations and disco balls around here, I'm sure it'll be quite the sight to see come sunset.

I stop at the railing and take a deep breath of the salty air, letting it put me at ease. The breeze makes it cold with just this silk slip dress, and I pull my wrap tighter around my shoulders.

Footsteps pad quietly on my right, and I turn, expecting Liam, but it's Asher who offers a smile that looks more like a grimace as he steps up beside me.

"Hey, Gracie."

"Hi."

He finally did away with the strange near-mohawk he had going all summer. I almost didn't recognize him without it. Now he's left with little more than a buzzcut, and it looks like he's trying to grow a mustache. He chews on his lip and shoots a look over his shoulder before leaning against the railing and facing me. "So I've been meaning to talk to you."

"Oh?"

He tugs on the collar of his shirt. "About Miles."

My stomach drops, and I turn back to looking at the water.

Thankfully, I haven't had to see him again since that night. But of course I've thought about it. Admittedly less so once Christine assured us she'd handled the legal side of things, and after weeks passed without hearing from him, my anxiety about the situation finally relented.

Asher swallows audibly and shifts his weight, that usual carefree, frat-boy swagger of his noticeably absent. "I was shocked when Liam told me what happened. I had no idea. And I just wanted to say I'm really sorry. You didn't deserve that. And I guess I wanted you to know that he and I...well, we don't hang out anymore."

The look in his eyes is earnest, almost pleading, like he's looking for my forgiveness. Not that he needs it. I never blamed him.

"Thanks, Asher."

I think that'll be it, but he doesn't walk away. I peek at him sideways, but he isn't looking at me. His gaze is trained on Liam, who's currently taking two drinks from the bartender.

"He's happy with you," Asher says quietly. "Happier than I think I've ever seen him." He turns back to me with a rueful smile. "And I know our family is capable of scaring off the best of people, so I guess I'm saying I hope you won't let them. You've got me in your corner, at least."

"You better not be trying to steal my date," Liam says as he approaches.

Asher smirks and takes a step back as Liam hands me a glass of champagne.

"Getaway car will be out front in five," says Asher with a wink before he takes off to the bar.

"What'd he say to you?" Liam asks as he sets his drink on the rail and slips off his suit jacket.

"Nothing bad."

Liam wraps the jacket over my shoulders and gives me an unconvinced eyebrow raise.

I laugh. "I promise. How are you doing?"

"Me?" He frowns and sips his beer. "Fine."

"That was really convincing."

"So I'm counting down the seconds until it's acceptable for us to leave. Sue me."

"So you *don't* want to take a picture with the flamingos?"

He scowls. I smile and bat my eyelashes.

"Have you even tried the new candy yet?" I ask.

"Yeah." He scrunches up his face. "Foul."

"Is it really?"

He tilts his head back and forth. "Okay, so it was pretty good. You want some?" He grabs the collar of the jacket around my shoulders, pulls me a step closer, and reaches for the inside pocket.

"You did not shove some in your pockets for later," I whisper.

He smirks and pulls out a handful of gummy bears. "Want one?" he asks as he pops one in his mouth.

I can't help but laugh. "No, I don't want your pocket gummy bears."

He shrugs and eats another. "You want me to go get you some *fresh* ones?"

I shake my head and eye the stairs that lead to the rest of the grounds. Liam follows my gaze.

"You hatching an escape plan?"

I shrug innocently. "No one will probably notice we're missing until all the guests are arriving, right?"

Liam throws his arm over my shoulder and steers us that way. "Have I mentioned that I love you?"

We pace around the grounds, admiring the flowers, landscaping, and ocean views. Eventually we come across a small gazebo lined with flowers and string lights, and I huddle against Liam's side for warmth as we slide onto the bench. He drapes my legs over his lap and runs his hands up and down them.

"We can go back inside if you're cold."

I shake my head and wind my hands around his torso. "I'm just going to steal all of your body heat."

He chuckles and kisses the top of my head. After a moment, he murmurs, "Thanks for coming with me today."

"Of course." I debate the wisdom of my next words, if I want to risk ruining this moment, but I've been dying to ask since it happened, and it's just never felt like the right time. "Can I ask you about something?"

He nuzzles his face against the side of my neck. "Mm-hmm."

"It's something Leo said at the party."

He pulls back, a hint of concern drawing his eyebrows together. "Okay?"

I stare at my hand on his thigh. "What did he mean when he said you promised you'd never go there with me?"

He takes a deep breath and tilts his face up to the sky. "Oh. That." He says nothing for what feels like a long time, but when he rolls his head to look at me, there's a faint smirk tugging at his lips. "Leo has always been perceptive," he says, as if that answers everything. "Even in high school. Or maybe it was just obvious. Where my attention was. I guess he wasn't worried while I was dating Hailey, but she and I were broken up for a good six months during your freshman year. That's when he gave me *the talk.*"

Freshman year? "I—I didn't think you noticed me back then."

"Gracie." He says my name like a prayer, like a promise. He

306

tucks his knuckles beneath my chin and tilts it up. His eyes are soft as they trace over my face. "I've always noticed you."

I try to fight my smile, I really do, but it feels like my heart is doing flips in my stomach the way it always does when he looks at me like this. "So what you're saying is my stupid, embarrassing crush on you *was* noticeable."

He stares at me. Blinks. Stares some more.

I shove him lightly on the shoulder. "Oh, don't pretend to be surprised."

He shakes his head as if stunned, and a slow, disbelieving smile grows. "Gracie, I—I had no idea."

I cock my head. "Really?"

"Really." That smile turns into a full-on grin as he brings my hand to his mouth and kisses my knuckles. "How long?"

"How long, what?"

"How long did you have this crush?"

My face burns, and I purse my lips and look away. "Don't make me say it."

"Please."

There's something about the quiet, sincere quality of his voice that makes me turn. And the look in his eyes...it's almost like a younger version of him is looking at me right now.

"I don't even know," I say quietly. "Pretty much always."

His smile turns soft, tender, as he brushes my hair behind my ear. "Yeah, it was pretty much always for me too."

I have to break the eye contact because this conversation is veering into dangerous territory. The kind that might make me do something stupid like sneak off somewhere so I can tear off all his clothes.

I clear my throat. "Have you and Leo..."

He shakes his head.

I was hoping Leo would've reached out to him by now. Maybe it was naïve of me to think the rift this caused would be so easily fixed. But the guilt from it is a constant presence in the back of my mind. Not just for hurting Leo—because that's the worst part. I can tell he isn't *angry*. He's *hurt*—but also for being the reason Liam's lost access to his closest friend.

"I don't want you to worry about it. I mean it. We'll work it out."

He seems so calm, so certain. I settle in against him again, and he kisses the side of my head as his arms wrap around me, blocking the worst of the cool breeze. And I think I could sit here like this with him forever. No matter the amount of lingering guilt, I can't find it in myself to feel sorry. Because nothing about this feels wrong.

His gaze is trained on the horizon, a thoughtful look on his face as his eyebrows pull together. I run my hands up and down his arms.

"What's on your mind?" I murmur.

One side of his mouth kicks up in a smile that's not quite happy, not quite sad. "My mom."

My hands pause.

"She used to love things like this," he says. "You could never really tell she came from money, except at these kinds of events. She always made it look so natural. She... I think she would've really liked today."

Slowly, he pulls his gaze back to me. I push the hair from his eyes, then leave my hand cradling the side of his head.

"You don't talk about her much, so I've never wanted to bring it up in case you didn't want to... But I want you to know that I'm here if you ever do want to talk about it. About her."

He smiles. "I think she would've really liked this—you and me—too."

I rest my head on his shoulder and trail my hand down to interlace my fingers with his. Admittedly, I don't remember a lot about his mom. I remember her always being kind to me and how well she got along with my parents. That she and Liam had the same smile. But now I wish I'd paid more attention. "You know, I think she is here. In her own way."

He lets out a slow breath. "You think so?"

"I do. I don't think she's missed anything. I think she's been with you for it all."

His hand tightens around mine as he rests his cheek against the top of my head. "Sometimes I think I can feel her," he says so quietly I almost can't hear him, but I don't miss the choked-up quality of his voice. "Or it seems like she's sending me signs."

"Have you felt her today?"

"I have." He laughs a little. "I feel her right now, actually."

I nestle in closer, close enough to hear his heart beating in his chest, to feel the way our breaths sync up.

"I think she'd be really proud of you, Liam," I whisper. "I know I am."

We sit there for what feels like a long time, listening to the waves crash against the shore and the music from the party gradually grow louder in the distance.

"We should probably head back," he says after a while.

I nod. He tightens his hold on my legs before I can move to stand though.

"Just…a few more minutes, maybe."

I smile and relax against him. "A few more minutes."

Chapter Forty

LIAM

"But it's like I was telling 'em, definitely wasn't up to code. But no one wants to listen to me, and so I..."

Bill's voice fades in and out of my awareness. I can't even say I stopped listening halfway through his story. I haven't been paying attention since the start. But after half a dozen sessions with him, I've come to expect it. Luckily he's the type of talker that can have an entire conversation with himself. The occasional nods and grunts on my end are usually enough to keep him satisfied.

The rest of the event the other night wasn't nearly as painful as I'd been expecting. Maybe it would've been under different circumstances, but with Gracie...she made getting through the whole thing easy. Maybe even *fun* at times. The endlessly shaking people's hands, forcing smiles for pictures, having to stand on stage with the family as Dad gave some bullshit speech—as long as I could find her in the crowd or go back to holding her hand after, the rest of it didn't matter.

For someone who didn't grow up in that world, Gracie

navigated the whole night...well, like my mother did. With ease and grace and a smile the whole goddamn time.

She even took the edge off running into Hailey, which I'd be lying if I said I hadn't been dreading.

Hailey's eyes locked on me the moment Gracie and I returned to the terrace. She'd taken a few steps forward like she was planning to come talk to me, but then Gracie—my five-foot-three, deer-in-headlights, nonconfrontational Gracie —all but shoved me behind her like a guard dog and stared Hailey down until she turned away.

Once the threat was neutralized, Gracie snapped back to her usual self, a faint blush on her cheeks as she looked at me, like she was worried how I'd react.

It shouldn't have turned me on nearly as much as it did.

"Remind me to never get on your bad side" was all I said, and she blushed harder.

Which just had my imagination running wild with ways to make that blush spread further.

I blink back to Bill's calf, wipe the excess ink, and crack my neck before coming at it from a different angle, my eyes flicking to the front door of the shop every few minutes, even though I know I won't find what I'm looking for. I gave Gracie the day off since she's been putting in so many hours outside the shop.

I haven't seen her since the launch party the day before yesterday.

Which is fine. I've been busy getting caught up with work stuff, she's been spending time with her family. We've exchanged a handful of texts over the past few days, but this is still new. We're still learning each other in this way, and I don't want to come on too strong, so I've been giving her space.

But it's like fucking withdrawal at this point. We wouldn't even need to talk. I just want to *see* her. To be near her.

The shop was too quiet when I opened it. Too empty. Prepping for the day's clients alone felt all wrong, even though I've done it a hundred times before. I kept expecting to hear a camera shutter go off, or Gracie's voice asking if I could jump into a quick video. To hear her humming while she worked on admin stuff, which I'm pretty sure she doesn't realize she does. Or even to just look up from what I'm doing and see her sitting at the front desk.

I didn't realize how used to it I'd gotten.

What the fuck is going on with me?

I wrap Bill's piece up around noon, then pace around the shop while I shove a protein bar down for lunch and wait for my next appointment at one.

The bells above the door ring, and I practically break my neck as my head snaps up to see…

"Leo?"

He's standing several paces away with his hands in his pockets, shifting his weight uncomfortably back and forth like he hasn't been here a million times before. He grimaces when he meets my eyes, the twist of his mouth identical to Gracie's when she makes that face.

We haven't spoken since Gracie's birthday—the longest we've gone without talking since we met, I think. But if there's one thing I've learned over the course of our friendship, it's he can't be rushed. His immediate reaction to something is almost never how he feels about it in the end, but the only thing that can change his mind is giving him time to process it on his own.

So I've held off from reaching out to him, no matter how many times I wanted to. Though I admit, I was starting to doubt waiting it out was going to work this time around.

"Is Gracie here?" he asks.

I can't read whatever that expression is on his face, so I try not to look too eager about him being here. "Uh, no. I gave her the day off. I think she said she had plans with her friend Carson."

"Oh." He frowns.

But he doesn't leave.

For a moment, I think that'll be it, but then he sighs and glances around even though we're the only ones here. "I don't like this."

"Leo—"

"Let me finish."

I pinch my lips together and nod.

"I don't like this. But I also..." He meets my eyes again and sighs. "But I also trust you with my life. And sometimes I forget that Gracie isn't a kid anymore who needs me to look out for her. I want her to be happy, and I want you to be happy. And if this is what does it... I don't know if this is ever not going to feel weird, but I'm going to try to get used to it."

I crack half a smile. "Did Keava write that script for you?"

He rubs his eyes. "We came up with a few different ones."

"Is she here?"

"She's waiting in the car."

I chuckle, and when he lowers his hand, he's smiling too.

"I'm sorry about the way you found out. I wanted to be the one to tell you. And I wish I'd done it sooner—"

"I know it's not your fault. She told me she asked you not to." His eyes flick to the shop behind me. "I'm sorry about some of the things I said."

I shrug.

"No, really, Liam. I didn't mean...obviously I know that you're not..." He scratches at the back of his neck as he fights for words. "I was being selfish."

I blink and shake my head. "No, Leo—"

"No, I was," he insists. "I didn't realize it in the moment, but

I think what I was really worried about was if this doesn't end well, then what am I supposed to do in that position? I've always been on your side, but I've also always been on Gracie's. And if the two of you don't work out, that won't be an option anymore."

"I can't speak for Gracie, but I'm pretty sure she'd agree that we'd never want you to pick sides if it came to that, Leo. But I know it's an awkward position to put you in. I'm sorry." Slowly, I rise from my chair and offer my hand. "So we're good?"

We shake hands, but he tightens his grip before I can let go. He stares at me, hard. More serious than I ever think I've seen him, at least when it comes to me. "Don't think just because we're friends that I won't kill you if you hurt her."

"I'd be disappointed if you didn't."

Chapter Forty-One

GRACIE

Carson pulls into a spot down the street from Brooks Tattoos and shifts the car into park. For one of the first times this summer, our days off lined up, so we spent the afternoon lying out on the beach and then binge-watching old reality shows we loved in high school. I'm a little sunburned and still fighting my way out of a food coma from the amount of chips and guac we consumed, but I wouldn't have it any other way.

"Thanks for the ride," I say as I gather my bag and jacket sitting at my feet.

She smiles, her cheeks also looking crisp and red. It's less noticeable on her though. Maybe it's having less contrast with her hair so dark, or it's because she already had a much better base tan than I did. "Tell Liam you need days off more often. This was fun."

I snort.

"I'm serious! What's the point of banging your boss if you don't abuse the perks?"

"I—we are not—"

Carson pats me on the head. "We both know you are."

315

I scowl, but before I have a chance to reach for the door, my phone rings.

I fish it out of my pocket and almost let it go to voicemail when I see it's an unsaved number, but something about it makes me pause. "Is 267 a Philly area code?"

"Yeah, why?"

I turn the phone to Carson. "It might be one of those jobs I applied for."

She flaps her hands frantically. "For God's sake, pick it up before it goes to voicemail!"

"Hello, this is Gracie." I cringe at the squeak in my voice.

"Hi, Gracie, this is Savannah with Bezzels. We spoke at your interview a few weeks ago."

"Of course! I remember."

"I wanted to deliver the good news to you myself. We're pleased to offer you the position…"

Carson watches me with wide eyes, and I have to keep pinching myself to stay focused on what the woman is saying enough to process her words, my brain still tripping over *We're pleased to offer you the position.*

I was really beginning to think this day would never come. But I'd done it. *I'd done it.* After dozens upon dozens of form rejections or no response at all, I managed to find a company who thought I looked worth hiring. One in my field—not that I'm particularly passionate about fashion or designers, but it's a huge company, and some experience there could open even bigger doors. And they have lots of other designers working there, ones I could hopefully learn from. Keep improving. Network.

First is the shock. Then the delight, the excitement. And then…

I feel the blood drain from my face as my gaze slowly swings to Liam's shop.

If I'd gotten the call months ago, even weeks ago…

But *now*? When it feels like things are finally all going so well?

I must start responding at some point, but I think I black out because the next thing I know, I'm sitting with the phone in my lap and Carson shaking me by the shoulders.

"You just got the job!"

"I got the job," I repeat numbly.

"Gracie is employed!" she cheers.

I blink, coming back to the car. This is a good thing. It *is*. The thing I've been killing myself for all summer.

She cocks her head to the side. "How are you not so totally thrilled right now? Wait—is this not a good one? We didn't want this one?"

"No, we did—I *do*."

She follows my gaze to Liam's door, her expression softening.

I open the car door before she can comment on it, my brain already running a hundred miles an hour trying to figure out how I'm going to tell him. "I'll see you later, okay?"

She nods as I climb out onto the sidewalk, then leans across the seats before I shut the door.

"Congratulations, Gracie."

I wave as she drives off, but I don't start walking. Not right away.

The Closed sign is already hanging in the window, but the lights are on, so he's here. Working late, as always.

He's sitting at the front desk when I step inside, and his grin when he sees me is immediate. I barely make it a few paces into the room before he jumps up, throws his arms around my waist, and lifts me in a hug so tight it steals my breath.

"You just couldn't stay away, could you?"

"What can I say? I'm a workaholic," I mutter.

He's grinning as he sets me on my feet, but the smile falters as he takes in my face. "Is everything all right?"

"Yeah, yeah!" My voice comes out too fast, too high. "I wanted to surprise you. Thought maybe we could get dinner. And there's something I need to tell you."

His eyes sweep my face like he can read my thoughts there. "Okay."

"Do you want to...come sit down?" I gesture to one of the stations.

He nods and takes the rolling chair he usually tattoos from while I sit cross-legged on the table.

"What's going on?"

I take a deep breath and stare at my hands in my lap. I smile when he reaches over and lays his hand over mine.

"I got a phone call," I explain. "From the hiring manager of a company I applied to a few weeks ago. I did an interview with them over Zoom, but then never heard anything, so I assumed I didn't get the job. But...I guess I did."

He blinks once, twice. "You got the job?" he repeats.

I nod.

His entire face breaks into a grin. "Jesus fuck, Gracie. You were acting like someone died or something." He rolls his chair closer and takes my face between his hands. "Congratulations. I'm so proud of you! Why don't you look excited about this?"

"It's in Philadelphia," I say quietly.

The look on his face doesn't change. "Okay?"

My brow furrows as I look between his eyes. "So I...I'm leaving."

He runs a hand over my hair until it comes to rest at the nape of my neck. "Not ideal, obviously. But it's not that far. That's, what? An hour and a half drive? I'll come up to see you a few times a week or on the weekends, we'll talk on the phone

—we'll make it work. I knew it was never your plan to stay here."

He says it so confidently, so casually, like it's obvious. The relief that surges through me is immediate and violent.

Tears break free onto my cheeks, and my lower lip starts to wobble.

"Hey, hey. What's wrong?"

"I thought—I thought you'd break up with me."

He shakes his head a little, looking absolutely bewildered. "Why would I do that?"

I throw my hands up. "I don't know. We've been together for, like, a second. And I wouldn't blame you if you didn't want to do long distance again, and—"

He kisses me, his hands coming to cup my cheeks. "I wouldn't care if you told me you were going back to Portland," he murmurs. "I would want to make this work with you no matter what. And I *want* you to take this job. This is everything you've been working for. This is a good thing, Gracie. Are you not excited about it?"

I wipe my cheeks with the backs of my hands. "No, I am. *I am*. I just... Well, I'll miss you."

"Sweetheart," he breathes, and it almost sounds like a laugh. He pulls me into his chest and kisses the top of my head. "You and me, we're going to be fine. Please don't let that ruin this for you. Tell me everything. When do you start? Are you planning on looking for an apartment? That's too long for a commute, right? Wait, what company is it? What part of town? Do they pay as well as I do?"

I pull back, and the complete sincerity on his face makes my smile widen. I take his face between my hands and gently press my lips to his.

"I love you," I murmur.

He brushes my hair behind my ear. "Of course I'm going to

miss you around here, but did you really think I wasn't going to be happy for you?"

"It's not that, I just…I don't know. I got worried."

He gives me a slow smile, then pulls me into a headlock of a hug. "If you're trying to get rid of me, you're going to have to try a lot harder than that." He loosens his grip but doesn't release me. "Come over to my place tonight. Let me make you dinner."

I lift an eyebrow. "You cook?"

He shrugs. "You'll find I'm a man of many talents."

Liam squints from his phone to the bustling grocery store aisles around us, the basket hanging from his forearm. "Let's start at produce," he decides after staring at the recipe for another minute. "I definitely don't have any avocados."

"We really don't have to do something fancy—"

"We're celebrating a fancy job offer. Yes, a fancy dinner is required." He stops beside the avocados and carefully sifts through and squeezes them until he finds three he likes. "Speaking of the job offer, I want to know everything." He frowns at his phone again, then throws a few limes into the basket.

"It's an apparel renting service, so people can rent higher-end pieces for special occasions or whatever. The position is technically junior graphic designer and social media coordinator."

"So it's two jobs, basically."

"With the paycheck of one, yeah." A very sad, very small paycheck, especially considering what I've been getting from Liam. "*But* they offer corporate housing, which was one of the big sellers for me."

"Corporate housing?" Liam asks as he takes my hand and wanders until he finds the spice aisle.

"It's a fully furnished apartment in the city, so I wouldn't have to worry about a long commute, *and* it's fully paid for by the company."

"Oh nice, so you don't even need to worry about looking around for an apartment. Have you looked up the building? Do you like it?"

I shrug as he throws another few ingredients into the basket. "It's a studio, but it's no smaller than Leo's basement. No amenities really, other than a common workspace and a tiny gym, but it has in-unit laundry!"

He glances at me sideways. "I don't think I've ever seen someone more excited about a washing machine."

I swat his chest and gesture for him to move on to the next aisle. "Like you'd want to drag your laundry around the city to a laundromat."

"Fair enough." He swings our arms between us. "Does your building have parking?"

"Yes! And they pay for that too!"

"Damn. Rolling out all the stops."

I don't bother explaining the living accommodations basically *is* my compensation, and the starting salary is basically a little *here's a treat* offering because there is no way someone would be able to afford to live in the city on that alone.

"When do they want you to start?"

"Next week."

His hand tightens on mine for a moment before relaxing again. "Next week," he repeats softly.

Chapter Forty-Two

LIAM

She's leaving next week.

I don't let it show on my face. I can't.

I have to keep smiling for her sake. I have to stay excited for her sake. She worked so damn hard for this. She must have submitted at least a hundred applications, and her talents have been wasted on me and my tiny shop in this tiny town. This is her big opportunity. I can't ruin that for her. I won't.

So I cook her dinner and pour her wine and ask every question I can think of about the new job.

And I smile. And I laugh.

And I tell her it'll be fine.

And I don't, not even for a second, think about Hailey.

I don't think about having these exact conversations with her when we first went long distance.

I don't think about how certain I'd been then that everything would work out. That nothing would change between us, not really.

That I could trust her.

But this is different.

Gracie is different.

She's so different from Hailey I could laugh. She's soft everywhere Hailey was hard, kind everywhere Hailey was cruel.

But Gracie and I, we've barely gotten our feet off the ground. This is still so new.

On the other hand, with Hailey, we'd had years of history, and look what good that did me.

Gracie smiles at me across the table as she takes another bite of her taco. I don't think she has any idea how fucking cute she is. When she smiles, her nose crinkles, and her round cheeks shoot straight up. She just radiates pure light.

"Best tacos I've ever had," she says.

She's a terrible liar, but I think I did okay for my first time trying to make tofu.

"Are you excited about living in the city?"

She tilts her head back and forth as she sips her wine. "Intimidated. Portland is so small in comparison, and even then, my school wasn't *downtown*. It'll be totally new to me." Her lips twist into a shy smile. "I'm kind of scared."

I reach for her hand across the table. "Everything new is scary. Then you get used to it, and it's not new anymore, and it loses that power. Plus, you're like the bravest person I know."

She guffaws as if I've said something absurd.

I tilt my head to the side when I realize she's serious. "I mean it. You didn't know *anyone* on the West Coast before you chose that school. But you just picked up and moved about as far away from home as you possibly could. I know you were scared to do it, but you did it anyway. *That*, to me, is real bravery." Her cheeks redden, and I squeeze her hand. "This is a new chapter for you, and it's going to be amazing. I'm so excited for you."

"Thank you," she murmurs, "for being so great about all of

this. It means a lot to me. I know this affects you too. And I know it's probably...well, it might..." She grimaces as she fights for the right words.

"It is going to suck not having you around. Every day I walk into the shop and don't see you, I'm going to hate it. I'm going to hate not being able to drive five minutes to see you, that I won't be able to take you out as much as I want. I'm going to miss you every day." She chews on her bottom lip, and I run my thumb over the back of her hand. "But I would hate it more if you stayed," I murmur. "Because I know this is the right thing for you. And I don't ever want to be the thing that holds you back."

Her smile is small, sad, as she drops her gaze to her lap. Now that I've driven us into this somber mood, I'm not sure how to get out. But I don't want to leave things on this note. Don't want to leave them at all, actually.

"Stay here tonight. You can catch me up on all your zombie movie news."

A spark flicks to life in her eyes.

I grin and reach for the wine bottle to refill her glass.

Chapter Forty-Three

GRACIE

"Gracie? You good?"

"She short-circuited. Give her a minute to reboot."

"No one thinks you're funny, Leo," I mutter.

"Ah, there she is."

There's still a fifty-percent chance of me passing out, but the light-headedness fades, and the world around me slowly comes into focus. The worst part is Leo is kind of right.

I've been through Philly before. Not a lot, but enough. And as soon as I got the job offer, I spent hours scouring the internet for every detail of the area I could find.

But it wasn't until we were actually driving through the city with my entire life in boxes that it hit me we aren't just passing through.

They're going to leave me here.

All by myself.

Everything here is so fast and *loud*. So many people. So much activity.

My heart is racing by the time we make it to center city, and I've all but forgotten how to move my limbs when Keava and Leo start unpacking the car. Leo's waits behind us with a few bags we couldn't fit in mine.

And also because we needed two cars. Mine is staying here. Because *I* am staying here.

And they're leaving.

"One foot in front of the other," murmurs Liam beside me. He smiles when I meet his eyes, then squeezes my hand and pulls me from the car. "Come on. I can't wait to see the place."

I never thought I'd be living somewhere with a doorman, and I almost expect them to take one look at me, decide I don't belong here, and shoo me away. But then we're in the elevator, and I have a brand-new set of keys in my hand.

Luckily, since the place is already furnished, the moving-in process is fairly minimal—just my clothes and personal items.

"Damn," Liam says under his breath as he sets the box in his hands on the kitchen counter and ventures to the windows on the far wall. "You can see Rittenhouse Square. This view must be amazing in the fall."

The space is undeniably small. A double bed is tucked in the far corner with a desk beside it and a TV mounted on the opposite wall. They attempted to separate the kitchen from the "bedroom" with a love seat and a tiny bar table. Even with the small furniture, it feels overcrowded, but it's not much different than the dorms I'd had in college.

"It seemed like you have a ton of restaurants and stuff around here, so that'll be nice," Liam goes on. "And there was a grocery store two blocks down. And I like the building. Seems really safe."

The panic on my face must be really fucking obvious if he's trying this hard.

His eyes soften, and he pulls me over to the windows so I'm standing with my back against his chest as he wraps his arms around me.

Liam's right. That view really is amazing, especially compared to feeling like I was living in a cave in Leo's basement. But instead of the dread I'd felt moving in there, without me noticing it, I guess it started to feel like home. Leaving it behind feels so much more bittersweet than I was expecting.

Not just the basement. But seeing Leo every day. Seeing Carson, Liam. Being close to the water. Being close to my parents, but not too close.

When I used to close my eyes at night and picture the way I thought my life would go after college, it looked a lot like this. A new city. An apartment that was tiny and cramped but at least it was all mine.

A small smile brushes my lips. I can picture myself going for walks through the park in the morning, grabbing coffee down the street. Maybe finding a fitness studio, though that might be stretching my new salary a bit too far. So, the gym in the building then.

And somehow, someway, this feeling of mourning my time back home will fade until *this* feels like home instead.

"What are you thinking?" Liam murmurs.

I take a deep breath, letting in the nerves and the overwhelm and the fears instead of fighting against them, so when I turn, I don't have to force my smile.

"I like it."

Between the four of us, the unpacking doesn't take long. After taking me on a "practice commute" so I'll know how to get to my building on the first day, the sun is already setting and it's time for them to head home.

Leo hesitates in the door, a strange look on his face. "You have that pepper spray I got you?"

I roll my eyes. "Yes, Dad."

"And you need to be careful about where you park that car. There are break-ins all over the city."

"I know."

He opens his mouth, closes it, then frowns, like he's out of things to say but doesn't want to be.

"I'll miss you too, Leo," I say quietly.

He looks away and clears his throat. "We still have all your furniture in your room. Just. If you change your mind. You can always come back."

Your room. Not *the basement.*

I hug him before either of us can get emotional because neither of us will know how to deal with that.

"I'm sorry to rush out of here," he murmurs. "But, you know, Keava has to be up early and—"

"Leo, it's okay. Go. Get out of here."

He ruffles my hair, and I swat him away until he ducks into the hall.

"You've got sixty seconds, Brooks, before we leave your ass behind!" he calls.

I turn to where Liam's standing in the kitchen with his arms crossed.

"You're sure you have everything you need?" he asks.

I nod. I don't think I can speak around the emotion rising to the back of my throat. He wraps his arms around my shoulders and pulls me close, the scent of him momentarily blocking out everything else.

"Thank you for helping today," I mumble into his shirt. "Text me when you get home so I know you made it back okay?"

"You got it." He kisses the top of my head then holds me out at arm's length. "I'll see you soon, okay? We'll FaceTime tomorrow so you can tell me about your first day."

He kisses me goodbye, and I last an entire sixty seconds after the door closes behind him before the tears spill over.

The apartment barely looks different with my minimal belongings. There's a small stack of books on the nightstand, a plant on the desk, my fuzzy pink blanket on the foot of the bed. The portrait Liam painted of me on our first date is the only thing on the wall.

It's so empty, so quiet. I pace the length of it, looping around the furniture, taking in every square inch. The AC thrums loudly in the background. I grab a leftover slice of the pizza from lunch and a pillow from the couch, then plop on the floor in front of the windows so I can peer out at the city lights as night falls.

I chew the cold pizza, barely tasting it, and hug my knees into my chest. The world looks so much bigger from here. Cars are parked along the sides of the streets, and people walk back and forth on the sidewalks. Traffic stops and starts as the lights change.

Nothing about it looks familiar. Nothing about it looks like home.

But for some inexplicable reason, through the tears running down my cheeks, I smile.

Chapter Forty-Four

GRACIE

It's immediately apparent that my wardrobe is not up to par. I opted for a plain black dress and cream cardigan for the first day to play it safe until I saw what everyone else was wearing, but instead of blending in, it paints a neon New Kid sign on my forehead.

Because everyone here looks fucking fabulous.

People stream in and out of the elevator as it stops a dozen times. Everyone looks older than me. More polished. I smooth the hairs that escaped my low bun and tuck them behind my ears.

When I reach the fifteenth floor, it's easy enough to find the suite I need because Bezzels is an explosion of color through the glass doors. The furniture, the decorations, the clothes.

I swallow hard as I step up to the front desk. A woman with cat-eye glasses and bright purple lipstick types away on a computer, her complexion tinted pink from the neon sign behind her.

I wait and wait, but she doesn't acknowledge me.

I clear my throat and drift forward another step.

Still, nothing.

I double—triple—check the time, then the welcome email. But no, this is exactly when I'm supposed to be here.

"Excuse me?" I ask.

Finally, the woman glances at me over her glasses.

"I'm Gracie Collins." I force more confidence into my voice than I feel. "I'm a new hire. I'm supposed to start today."

She looks me up and down. "I'll get Selena for you." She picks up the phone then cuts her eyes to the waiting area behind me. "Have a seat."

I sink onto one of the bright red leather chairs that's shaped like a pair of lips and try to keep my eyes from widening too far as I take everything in.

The office seems to be mostly an open floor plan, and the offices that have walls are made of glass. Girls in dizzyingly tall high heels stream this way and that in a blur of leather, fur, and sparkles. I melt a little at the sight. I might not be super into fashion myself, but I can only imagine how well all those looks would photograph.

"Gracie?"

I jump to my feet as a woman rounds the corner.

"I'm Selena." She holds out a hand for me to shake, and something about her presence is relaxing. Maybe it's how wide her smile is, or the simplicity of her outfit compared to everyone else. She still looks like she stepped straight out of a magazine, but the oversize blazer and jeans combo is much easier for my brain to comprehend than some of these other outfits. "I'm the art director here at Bezzels. I'm so excited to have you join our team. Come, come."

I hurry after her as she heads down the hall, smiling and waving at the cubicles we pass. "I have three other designers on my team, who you'll meet later today. They're in a meeting right now. You'll answer to me for the most part, but when I'm busy, you'll be under Aria, our senior graphic designer."

She grabs my wrist and pulls me against the wall as a man and a woman sprint by us with a box full of scraps of fabric.

"Sorry, Selena!" the man calls before they disappear around the corner.

I turn to her with wide eyes, but she looks completely unfazed. "You get used to it. We'll start slow until you get a better grasp for how things run around here. Your desk is this way. You'll find a sheet with all of your logins and passwords there. I'm afraid I don't have too much time for training right now as we're getting close to the deadline for a major campaign, but Heather, one of my other designers, has quite a few tasks she doesn't have the time for and would love to pass them on to you. Ah, here they are."

We pause at a collection of cubicles near the corner as the door to the conference room across from them opens.

"Heather?" calls Selena as people flood into the walkway carrying laptops and folders.

A very tall woman with very black hair and a very deep tan turns to us.

"This is Gracie, our new junior designer."

Heather offers her hand to shake as Selena checks her watch.

"I have a meeting—can you take over showing her around and getting her started?"

Heather bows her head slightly. "Of course."

"I'll swing by again around lunch to see how you're settling in, Gracie!" says Selena as she takes off, walking much faster than she had with me. "Welcome to Bezzels!"

"Come on," says Heather. "Your desk is next to mine."

Mine is entirely plain and devoid of personality, especially in comparison to the ones around me. Just a white L-shaped desk, plain black monitor, and a sheet of paper beside the keyboard with Selena's welcome instructions.

Heather's is absolutely covered in plants, bright pink sticky notes, and random trinkets.

"Are you from the Midwest?" she asks suddenly.

I stare at her. "I—no. Why?"

She shrugs one shoulder and boots up her computer.

Do I give off Midwest vibes? What does that even mean?

"You should familiarize yourself with our social media accounts today. Take a look at what we've done in the past, our captions, engagement. I'll email you a list of some upcoming announcements, sales, and whatnot, and you can draft some sample captions and concepts. If I like any of them, I'll give you the go-ahead to make the posts. It'll be good practice, and if they're no good, it'll help teach you what we're looking for instead."

Draft concepts.

If I like them.

Practice.

This is fine. Of course I'm not going to hit the ground running on the first day. Learn the ropes. Pay my dues.

It's a bit of whiplash coming from Liam's shop where I started everything from scratch, had complete creative control, and made all of the decisions myself. I can't help but feel like I'm taking a dozen steps backward.

But this is fine. It's just going to be an adjustment. And once I show them what I can do, hopefully the training wheels won't last for long.

The training wheels have been surgically attached to my ass.

I barely see Selena for the rest of the week, and the tasks

Heather gives me never take me more than an hour or two. Which leaves me with six or so hours a day sitting at my desk doing…nothing.

I comb through every single thing the company has ever posted on social media, dissect every caption, every hashtag, every inch of the website, every competitor, every name and role at the company. I even end up Facebook stalking some of my coworkers.

By Thursday, I start making my concept emails more detailed, throwing in more ideas, taking more time to create the mock-ups so they look closer to finished products.

They never use anything I make.

The highlight of the week is when they use a minor color correction I made for a social post.

By Friday, I find myself scrolling through the accounts for Liam's shop.

He's gotten better about posting things himself—mostly before and afters of recent tattoos, a new timelapse video of him working. The number of reviews for the shop online have skyrocketed, and pretty much any video where he shows his face gets ten thousand or more views, easily.

I hope it's enough.

"Thank God it's Friday, right?" says Waverly, the third member of Selena's design team.

"Thirty minutes until happy hour ends." Aria throws her bag over her shoulder as she stands from the cubicle across from mine. "You in, Heather?"

"Obviously." She finishes reapplying her lip gloss and fussing with her bangs, and there's a moment of awkward silence as three pairs of eyes turn to me. I can practically see the gears turning in their brains, debating whether they should invite me.

I pretend to be utterly enthralled with packing my bag.

"Gracie," Heather finally says. "Do you drink?"

I freeze. "I—yeah."

She cocks her head as she considers me. "We're heading to Smith's around the corner."

I think that's as close to an invitation as I'm going to get.

I've passed this bar every night this week on my walk home but never ventured inside. It's about as colorful as the office with pink decorations and disco balls dangling from the ceiling. The sight sends a weird pang through my stomach. It looks like something Christine would do. The girls head for a small booth in the back corner in what's clearly a routine for them.

"I'll grab the drinks," announces Aria. She pauses, eyes cutting to me.

"Whatever you guys are having. Do you need help carrying them all?"

She waves me off and disappears into the crowd that seems to get thicker by the minute. It's a mostly women crowd, unsurprisingly, given the décor.

Heather and Waverly slide into the booth side, and I take the chair across from them. The music overhead is so loud I can barely hear myself think, let alone whatever the two of them are saying. They don't seem to mind. They lean back and forth, yelling into each other's ears and laughing.

I subtly check the time on my phone. Liam and I have been FaceTiming every night at seven. It's become a routine—leave work, grab dinner on my walk home, do some yoga as I watch the sunset through my window, then end the night talking with him, sometimes for hours. Honestly, it's the part of my day I most look forward to.

"Here we are." Aria appears through the crowd with four beers balanced against her chest. I jump up to help her set them on the table while trying not to let my disgust show on my face. I don't know why I assumed they'd get cocktails or something. I've never met a beer I liked.

"I have some cash," I say, but Aria waves me off and holds her beer up for a toast. "To Gracie's first week!"

"Gracie!" the other girls chorus.

I smile and take a sip of mine. Yep, just as bad as I'd thought it'd be.

Aria leans across the table and says something to Heather I can't hear. My face starts to hurt around my smile as I shift my weight and wonder how early would be acceptable to leave.

Liam says I should spread my wings, lean into all of the new experiences I have available to me now.

But this…this isn't fun. It's loud and bright and I can't hear anything anyone is saying. My drink tastes bad, my feet hurt from being in these shoes all day, and I'm starting to annoy myself with all of my internal complaining.

Maybe I'm not giving it a fair chance. Of course I'm uncomfortable being around girls who already know each other, not to mention they're all at least five years older than me. But I was uncomfortable at first around all of the people I now consider friends too. I force down a big mouthful of beer and lean forward, trying to hear some of the conversation.

Waverly's eyes flick to me and she tilts her head to the side. "Where are you from again, Gracie? Did you grow up in PA?"

"Jersey."

"Ah." She nods slowly in a *that makes sense* way.

Heather narrows her eyes thoughtfully. "What's your sign?"

Aria snorts out a laugh. "Heather's God is astrology."

Heather shrugs.

"Um, I'm a Cancer."

"June or July?"

"July."

Her eyes light up, and she leans her forearms on the table. "Oh my God, I'm so sorry. No wonder. You must feel so uncomfortable with us. We're all fire signs." She wags a finger between herself and Waverly. "Sagittarians." She points at Aria. "Aries."

Aria rolls her eyes. "Aria the Aries. I know, it's tragic."

"Do you know much about astrology?" asks Waverly.

I shake my head.

Heather smiles warmly and pats my hand. "Fear not, little water sign. We'll adopt you."

"You know, every single one of us originally started out in your job," says Waverly.

"She means to say we all know it kind of sucks," says Heather.

Waverly swats her arm. "Don't be a bitch."

"I meant that in a comforting, comradery way!"

My head whips back and forth with each volley of the conversation, but as quickly as the focus had shifted to me, Heather and Waverly turn to each other and launch into a different conversation too low for me to hear over the music. It happens so fast, I feel kind of dizzy.

Aria bumps her shoulder against mine. "Welcome to the shitshow."

LIAM

Christine and I don't talk much. Especially not one-on-one. The few times she *has* called, it's been about Casey.

And it's never been good.

So seeing three missed calls and a voicemail from her today was nearly enough to give me a heart attack.

I pull into the driveway of the address she sent me—one of the little Victorian houses on Main Street that has been converted into a business. A divorce law office, by the looks of the sign.

Christine and my dad are standing near the front porch yelling at each other, and Casey is sitting on the ground behind his mom with tears streaming down his face.

I throw the truck's door open and jump out.

"How could you not talk to me about it first?" Christine demands. "We don't have anyone else—"

"She needed to go!" my dad yells. "If she can't handle a single six-year-old, we're better off!"

"It wasn't her fault!"

"Liam!" Casey jumps up when he sees me. He lunges in for a hug, then practically collapses in my arms until I'm the only thing holding him up. His little face is bright red and puffy like the crying has been going on for a good long while now.

"Hey, bud," I say.

Christine and my dad stop, apparently just noticing me.

"Finally," Dad mutters, then turns and heads into the house without another word.

Christine is practically vibrating with anger, but she takes a deep breath before turning to me with a small smile. "*Thank you. I'm so sorry—*"

"Don't mention it. I was already done with clients for the day anyway."

She flicks her wrist and rubs her eyes. "He fired Casey's nanny this morning, and I couldn't get a hold of anyone else, and—" She glances at Casey, her face falling, and lowers her voice. "You really seem to be the only one he wants around right now anyway. I don't think this will take longer than an hour..."

I wave her off. "Don't worry about it. We can find something to do. Right, Case?"

She nods a few too many times and shoves her blond hair behind her ears. Now that I'm looking at it, I realize how messy and tangled it is, how wrinkled her dress is, how dark the bags beneath her eyes are. I don't think I've ever seen her like this.

"Thank you, Liam." She squeezes my shoulder and turns for the door. "I'll text you when we're done?"

"No!" Casey latches on to her leg before she can go inside, big, fat tears streaming down his cheeks. "Don't leave. Please."

Christine sighs and crouches down to his level. "I won't be gone long, I promise. You're just going to hang out with Liam for a little bit. Doesn't that sound like fun? Then you and I can do whatever you want for the rest of the day."

He sniffles but still doesn't let go of her leg. "You promise?"

She gives him a serious nod. "I promise."

"How about the arcade, Case?" I offer. "What do you think?"

That gets a smile out of him.

The door opens, and a woman in a crisp black suit steps one foot onto the porch. "Christine." She glances at her watch. "We really need to get started."

"I'm coming!" After giving Casey a quick hug, Christine stands and dusts her hands off on her dress. If I didn't know any better, I'd swear her eyes looked a little misty too.

"Go on." I grab Casey's hand. "We're good here."

Casey tucks himself against my leg and waves goodbye to his mom.

She gives him a watery smile before steeling herself with a breath and heading inside.

I don't think I'll ever be able to pry Casey off this motorcycle. I have no idea if this game has an age limit—his little feet can't reach the footrests, and I had to pick him up to help him get on it—but he's somehow still kicking my ass.

We don't talk for the first game, or the second, but I wait for him to come to me. It pays off because after the third race when I suggest taking a break to get some water ice, we camp out on the bench outside the arcade, and he turns to me.

"Dad made Nanny Dina leave."

"Did you like her?"

He nods, tears welling up in his eyes again. "She was the best at playing dinosaurs. She got in trouble because I was hiding and she couldn't find me. I didn't mean to get her in trouble. They were just yelling a lot, and I don't like it when they yell."

I sigh and wrap my arm around his shoulders. "I know. It's not your fault, Casey. Dad shouldn't have done that."

"But he's a grown-up."

"Sometimes grown-ups mess up too."

"Ow! Freezy-head." He smacks his hand against his forehead, his spoon sticking out of his mouth.

I chuckle and pull it out. "Yeah, doofus, you can't eat it all at once."

Undeterred, after a few seconds, he resumes shoveling it in his mouth.

I lean back against the bench and look out at the waves. The beach is quiet with only a few people lying out on towels. There's a girl a few yards away on her front with her book propped in the sand.

My stomach twists at the sight, and I check my watch. Gracie and I are supposed to FaceTime in an hour. She's only been gone a week, but her absence is already glaringly obvious.

It was obvious when I swung by Milano's and had to correct the barista that I was ordering only one coffee. It was obvious when I opened the shop and the front desk was empty and there was no bike out front. It was obvious every time I looked up from work, expecting to see her smile or a flash of her hair.

I'm trying to give her space to grow into this new phase of her life, but all I want to do is jump in the car and drive out there so I can see her face light up about how amazing her new job is in person.

At least I know she hasn't been alone all week. Her parents went up to visit her one day, and she was telling me about her plans to get lunch with her friend Carson this weekend. And I'm sure Leo's itching to get back up there too.

Still no word from Christine though, so it's looking like I won't even be able to make our call. I've been looking forward to it all day.

Casey and I head back into the arcade once we've finished our water ice. We do a lap and try every game he can reach—most of them are too big for him—then he starts pointing out which ones he wants me to do to win more tickets. I dutifully play the basketball, Whac-A-Mole, and Skee-Ball machines until he's able to afford the ugliest stuffed sea lion I've ever seen. Its eyes are tiny, and the stringy white whiskers are... something else. But Casey jumps up and down with excitement as the worker behind the counter hands it over, then clutches it to his chest like it's now his most prized possession.

By the time Christine texts me, it's dark outside, and she comes to meet us at the arcade to pick Casey up.

"Thank you again, truly." She sighs as she helps Casey into his car seat, his eyes already half-closed. I'm pretty sure he passes out before she closes the door behind him, that sea lion tucked tightly beneath his chin.

"It was no problem." I turn for my truck, but she stops me.

"Liam..."

I tuck my hands in my pockets and wait.

"I just wanted to say I'm sorry again, about how the whole thing with Hailey and True Sweets went down."

I wave her off. "Don't worry about it—"

"No, no, I do. Especially after what Asher told me. I tried to talk them out of moving forward with her after that meeting, but as you can probably imagine, my vote didn't get too far."

I shake my head, not sure I heard her right. What could Asher possibly have told her? "Asher?"

Her eyes flick between mine, and her brow furrows. "He said…well, he said she was pretty abusive."

I rock back on my heels. I *never* talked to Asher about Hailey.

She gives me a small smile. "I think he's more observant than people give him credit for."

I glance at Casey through the window. His head is lolled back and mouth wide open as he sleeps.

Christine sighs. "Look, Liam, I know you don't like me, so my opinion won't count for much, but—"

My eyes snap back to her. "That's not true."

She raises a single eyebrow.

"Okay, so it *was* true. I didn't like you at first. But I didn't know you. And it had a lot more to do with my dad than you."

She smirks. "My point is, my mom had me when she was a teenager, and my dad left before my first birthday. My grandparents on both sides have pretended I don't exist all my life. And when I left home at sixteen, my mom didn't even try to stop me. So shitty families? I get it."

I stare at her for a second, the image I'd had of her all this time crumbling. Her sunny disposition, always smiling, always jumping in to help—always trying a little too hard, if you asked me. The clothes and the parties and the way she never seemed to have a care in the world. I guess I assumed she'd always been that way.

"I had no idea," I murmur.

She gives me a wry smile. "It's not exactly something I advertise. My point is, yours? They may do a shit job of showing it, but they *do* love you and want you around. That's not nothing."

I have to resist the urge to scoff. *Sure, they want me around. As long as I'm in a tie, hide the tattoos and piercings, and pretend to give a fuck about so-and-so's latest golf game or new boat or trip to Ibiza.*

"The version of me they want around doesn't exist," I mutter.

She tilts her head to the side and nods. "Your dad, yeah. Taylor and Makayla, maybe. But not me and Casey. And not Asher. It doesn't have to be all or nothing." She laughs at whatever look is on my face. "Ash is a pain in the ass, but he's young. And can you blame him? He grew up in that house too. He was even younger than you when your mom died. I think he's just lost, Liam. And we both know your dad shipping him off to rehab so he doesn't have to deal with it isn't going to help him. I guess what I'm saying is...maybe you should give him more of a chance. He looks up to you."

I glance at Casey again, but this time, I see Asher at that age sitting in the car seat next to me as my mom drove us to school. I was in fifth grade when he was in second, so it was one of the rare times we overlapped and went to the same school. Taylor had already moved on to middle school, so naturally, he was too cool to be seen with us. Makayla was already in high school, which might as well have been a different planet. For a while there, it was Asher and me against the rest of the world.

I'm not sure when that changed.

Maybe I was unfair to him. Resenting him because the more he grew up, the more he fit into the family, when the opposite was happening to me. Taylor and Makayla always felt apart, but watching Asher join them...I guess it felt like a betrayal, in a way.

Maybe he was just trying to survive being a Brooks too.

I say nothing. I don't know if I could if I tried.

Christine shrugs and opens her car door. "Just something to think about. Thank you again for the help."

"Hey, Christine—"

She pauses.

"I don't know if I ever properly thanked you for getting Michael Cushing not to press charges. But...thank you."

She smiles. "Whether I'm married to your dad or not, we're family. That means something to me."

I smile back and watch until her brake lights disappear around the corner.

Chapter Forty-Six

GRACIE

Liam: I'm so sorry. Something came up with Casey. I won't make it for 7. Can we try closer to 9?

I hesitate at the outskirts of the park with my store-bought sandwich. So much for hurrying home. Not that I would've stayed longer otherwise. Less than an hour there and I still left the bar feeling like I needed a nap. I backtrack through the path until I come across an empty bench, sit, and tear open my clearance bin dinner.

We're still hanging on to those long days of summer, so the sun hasn't quite set yet, casting a golden tint to the surrounding park. The paths are full of people heading home from work, jogging, or walking their dogs. I close my eyes for a moment and breathe in the fresh air. It's not quite as peaceful as I'd been hoping for with cars honking and music from the surrounding bars in the background.

I wanted this. More than anything, I wanted this, I remind myself.

I worked so hard to be here. I spent nights crying into my pillow when I thought this day wouldn't come.

Across the street, I catch sight of a man rolling by on a skateboard.

My stomach twists.

All I can think about is the summer. Sitting in coffee shops, on the beach, the skatepark, the shop. Laughing with Carson or Liam or Leo, working day and night because I so badly wanted to see the shop improve. Because it felt like that mattered. Like everything I was doing had the potential to make a difference.

I glance around the park, at all the strangers passing by, people I'll probably never see again and whose names I'll never know. And I desperately try to remember when it was that I decided I wanted this. And why.

When nine o'clock rolls around and I still haven't heard from Liam, I FaceTime Marti instead. The odds of her being available on a Friday night are slim, but at least since she's on the West Coast, it's only six o'clock for her.

"Gracieee!" Marti squeals as her face blurs across the screen. She sets the phone up in what seems to be her bathroom, her hair half pinned up like she was in the middle of straightening it. Rap music blares somewhere in the background, and she shouts over it for her speaker to pause. "I'm so glad you called! I was wondering how your first week in the big city went." She fishes around in a makeup bag on the counter until she finds a brush, then disappears from view as she leans closer to the mirror.

"Oh, you're busy. This can wait."

"No—no!" She snatches the phone off the counter, a close-up of her face abruptly coming into view. "I wanted to talk to you anyway! I have *newsss*."

"Oh yeah?"

"Yes!" she squeals and sets the phone down, leaving me to stare at her ceiling. She snatches me up again just as quickly, and I have to look away from the screen for a moment, starting to get motion sick. "Gracie, I got the part!"

"I—*what?*"

"Yes!" she screams. "I just got the call from my agent like thirty minutes ago. I. Got. The. Part! I'm screaming. I'm dying. I'm levitating. I'm dreaming, right? This isn't real."

"Oh my God, Marti, that's amazing! I'm so happy for you!"

"I really thought I didn't stand a chance," she gushes, props the phone up, and goes to town blending the blush on her cheeks. "So I wasn't getting my hopes up. My agent was a little more optimistic since they got the big name for the male lead, so they had a little more leeway with my part, but I didn't think they'd cast a *nobody*."

I roll my eyes. "You're not a nobody."

"You know what I mean." She drops the brush onto the counter and leans her face close with a goofy smile. "I don't know, Gracie, I just really feel like this is going to be my big break, you know? If this goes well, this could open so many doors for me. I'm just—I'm so—" Tears fill her eyes. "Ugh." She looks up and fans her face with both hands. "I'm going to ruin my makeup!"

"So are you going out tonight to celebrate?"

"You bet your ass I am! I want to stay out until the sun comes up. Ugh, I wish you and the girls were here too. You'd love LA..." She grimaces. "Okay, you'd hate it. But *I* would love having you here."

"So what's next? What happens now?"

"I don't have all the details yet, but it sounds like it's going to be a *lot*. Rehearsals, trainings, choreographing, table reads. It sounds like we'll be jumping right into prep here pretty soon."

"God, Marti, I'm, like, in shock. This is so amazing."

"I know, me too!" She does a little dance as she sifts through her lip gloss options, then pauses. "Wait, you called me. What's up? Tell me alllll about the new job!"

"Oh. Um. Great. Everything's great. I actually just went out with some coworkers for drinks."

"Oh my God, that's *great*. I'm so happy for you. So you guys get along well?"

"I—yeah, yeah." I cringe at the way my voice shoots up an octave. "They're very…passionate, but nice. More welcoming than I was expecting."

"And how's the new apartment? It must be so nice being out of the basement, right?"

A weird longing settles into the pit of my stomach, but I clear any trace of it from my face by the time Marti looks back at the screen.

"Yeah. The building is nice. It feels really safe, and it's close to work, so I've been walking there every day."

"Ugh. A dream. LA is so *not* walkable."

A dream.

"Wow, I love this for us." Marti beams. "Everything's working out for all of us right now, isn't it?"

I don't correct her. How can I? Especially not today, the day she got the most amazing news of her life. She doesn't need my pity party energy right now.

"Well, have fun tonight!"

"Tell Liam I said hi!" She air kisses the camera and waves before hanging up.

The following silence rings in my ears.

I didn't lie to Marti. I *am* happy for her. Of course I am.

But that conversation did the opposite of make me feel better.

Another text from Liam waits in my notifications, apologizing that he's still too busy and he'll call me tomorrow instead.

I change into one of his T-shirts that still smells like him and shuffle my way to the bed. Hugging a pillow to my chest, I curl into a ball on my side and look out at the city below. As the tears roll down my face, I don't bother trying to stop them. I just let them flow on and on.

It'll get better. Eventually, it will.

It has to.

Chapter Forty-Seven

GRACIE

Weeks pass, and my days start to feel more like a routine. The girls are nice in the office, but I decline the next time they invite me to happy hour, then they don't ask again. The only people I've run into in my building so far have been much older than me. I'll get an occasional smile in the elevator, but everyone for the most part minds their own business.

The check-in calls and texts from family and friends die down as the novelty wears off. All except Liam. Talking to him every day is one thing I can count on.

But other than driving up to see me the first weekend I was here, I haven't seen him in person. He's had a lot going on with his family, so it seemed even if I made the trip out there, it wouldn't have been a good time.

But now as my third weekend in a row with no plans rolls around, I throw together an overnight bag, climb in the car, and drive.

"Oh my God, Gracie! What a surprise!"

"Hey, Mom."

She opens the door wider and waves impatiently for me to come inside, her eyes on the duffel bag in my hand.

"I hope this isn't a bad time."

"Of course not! Your father is at the grocery store. I'm just baking some banana bread."

"So *that's* what smells so good in here."

She beams, and I follow her to the kitchen. The counter is covered in junk, as usual, and I grab a bar stool and start clearing myself a little area.

"So are you just back for the weekend?" she asks lightly.

My hands freeze around a pile of mail. I have no idea why *that's* what tipped me over the edge. I thought I might cry it out on the drive over here, but the hour and a half passed in a daze, like my body was moving on autopilot and I was barely conscious the entire time. But now with my mother staring at me, surrounded by the house I grew up in and the comforting smell of my favorite treat, my lower lip trembles.

Mom turns when I don't respond, her eyes going wide when she sees my face. "Oh, honey, what's wrong?"

I laugh. I cover my face with my hands and *laugh*, softly at first, then it turns into something of a sob, then it rises a few octaves and borders on hysterical.

Mom drifts toward me. "Gracie…"

"Everything," I say around a gasp. "Absolutely everything is wrong, Mom."

We end up at the kitchen table, and she makes me a hot chocolate to go with my banana bread, just like when I was a kid. A graveyard of used tissues surrounds us as I recount the past few weeks and talk in circles trying to explain what the hell is going on with me.

When I'm done, the concern has faded from her eyes, like she's...relieved?

"You want my honest advice?" she says.

"Of course."

She tilts her head back and forth like she's arguing with herself over her next words. "I think you should break up with Liam."

"I—*what*? Wh-why?"

She shows me her palms in a *what can I say?* gesture. "I don't think you're giving this new chapter a fair chance. And I don't see how you can like this. If you had been in a relationship before you'd gone off to college, I would've given the same advice. I think you need a truly clean slate. How can you really say you gave this a fair shot when you're always wondering when you'll talk to him next, or waiting for him to call, or coming home as much as you can to see him? You're living your life with one foot in the past, one in the present. And Liam—I love him, I really do—but he is never going to leave this town. And I think deep down, you know that. So you feel like you can't leave. Like you can't find somewhere new to love, because if you do, there's no way the two of you can work. Because he won't follow you. He might wait around for you to come back, but he won't move forward into this new phase of your life with you. So you feel like you can't move into it either."

"You think he's holding me back," I whisper.

The smile she gives me is the saddest thing I've ever seen. "I do. If you want to come back here, Gracie, by all means, you know how much I would love to have you close. But I want to make sure you're making that decision for you. And that's an impossible choice to make if you don't know what other options are out there—if you're not in a place to give those other options a fair shot. I want you to be the happiest you can be, my love. I don't want you to look back on this ten years from now and wish you'd seen it through."

I scrunch my nose against the burning sensation as tears threaten to boil over again. I try to picture what she's saying. But Liam is one of the few things in my life that feels *right*. How could cutting out the one thing that's making me happy help?

"I love him," I choke out.

She grasps both of my hands in hers. "I know you do. But loving him is not a replacement for loving your life. You're still gonna have to work that one out on your own. He makes you happy. Anyone can see that. But he can't be the only thing that does."

Chapter Forty-Eight

GRACIE

I don't have a plan for what to say when I show up at Liam's door. Don't have any plan at all, really.

"*Gracie?* I—what are you doing here? I didn't know you were coming to town—" Liam stops short when he opens the door and his gaze falls on my face. Wordlessly, he steps aside so I can pass.

"I'm sorry if this is a bad time. I know you've had a lot going on."

"No, no. It's fine. I'm sorry I've been so busy. Here, sit down."

I take the kitchen chair he pulls out, a wave of déjà vu rolling over me from the conversation I had an hour ago.

"Is everything okay?" I ask.

He sighs as he takes the seat across from me. "Casey's been getting into some trouble."

"*Casey?*" Granted, I don't know the kid well, but he didn't seem like the troublemaking type.

Liam pinches the bridge of his nose. "Yeah. And my dad has no patience for it, as you can imagine, and Christine is at her wit's end with my dad. Anyway. What's going on with you? Is everything okay?"

I thought I'd cried myself out at my mom's, that it wouldn't be physically possible for me to do it anymore, and yet...

Liam's eyes widen, and he pulls his chair around so he's beside me.

"I think I made a mistake with this job," I whisper. "I feel like I'm playing dress up in someone else's life. And I thought at first it was just new and I needed to give it time for it to start to feel like home. And I have. I've tried. But it doesn't feel right... But if it's not this, then I don't know. I don't know what I want. I don't know what to do. I went to talk to my mom today."

"Okay." He rubs his thumb over my knee. "What did she say?"

I throw my hands up. "That I'm not giving it a fair chance. That I went into this with one foot already out the door because of..."

"Because of what?"

My shoulders slump. "Because of you."

He leans back in his chair, his eyes searching my face. "Did you... Did you come here to break up with me?"

"No!" The tears break free onto my cheeks. "I mean, I don't —I don't know. I don't want to. But what if she's right?"

He stares at me for a long moment, and the look on his face gives nothing away. I have no idea what he's thinking.

"You said the city doesn't feel right, so then tell me what does."

I open my mouth, but nothing comes out.

"Come on. You have things that feel right. No matter how small."

I swipe the tears from my face with the back of my hand

and flick my wrist. "The water. Being close to the water. The ocean, I miss it."

He leans closer, his gaze boring into mine. "What else?"

I shake my head.

"You know, I can probably think of a few things," he says. "Your books. Being a vegetarian. Photography. You know what else I think feels right to you? Us. And I think that scares you. I know it scares the hell out of me."

I bite my lip, and he moves closer.

"Tell me what you want, Gracie," he says lowly. "Not what you think you're supposed to want, not what everyone says you should want. What do *you* want, Gracie?"

I throw my hands up, hot, frustrated tears filling my eyes. "I don't know."

"I don't buy that. I think you do know. What do you want?"

"I don't know!" I repeat, louder this time, but Liam doesn't back off. He leans in closer.

"What do you want?" he pushes. "Come on, Gracie. Stop overthinking every little thing. Stop trying to find the perfect answer. The first thing that pops into your head—what do you want?"

"I want to come home," I croak, and as soon as the words hit the air, it's like all of the tension in my shoulders deflates. "I want to come home," I repeat in a whisper. "But if I do, I'll feel like I failed." I roll my eyes against the tears and the cracks in my voice. "Again."

And Liam, like a complete psychopath, as he watches me crumble into a million pathetic pieces at his feet, smiles.

"Why are you smiling?" I demand.

"Because I'm a selfish bastard and I want you here, but also because I can tell you meant that. So now all that's left to do is for us to find a way for you to get what you want without you feeling like you failed. We're going to work this out. You and me. So break it down for me. You don't like the job."

"I hate it," I whisper.

He nods thoughtfully. "What would make you like it? What is it missing?"

"It feels like...filler. Like filling time just for the sake of it. Wasting time. I feel like I could be doing so much more. Even the small tasks they occasionally throw my way feel so...lifeless. Like I can't remember why I enjoyed designing in the first place anymore."

"But you didn't feel that way working for me?"

"Liam," I sigh.

He holds up a hand. "I'm not trying to get you to come back to the shop. I'm trying to understand why it's different."

I pause, turning the words over in my head. Why *is* it different?

"I guess when I look around at other people in the company —the people higher up than me, the jobs I could have one day if I stick it out and pay my dues—there isn't a single job there that I want. I think I'd have the same complaints."

He runs his thumb over the back of my hand. "Is it the company? Do you think you'd like it somewhere else if you were more passionate about what they were selling?"

"I don't think so."

A slow smile stretches across his face as he looks at me.

"What?"

"Come on," he murmurs. "You have to see the answer. It's right there in front of you."

I frown.

"You liked working at the shop because you had free rein," he says slowly. "You were never waiting around for approval or having to clear your ideas. You just got to jump in, get your hands dirty, and figure out what worked on your own."

Well, yeah. But I don't see how that—

"Gracie." He chuckles and smooths his thumb over the tension between my eyebrows. "It's not that you don't like design anymore. You don't like working for someone else."

I lean back. Cross my arms. Uncross them. Lean forward.

"Well fuck," I breathe.

That's the opposite of an easy fix. That's every plan I've ever had for myself, every possible version of my future I've pictured gone up in smoke.

But it's also the first time I've felt like I could breathe in over a month.

Because I could do it. I know immediately that I can. That I'd like it.

But no more fixed salary, job security, health insurance— my head starts to pound as each new consequence clicks into place.

Liam smirks as I refocus on his face. "Welcome to my world."

But even with how much that makes sense...

"I can't quit," I murmur. "I can't come back here and move in with Leo or my parents again. I can't feel like I'm starting from scratch. I need to feel like I've—I don't know. Like I've progressed? Like I can support myself now? I just don't want to jump the gun, you know?"

Maybe if I'd saved what I made from the shop this summer things would be different. It would be enough to coast along for a few months, at least. But nearly all of it went toward paying off my student loans. And who knows how long getting a new business off the ground and consistently bringing in enough income could take me?

"You know the shop's doors are always open. You want your job back, you just say the word. Or I could be your first client, if you want to look at it that way."

"I appreciate that. But I…" I trail off, not sure how to put it into words. I need to feel like I did this myself. And depending financially on a boyfriend, no matter how qualified Liam sees me as, it just wouldn't feel good. And if I leave Bezzels now, no matter the circumstances, it'll feel like giving up. The job itself might be a bad fit, but the city…I really don't feel like I've given it a fair chance yet. I settle on: "I need to see this through."

He rolls his lips together and nods slowly. "So you're not coming home."

"Not yet." I take his hands in mine and squeeze. "Thank you for talking this through with me. It's given me a lot to think about."

His eyes search mine. "And us?"

As much as I want to pretend otherwise, my mom was right. I've been leaning on the idea of a relationship being the one thing that would make me happy for so long. And it *does* make me happy. Liam makes me so unbelievably happy. But I need to find a way to feel that on my own too.

"I don't want to break up, but I think I need some time to figure out how to stand on my own two feet. I want to *want* to be with you. Not *need* to be."

He takes a deep breath, that unreadable look still on his face. "So you want to take a break?"

I chew on my lip, hoping he can see in my eyes how sorry I am, how much I know I'm not being fair to him. It feels cruel, even, knowing what happened with him and Hailey.

"I'm sorry to even ask. I know it's unfair, and I can't expect you to just wait for me—"

He pulls me into his chest and kisses the top of my head. "How long?"

"You mean…you'd…"

"Of course I'm going to fucking do it, Gracie. I don't like it. I don't want to be apart from you. But I understand what you're saying. If this is what you need, of course I'm going to give it to you. I'd give you anything you asked for. So how long?"

My lower lip wobbles, and I suck in a shaky breath. "A few months, I think."

He runs his hand up and down my back. "So what does this mean? No contact at all?"

I want to say no, that checking in with each other here and there would be fine, but I know myself too well. If there's even a chance I'll hear from him, some part of me will be waiting for it, hoping for it, lunging for my phone at every notification, devastated when it isn't him. It'll feel like a holding pattern—and how is that any different than the way things are now? I'm not capable of going back to being friends or whatever we were before. I wish I was, but I'm not.

"I think that would be best," I whisper.

He doesn't say anything for what feels like a long time. Maybe he knows once this conversation is over, I'm going to leave, and he's not any more ready to let go of me than I am of him.

Finally, he says, "I'm guessing you'll be home for Thanksgiving? So we'll talk then?"

Nearly three months from now.

Three months of not seeing him, hearing his voice, feeling his touch. Three months of no calls, no texts, no inside jokes, no random pictures of his day.

Three months to pull myself out of this hole and stop feeling so damn sorry for myself.

I close my eyes and tighten my arms around his waist. "Okay."

Chapter Forty-Nine

GRACIE

I give myself a weekend. One weekend. Where I do little else but mourn and sulk and shuffle around my apartment wearing Liam's clothes and going through a box of tissues a day. We agreed to no contact, but I find myself constantly checking my phone just in case he reached out all the same. I have to delete our text conversations entirely to force myself to stop rereading them.

And I wonder, at least a dozen times a day, if I've made a huge mistake. If I'm taking the hard route of my life for no reason.

I could've stayed with Liam. I could've stayed in Sweetspire. Maybe forever. I could've let Liam continue to finance my life and let Leo put a roof over my head.

I could've called it quits the second this new life didn't turn out to be as shiny as it was in my daydreams.

And maybe it would've been enough. Maybe the happiness would've lasted.

But I don't know if I'd ever be able to meet my eyes in the mirror if I did.

So even though my face is puffy and red from crying and I only got a handful of hours of sleep, on Monday morning, I roll myself out of bed, put on the cutest dress I can find, and stop to grab a fancy coffee on my way to work.

The day passes mostly the same as every one that came before it—minimal mind-numbing projects slid my way and an ungodly amount of time to fill on my own.

But today, I look at it differently. Today, I use that time to plan. And research. And prepare.

Luckily, my website and portfolio are already in great shape since I worked on them so much this summer. But instead of acting as a digital résumé, I'll need to tweak things now to look like a business. A business I don't even have a name for—or frankly, any idea how to run. That, I guess, is as good a place as any to start my research.

I wrap up the small tasks Heather and Aria assigned me by noon. The floor mostly clears out as people take their breaks, leaving me alone in what I've come to think of as the design corner. I carry my microwave lunch to my desk to hunker down. I've had virtually no appetite since I returned to the city, but I'm determined to force at least a few bites down. Even though it makes me feel a bit silly, I type *how to start a business* into the search bar.

I ignore the slight pang in my stomach as it occurs to me I could've asked Liam for help.

But then again, he had to figure all this out at some point too. If he could do it, so can I.

I think the hardest part is going to be finding clients in the first place. And if I want to grow relatively quickly, I might need to seek them out myself.

I open a new tab to search for small businesses in the area.

"Oh, hi!"

I blink, my eyes burning from staring at the screen. A girl

who looks about my age in hot pink trousers and a matching waistcoat stands a few feet away, holding some pasta in a Tupperware bowl.

She smiles when I meet her eyes, exposing the rows of silver braces on her teeth. "You're new!"

"Um, yeah." I hop up to offer her a handshake. "I started a few weeks ago. I'm Gracie."

She shakes my hand, the warmth in her smile never wavering. "I'm Sloane. I'm over in accounting. I'm new too. Been here about a month."

"Oh, cool. Nice to meet you. I love your outfit."

"Thank you! I just got it from this thrift shop a few blocks from here. I *love* your dress too. The little bows on the sleeves are so cute. Do you thrift at all?"

I shrug. "I've never really tried it. I'm from a pretty small town. Didn't have a lot of store options."

"Oh my God. I'll have to take you then! They had so much stuff there that looks like it would be your style."

She says it so confidently, as if we're already friends. Compared to my happy hour attempts, a thrift store sounds a lot more my speed. "That would be great."

Voices carry through the halls as people filter in from their break. Sloane smiles and steps back to let a group pass her. She points at me before waving and heading toward her desk. "I'll come find you later!"

I smile and wave. When I return my gaze to my computer, I find myself fighting the sudden urge to cry. Not about Liam or this job or any of that. Maybe it's small, and maybe I'm being ridiculous, but I can't help but feel like this was the universe trying to give me a sign that everything's going to be okay after all.

Chapter Fifty

GRACIE—THREE MONTHS LATER

Well, it's finally time.

I pushed it off for as long as I could, but there is no way I'm hitting the running trail out there today with snow flurries, wind, and twenty-degree weather.

It's a little before 5:00 AM when I step into the apartment gym. I stifle a yawn as I grab a treadmill in the corner. One other person is on the opposite side of the small space doing dynamic warmup moves. I've seen her in here a few times when I've come at night for the weight section.

She smiles when I meet her eyes in the mirror, and I offer a smile back before increasing the treadmill speed to my warmup pace. It's taken me a few months, but I've managed to get my miles under eight minutes for my longer runs.

Can't wait to see Leo's face when I beat him for the first time ever at the family turkey trot this year. I'll never be able to do the distances he can, but he's never been particularly fast.

By the time I'm showered and ready for the day, it's nearly seven. I pack up my work bags, throw on a few extra layers to fight the cold, then brace myself for my walk to the coffee shop halfway between my apartment and Bezzels.

"Hey, Gracie," says Kayla, the barista, as I step through the door and shake off the snow clinging to my jacket. "Usual?"

I blow on my hands as I approach the counter, trying to thaw them out. "Make it hot today, please."

It's a lot quieter in here today—maybe people heading out of the city early for the holidays. Or maybe their companies were a little more generous giving them the entire week off. No such luck for me.

I smile and drop some change into the tip jar as Kayla hands me my coffee, then slide into my usual table in the back corner, which is, thankfully, as far from the cold draft of the door as possible.

One by one, I pull my things out of my bag and set them on the table in my well-practiced routine—laptop, planner, notebook, pens. I set the timer on my phone so I don't spend too much time in one area. I only have about an hour and a half before the day job—no time to get distracted.

I start with checking emails and DMs as usual, replying to current and prospective clients. Considering I just wrapped my largest project I've had to date last week, this doesn't take long. Then I switch over to monitoring my ads, double-checking my calendar, due dates, invoices, and spreadsheets, before using the rest of my time for content creation.

Most of it is for my website and socials, trying to market the business and draw in new clients, but I do have a few lingering client pieces—mostly full-time influencers Marti introduced me to who don't want to edit their own photos or make thumbnails for their videos. Those projects don't pay much, but they don't take much time either, and I'm not in the position to turn anything down right now.

My goal is to transition to mostly working with small businesses. I've only worked with a few so far. Liam's shop, Consign Couture—the thrift shop Sloane introduced me to— and Body by Brittany—a personal trainer in my apartment who wanted to expand to offering online video memberships. But in the meantime, I'll take all the additions to my portfolio and testimonials I can get.

And the extra income. I can't say no to that. It's the only way I can justify these daily overpriced coffees. Nearly every other penny goes toward my student loans and savings until I build a big enough safety net to feel comfortable quitting Bezzels. If I was still making what I was at Liam's, I'd be a lot further along.

My fingers freeze over the keyboard.

It's gotten to the point where I can go hours without thinking about him. Not quite days, but nearly. But sometimes a thought will creep in there and hit me like a punch to the stomach.

My gaze drifts to the date in the corner of the screen. My heart rate kicks up, and it isn't from the caffeine.

"Gracie," calls Kayla.

I blink, the rest of the shop coming into focus, then glance at the timer on my phone.

Shit.

"Thank you!" I wave at her, shove everything into my bag, and hurry down the street for work.

I end up driving to Jersey the morning of Thanksgiving instead of the day before to avoid the snow. Usually we do the turkey trot the morning of, but everyone agreed in the family group chat to push it to Friday since it looked like the storm would pass by then. When I pull into the driveway, I hesitate a moment before getting out, wondering if I somehow managed to end up at the wrong house.

An eerily identical, but clearly not my family's, house.

Festive is not a strong enough word. *Decorated* doesn't begin to cover it.

The house has been *ambushed.*

Autumn leaf garlands are wrapped around the porch railing, and little trios of fake orange and white pumpkins are arranged every few feet. Stained-glass turkeys hang from every single window in the house, along with white and orange twinkly lights.

I didn't even know there were people who decorated for Thanksgiving, but if there are, I know without a shadow of a doubt it's not my family.

I climb out of the car with my store-bought pie and tilt my head to the side, taking in the twinkling acorn-shaped lights surrounding the front door. Where does one procure acorn lights?

Judging by the number of cars in the drive, not everyone is here yet.

At least, there's one noticeable truck missing.

Or is it? Maybe he's not planning on coming at all.

We didn't get into the details of what would happen today, and we haven't exchanged a word since all those months ago. I didn't realize how much I was counting on him being here until that sinking feeling in my stomach hits.

What if he doesn't come?

Am I supposed to reach out?

Will he?

Snapping myself out of it, I hurry and let myself through the door.

The inside was not spared either. Every inch of space is covered in lights, turkeys, acorns, pine cones, pumpkins, and leaves. Even the entryway rug has been replaced with an orange-and-white-checkered runner.

"Mom?" I call.

"Oh, Gracie! Hi, honey! Kitchen!"

The house is about a million degrees, so I shrug off my vest and leave it on the entry bench. I hadn't thought ahead enough for today's outfit, so I'm wearing the same sweater, skirt, and boots combo as last year.

I grimace as I round the corner and take in the kitchen counter. Seems everyone else decided to bring a pie too.

Mom smiles with an oven mitt on each hand. "Oh, that's perfect! We don't have an apple one!"

The decorations continue in here. I'm afraid to look in the dining room.

I eye my mother as she pulls a casserole from the oven. Is this her doing? Some kind of eccentric midlife crisis?

"Okay, place settings are good to go! You did say nine, right?"

The clack of her high heels proceeds her entrance, but then there she is—Liam's stepmom. In my house. On Thanksgiving. Looking like she just stepped out of a Hallmark movie in a burnt orange jumpsuit and wide-brimmed hat.

"Yes, nine!" Mom smiles as she whips off the oven mitts. "Gracie, you've met Christine, right?"

I force my jaw shut. "Uh, yeah."

"I hope you don't mind that Liam let us tag along," says Christine.

My brain doesn't know what word to latch on to first.

Liam.

Us.

So he is coming. I don't know quite what to make of the nerves that buzz around in my stomach like insects at the news.

I do the mental math. Nine people? Mom, Dad, Leo, Keava, and I make five.

Her, Liam, and…

"The house down the street has a blow-up turkey!" Liam's little brother Casey skids around the corner, his socks sliding on the wood floor. He barely acknowledges anyone else in the room, his eyes locked on his mom. "Why didn't we bring one of those?"

Christine pats his head. "Next year."

Ah, so they're responsible for the house looking like a craft store. I should've known.

My eyes dart the way Casey had come, but there's no one else there.

"Christine had a wonderful idea," says Mom, drawing my attention to her. "Everything that's safe for you to eat is on a white plate. The red ones have meat."

I eye the spread covering every inch of the kitchen, my heart warming at the number of white plates. It seems there are two versions of everything.

"Thanks, Mom," I say quietly.

"Oh, I had plenty of help! Now can you start carrying these into the dining room? We're starting in twenty minutes!"

Christine and I get to work laying the dishes along the runner in the center of the table. Every time I head to the kitchen for another plate, by the time I make it back, she's rearranged everything I brought in the previous trip. I glance at her out of the corner of my eye as I set the final bowl of cranberry sauce down.

I've never spent much time around her, and definitely not alone. I don't know if I've ever realized how *young* she is. She looks far too expensive and polished to be in this house. And as far as I know, despite Liam's love for Casey, he and Christine have never been close. So *why*—

"Casey's father and I are getting a divorce," she says without looking at me.

I freeze.

"I don't speak with my family. Casey and I were going to spend today at the hotel we've been living out of, until Liam... well, I hope you don't mind that he invited us."

"Of course not."

The entire house reverberates as the front door bangs open and several sets of feet kick off shoes in the entrance. "We're back! We're back!" calls Leo. "Crisis averted!"

I glance sideways at Christine. "Crisis?"

She smirks. "Your brother forgot the alcohol at home."

Alcohol. Thank God.

"Not sure you have enough there, man."

My body does a full reset at the sound of his voice.

Someone scoffs. "This whole case is just for him." Is that Asher?

"Excuse me," I murmur before hurrying in the opposite direction of the voices and slipping into the bathroom.

The voices continue, muffled behind the door, punctuated with the occasional laugh. My hands tremble as I fill them with water in the sink, focusing on the cold against the inside of my wrists.

I'd be lying if I said I hadn't thought about this day. Dreamed about it.

Had nightmares about it.

Three months is a long time. A lot can happen. A lot can change. I know I've changed.

It's longer than we were together in the first place, though it doesn't feel like it. That summer feels like it lasted forever.

But I'm not naïve. The distance, the time, the no contact—it could have given him clarity. Made him realize he was just swept up in the moment with me.

371

He could have changed his mind by now.

He could have moved on.

And it would be my own damn fault because I asked for this.

I stare at my reflection for a moment, but only a moment, before shoving the door open without giving myself a chance to think about it.

"What is *tofurkey?*" Casey asks.

"Turkey without the turkey," Leo says as he reaches across the table to load his plate with gravy.

Casey's nose scrunches as I pull a piece of the offending dish onto my plate. "Then what is it?"

"Mostly tofu," I say.

His nose scrunches further.

Unsurprisingly, no one else touches the dishes made for me. That is, until Liam clears his throat, rises slightly out of his chair near the opposite end of the table, and slides a piece onto his plate too. Which, now that I've gotten a better look at it, is nearly identical to mine. He hasn't taken any of the regular dishes.

I meet his eyes for the first time tonight as he sits down.

And suddenly there's no one else at the table. There's no one else in the room. He doesn't smile as he holds my gaze, but the look in his eyes softens, and it does criminally unfair things to my stomach.

"Liam, Asher, you guys staying for the game?" my dad asks around a mouthful of mashed potatoes.

I can't quite put my finger on it, but the dynamic between Liam and his brother seems...different now. I guess Asher's presence here in the first place is a testament to that. He's never spent holidays with us before. It shows in the way he carries himself—smiling and laughing along with everyone else, but with a hint of discomfort in the tension in his shoulders, like he's somewhere he doesn't quite belong.

"Act civilized!" Mom swats Dad's arm with the back of her hand. "We have company!"

"I want to watch!" says Casey.

"You like football, Casey?" asks Leo.

Casey nods vigorously.

Christine leans over and murmurs in my ear, "He has never once sat through more than ten minutes of a game."

I press my lips together to hold in my laugh.

The conversation quickly devolves into compliments for Mom's cooking, and it doesn't take long for people to finish their plates. Or to go back for seconds, and thirds... It's all so damn good that even I can't help myself from piling more on my plate despite my stomach screaming at me that it can't take any more.

Leo clears his throat and glances around the table with an uncharacteristic nervousness as he lays his hand over Keava's on the table.

"We actually have something we want to tell you all." He glances sideways at his wife, and she gives him a supportive nod.

My eyes widen in realization as Leo opens and closes his mouth a few times, like he's fighting for the words.

"We're having a baby," Keava cuts in with a laugh. "I'm due in June."

The table erupts with noise, and Mom all but breaks down in tears as she hurries to embrace Keava.

I give it a few minutes for everyone else to complete their fawning before rising from my chair to give Leo a hug.

"Good thing I'm not camping out in your basement anymore then, huh?"

"Are you kidding?" says Keava. "I would've *killed* for the babysitting help."

"Oh, I still have first dibs on babysitting." I hug her next. "Congratulations."

I slip into the kitchen as Dad starts some monologue about the first Collins grandchild, not sure why the smile I'm forcing feels so heavy. I get to work rinsing the dishes in the sink just to have something to do with my hands and try to shake off this weird feeling clinging to me.

"Here, I got it." Liam slides in on my right and takes the stack of plates to load in the dishwasher.

"Thanks," I murmur, probably too quietly to hear over the surrounding chaos.

He says nothing else, and neither do I. This is the first moment we've been alone today, and it has adrenaline coursing through my body as if I'm about to jump out of an airplane. Somehow he went from the person I was the most comfortable around to making me so nervous I feel like I'm about to be sick. I can't tell if it feels the same for him—if he's feeling much of anything at all right now. His expression is normal, calm. We work in silence as I rinse each dish then hand it to him.

It's so *hot* in here from the oven being on all morning, and standing this close to Liam isn't helping. God, I feel like I can't breathe. And every time I feel him look at me, the tightness in my chest gets worse.

Once the bulk of the work is done and people start drifting to the couch, Liam tilts his head toward the back door. *Oh God, this is happening now.* I nod and step onto the patio first, desperately breathing in the cold air.

The noise fades to the background as the door closes

behind me, and I pace away from the view of the windows and shake out my hands, trying to calm myself. I crane my head back as a few flurries find their way to my cheeks. It's barely snowing now, just some stray flakes swirling in the breeze.

Christine decorated here too, though it's not as gaudy as the front of the house. Orange string lights are wound around the railing and a few of the trees in the yard. It makes everything glow. Even I have to admit, something about it feels magical and warm.

The chatter inside doubles in volume as the door opens again. His footsteps crunch softly through the snow as he makes his way toward me. Wordlessly, he drapes his jacket over my shoulders.

I turn to meet his eyes. I don't know what I expect to see there—indifference, discomfort.

Anything but this soft warmth. Like nothing happened. The way he looked at me before.

I curl my fingers around his jacket and pull it tighter around me. "Thank you."

He bobs his head once and steps up beside me against the railing, not quite touching me but close enough it makes me ache that he's not.

"How are you?" I ask. "How's the shop been doing?"

He cracks half a smile. "Promise I haven't screwed up all your hard work yet. How have you been? How's the job?"

I bump his shoulder with mine. "I know you're being modest. I've seen how well it's doing."

"Ah, so you've been stalking me." He grins like he's genuinely delighted by this. "And *I* happen to know things have been going pretty well for you too. At least based on your website and the reviews." He tilts his head. "And all the additions to your portfolio."

My chest warms, melting away a layer of the nerves. *He's been keeping tabs on me too.* "Oh, so now who's the stalker?"

His grin widens, but the amusement in his eyes fades. "But how have you been, really?"

Embarrassment tinges the tops of my ears as I remember the last time we talked—when I was a sobbing, blubbering mess. "A lot better. The day job still sucks, but my business is growing every month, so I'm hopeful about where it could go. I've made some friends. Gotten into a routine. It's good."

"I'm glad," he says softly.

I turn toward him and lean my side against the railing. "You skipped my *how are you doing* question."

He shoves his hands in his pockets and blows the air out of his cheeks. "Good. Learning how to delegate more. Promoted one of my artists to help manage the shop so I don't have to be there every day. Shop is turning a profit now." He winces and scratches the back of his neck. "Started going to therapy."

Half a dozen follow-up questions are on the tip of my tongue, but I bite them back, not sure if it's my place to ask anymore. "I think that's great, Liam," I say instead.

He squints in the distance and clears his throat. "I don't know if you heard about Christine and my dad."

"She mentioned they're getting divorced."

"Casey's taking it pretty hard. So I've been spending a lot of time with him."

I nod slowly, the pieces clicking into place. He told me months ago that Casey had started getting into trouble. Who knows how long things were tense in that house before they actually filed?

"Are you, um, have you been seeing anyone?"

My stomach does a somersault. "No," I say quietly. "I'm not seeing anyone." I hold his eyes, wanting to know—*needing* to know—but I can't bring myself to ask. Because *this* is what I've been afraid of all day. The wrong answer will break me. If he's already moved on, if the time apart has changed his perspective, and now when he looks back at that summer, what we had has been reduced to some fleeting, exciting fling. Just a stepping stone to help him get back out there after Hailey.

I swallow hard and look away.

"Me neither."

My head snaps to look at him, the relief enough to choke on.

Neither of us says anything for what feels like a long time. We just take each other in. He's lost a bit of his tan, and he must have cut his hair recently. The dark waves barely brush his ears now. I wonder what he sees when he looks at me. If I look different to him now. If he's spent more nights than not with me in his dreams the way I have, wondering if my brain has started to lose all the little details of him.

"Are you happy?" he asks. "In the city?"

There's more weight to his question than the simple words imply. This is the chasm between us.

Because I want him back. That's never changed. But I can't help but wonder, would it feel any less like limbo than it did before? Long distance with no end in sight? A relationship broken into bits and pieces—a few hours here, a weekend there—never quite fitting into each other's lives completely? Because it's about more than just the physical distance between us now. It's the directions our lives are heading. The lifestyles we want to lead. If those will ever align again.

I meet his eyes, and I'm frozen, unable to lie to him. My voice comes out small. "I am. Are you happy?"

He gives me a small smile. "I'm getting there. Is this still..." He gestures between us. "Is this still something you want to talk about?"

There are so many things I'm desperate to say to him right

now. How much I've missed him. How good it is to see him. How sometimes, on the harder days, I curl up in one of his T-shirts even though it stopped smelling like him months ago.

But even now that we've hit our deadline, I don't know what to say because so much has changed, but so much hasn't. I don't feel ready to come home yet. The homesickness is still there a lot of the time, but the city has grown on me too, just like everyone said it would. There are so many parts I would miss if I left.

And my mom was right about a lot of things. I don't think I would've been able to come as far as I have in such a short period of time without being a little selfish. All of my time, all of my focus, has been on me. And now that I know what that feels like…well, I don't know if I'm ready to give that up. If it would even be possible for me to have both.

If this new version of me is someone Liam would want anymore.

Because there's something else my mom said that's been playing on repeat in my mind for months.

He is never going to leave this town.

He might wait around for you to come back, but he won't move forward into this new phase of your life with you.

But none of that logic does anything to extinguish the bone-deep ache inside of me that I've never felt for anything other than him.

Laughter inside draws our attention to the window.

"Liam!" calls Casey. "*Liiiiam!*"

I wave a hand in front of my face. "It's okay. It can wait."

A troubled line deepens in his forehead as he searches my face, but he nods and takes a step back.

He's nearly to the house by the time I find my voice. "Liam—"

"Gracie—" he says at the same time, pausing a pace from

378

the door. His jaw works like he's arguing with himself over his next words. He settles on: "You look beautiful."

My fingers tighten around his jacket, not ready to let it go yet. I stare at him, silently, desperately, because there is nothing I can say right now that would be fair. Nothing that will ease this gaping hole in my chest that's my own doing.

It's stupid, what I'm feeling. Selfish. Unreasonable. This is what I wanted. This is what I chose. And I don't feel any closer to having an answer for him than I did months ago.

But seeing him in person, if I made any progress over the last few months, it's long gone now.

His footsteps crunch through the snow, harder and faster this time.

I barely have a chance to pull in a breath before he has my face between his hands, and then he kisses me.

My hands fist in his shirt. I stumble back a step, and he follows, his body caging me in against the railing and his hips pressing into mine. I all but moan as his tongue sweeps into my mouth.

I can't stop. I kiss him back just as desperately, both of us barely coming up for air. I've imagined touching him, feeling him, tasting him a thousand times since we last spoke, but it's nothing in comparison to the real thing.

I trail my hands everywhere I can reach—his face, his hair, his neck, his chest, his arms, like I need to feel every part of him before I can convince myself this is real. That it's not just another dream.

I don't know how I end up in his truck, if he initiates or I do. It's parked far enough back on the property that it's shrouded in shadow from the surrounding trees and I can barely hear the music from the house once we're inside.

This is a bad idea.

We should stop.

We should be talking.

I say none of these things as I push him onto his back and climb onto his lap in the back seat. He grips my hips and stares up at me with parted lips, his chest rapidly rising and falling with his breath. I bring my lips to his before he can say it either. He groans into my mouth as I grind against him.

Nothing, *nothing* has taken the edge off missing him but this. And maybe it'll hurt more after, but I think I'm desperate enough to take that risk.

"God, I've missed you," he breathes. His fingers tangle in my hair as he deepens the kiss and takes over control. Holding my back with one arm and my head with the other, he flips us so I'm on the seats and he's crouched over me in the small space. I keep my legs wrapped around his waist as his mouth finds my neck, my jaw, my collarbones.

"Do you have any idea what you do to me?" he asks in a voice so rough and low that I feel it down to every cell in my body.

Liam Brooks kisses me like he was made for it. Like it's the one thing he knows how to do and he's spent his entire life perfecting it. He's an expert in exactly how to touch me, exactly what to say to make me burn, exactly how to make the rest of the world turn off.

"Gracie, I need you to tell me if you want me to—"

"Don't stop," I pant, my hands shaking as I unfasten his belt. "Please, God, don't stop."

His lips crash against mine before I can finish the sentence, and he shoves my skirt up to my waist. We both frantically try to pry my tights down my legs, but we keep bumping into each other in the small space. My head hits his collarbone, and his chin clips the top of my shoulder. My knee knocks beneath his ribs, and his other hand gets caught in my hair as he tries to balance himself against the seat.

I let out a laugh as he finally manages to get the tights off, and by the time he positions himself over me, we're both completely out of breath.

He slides his hands from my hips to my ribs beneath my dress, and I hiss.

"God, your hands are cold."

"Sorry. Sorry." He readjusts on the seat, then glances around the truck, a muscle in his jaw flexing. "I don't know if this…"

"Don't say it."

"Hold on." He wedges his arm around the front passenger seat and hits the control for the seat to move forward as far as it can. He lowers to his knees in the cramped space, grabs my hips, and pulls me to the end of the seat.

I sigh and let my head fall back against the seat…but his touch doesn't come.

I prop myself on my elbows to see him breathing into his cupped hands. "What are you doing?"

"Making sure my hands aren't cold!"

My laugh starts small—just a breathy giggle, but it builds uncontrollably, and then Liam is laughing too, and God, his laugh is so fucking contagious. I've missed it. I've missed it so goddamn much.

Even after moving the seat, the angles are all wrong for what he's trying to do, so he leans over me again, his lips brushing mine as he murmurs, "Get on your hands and knees for me."

I don't know what it says about my current desperation that I do it without hesitation. And Liam sure as hell doesn't hesitate before pushing my skirt up, grabbing my legs with both hands to spread my thighs wider, and then his tongue—

"Oh my God," I moan.

He devours me like a man starved, and I dig my fingernails into the seat just trying to hold on.

"As much as I love hearing you," he breathes against the back of my thigh as he works a finger inside of me, then a second. "I need you to be quiet for me this time."

I blink, almost having forgotten where we were. A wave of ice rushes over me at the thought of anyone in my family...

"I'm keeping an eye out. You're okay." He dives back in, but not before murmuring, "As if I'd ever let anyone but me see you like this."

I let out a hiss through my teeth to keep from moaning as his tongue works agonizingly slow and firm circles against my clit while his fingers curl inside me. It's going to become blatantly clear how embarrassingly desperate I've been for this in about thirty seconds if he keeps it up.

But sensing it—because of course he does—he backs off, then I feel his touch leave me completely. I look at him over my shoulder as he rifles through his pants pockets, then the truck center console. If he can't find a condom, I think I'm far gone enough at this point to say fuck it. But then he locates his wallet, and the crinkle of foil tearing fills the quiet.

"It's a damn shame I can't take my time with you the way I want to right now." He leans over me until his chest presses against my back as he lines himself up with my entrance, his lips brushing my ear as he says, "You sure about this?"

The words feel heavier than every time he's asked me before, but I know without a doubt that my answer would be the same, no matter which meaning I chose.

"Yes," I gasp.

He pushes inside slowly, inch by inch, and it steals what little air was left in my lungs. He presses his forehead to the center of my back with a muffled groan as he holds on to the seat above my head for balance with one hand, the other winding around my hips to rub my clit.

I whimper as he gradually picks up his pace, his thrusts slow and deep. I've never taken him like this before and didn't realize how *different* it would feel.

"You doing okay?" he whispers.

"Much...much better...than okay," I manage between gulps of air.

I can *feel* his smile as he kisses the back of my neck, then my cheek.

"You feel better than I remembered. If that's even possible."

His fingers keep the same pace, but he drives into me harder, faster, and I squeeze my eyes shut, my nails probably leaving behind marks in his seats as I helplessly careen toward the edge.

"Do you know how many times I've dreamed about making you come again?" he murmurs.

I duck my head between my shoulders, desperately needing to move more, but there's no room, so my hands scramble against the seats. Liam's hand falls on top of mine, holding it there.

"Have you touched yourself since you've been gone?" he rasps.

Every breath in my lungs is like fire, each growing shorter and faster.

"Have you?" he demands.

"Yes."

"And what did you think about while you did?"

He thrusts into me harder, deeper, and I bite my lip to keep from crying out.

"You," I all but whimper.

He grabs my chin between his thumb and pointer finger,

turning my face to meet his. His eyes burn into mine. "Only tell me that if it's the truth."

"It is."

His mouth lands on mine as every last muscle in my body coils to its breaking point, and he swallows every sound I make as I fall apart in his arms. I feel it the moment he finishes too, his body slackening against mine, and for a moment, only our ragged breaths fill the car.

He doesn't move, not at first. He just brushes my hair over my shoulder and gently kisses the back of my neck. My eyes fall shut, and I revel in the warmth of his chest pressed against my back, never wanting to break the contact.

But then all too soon, he sits back, pulls my skirt down, and grabs my tights from the floor. "Maybe we should talk now?"

I chuckle and take the tights from him. "Yeah. I guess so."

Chapter Fifty-One

GRACIE

I've always loved the beach during the colder months. It's quieter, sure, but there's something so peaceful about listening to the waves crash against the shore while you're bundled up in layers, the cold air against your face making you feel fresh, awake, and alive.

No one seems to mind—or seems surprised—when we head out together while they're watching the game. We end up in the same spot we had our first official date, and Liam pulls a blanket out of his truck to throw around our shoulders. We sit with my legs across his lap, our intertwined hands sitting on top as I lean against his chest and watch the ocean ebb and flow. His heart beats steadily beneath my ear, and I feel like I could melt into it. His fingers trace along the back of my hand, then thread through mine, then dance along my palm before he starts all over again, and it sends shivers down my spine.

"So I've been thinking about this a lot since you left," he says quietly. "And if Philly is where you want to be right now, then that's where I need to be too."

I stiffen against him, the words not quite registering at first. "You want to…come to the city? You would leave?"

"Like I said before, I've brought on some help managing the shop, and the drive's not that bad. I could find a spot to rent and tattoo a few days in the city, commute out here a few days. I can make it work."

"You would leave," I repeat because my brain refuses to process it. "But…your whole life is here."

He nods and runs a hand up and down my back. "Yeah, and I've never left. I've never had a reason to. But now I do. You made me realize maybe it wouldn't be so bad to get out of my comfort zone. I've been so in awe of you, Gracie. You find these things that terrify you, and you just do them anyway. I want to be with you, but I also want you to have everything you want. And if that's Philadelphia, Gracie, I will follow you wherever you want to go…if you'll still have me."

I turn around in his arms, tears building in my eyes.

"I want to make this work with you, Gracie," he murmurs. "Whatever it takes. But I know this wasn't just about the distance. I know you had stuff in your life you wanted to figure out too, so if you need more time and space—"

"I don't. I don't want time, and I don't want space."

The line between his eyebrows finally relaxes, and I smile as I frame his face with my hands. "I'll need to stay in the city until I'm able to quit my job. But after that…the idea of finding some way to do half and half sounds amazing. I mean, with Keava pregnant now, I want to be around. I want to be the coolest aunt ever. And I want to be close to the water, and my parents." I jab him lightly in the chest. "And I want to make sure you don't screw up all my hard work with the shop."

He grabs my hand before I can pull it away, holding it above his heart.

"But what if you hate it?" I whisper. "What if you try moving out there and hate it?"

He nods his head to the side, acknowledging this. "Then we'll talk about this again. That's how this works, Gracie. Everything isn't always going to run smoothly. But we agree to work it out together."

I wince a little, seeing as that's the exact opposite of how I handled this. But it had seemed like the right thing to do at the time. "I'm sorry about the past few months—"

He shakes his head and tightens his hand around mine. "Don't be. I think it was good for both of us."

I know I feel different now. Better. More capable. Proud of myself for seeing it through. But I've never been able to shake the guilt that I was being selfish and unfair, and it was only a matter of time until he'd see it that way too.

"Really?" I whisper.

He nods and runs a hand down my hair. "I've been putting so much of myself into work for so long, I guess feeling like I had something to prove. And I didn't realize I might have been neglecting some other parts of my life."

"I meant to ask—I was surprised to see Asher today. You two seem to be getting along."

"He's still a little punk half the time." He rolls his eyes as a begrudging smile pulls at his lips. "But yeah, we've been spending more time together."

My heart warms for him. His family has always been such a weird, touchy subject. From the outside, it might look like Liam's the one who's pushed them away. But after spending some time around the Brookses, I can't help but think it had more to do with self-preservation. He distances himself so their lack of acceptance can feel more like his choice than theirs. Despite him having so many more siblings than me, it's always been obvious that he's never had a bond like Leo and I do. Not with any of them, except for maybe Casey. He'd probably never admit to it aloud, but I think a part of him has always wanted that.

"But if you want to try this again," he says, "I'm going to need something from you."

My eyebrows lift. "Oh?"

He nods seriously. "I'm going to need to hear you say it."

I shift so I'm straddling his lap. He tries to show no reaction to this, but I don't miss the way his pupils dilate, how his throat bobs as he swallows.

"Liam Brooks."

His hands land on my hips. "Mm-hmm."

"Will you…" I slide my hands around his shoulders and let my fingers tangle in his hair. "Pretty, pretty please…"

His smirk breaks into a full-on grin.

"Be my boyfriend again?"

He leans forward and kisses me so hard it sucks all the air from my lungs.

And I let him.

God, do I let him.

Epilogue

LIAM

Gracie is practically vibrating in her chair. We've been sitting here for hours, but it hasn't dampened her spirits in the slightest. She keeps her palms pressed together between her knees, one leg bouncing vigorously against the ground, her lips folded so tightly together they're white.

"Sweetheart, take a breath, or you're going to be admitted next."

Her round eyes snap to mine. "I am breathing."

I can't hide my smirk, and I throw my arm over the back of her chair. As far as hospital waiting rooms go, I suppose they could be more uncomfortable.

But not by much.

Gracie bites her lip, that leg going back into overdrive. "I hope everything's going okay."

I grip her knee and trace circles with my thumb. "I think C-sections generally take less than an hour, right? So they're probably done already, and now it'll be until Keava feels up to having visitors. Probably wanted some time with just the three of them first."

"What if it's not actually a girl? You know, sometimes they get that wrong." She stares in horror at the pink *It's a Girl!* balloon tied to the care basket she made for Keava.

I shrug. "Then he'll learn early on it's okay if he likes pink too. Or I can run to the gift shop for a new one."

Her shoulders relax a bit at that, and it takes everything in me to hold back my laughter. *This girl.*

She goes back to staring down the hallway, where she's hoping someone will appear with news, and I go back to staring at her. Her freckles have been making an appearance as we've transitioned into June and started spending more time on the shore than in the city. They brighten her whole face, especially when she wears her hair back like this.

I subtly slide the hand not on her into my pocket for the millionth time today. I'd been *hoping* to ask today, but now it seems like the wrong time. I don't want to take away from Keava and Leo's moment, and I want to make sure it's special for Gracie.

I run my fingers along the grooves of the key. We've been renting separate apartments in the city for the past six months, but now that my lease is up, and Gracie feels ready to quit her job—which would take her apartment with it—it feels like the right time to find somewhere new…together.

We can still use my apartment here for the days we spend on the shore, but even with her things in the closet and drawers, I know it must feel more like my space than hers. A new apartment in the city though, it's a chance for something to feel like ours.

She's been talking for months about everything she doesn't like about her current apartment, what she'd rather have. Finding someplace with all her specifications was no easy feat, but the moment it became available, I couldn't risk losing it. Hopefully that wasn't a bad call.

I press my thumb into the sharp point of the key until it hurts, forcing my mind back to the room.

Gracie gasps, her hand flying out to grip my arm, as a nurse rounds the corner and makes eye contact with us. She smiles at us and nods. "You can come on back now."

Gracie squeals and does a little dance that I think is purely involuntary.

I wave her off when she goes for the basket. "I've got it."

She squeals again and wraps an arm around mine, all but dragging me down the hall in her haste. She starts dabbing at her cheeks with the back of her hand before we even make it to the room.

"Oh, look! It's your auntie Gracie. That's Auntie Gracie!" Keava coos to the baby in her arms. Leo stands beside her, one hand on her head, the other on his daughter.

Gracie covers her mouth with her hands and takes a few tentative steps forward.

"How are you doing, Keava?" I ask from the door.

She gives me a tired smile. "Good. Thanks for asking."

"How's our godchild?"

Leo grins up at me, his eyes looking a little watery. "Perfect."

"Your parents said they're on their way," I add. "Stuck in traffic."

"Did you decide on a name?" asks Gracie.

Keava beams. "Rowan. Rowan Isla Collins."

"Oh, I love it. Rowan, you and I are going to be very good friends. I've already called first dibs on babysitting. Me and your uncle Liam. That's right. That's right."

She glances at me over her shoulder, her cheeks going a little red as everyone laughs at her babytalk, and I can't take my eyes off her.

I know she said *uncle Liam* because Leo and I are practically brothers. But there's a very different circumstance that would also give me that title.

I think I've always known it was only a matter of time, but in this moment, my future has never been clearer.

Turn the Page

For character art of Gracie and Liam and a sneak peek at Sweetspire book 2, *Tell Me It's Wrong.*

Chapter One

CHRISTINE

There is nothing more pathetic than a woman getting drunk at a bar alone.

That's what my husband always says—ex-husband.

A hysterical cackle bursts from my lips as I finish off my glass of Riesling. How fitting that I ended up here on the day we finalized our divorce.

And I do mean day. That's definitely sunlight coming through the windows.

I've passed this bar a hundred times on my way to the yoga studio down the street, but I've never been inside. Julian wouldn't have been caught dead in a place like this, and since he owns half the other bars around here, we usually just ended up at one of those.

Not that we had many nights out together.

I hadn't planned on coming here. After leaving the lawyer's office, I was driving back to the hotel I've been living out of these past few months. But then I remembered I'd be there alone.

My son, Casey, has been staying there with me, but Liam,

his half brother—who is closer to my age than his by a land-slide—offered to take him for the weekend while we finalized the divorce. I hadn't realized how much I needed that until now. I just don't have it in me to put on the *everything's fine* face today.

Julian has barely been involved in his life as it is. But now? And like most seven-year-olds, Casey doesn't know any better and worships his father.

I don't know how much longer that'll last.

Driving through town after that meeting was its own kind of torture—my ex-husband's last name plastered on every other building.

Until I came across this shabby little place. And there was just something about it that drew me in today.

Maybe because it reminds me of another life.

The neon lights, the pool tables, the shitty cracked leather bar stools—it's the kind of place I would've gone before him. Before this current version of me.

If past me could see me now... I let out another laugh. She'd fucking choke.

The bartender sets down a cup he'd been drying when he notices my empty glass and heads over. He barely looks old enough to be in here.

"Can I get you anything else?" he asks.

I tap the top of my wineglass.

He nods and pulls a new bottle out. His eyes flick from the glass to me as he pours. They're nice eyes. Unique. Somehow green and brown at the same time. Is that considered hazel?

"Rough day?" he asks as he slides the glass back to me.

I snort out a humorless laugh as I take a sip. There's no way this poor kid wants to hear my middle-aged sob story. Is thirty-one considered middle-aged? Everyone spent the last seven years preening over how young I was next to Julian, but now without him in comparison...

But then again, there's no one else in the bar, so maybe he's just bored.

I swirl the wine around in my glass. "I just became a multi-millionaire. I should be thrilled."

A million for each year we were married, per our prenup. Plus the twenty grand monthly child support. I could have asked for more—assets, properties—probably would've gotten it too. Maybe a younger version of me would have.

His eyebrows lift, and his eyes flick around the room. Slowly, a smirk tugs on the corner of his mouth, and he leans closer to me. "And you're drinking *here*?"

I snort, and that smirk turns into a grin.

He has nice teeth too. Is that a weird thing to notice? Very white, very straight.

"So are we talking a lottery win or a bank robbery?"

I sigh and rest my chin in my hand. "Divorce."

He winces. "Sorry."

I shrug. I'm sure a lot of people are thinking I got what's coming to me, marrying for money like that.

That's a real easy thing to say if you've never had to go without it.

"How long were you together?"

I blink, surprised he's still standing here. Most would run before having to hear any more.

"Seven years." I roll my eyes. "Which I'm pretty sure is the average for marriages that end in divorce. Even statistically I'm a cliché."

He shakes his head with a smile. "You seem about as far from a cliché as they come."

I cock my head to the side, not sure if he's just trying to be nice or he really doesn't know who I am. He carded me when I first sat down—something that definitely fluffed my poor beaten-down ego—but maybe he hadn't paid attention to the last name on there. Seems like everyone knows everyone around here—and everyone's business.

But maybe that's just the circle I run in.

Ran in.

"That's a big assumption for a stranger I've exchanged half a dozen sentences with."

"Fletcher." He extends a hand over the bar for me to shake, and he clasps my hand firmly, not the wimpy way some men do when they shake hands with a woman. "Now we're not strangers. Well…" He raises his eyebrows as he waits for me to fill the silence.

"Christine."

His smile returns. "I'm also good at reading people. I've seen plenty of clichés walk through that door. Don't think you're one of them, Chris."

Now it's my turn for my eyebrows to shoot up. Is this twentysomething bartender *flirting* with me?

Before I can respond, he ducks beneath the bar again and returns with a tall cup. He meets my eyes as he grabs the soda gun and fills the cup with water.

"Passive aggressive," I mutter, but pull it toward me anyway, then frown as the light catches my ring.

The ring, for some reason, I'm still wearing.

"How many drinks could I buy with this?" I ask, slipping it from my finger.

He lets out a low whistle. "Think you could buy the bar."

I glance around the musty, dark space, and my upper lip curls.

Fletcher laughs, the sound deep and rich, an almost musical quality to it.

I press the ring to the bar, my finger in the middle, and spin it around and around.

It's giant and expensive and hideous. I've always thought so.

It's silver, for one, which I never wear. The emerald cut does not complement my fingers at all, and the band is thick and gaudy with all of the extra stones crammed into it.

A ring someone who didn't know me at all would buy.

But I didn't care. At least, that's what I told myself at the time. Because I'd done it. I'd found a man who could take care of me for the rest of my life. I finally would never have to worry again, and I'd done it all before the deadline my mother and I set when I was five.

I can't remember the first time she brought it up, me needing to marry for money. It must have been around there.

Your beauty is your best asset, Christine. Use it while you can, because it won't last.

The only thing she talked about more was her regret not doing the same thing for herself.

I could have had everything, she'd say. *Don't you dare repeat my mistakes.*

Her mistakes being...me, mainly. Having me at seventeen, marrying my dad. Him leaving less than a year later, never to be heard from again. And the two of us struggling day in and day out on food stamps, other people's couches, and eventually another man's paycheck until I finally packed my bags at sixteen and never looked back.

"I think there are way more fun things you could do with that money though," Fletcher says lightly, pulling me out of my thoughts.

I sip my wine. "Oh, really? What would you do with it?"

He hums thoughtfully. "An African safari. Swim with dolphins. Super Bowl tickets. Ooo, rent out an entire cruise ship."

"What would you possibly need an entire cruise ship for?"

He shrugs. "Bring people you like with you. All you can eat and drink. You'd never have to wait in line. Don't have to worry about someone peeing in the pool."

"Is that something you worry about often?"

He frowns and tilts his head back in forth in a *more than you'd think* gesture.

I chuckle and shake my head. "I will take those suggestions under advisement. Thank you."

He salutes me with two fingers and heads back to where he was cleaning the glasses. "I'll be here all night."

Chapter Two

FLETCHER

The bar fills pretty quickly once five o'clock rolls around, as it usually does.

But Christine doesn't leave.

Every time I get pulled aside by another customer, by the time I make it back to peer at her spot, I keep expecting her to be gone, but she's not.

At least half a dozen men have taken the seat beside her at this point, trying to flirt and buy her a drink.

For some reason, my shoulders tense every time.

But they don't last long. After a few minutes, sure enough, they leave, and Christine sits there sipping her wine with a smug little smile on her lips.

God, what I wouldn't give to be a fly on the wall for those conversations.

It's obvious why they all keep flocking to her despite witnessing the failures of the men before them. She's like a neon light sitting there, everything about her screaming she doesn't belong in here. From the blatantly expensive dress and purse, to the shiny blond hair and perfect posture, to the jewelry I'm a little afraid someone is going to mug her for in the parking lot...a green-skinned alien would blend in better than her.

Something about her is so damn familiar, but I just can't put my finger on it.

After a *seventh* guy strikes out with her, I make my way over.

"How are you doing over here?"

She smiles up at me, and that's how I know she's drunk. Even when I'd gotten her to laugh earlier, the corners of her mouth never quite passed the middle line, like they were fighting against it. Her eyes are a little glassy now, and I double-check she still has that baseball of a ring on the bar and no one swiped it.

But no, it's there. She's still spinning it around and around.

"No more for me," she says, pushing her half-full wineglass toward me.

"Glad we agree on that."

"Thank you for talking with me earlier," she says, her words starting to slur together. "That was nice of you."

"I enjoyed it. You're the most interesting person I've had in here in a while." She rolls her eyes, and I lay my hand palm up on the bar top. "But I'm going to need your keys."

She purses her lips like she knows I'm right, but makes no move to give them to me.

"I can call you a cab," I add.

Her nose scrunches as she looks up at me. "I don't want to leave my car here. My hotel is only a few blocks away."

"Come on, you know that's not a good idea."

"Didn't I see on the news you keep having break-ins in your parking lot?" Her nose scrunches again. "No offense."

I wince because she's not wrong. People have definitely caught onto the number of people who regularly have to leave their cars here overnight and taken full advantage of that.

I sigh and glance at the clock, then the second bartender who showed up an hour ago. "Which hotel are you staying at?"

"The Ridley."

Damn, that is really close.

"All right." I curl my fingers for the keys, and her lower lip pushes out a little in disappointment. I don't even think she realizes she's doing it. "I'm going to drive you. Come on."

She blinks, a crease forming between her eyebrows. "You won't get in trouble for leaving?"

I shake my head. "It'll take less than ten minutes."

"But how will you get back?" She seems genuinely baffled.

I chuckle. "I've got it taken care of. It's me or the cab. Your pick."

Slowly, she pulls her keys from her purse and drops them into my waiting palm.

Thank God she didn't leave her car here. This thing must have cost at least a hundred grand. It wouldn't have stood a chance.

It's nothing too flashy—a sleek black SUV. I would've taken her more for the sports car type, that is, until I open the back seat to toss my skateboard inside and notice the car seat.

Damn. She seems really upset about the divorce as it is, but that adds a whole new layer to it.

I have a million questions I want to ask, but I don't know where the line between friendly ends and nosy begins.

She climbs into the passenger seat with a sigh, and I drop the ring she left on the bar into the cupholder.

"Oh." She stares at it as I adjust the seat. "Oops."

A laugh gets stuck in my throat. That ring looks like it was a million dollars. *Oops?* Who the fuck is her ex-husband? God?

"Are you even old enough to drive?" she says as I pull out of the parking lot.

"I am *not* that much younger than you."

She scoffs. "I could be your mother."

My head whips toward her. Is she *serious?* "How old do you think I am?"

She frowns and squints at me. "Sixteen?"

I give her an unimpressed look. "And bartending? Try again."

"Eighteen?"

"That's more legal, but still no."

She purses her lips. "Twenty-one."

"Twenty-two," I admit. "But you can't be that much older. Definitely not old enough for the age jokes."

She groans and covers her face with both hands. "Try ten years."

Huh. Looking at her, I would've guessed less, but still. "That's nothing."

"That's a *decade.*"

"So?"

She shakes her head like she can't believe I just said that.

All too soon, I pull into her hotel's parking lot, and I find myself grasping for something else to say to make her stay longer.

"You have your hotel key?"

She frowns and digs in her purse until she finds it.

"Phone?"

She digs for that next.

"Wallet?"

She throws her hands up, but then she sees me smirking at her and presses her lips together like she's trying not to smile.

"So I forgot one thing," she mumbles as she fishes the ring out of the cupholder. It takes her a few tries, but she gets there.

I grab my board from the back and hop out to get the door for her, and she stares at me for a moment before finally climbing out.

"These too," I say, slipping the car keys into her purse.

"Thank you," she says softly, not quite meeting my eyes now.

"For what it's worth, coming from someone with zero knowledge of the situation, your ex-husband must be an *idiot.*"

She blinks up at me—blue eyes. I hadn't been able to tell in the bar lighting, but yeah, they're definitely blue. The deep kind, like the ocean. She was beautiful sitting there in the bar, but up close? She's fucking breathtaking. Down to every little detail—the curve of her lips, the freckles on her nose. Without a doubt, she's the most beautiful woman I've ever seen.

I'm seized with the sudden urge to kiss her, but that would probably be the worst possible thing I could do right now. If she were sober…I'd probably try to get her to invite me inside.

Reluctantly, I take a step away. "I should get back."

She blinks and takes a step back too. "Of course. Thank you. For the ride."

"See you around, Chris." I set my board down and kick off with a wave. "I work Thursday through Monday!"

Even as I round the corner and her form disappears into the dark, I still manage to catch her smile. "I'm never going back there!" she calls.

I smirk. We'll see.

See What Happens Next

Thank you so much for reading *Tell Me It's Right!* If you enjoyed it, **it would mean so much if you left a review!**

Continue the Sweetspire series with book two, *Tell Me It's Wrong*, now available for preorder.

If you want more of Gracie, she also appears as a side character in *The Anti-Relationship Year*!

About the Author

Katie Wismer writes books with a little blood and a little spice (sometimes contemporary, sometimes paranormal.)

Be the first to know about upcoming projects, exclusive content, and more by signing up for her newsletter at katiewismer.com. Signed books are also available on her website, and she posts monthly bonus content on her Patreon (including a Patreon-exclusive book!)

When she's not reading, writing, or wrangling her two perfect cats, you can find her on her YouTube, Instagram, or TikTok.

patreon.com/katiewismer
tiktok.com/@authorkatiewismer
instagram.com/authorkatiewismer
youtube.com/katesbookdate
goodreads.com/katesbookdate
amazon.com/author/katiewismer
bookbub.com/authors/katie-wismer

Made in the USA
Middletown, DE
10 December 2024

66673201R00250